Outstanding praise for the novels of Scott Nicholson

The Home
"With *The Home*, Scott Nicholson has cemented his position, along with Bentley Little, as one of the most consistently good horror writers being published today."
—*Baryon Magazine*

"Writing with the confidence of a seasoned pro, Nicholson weaves his tale in fine style . . . don't be surprised if he—like Koontz and King before him—becomes a genre unto himself."
—*Hellboundbooks.com*

"Readers will find a cast of well-woven characters who find themselves in the most dire and terrifying straits."
—*The Mountain Times*

BOOKS BY SCOTT NICHOLSON

The Red Church
The Harvest
The Manor
The Home

Published by Pinnacle Books

THE
FARM

SCOTT NICHOLSON

PINNACLE BOOKS
Kensington Publishing Corp.
www.kensingtonbooks.com

PINNACLE BOOKS are published by

Kensington Publishing Corp.
850 Third Avenue
New York, NY 10022

All Kensington titles, imprints, and distributed lines are
available at special quantity discounts for bulk purchases
for sales promotions, premiums, fund-raising, educa-
tional, or institutional use.

Special book excerpts or customized printings can also be
created to fit specific needs. For details, write or phone the
office of the Kensington special sales manager: Kensington
Publishing Corp., 850 Third Avenue, New York, NY 10022,
attn: Special Sales Department; phone: 1-800-221-2647.

This book is a work of fiction. Names, characters, businesses,
organizations, places, events, and incidents either are the
product of the author's imagination or are used fictitiously.
Any resemblance to actual persons, living or dead, events,
or locales is entirely coincidental.

PINNACLE BOOKS and the Pinnacle logo are Reg. U.S.
Pat. & TM Off.

ISBN 0-7860-1712-0

First printing: July 2006

10 9 8 7 6 5 4 3 2 1

Printed in the United States of America

For John Scognamiglio, daydream believer

Chapter One

Lilacs.

The scent drifted from the cupboard and crossed the kitchen as if riding a late spring breeze. Katy Logan sniffed and frowned. It was late September, too deep in the Appalachian autumn for any flowers but goldenrod, jewel weed, and hummingbird plant. She hoped Gordon wasn't the type of man who believed in packaged deodorizers, those little plug-in things that looked great on a television commercial. The kind featuring a fashionable mom who could clean the house, build a career, raise three kids, and still manage to be dynamite in the sack, all without rumpling the pages of *Cosmopolitan*.

Katy had no doubt the scent was lilacs. Her mother, Althea, was a gardener, though her Floridian climate was eight hundred miles and four thousand feet of elevation removed from the North Carolina mountains. Mom had a string of blue ribbons from flower shows across the panhandle. Katy's green thumb had turned a sickly shade of chartreuse somewhere at the age of six, when she'd dumped a bucket of mud on a prize species of two-tone rose. Sent to bed without supper, Katy had fantasized about ripping Mom's flower garden up by its roots, starting with the lilacs.

She let the pot she was scrubbing slide into the soapy water. The scent came again, stronger. It wasn't a pure smell. The lilac had a faint musky undertone. Like old fish.

God, she shouldn't have cooked Gordon swordfish last night. At least the heady lilac disguised the odor a little. She was as hapless in the kitchen as she was in the garden. She had always resisted the petty tyranny of the kitchen, its perfect order and shiny regimen, the confusing array of spices. Did tomato-based sauces need basil or garlic? Was it cinnamon or was it cloves that dominated a pumpkin pie? Did swordfish demand a freshly squeezed lemon or a splash of soy sauce?

Katy had gone with both lemon and soy last night, determined to be a good wife for Gordon. A textbook wife. An Old Testament wife, if necessary. She'd been the other kind of wife and didn't have much to show for it.

Except Jett.

Katy dried her hands. A door slammed beyond the kitchen. Jett must be coming in, ready to hit the books and prepare to wow the sixth grade teachers at Cross Valley Elementary tomorrow.

"Jett?" A smile slipped across Katy's lips, and she could practically feel the furrows in her forehead smooth out. Like a *Cosmo* mom. No stress. Wrinkles were for those who succumbed to gravity.

Katy waited for the footsteps of her daughter. Jett was on the threshold of blossoming, getting swells on her chest, and the subsequent adolescent turmoil made her unpredictable. She was as likely to break into tears over an imaginary slight as to crawl on her mother's lap for a good cuddle. Her first expression would reveal the mood of the moment.

Katy was glad to be done with the kitchen, anyway. That lilac smell had given her a headache and she was going to thaw some pizzas for dinner. Last night's swordfish experiment had taught her that she'd better take it easy on becoming Supermom. Simply slapping an S on her chest hadn't eased today's stink any. She sprinkled baking soda into the trash can, hoping the odor would fade before Gordon came home.

"Jett?" she called again, closing the freezer.

Foot *stomps*, not steps.

Her daughter was in a mood that could only possess a twelve-year-old. Anger, anger, anger with fat leather heels. A hard day in the classroom, no doubt. Or a boy. Probably both, since those went hand in hand when you were in your first year at a new school and real boys were just starting to rival Goth bands and horses for your attention. Except Jett had made an art form of being an outsider. Black wardrobe and attitude to spare.

Katy left the kitchen without a backward glance, the lilac-and-fish aroma and the whirring microwave occupying the room. Even after four months here, she still hadn't become comfortable with the layout of Gordon's house.

No, not Gordon's house. Our house. Until death do us part, just like I promised.

For the second time.

The front door of the two-story farmhouse opened onto the living room, with a foyer that was barely big enough for dirty shoes and damp umbrellas. The kitchen stood off to the right, interrupted by a stretch of hardwood floor that contained a dining table. Four chairs. Gordon must have always been an optimist, even during those last five years of bachelorhood.

Katy almost called for Jett again, but stopped herself. That might be construed as nagging. Katy had dropped the two of them into the middle of this new situation, so she owed her daughter a little slack. If Katy were compelled to be honest with herself, something she desperately avoided, she would admit Jett had endured the tougher transition.

Katy had done nothing more than say "I do" and turn in her resignation at Wachovia Financial Services. Sure, she'd hated Charlotte anyway, and a small town called Solom in the Blue Ridge Mountains of North Carolina seemed like the perfect escape from the thirty-two years that had given her nothing but a beautiful child and a bottomless well of insecurity. But for Jett, this move had been the equivalent of an emotional tsunami.

Not only had Jett left her father behind, she'd said good-bye to a small private school and a number of friends she'd known since diaper days. The two-bedroom apartment on Queen Street had been traded for a restored wooden-frame house on thirty acres of slanted land. Jett couldn't even get a decent cell phone signal out here, a point she'd drilled into Katy at every available opportunity. So

Katy didn't completely blame her for storming up the stairs to her room.

As a mother, Katy had the duty to go up and tap quietly on Jett's door. On her way, she made a halfhearted swipe at the dust that covered a curly maple coffee table. How could dust collect so fast? As a wedding present, Gordon had hired a professional cleaning service to perform a top-to-bottom wipe-down. But already the weight of domestic responsibility had settled in Katy's heart as heavy as the dampness from the stream that ran behind the house.

As she climbed the stairs, she expected to hear the floor-shaking beat of industrial Goth, music that Katy dared not criticize lest it gain a permanent slot on her daughter's playlist. Katy had helped Jett shop for her first studded dog collar, a possibly scarring experience for them both. Since then, Jett had eschewed the collars as part of her black leather-and-vinyl outfits, along with the occasional denim complement, and Katy had withheld fashion advice. Katy didn't relate to the Goth look, but she recalled her own youthful experiments in hippie chic, frayed bell-bottoms and paisley blouses worn without a bra. She shuddered to imagine herself in such a costume now, and figured Jett had the right to make her own choices she would later regret. Except the choice to do drugs.

Katy paused at the top of the stairs. Below, the footsteps crossed the living room, headed for the kitchen.

"Jett?"

A snack. No adolescent's afternoon was complete without an apple or a peanut-butter-and-jelly sandwich. They were growing, after all, pushing toward adulthood, shoving aside the generation ahead.

Swordfish, for God's sake. What had she been thinking? Katy knew swordfish was loaded with mercury, but figured the toxicity wouldn't do any lasting damage upon first exposure. She'd been trying to impress Gordon, plain and simple. Jett liked it okay, she barely ate dinner these days anyway, what with all that after-school snacking and chronic dieting. Gordon had taken a first bite, lifted his eyebrows, then shifted his attention back to the book he was reading. He'd turned the page before wiping his lips and saying, "Honey, you've outdone yourself. I've never tasted such exquisite brook trout."

Katy had smiled, sipped at her glass of white wine, swallowed the lump in her throat, and said what any newlywed would say. "I'm glad you like it, dear."

Instead of going back downstairs in search of her wayward daughter, Katy went down the hall to her and Gordon's bedroom. She opened the walnut door with a creak of century-old hinges. The room was always dark, even now with the five o'clock sun at the windows. The room was thick with Southern Appalachian history, outsider sculptures in seven native woods, stacks of tapes from old evangelical radio stations, dozens of family Bibles arrayed in rows across the shelves. Gordon's work was his life, had apparently always been. She wondered if he would ever be able to change. She'd married him on the off chance that he'd be one of the very few men to pull it off.

No, that wasn't entirely true. She'd married him for a number of reasons that were as shallow and tangled as the roots of a black locust tree.

A rustling arose from inside the closet on Gordon's side of the room.

Had Jett hidden in there, playing hide-and-seek like a four-year-old? The closet was barely big enough for a person to stand inside, and was filled with the regalia of an academic's profession: black and blue suits, white shirts, polished shoes, and a tuxedo. The closet was open, the ancient door handle missing its knob.

Jett wasn't in there.

Nobody home.

She'd heard no footsteps.

Stress.

From slapping the old S on the chest.

The noise came again from the hollow of the closet. Mice. A house developed holes over the years, especially in a rural setting. Generations of mice had the opportunity to search for crevices, to explore the corner boards and probe the openings where utility lines entered the walls. Supermom would have to learn to set traps. Smith mice for the Smith house.

She'd mention it to Gordon. Maybe he was the type who would insist on taking care of the problem. He'd never been much of a traditionalist in other gender areas, though. He'd let her keep her maiden name of Logan. Katy had said she wanted to remain a Logan for sentimental reasons, because her grandmother had died a few years before. In truth, changing her name back after her divorce had been so troublesome she never wanted to endure it again. Not that she was planning to get divorced again. Of course, she'd also said she'd never get married again, and here she was, in Gordon's house, her Supermom cape already in need of a good drycleaning.

The front door swung open and banged closed. "Mom, I'm home."

Katy frowned at the closet, wondering if she should peek inside and scare the mice away. No, might as well let them get comfortable. Made them easier to snare. She hurried from the room and called from the top of the stairs, "Honey, what's going on?"

"Nothing. I just got out of school. I caught a ride from Mrs. Stansberry up the road. You know, the math teacher."

Katy was halfway down the stairs when Jett came into view. Freckles like Mom, but black hair instead of red, cut short in bangs and the back spiked with mousse. The darker hair was one of Mark's genetic contributions, along with a gangly frame, though Jett had dyed it a shoe-polish black for dramatic effect. Jett had taken to slumping so she wouldn't tower over the sixth grade boys. Jett smacked her gum, a habit she'd picked up in Charlotte and clung to with all the defiance and resentment of a quarantined goat.

"I haven't met Mrs. Stansberry," Katy said. "I'd rather you not ride with strangers."

Jett let her book bag drop to the floor. "She's not a stranger. She lives up the road. She knows Gordon."

Gordon. It was odd to hear Jett call him by his first name, as if he were an acquaintance instead of her stepfather. But "Dad" wouldn't do. Mark, for all his faults, deserved the sole right to that title. Even if he'd done little more than squirt a seed invisible to the naked eye, then roll over and snore.

"You could ride the bus."

Jett was already headed to the kitchen, heels clopping on the floor. Just like the footsteps Katy had heard minutes before. "The bus is lame," Jett said. "That's for third graders. Bethany's getting rides from a high school boy."

Katy descended the rest of the stairs, following into the kitchen. "This Bethany, she's in your class?"

Jett pulled her head from the refrigerator. "Mom, she's in, like, seventh grade already. And he's only a sophomore. He flunked a grade, plus he's on the football team."

"I hope you have better judgment than that."

Jett kneed the refrigerator closed, hands full with a yogurt, Diet Sprite, celery, and a microwave burrito. "Jeez, Mom. I'm not a kid anymore, okay? Remember last month?"

The period. Even after all the mother-to-daughter talks about what it meant to be a woman, how puberty came earlier to females than males, how blood was all part of being a woman, Jett had still panicked when she'd awoken to find a red splotch on her sheets. Gordon had been in the bathroom, suiting up for the commute to Westridge University, so they'd both been spared an awkward moment. Katy had helped her daughter clean up and choose an appropriate feminine hygiene product.

"Okay," Katy said. "Just because you can have a baby doesn't mean you're ready to date high school boys."

"Mom, don't get in my face about it. I haven't done anything wrong." Jett leaned against the counter, set down her snacks, and peeled back the lid on the yogurt.

"Sorry, honey." Katy went back to the sink and the never-ending demand of dirty dishes. "I know the move has been hard on you."

Jett shrugged. "One place is as good as another."

"Do you smell lilacs?"

"All I smell is stinky fish. That swordfish was *so* not right. I mean, it tasted good and all, but there's not enough Lysol spray in the world to hide it."

Katy plunged her hands into the dishwater. "I'm sorry you had to give up Charlotte. I know you had a lot of friends there and—"

"We talked about it, okay? Jeez, you wouldn't even get married until I gave my permission."

"Please stop saying 'Jeez.' You know Gordon finds it disrespectful."

Jett looked up, gave a theatrical lift of her arms, and said, "Do you see Gordon? I don't see Gordon. In fact, you never see Gordon. He's practically a ghost in his own life."

"He works hard, honey. He has a lot of responsibilities at the university."

"Assistant vice dean of continuing something-or-other? Sounds like a job he could do over the Internet."

"He also teaches."

"Like, what? One class this semester? A seminar on obscure hillbilly cults?"

"He's well known in his field."

"What field is that, exactly?"

"I don't know. Appalachian religion, I guess."

Jett dug into her yogurt. The Yoplait painted her lips a milky green. "So how are you handling giving up your career?"

"I have a career. I'm your mother and Gordon's wife."

"I meant one where you make money and get to dress up and do stuff. Get out of the house."

"I'm very happy, honey." Katy glanced at the orange rings of greasy suds floating on top of the dishwater. She forced her focus through the window, to the barns outside and the barbed-wire stretch of meadow. Gordon had seven head of cattle, two of them the black Angus variety. Gordon said that was where the breeding money was. Breeding money. Sounded a little obscene to Katy, like a prostitute's tip. But the goats were his real pride. She could see a few of them, young bucks separated from the rest because they would try to mount anything that moved, including their mothers.

"Maybe you can be happy enough for both of us." Jett had bottomed out on the Yoplait and popped the tab on the Sprite.

"It will get easier for you."

"Sure. In two years, when I start high school. By then, nobody will know I'm the new kid and I'll lose these Frankenstein wires." Jett grimaced, flashing her braces.

"They go fine with your studded bracelet."

"Cute, Mom."

"Solom isn't so bad. I kind of like the peace and quiet."

"That's the problem. It's as quiet as a graveyard. And what's with that creepy tabernacle up the road, with the steeple that looks like a KKK hood?"

"Gordon said it's a family tabernacle, charismatic Baptists."

"Did Gordon get baptized there or something? What do they dunk you in, goat's milk?"

"Honey, Gordon is taking good care of us. He opened up his home and heart. I know he's not your dad, but he's trying his best. Let's give it some time, okay?"

"Time. You're already old and over with and you've got all the time in the world. I'm only twelve and every second counts." Jett walked her burrito to the microwave.

"Don't get too full before dinner. I'm planning spaghetti."

"From a can, I hope."

"Jett."

"Sorry, Mom. I'm on a diet, anyway."

"Girls shouldn't be on diets." Katy wished she had canceled her subscription to *Cosmopolitan*. Katy had never been able to measure up, and Jett had often thumbed through those same magazine pages. The Buddhists said desire was the cause of all suffering. But Buddhists occasionally set themselves aflame to prove a point.

"It's okay," Jett said, then began reading aloud from the burrito wrapper. "Calories, three fifteen. Grams of fat, fifteen. Serving size, two ounces." She turned the wrapper around. "Apparently this single burrito contains three servings, so I won't have to eat again until lunch tomorrow."

"You'd better be hungry in time for the spaghetti or I'll start serving up goat meat."

Goats had become a joke between them because half the local farms raised the animals. Beyond Gordon's cow pasture was a hillside dotted with the stunted white creatures, their heads constantly down as they gnawed the world to its roots. They preferred to browse in the forest, only coming down at dusk when Gordon fed them grain or hay. Gordon's breeders had been fruitful this fall, and the herd seemed to have doubled in size since the wedding.

"Do goats smell worse than swordfish?"

"Depends on which end you stick your nose in."

"Gross, Mom." Jett gathered up the remnants of her snack, leaving the empty yogurt cup on the counter. "I'm going upstairs to study. If the phone rings, I'm not home."

"Expecting a call?"

"Not from anybody you know." And Jett was out of the room, leaving Katy with a kitchen that had too many items out of place. She glanced at the clock. Gordon might be home soon. Or maybe not. This was Tuesday, and the departmental staff often went out together on Tuesdays. Something about celebrating almost getting through half a week.

She decided to put a pot of water on just in case. Spaghetti only took fifteen minutes. She would be brave and not resort to the prepared sauces in the pantry. Instead, she would go for diced tomatoes and fresh mushrooms. Except, what did you spice a spaghetti sauce with? She ducked into the pantry and pulled out the Gregorio. She held the jar near her face and read the ingredients. Salt, oregano, basil, garlic. Okay, she could handle that. She didn't know the proper ratios but if she was conservative, then it might balance out. If worse came to worse, she could fry up some hamburger, greasy mad cow that would wipe out all the other flavors. Or goat. Goat would do the trick.

Goatghetti. A traditional Appalachian-Italian dish.

She tucked the jar back on the pantry shelf, then paused.

The smell of lilac rose like a solid thing, brushed against Katy, embraced her. She shivered, though the pantry was dry and breezeless.

Footsteps sounded again, those hard heels leading from the pantry and across the kitchen.

No.

She doesn't exist.

No matter what Katy had seen and heard and imagined these past few weeks, this kitchen belonged to her. This was her house now. Until death she and Gordon did part.

Behind Katy, the Gregorio fell to the floor with a brittle shattering of glass.

Chapter Two

Lame, lame, lame.

Jett tried to concentrate on her homework. World history, memorizing the long list of white Europeans, whom they killed, and when. The problem with history textbooks was they never got into the *why* of it all. Of course, the sixth grade spent a day each on India and Africa, and China, the world's most populous country, earned a shared chapter with Japan. Jett decided world history could be summed up in a single word, and she'd write it in on the next essay test: B-O-R-I-N-G.

Make that two words. F-U-C-K-I-N-G boring.

Her attention wandered from the book in front of her. If only she had an Xbox or a TV in her room. Too bad she'd gotten stuck with one of those weird moms, the kind who checked up on their daughters and paid attention to their moods. Why couldn't she have Bethany's mom, who had signed for birth control pills, given her daughter a cell phone with unlimited minutes, and turned her loose with a football stud? Now *that* was love. That was understanding. That was knowing what a daughter needed.

Jett looked out the window. Anywhere but at her book. The hills crawled away toward the horizon, a few barns and houses scattered among the green hills. *Solom, North Carolina. Whoopdie-shit.*

She'd taken to cussing in her mind. Rarely out loud, because Mom was one of those old-fashioned types who said cussing was the cheap tool of small minds, and Gordon was a bastard about blasphemy. Better to think up something clever and leave them baffled and off-balance, Mom always said. Of course, it was easy for Mom. She hadn't been twelve years old in a century or so. She'd forgotten what it was like.

Solom. Population what? Three dozen, unless you counted the horses and goats and cows?

Fucking Solom.

Three churches, a post office, a general store, and five Rebel flags.

Charlotte wasn't all that great, either. At Jett's last public school, a kid had gotten knifed at the bus stop over a dope deal. Dope was one of those things that horrified the teachers and parents, but most of the kids didn't pay attention. It was there if you wanted it, and if you could hang with that crowd. Jett didn't hang but she'd tried a joint and then she was lighting up every morning before school. That led to other things, some of which had erased their tracks through her brain. Like father, like daughter.

Of course, Solom might not even have dope, as backwoods as it was. The big deal here was joining the 4-H Club, breeding prize-winning livestock, and growing cabbage. And going to church. No fewer than a half dozen girls had invited Jett to their churches in her first week at school, and every one of them attended a different one. Drip Creek Union Baptist, Cross Valley Living Water Fellowship, True Light Tabernacle, Solom Free Will Baptist, Solom Methodist Church of the Cross, Rush Branch Primitive Baptist Church. Gordon could probably explain the differences, but if he even tried, Jett would fall asleep by the second sentence.

Not that Gordon was completely bad. Mom had spent months and months telling Jett all about it. About how Gordon was nice to Mom, how he took care of the family, how he opened up his home and gave them a future. About how Gordon would be a good father, not her *real* father, of course, but he would be there if she ever needed him. Gordon was rock solid, reliable, ready to take on arrogant teachers and subscribe to *Parent* magazine, preview every PG-

13 movie before Jett could watch it, and frown at every CD that had a black M stamped on the cover.

Sure, Gordon was all right. His eyes were dull and kind behind those thick lenses. He read a lot, and must be pretty smart, judging by all those degrees and certificates on the wall of his downstairs office. If world history started to mess with her, Gordon would probably have all the answers. But there was one major problem with Gordon.

He wasn't fucking goddamned her dad.

He was Gordon. *Mark* was Dad. Dad wasn't even Mark, just Dad. He didn't need a name. If she had a working cell phone like everybody else in the world, she'd give Dad a call right now and tell him about this hick shit hole called Solom.

The wind blew the curtains apart, giving Jett a full view of the barn and its dark windows. She imagined ancient creatures flitting and fluttering around in the eaves.

Inside the hayloft, a light flashed. Must be a lantern, because it flickered and bobbed instead of cutting a solid arc the way a flashlight would.

Jett was no hick, but even *she* knew better than to carry a lantern in a barn. With all that straw and stuff, a dry barn was like a whatchamacallit on a galleon, the kind of ship the English sank in the Spanish Armada in 1588. A powder keg. Where one spark meant ka-blooey.

She went to the window. The sun was low in the sky but not yet touching the horizon, so it was probably a little before seven. Why did some lamebrain need a lantern in the barn when it wasn't even dark yet?

The light came again, flashed once, then twice. Like a signal. One if by goat, two if by cow. Jett pressed her face against the glass and peered up the slope that faced the barn's opening. Under the dark canopy of trees came a flurry of movement, as if something or someone had been beckoned by the light.

Holy shit. This was like Nancy Drew or something. A real mystery.

Jett thought about telling Mom, because Mom kept saying they were in this together and would "get through it together." But Mom had enough to worry about, what with a smelly kitchen and dirty dishes and a new husband and nothing to do all day but clean house. Actually, Mom would enjoy a good mystery, but if things got the slightest bit squirrelly, Jett would be sent to her room until matters calmed down. Who wanted calm? Certainly not a girl who was now a woman, almost, at least in the ways that counted.

She glanced at the textbook on her desk. The F-word was getting lame and she should come up with a better alternative. But for now, it would have to do.

"Fuck off, Archduke Ferdinand."

She left the room, pausing at the head of the stairs to make sure Mom wasn't lurking. A pot clattered to the floor in the kitchen downstairs. "Shooty-booty," Mom yelled, not aware she had an audience.

Mom was busy making the perfect meal, all four food groups represented, as colorful as anything in *Women's World Weekly*, the calories toted up, the serving dishes neatly spaced on the dining room table. When Mom was in housewife mode, Jett could get away with murder. She slipped down the stairs and out the back door. The barn was thirty yards away, weathered and gray, the sun bouncing off its dull tin roof.

Gordon's barn was weird. The boards on the top story slanted upward in the angle of a V, and the loft opening was a black, upside-down triangle. The barn leaned slightly to the side in a wobbly geometry. The other barns in Solom had the same appearance, like something M.C. Escher would draw while stoned. Jett's secret obsession with art might come in handy if she ever needed to sketch a picture of her pathetic life.

The barn was separated from the house by a brown stretch of garden. The vegetables were mostly played out for the year, the tomato plants hanging like crucified black witches from their stakes. The only green was from the rows of fat cabbage heads, thick bottom leaves curled and yellowed, evoking an image of blondes buried to their necks in the dirt. That would be sweet. Jett despised blondes, resented their vacant faces and blue eyes and the amount of silliness that the boys expected from them. Plus, Bethany was blond.

The frost had come two nights before, sending the garden to

seed. Jett had been delighted by the sight of it, waking up to see the billion silver sparkles across the landscape. Then she'd had to wait for the bus at the end of the road and decided that cold was for the Eskimos, she'd take a sunburn in Charlotte any day. She dreaded the coming winter. Snow was a rarity in the Piedmont, but these mountains on the Tennessee border received four or five feet of snow per year. Probably glaciers, too, cutting through the valley and scooping up goats, cows, donkeys, and enough rednecks to fill the stands at a tractor pull.

Now, Jett, she could hear her mother say. Mom had a way of doing that, popping into her head with a voice of common sense when all Jett wanted to do was make fun of people and turn her back on the fucked-up world that never seemed to heed her wishes. She was an artist and an outsider, and that gave her a hammer. She could knock down anything that stood in her way.

Including the goat that stood between the edge of the garden and the barn.

Gordon's pet goat.

It was mostly white, with a few tan splotches on its belly. Two worn stubs of horns grew out of the skull like the thumbs of dirty gloves. The eyes were the color of a storm ditch, and the black pupils were horizontal slits against them. The goat raised its head and stared at Jett. A long tuft of hair trailed from its gut to the ground, matted with the animal's own urine. Somewhere in there was its mysterious penis, but she didn't look too closely.

Abraham, the goat was called. One of Gordon's religious jokes, the kind he let loose out of one side of his mouth, sitting in his overstuffed chair while reading a book, not caring if anyone heard him or not. Gordon had a lot of inside jokes. He would chuckle to himself, the sound rolling up from his ample belly and squirting out beneath his mustache. Poor Mom tried her best to keep up, to ask him to explain, but lately she'd taken to answering with a half-hearted laugh, a nod, and a stare off into the corner of the room.

"Howdy, Abraham," Jett said. "Good kitty."

Abraham dipped his head, swiveled his neck to look at the worn patch of meadow behind him, then swicked his short tail to scare up some flies.

"Nice kitty, kitty, kitty."

Jett approached the hog wire fence, getting a foothold in one of the wire squares along a locust post. The fence was topped with a single strand of barbed wire, but that would be no trouble for an athletic twelve-year-old. All it would take was a hop and skip, then a jump and roll like an Olympic gymnast finishing up a spastic routine. Abraham twisted his jaws, bits of green dribbling from the pale lips.

Halfway over the fence, her legs splayed on each side, Jett glanced up at the barn loft. The light flashed again, penetrating the center of the black triangle. Jett's hand hit the top wire and one of the rusted metal barbs pierced her palm.

"Shit fuck damn ass-wipe me, *Jesus*," she said, depleting her entire repertoire of bad words. She put the wound to her mouth and sucked, hoping to draw out the tetanus and West Nile virus and herpes and whatever else you caught from farm animals. Abraham lifted his head, ears perking. His nose wriggled as he sniffed the air. He took three steps toward Jett.

"Nothing to see here, folks," Jett said. "Just move on along."

The only moving Abraham was doing was *closer*.

"Seriously," she said, her voice cracking just a little. "No harm, no foul."

Abraham snorted and his head doddered, the filthy white beard waving in the breeze. Jett looked back at the house. Mom was busy in the kitchen. Not that Jett would call for help, even if her life depended on it.

What's the f-ing deal? Scared of a doofy goat. No wonder the kids at school make fun of you. You ain't country, you ain't mountain, you ain't from round here. You're freaky. You like to draw and read Vonnegut and Palahniuk. You have purple bootlaces, a black leather bracelet, and a button of Robert Smith in silhouette on your backpack. A Gothling in the land of Levi's and plaid cotton. A confused pilgrim in the Promised Land. No wonder you look like billy-goat bait from Abraham's point of view.

Easy meat.

"I'm not scared," she said to Abraham. "I'm the human here. I'm the one who can toss your ass on the altar or serve you up as stir-fry."

Abraham was unimpressed. He eased closer, his musky stench

assailing her. Jett dangled from the top of the fence, her crotch dangerously close to the barbed wire. She couldn't flip herself to either side without risking some sort of unimaginable disaster, the kind that no amount of feminine products could stanch.

Maybe Mom would hear her if she yelled. But she pictured the scene that would greet Mom, her daughter straddling the fence, held at bay by a goat. Christ, she wasn't a four-year-old anymore. This wasn't a Charlotte playground where the crack kids would mug you for a nickel. This was her new home, the place where she would grow to womanhood, where she would crawl through her defining moments. High school, soccer team, first boyfriend, junior prom, and with any luck, the place where she would lose her virginity. All those things were much scarier than a fucking goat.

She clenched her jaw and launched herself toward the meadow. Abraham, startled, stepped back. Jett landed on the balls of her feet, raised herself into a jujitsu stance, and said, "Bring it on, crap sack."

Apparently the crap sack was awed by her display, because Abraham backed away, the horizontal pupils fixed on his sudden adversary. Jett waved her hands in a shooing motion and headed toward the barn. The center of her palm threw off bright sparks of pain, but she focused her attention on the loft. Whoever was in the loft must have seen her. The space beyond the triangle was dark and still.

Jett hurried to the open mouth of the barn, expecting Abraham to charge at any moment. She'd prowled the barn before. That was one of the first things that caught her eye when Gordon had brought his new family to the mountain farm. Gordon had flashed a pleased grin at Jett's interest, but in truth, Jett had been desperate to get away from him. A two-hour car ride up from Charlotte had been about as much of the Gordon experience as she could handle for one day. So the barn had been both an adventure and an escape, and she'd explored it a couple of times since, imagining a roll in the hay with a boy, though she couldn't picture the boy's face or exactly what they were supposed to be doing, only that it was something that would make grown-ups mad.

The bottom floor of the barn was nothing to get excited about. Strands of hay and dried waste laid a mottled carpet, and a few stalls at the back were empty. Apparently Gordon's ancestors had killed cattle and pigs here, but Gordon said it wasn't right to slaughter the innocent. Only the guilty. Not that Gord was a vegetarian; he just let other people do his killing for him.

A set of crooked stairs led to the loft. Black squares in the floor above allowed hay to be thrown down to the animals. Jett listened, expecting footsteps. The mystery person upstairs must have seen her enter the barn. A delicious shiver ran up her spine. She twisted the leather bracelet for courage.

Maybe she wouldn't die of boredom in Solom. Not with all the delightful conspiracy theories she could spin. The person upstairs could be a terrorist, Al-fucking-Qaeda, Osama's long-lost twin gone country bumpkin. Or a militant white supremacist. She'd never seen as many Confederate Stars and Bars as she had on the two-mile stretch from the main road to Gordon's house. The cluster of them around the tabernacle gave the feeling of an armed compound, as if the natives would disappear into their bunkers at the first sign of a government license plate.

Sure, it was a weirdo, a freakazoid child rapist. In that case, what in the F was she doing standing there? Entering its lair, its zone?

Probably it was Odus Hampton, the stubble-faced guy in overalls who sometimes did farm chores around the place. Odus didn't talk much, worked hard, and kept to himself. To Jett, Odus was the typical redneck, with big, rough hands and crooked teeth. As crooked as hers would be, if Gordon hadn't been wealthy enough to pay for braces.

Jett peeked through the gap between two siding boards. If the person upstairs was signaling someone, then maybe she could decipher the message. Turn the tables on him, get the goods and pull a little blackmail game. Accuse him of trespassing, maybe score some points with Gordon, for what that was worth. The stand of hardwoods where she'd seen the answering light was unwaveringly dark, the evening shadows creating a thick morass beneath the tops of the trees.

She leaned against the wall, held her breath, and listened. She peeked through the boards once more, and a rheumy green eye looked back at her. She yelped and fell on her rump, crab-crawling away from the eye. Then Abraham gave his moist snort, and Jett sighed, dust filling her nostrils.

Scared out of her wits by a fucking goat.

Some Nancy Drew she was. More like a lame Olsen twin.

Jett stood and brushed herself off, determined not to be girly. Someone was upstairs, in Gordon's barn, without permission. In *her* barn. After all, she was family now, whether she liked it or not. She was part of this fucked-up stretch of uneven ground, it was her turf, home territory, the farm. Besides, if worse came to worse, she could yell for Mom and have an ally. Mom was always on her side, no matter the battle.

Some old bits of hardware hung from pegs on the wall: a length of chain, stinky brown rope, a hackamore, rusty branch clippers, and a backpack spray tank that looked like a leftover prop from a fifties big-bug sci-fi movie. Jett pictured herself slipping on the backpack, finding some goggles, then clambering up the stairs and scaring the living bejesus out of the intruder. No time. Besides, that was a little over the top. Just being a Goth Lite was edgy enough. Maybe the tiny bit of black eyeliner that Mom allowed would be enough to frighten her adversary.

She eased up the stairs. The second tread creaked like an arthritic toad. She paused, letting her weight settle. No sound from above.

At the top of the stairs stood a rough door, sagging, the boards wired together.

Jett was in full Nancy Drew mode now, fueled with a little Wonder Woman and some Jennifer Garner thrown in for good measure.

Assuming the secret signaler in the loft hadn't noticed her approach, she could wait at the door, look through the cracks, and try to figure out what was going on.

She took the rest of the steps with all the patience of a widow. She sat on the top step, near the hinges, so she would be behind the door if it suddenly swung open. The interior of the barn had grown darker, and no doubt the sun was just beginning its slide down Three Hump Mountain in the west. She held her breath and put an ear to the door.

A snort.

From below. She looked down.

Abraham stood on the barn floor, head raised. Looking right at her. Jett could swear the animal was grinning, teeth glimmering wetly in the half-light.

"Go away," she mouthed, giving Abraham the benefit of a doubt. Goats were renowned eating machines, reducing forests to wastelands, eating the very fences that tried to hem them in. Maybe Abraham had a little bit of brains, since he didn't seem to be in the middle of eating something at the moment.

Abraham stared at her with those boxy pupils.

Jett looked around, found a dry corncob, and raised herself up to toss it. She flipped her arm forward and the cob spun end over end, striking Abraham just between the horns. He blinked and dipped his neck, grabbed the cob with his lips, and ground it between his teeth. The sound was like that of an alphabet block dropped into a whirring blender.

"Shh," she said. She looked about for something else to throw, maybe something with a little heft.

The hinges rasped behind her. She turned toward the door, lost her balance, and grabbed for the rail. The door yawned, shadows pouring out to match those that had risen from the floor.

The thing loomed, seven feet tall, a lantern in one hand that cast flickering shadows up into a face she couldn't see because of the straw hat pulled low. The other hand held a darkly gleaming sickle.

Chapter Three

Arvel Ward drew the curtains and turned away from the window. Nights like this were best spent indoors. Goats would be walking tonight, and him that held sway over them. Other things would be afoot, too. Autumn was a time of bad magic. Solom didn't need a Halloween midnight to open the door between the living and the dead; the door was already as thin as the pages of a dry Bible.

Arvel had first seen Harmon Smith, better known as the Circuit Rider, on a pig path on the back side of Lost Ridge. Arvel was nine years old and on his way back from a Rush Branch fishing hole when he stopped at a gooseberry thicket. It had been August, and the berries were fat and pink, with green tiger stripes. Gooseberries gave him the runs, so he knew better than to keep eating them, but they were so tangy sweet he couldn't stop shoveling them in his mouth, despite the three rainbow trout in the little reed basket he used for a creel.

Harmon came upon him while he was lying in the shade, his belly swole up like a tick's. Arvel squinted as the man stood with his back to the sun, the face lost in the wide, worn brim of the rounded hat. Arvel knew who it was right off. The Circuit Rider walked these hills looking for his horse, and had been looking ever since those other preachers had pitched in and murdered him. Arvel couldn't rightly blame Harmon Smith for doing all the terrible things people said he did. After all, he was buried in three different graves and that wasn't any way for a soul to find peace, especially for a man of the cloth.

Legend had it Harmon pitched Johnny Hampton under the water wheel at the old Rominger gristmill, and Johnny's foot got caught in one of the paddles. Over and over went little Johnny, shouting and blubbering each time his head broke free of the water, grabbing a lungful of air just before he went under again. Took about twenty rounds of the wheel before he tuckered out and drowned, while the mill hands desperately tried to stop the wheel. His death went down in the church records and the county deed office as an accident, but folks in Solom kept their own secret ledger.

Arvel's great-uncle Kenny was galloping down a moonlit road when he came to the covered bridge that used to cross the river near the general store. Everybody liked the nice echo of horseshoes clanging off those wooden runners, so Kenny had picked up speed and burst through. Trouble was, a carpenter had been doing repairs on the bridge's roof that day and left a level line in the rafters. The line had slipped during the night until it was about neck-high to a man on a horse. Kenny's head hadn't been cut clean through, but there was barely enough connecting meat left to stuff a sausage casing.

Others had fallen into hay rakes, caught blood poisoning from saw blades, and old Willet Miller had been gored by a goat, his intestines yanked out and hanging like noodles on a fork. So Arvel had had no expectations of ever getting up and walking away from the encounter that long-ago day. He was just glad for two things: he'd go with a belly full of gooseberries and he wouldn't have to clean the fish before supper.

"Boy," Harmon Smith had said in greeting, touching the brim of his hat. The voice held no fire and brimstone, not even the thunder of a preacher. It was just plain talk.

"You're the Circuit Rider." Arvel figured it was no time for fooling around; plus he ought to be on his best behavior. Free Will Baptists earned their way to heaven, and Arvel figured he had to do some making up for the horehound candy he'd pilfered from the jar down at the general store. Even stealing from a Jew probably counted as a sin in God's all-seeing eyes.

Harmon's head swiveled back and forth, offering just a hint of the man's angular nose and sharp chin. "Doesn't seem like I'm doing much riding, does it?"

Arvel squinted, trying to make out the man's eyes in that desperate black shadow beneath the hat. It almost seemed like the man had no face at all, only a solid glob of dark. His suit was black and pocked with holes, and he wore a tow-linen shirt, material only poor kids wore in those days. "You looking for your horse?"

"Why, have you seen one?"

Arvel made a big show of looking up and down the pig path. "I think I saw one down that way," he said, and nodded in the direction of the Ward farm.

Arvel couldn't have said the man exactly grinned, but the darkness broke in the lower part of the face, revealing a gleam of ochre enamel. "And I suppose you'd be leading me to it, right?"

"Why, yes, sir."

"Respect for elders. That speaks well for you, boy."

"I try to do right by people," Arvel said, as much for God's ears as for Harmon's.

"All right, show me that horse."

Arvel struggled to his feet, hitched up the suspenders he'd unhooked while digesting, and headed down the pig path, careful not to walk too fast. The Circuit Rider followed, scuffed boots knocking dust in the air. Arvel tried to sneak a look back to catch the man's face now that they were heading into the sun, but somehow the preacher stayed just out of plain view. Arvel had his cane pole over his shoulder, and wondered idly what would happen if his hook accidentally sank in the Circuit Rider's flesh. That would make some fish story.

They went through the apple orchard that divided the Smith and Ward properties. The apples were small and tart, still weeks away from ripening, and Arvel's belly was already gurgling from all the gooseberries. He wondered if he'd have to make a dash behind a tree before they reached the outhouse. Would the Circuit Rider give him privacy, or stand over him with the wooden door open while he did his business?

They came out of the trees and the Ward farm was spread out before them. Arvel's pappy was splitting wood by the house, and his brother Zeke was scattering seed corn for the chickens. Acres of hayfields surrounded them, and the crop garden was rich and green behind the house. There under the bright summer sun, Arvel felt protected.

"I don't see a horse," the Circuit Rider said.

"Sure, it's there in the barn."

"You're lying to me, boy."

Arvel's heart was pumping like water from a spring hose. He threw aside his pole and the basket of fish and broke into a run, screaming like a fresh gelding. Despite the noise in his own head, the Circuit Rider's voice came through clear from the shade of the orchard rows: "Liars go to the devil, boy. Know them by their fruits."

Pappy whipped him for raising a ruckus and startling the livestock, and Zeke had snickered and teased for days afterward, but Arvel was fine with all that, because he was alive. Still, he knew Harmon Smith never forgot, and the ride never ended. Sooner or later, Arvel would have to own up to his lie.

He just hoped it wasn't tonight. Zeke had been taken, but that was an accident, could have happened to anyone. Harmon Smith wasn't the type to rely on old age for stealing souls. No, violence was his way. He'd been taken by violence, and violence was what he had to deliver.

Arvel locked the doors. He should have warned Gordon's new wife and that little girl, no matter how peculiar they were. But they were outsiders. Plus, every fresh victim that stood between Arvel and the Circuit Rider meant a longer wait until his own day of reckoning.

After Mark, Katy had promised herself not to fall for a man, any man. She was on the type of post-divorce arc she'd read about in *Cosmopolitan*: no dating until a year after the breakup, then dating only nonthreatening men who didn't appeal to her all that much. The *Cosmo* rule declared no serious relationship could even be contemplated until two years after a divorce, especially if a child was involved. Katy ignored those kinds of rules, though she'd made a promise to herself to be cautious for Jett's sake. Jett, born Jessica, had gotten her nickname because of her inability to make sibilants as a toddler. When Jett had learned of eighties black-clad, bad-girl rocker Joan Jett, the name was sealed.

Katy had kept Jett away from the potential replacements for Mark, not wanting to parade men through her life. She'd dated a Roger something-or-other, an insurance adjuster with overpowering cologne and happy hands; a broody food columnist for a Charlotte paper who'd nearly had her in tears after just one lunch; and Rudolph Heinz, a tall blond Aryan she'd met in a coffee shop who'd given her a thrilling three weeks but in the end offered about as much mental stimulation as her favorite vibrator. After those experiences, part of her was ready to settle down again, but the rest was determined to hold out for the perfect situation.

Gordon changed all that. He was presenting at a conference in the same hotel where Katy's company had scheduled a seminar. Her bank had eschewed frugality and scheduled the event at a resort in Asheville, a vibrant community billed as a "gateway to the North Carolina mountains." In the tradition of such seminars, it combined networking with leisure, the kind of professional vacation that most employees endured for the good of their careers while cramming in as much recreation as possible. She'd skipped out of the session entitled "Tax Considerations of Mortgage Points in Refinancing" and was browsing the vending machines by the check-in desk when she saw the schedule for the hotel's other conference. Written in red marker on the dry-erase board were the words *European Mythology in Appalachian Religion,* with a room number and time listed. To Katy, bored nearly to tears and nursing a run high on one thigh of her stockings, the topic evoked images of snake-handling hillbilly preachers crossed with sacrificial burnings like the one in the old Christopher Lee film *The Wicker Man.* She knocked down a quick martini at the hotel's bar and slipped into the small room where she first saw Gordon Smith, who was keynote speaker.

Gordon resembled a slimmer Orson Welles, tall and broad-chested, projecting a vulnerable arrogance. He told the crowd of about twenty, mostly professors who were nursing tenure-track hangovers, about the Scots-Irish influence on Southern Appalachian culture, as well as contributions by the Germans and Dutch. Katy wasn't that interested in the Druids, and religious politics always seemed like an oxymoron to her, so she tuned out most of the speech and planned the evening ahead. The bank had paid for her room, the seminar officially ended before dinner, and she had hours looming with no responsibilities. Jett was staying with her dad, and she'd left her cell phone in her hotel room. She was about as close to free as a single mom could be.

Gordon pulled her from her reverie with a rant on Demeter and Diane, harvest goddesses who had to be appeased before they would prove generous with their human subjects.

"Human sacrifice was common among many primitive religions," Gordon said, his voice assuming an evangelical thunder as if to wake the drowsing audience. "Blood was not only a gift for Diane in the forests of Nemi. Central America, Scandinavia, the South Sea Islands, Africa, India, virtually every continent had bloodthirsty gods, and those gods often demanded the ultimate tribute. Certain Germanic tribes combined human sacrifice with nature worship. If someone was found guilty of scarring the bark of an oak tree, that person's belly button was nailed to the tree trunk, and then the body was circled around the tree until the offender's bowels served to patch the tree's wound."

Gordon had the audience riveted by then, and Katy found herself admiring the man's strong cheekbones, thick eyebrows, and dark, penetrating eyes. He went on to suggest that vestiges of the old worship still lived on in the form of scarecrows, horseshoes, jack-o'-lanterns, and Yuletide mistletoe. By the time he'd finished, she'd thought of a question to ask him derived from her own lapsed Catholic beliefs. She waited while he shook the hands of balding tweed-encased academics, and gave him a smile when her turn came. He nodded, impatient, as if he'd earned his honorarium and the show was over.

"Professor Smith, could you tell me how Jesus Christ fits into your theories of human sacrifice?"

Gordon first looked startled, and then he threw back his head and laughed from deep within his belly. "My dear, entire *books* have been written on the subject. Do you have an hour to spare?"

His question had not exactly been a come-on, but she didn't want to eat in the hotel dining room alone, or worse, with colleagues from the bank. So she said, "Yes, I do. How about dinner?"

She wasn't physically attracted to him, at least not in the rip-off-clothes-and-let's-wallow fashion. Even after their marriage, she questioned her original motivation in seeking him out. But somewhere between the oysters and the strawberry cheesecake, he'd become interesting for more than just his obvious intelligence. Gordon didn't flinch when she told him she was a divorced mother of one. If anything, he'd become more deferential and inquisitive. By the end of dinner, they agreed to a nightcap at the bar, Katy fully expecting the drinks to lead to an invitation to his room. She didn't have to decide whether she would have accepted the offer, because he never asked. Instead, he made her promise to join him for breakfast.

A flurry of communication ensued over the following weeks, phone calls at night, e-mails throughout the day, and even old-fashioned, handwritten letters showing up about once a week. It was the letters that eventually won her over. In person, Gordon was a little cool and distant, but his sentences burned with passion and a playful humor that belied his professorial persona. He invited her to visit Solom, and she drove up with Jett one Saturday, her daughter grumbling all the while, dropping into defensive mode over Dad. But Jett had frolicked on the Smith farm, exploring the barn, traipsing through the woods, playing in the creek, and by sundown Jett wanted to stay for another day. By then Katy was prepared to bed the evasive Dr. Smith, but he seemed old-fashioned about courting, reluctant to do more than kiss her cheek.

Katy's decision to accept his proposal came after a few sleepless weeks of soul-searching. She didn't want a replacement for Mark, especially in Jett's life, but as Mrs. Smith she would be a stay-at-home mother, something she had never desired until Jett's drug problems surfaced. Katy blamed herself for being so absorbed in her career that she let her marriage to Mark fail (though intellectually she knew they'd waltzed together over the cliff edge) and then compounded the error by neglecting Jett. Gordon and Solom offered a fresh start, a chance for her to rebuild her relationship with her daughter with a supportive man in her life.

Gordon had never explained Christ's position as the world's most famous sacrificial lamb, but it didn't matter now. The honeymoon was over.

The Blackburn River was old.

Geologists said it was the second-oldest river in the world, after the Amazon.

The people in Solom didn't care about history books. All they saw was the slim ribbon of silver that cut into the brown banks of the hilltops. The water brought sustenance in the spring, kept their stock alive in the summer, and in September it shot its narrow currents among the yellow and white stones. It slowed to a trickle in January, only to bust out white again during the March melt. Maybe the water, like the humans who clustered around its shores, had an instinctive understanding of ebb and flow.

Solom took its name from bad grammar. Some say the place used to be called Solomon Branch, after the Old Testament king. Others said it was Solomn, a misspelling of the word *solemn*, which meant everything from formal and serious in a liturgical sense to grave and somber, as in a funeral ceremony. The permanent valley settlers had eventually trimmed off the silent letter at the end. If it sounded like Solom, then it was Solom.

The original residents were the buffalo that trampled ruts across the hilltops as they made their way from Kentucky in the summer to the Piedmont flatlands of Carolina in the winter. The herds numbered in the thousands, and the ground shook as their hooves bit into the earth. The Cherokee and Catawba visited the region only in the fall, when meat was available. Otherwise, the natives had the good sense to stay off those cold and forlorn mountaintops. Then the whites came along and poured across the slopes like albino fire ants.

Daniel Boone and the early European trappers and hunters were cold-blooded enough to hang out on the trails and slaughter their quarry across the seasons, with no sense of a circular food chain. In a few short decades, the buffalo and elk that had sustained the natives for centuries were gone, remembered only in the occasional place name or flea-ridden floor skin. The Cherokee had their own problems, driven at gunpoint to Oklahoma, where the landscape was as alien to them as if they had been dropped onto the surface of Mars. The federal government later felt guilty enough to grant them control of gambling casinos, but by then their heritage and souls had been all but lost. They dreamed of spiritual journeys where they met up with buffalo, but they woke up to an artificially inflated Britney Spears, an artificially inflated Barry Bonds, and a cynical, media-inflated Republican leadership that encouraged fear in every sector of society, especially among the outcast.

Not that modern Solom paid any attention. The inhabitants were mostly the offspring of farm and lumber workers, the women thick and faithful, the men prone to drink when they weren't in church. All were raised with a sense of duty, and church records were often the final statement on the quality of a life lived. A man's obituary was set down by a barely literate family member, and if the man lived a good life, he was noted as a solid provider, a friend of the church and community, and an honest trader. If he failed in any of those areas, his obituary was nothing more than an opportunity to question the eventual resting place of his soul.

Women were measured within a narrower yet more sophisticated set of parameters. Were her hips broad enough to bear a goodly number of children? Did she sit quietly on her side of church, raising her singing voice only at the appropriate time, after the males had established the proper cadence? Did she keep the Bible on her lap instead of the shelf? Did her obituary list more than a dozen grandchildren?

No obit had ever been written for Harmon Smith, and his name was marked in no family Bible.

Many testimonials had once been recorded about the work of Good Harmon Smith, a Methodist minister who had crossed denominational lines in the late 1800s, whose horse Old Saint had touched half of three states. A rival minister, the Reverend Duncan Blackburn, had attended to the needs of Episcopalians and the few mountain Catholics. Blackburn had earned a resting place on holy ground while Smith had died on the slopes of what became known as Lost Ridge. Legend held he was on his way to a January bedside appointment with a dying widow when a blizzard swept down from the Canadian tundra and paid his holy debt in full. In the twenty-first century, Blackburn had a line-drawing portrait tucked in the back pages of a university library while Smith occupied graves in three different churchyards. No one knew where Smith's real remains were buried.

And some questioned if there were any remains left worth returning to the dirt.

But this was Solom, home of an old river, and questions only came from those who didn't know any better. From outsiders, and newcomers, and those who heard the soft sound of distant twilight hoofbeats.

Chapter Four

Cabbage.

Katy hated the stuff. When cooked, it stank almost as much as swordfish. But Gordon had grown it in the garden, and therefore it achieved all the sacred status of a scapegoat. She could cop out and make slaw, a little mayo, celery seed, and paprika and she'd be done. But she wanted Gordon to know she had broken a sweat, and she might accidentally cut her thumb in the bargain and prove herself a worthy mountain farm wife.

She lifted the heavy knife and was about to snick a fat green-white wedge when the scream pierced the air.

Jett.

Not from upstairs, so it couldn't be Jett.

Outside.

Maybe the cat had gotten a baby rabbit. Katy had been startled by the first bunny scream she'd ever heard, on a Sunday morning several weeks back. It was the keening of a raped woman, the grunt of a gutted man, and the mournful wail of an abandoned child all rolled into one. Gordon had chuckled at her leap from the bed. "City girl," he'd admonished.

But Gordon wasn't here and this was no laughing matter.

The scream came again, and this time it did sound like Jett, and it came from the barn, muffled by the chestnut walls.

Time for Supermom without a cape, her uniform stained blue jeans and beige sleeveless blouse instead of blue-and-red tights with a yellow S across her boobs.

She burst onto the porch, raising the knife as if she meant business.

Katy made a direct line toward the barn, kicking away the dormant lilies that had grown around the Smith house for decades. She plowed through the garden, her flip-flops throwing up brown bits of dirt and dead vegetation. The gate was at the end of the driveway, but it was thirty yards out of the way. The fence was right in front of her, sparkling silver in the sunset, but seemed as ephemeral as a spiderweb. Her heart beat monkey rhythms.

Where was Jett?

She was unaware of leaping the fence, though one foot had probably reached the top strand of hog wire, but she stumbled on the other side, the knife flying from her hand as she fell to her knees. The barn rose before her, a haunted vault of straw and cow manure, as ancient as the family that had erected it. Her daughter, her life, her soul was in there.

She scrambled to her feet and found the knife. Her breath was a sick series of dry heaves in her chest. As she entered the barn, she raised the blade like a talisman.

"Jett?"

No answer, only the wooden echo of her pulse.

The inside of the barn had gone to a bruised shade of purple with sunset.

Creeeeeek.

The loft.

She squinted and found the stairs and was halfway to them when a blur of motion came from her left.

"Jett?"

Katy's gasp tasted of dust. She stepped back as the body fell from above, its arms flailing in the half-light, the waist bent at an obscene angle. She cringed, waiting for it to fall in a splintering heap of bones on the crooked steps. Instead, the body bounced and sprawled on the dirt floor at her feet. She jumped away, slamming her back into a locust support beam.

The body was too large to be Jett's. It was facedown, the limbs askew. Katy waited for breathing or a wheeze of pain to come from the twisted figure. After a few moments of silence, she eased forward and nudged the body with her toe. It moved with a rodent rustle, too light to be flesh and bone.

Katy knelt and touched the flannel of the shirt, then lifted the head. Straw spilled from a split seam in the clothing. It was a scarecrow, mildewed and ragged. Her ascent up the stairs must have dislodged it from its seasonal slumber dangling from a rusty nail. A length of braided hemp rope was tied in a noose around its neck, the top end frayed. The head was wrapped in cheesecloth, with pale bone buttons for eyes and a piece of black yarn for a mouth. Its straw planter's hat had rolled away, a jagged crescent torn in the brim as if some animal had taken a big bite.

Maybe Jett had seen the scarecrow and thought it was a person and freaked out, just as Katy had done. After all, Gordon had told her the legend, too, and Jett's face had gone pale while listening, making her black eye shadow even more dramatic.

But there were worse things than legends. Like drugs. What if Jett had scored some angel dust or crystal meth, something that turned reality into a rocket ride down a nightmare chute to hell?

"Jett?"

Footsteps drummed on the loft floor above. Boots, too heavy to be Jett's ankle-high black leather things.

Katy mounted the steps, glancing at the four chicken-wired windows on the lower floor, wishing more of the fading sunlight would pour through and burn her fear away. But she had little room for fear, because worry took over. At the top of the stairs, she eased up the little metal hasp that kept the door fastened. She'd never been in the loft, and had only briefly visited the barn during Gordon's introductory tour.

Too bad she wasn't Supermom for real. X-ray vision would come in handy right now. The light was a little better up here, thanks to the large triangles cut into each end of the barn. Uneven squares of dirty blond hay were stacked around like an autistic giant's alphabet blocks. Stalks of tobacco dangled upside down at the far end of the barn, speared on poles, the drying leaves like the wings of reddish brown bats.

Could Jett be playing some bizarre game of hide-and-seek? She wasn't the type to scream. If Jett wanted to get attention, she usually came up with some mind-blowing observation or another. But Katy had been neglecting Jett in favor of Gordon lately, even though Jett's world had been shaken more than anyone's by the move to Solom.

"Okay, Jett," she said. "Fun's over. Come on out."

She heard a giggle, or maybe it was only a breeze rifling the parched tobacco.

"Dinner's probably burning," Katy said. "If you thought the swordfish was bad, wait until you smell scorched cabbage."

Katy felt silly holding the knife, so she tucked it behind her back as she headed between the rows of hay. The air was as thick as snuff, motes spinning in the shafts of dying sunlight. A few loose piles of hay were scattered here and there, near the black square holes in the floor through which food was thrown down to the animals. Katy expected Jett to jump from behind a stack at any moment, or burst up from one of the hay piles in a sneeze-inducing spray of gold. Good prank, except that would spoil dinner. She wanted Gordon in a good mood, so maybe they could finally finish consummating their marriage.

"Cute, honey. We can have a good laugh over the dinner table."

No answer. The time Jett had taken acid in Charlotte, she'd stayed out all night, hiding in a storm sewage pipe, showing up late for school the next day, dirty, wild-eyed, and ravaged by insects. Katy, who had waited up sleepless and had several times resisted the urge to call the police, had picked her up from school, taken her to the doctor, and let the school psychologist give the lecture. Something in Jett had changed after that, a drifting look in her eyes, a secretive smile that spoke of more journeys to come. Hopefully this wasn't one of them.

Katy made her way through the maze of bales to the far end of the barn. She looked through the triangle to the wooded hills above. A few goats dotted the slopes, browsing in the brush at the edge of the forest. In the adjacent meadow, separated by a stitch of fencing, cows worked the grass, their heads swiveling, ears twitching against the insects. She was about to turn back to explore the loft again when a light flickered in the distant trees.

Somebody with a lantern or flashlight. The ridge was Gordon's property. It was nearly hunting season, but Gordon's land was posted. Gordon said his neighbors were always welcome, as long as no bullets flew around and no drunken hunters mistook his cows for oversize deer. She'd have to tell him about the trespassing later, when such ordinary oddities would matter.

"Jett, seriously. Don't make me get mad." She tapped the knife against a post. "The scarecrow trick was a good one. Spooked the living daylights out of me. I bet you can't wait to tell Gordon."

No answer. Maybe Jett had already slipped down the stairs and was waiting at the dinner table, or in her room, cheeks swollen with the laughter she was storing up. At any rate, Jett was twelve and could find her way to the house with no trouble, even in the dark. Even stoned out of her eyeballs.

But that scream—

It hadn't sounded like a joke.

If there had even been a scream. Maybe, like the perfume in the kitchen or the footsteps that had no legs, the scream had been nothing more than invisible smoke. The farm wasn't haunted. Despite the way Gordon's first wife had died.

This was silly. Jett had promised to quit drugs as part of their new life. If a mother and daughter couldn't trust each other, they were hopeless anyway. Katy decided she would check on dinner, and if she didn't see Jett in the house, she would grab a flashlight and return. Without the knife.

"Okay, Jett," she yelled, her words stifled by the hay. "I'm going back to the house."

The lower floor of the barn was darker as she descended the stairs. The air was as cool as a cellar. A soft, moist sighing arose from the packed floor. She swallowed hard and took another step, nearly slipping to fall alongside the prone scarecrow. Something large and pale moved in the shadows, and Katy tightened her grip on the knife.

Damn Gordon and his mountain legends. The one about the haunted scarecrow, in particular. About how it only walked at late harvest, when the corn was turning hard and brown and the first frosts settled on the land. According to legend, the scarecrow climbed down from the stake where it had hung all growing season like a neglected Christ on the cross. Then it dragged itself into the barn, where it feasted on one of the animals, filling its dry throat with fresh blood. Sustained until winter, the scarecrow then returned to its stake, though on moonlit nights you might see rusty red spots on its sackcloth head. Gordon's eyes glistened as he'd told the story, and Katy had given the uneasy laugh he expected in response.

This was the right time of year. And the scarecrow that had fallen at her feet looked just like the one that leaned broken and sad in the cornfield at the end of the vegetable garden.

No. That was just a mountain folk tale. Not a wives' tale, because no wife would be so stupid as to pass along a story like that. Katy could come up with a rational explanation. Holder of a business degree from Queen's College, assistant to the board of directors at Wachovia Bank, she was made of stern stuff. Almost boring but ultimately practical.

So think.

Surely a big farm like this one had several scarecrows. Gordon's family had probably saved them, the same way frugal farm families had always hoarded things that could be used again. Besides, it was just a sack of straw. Flannel and old denim and scraps. No matter the legends.

The dim outline of the scarecrow made a lesser darkness on the floor, the gray socks of the feet poking out of the jeans, gloves at the end of each sleeve. The left sock, the one closest to her, twitched.

The wind, had to be. Except the air was as still as sundown.

Katy put out her own foot, meaning to kick the sock in case a frantic mouse was inside and upset that its nest had been disturbed. The straw toes flexed and curled, and then the foot kicked back at her.

The scarecrow would rise to its elbows and knees and haul itself off to eat a chicken or pig or maybe even a cow, ready to gnaw with those teeth—what would its teeth be?—kernels of giant, hardened corn, piercing flesh and grinding bone and—

The boots sounded above her again.

She hadn't imagined them. Despite her hallucinations in the house, she wasn't losing her mind. Scarecrows didn't move by themselves and her new house wasn't haunted. Never mind Gordon's goddamned legends.

Crumbs of straw fell in a snow between the cracks in the flooring planks above. Someone was up there for real.

The barn door beckoned. Twenty steps and Katy would be out of there, away from animated scarecrows and footfalls and demented goats.

And away from Jett.

Katy paused, heart like a horseshoe in her throat.

She couldn't leave Jett here.

If Jett even *was* here.

The barn had grown darker, the sun settling behind the trees on the ridgeline, fingers of deep red light reaching across the valley. The footsteps above had ceased. Katy's palm was a wooden knot around the knife handle. What good would a knife do against an animated scarecrow? Even if she shredded the cloth, dug into the chest, and found the rag-ball heart, would that even slow it down? Or would it keep crawling, rubbing against her, choking her with its chaff, that uneven grin never changing?

A knock came from one of the stalls. It was soft but insistent, like the hammering of a dying rain.

"Jett!"

Katy hoped to God Jett was back in the house. Even if the house was haunted, it couldn't be worse than this hell-shack of a barn. Katy backed away from the scarecrow twitching before her. Hallucinations and fleeting visions were one thing, and maybe a transparent woman walked the Smith house, but now she was dealing with a stack of rags and silage that did everything but talk.

Katy backed away, but the thumping in the stall was behind her. Whatever was making the sound couldn't be worse than the scarecrow. It had stopped moving, but she was sure it was holding its breath, waiting for her to come closer, tensing its fibrous muscles and licking its corn-kernel teeth with a parched tongue.

She turned and made for the stairs. Maybe if she reached the loft, she could signal Jett and tell her to go for help. Except what kind of help was there against a living scarecrow? Calling Ghostbusters and requesting a smarmy Bill Murray and his team to take the next flight down?

Gordon would be home any minute. He would know some mountain saying or folk spell to cast on the scarecrow, a secret passed down through the generations. That was the way these things worked, wasn't it? Evil countered by a good and courageous heart?

But if those were the weapons, what chance did Katy have? Her own heart was dormant, and besides her feelings for Jett, hadn't been used much in the last few years. She loved Gordon, but was no longer sure what the L-word meant. She couldn't really love God because of all the things he had visited upon her, but she was trying hard for Gordon's sake. But if Gordon, or God, or even Bill Murray, could get her out of this barn, she would be his emotional slave until the end of time.

The stall door opened to her right, and Abraham the goat emerged from the inky depths, his eyes glittering. He ignored Katy and went straight toward the scarecrow. The wad of dead vegetation probably smelled like a gourmet feast to the goat. Katy climbed three steps, stopping on a warped tread to watch the encounter.

The scarecrow regarded the goat with something approaching curiosity, as much as that expression could be suggested by the blank, stitched-up face. Ascribing human characteristics to the face was nothing more than projection, but Katy couldn't help it. She had seen its foot move. She'd heard the legends.

Abraham's nostrils flared; then he lowered his head and approached the scarecrow, the horns curled flat against his skull but still menacing. Twenty feet separated the two creatures—a little voice inside Katy admitted she had already accepted the scarecrow as an organic part of this strange, ancient world of Solom—when the boots sounded upstairs again.

"Jett?"

Please, God, let her be safe in the house.

Except why should God listen to Katy?

Abraham reached the scarecrow, which lay still and prone like a willing sacrament. The billy goat sniffed at the stuffed sock, lowered its bearded chin, and nudged the toes. Katy expected the scarecrow to kick out, to sit up and dig its teeth into the furry neck. Instead, Abraham clamped his teeth onto the sock and tugged, lifting the sock free, showering straw across the ground.

It was just a stupid goddamned scarecrow.

Katy was angry at herself for wasting the last moments of daylight letting her mind run wild. What if a stoned-out Jett had wandered off into the woods? Maybe that light in the forest had belonged to her, maybe she had taken a flashlight and run away from home. In Charlotte, she would head straight for Deidre's house, or the video arcade at the mall, or one of the music stores, to chill out until the drugs wore off. Here in the country, the only place to run was into the woods.

That didn't change the fact that *someone* was in the barn. Unless it, like the house, was haunted.

She went up the stairs to the loft door. It was locked. Had she slipped the latch herself, as she'd exited? She couldn't remember. Below her, Abraham ate the scarecrow's meat with a satisfied chuff.

Katy entered the loft again, determined not to leave until she'd found the owner of the boots, if one existed. The loft wasn't as dark as the space below, but the shadows between the stacked bales had grown deeper. The knife was heavy in her hand and her muscles ached with tension. A charred and pungent odor wended past, and she recognized it as scorched cabbage. She would probably burn the house down. Gordon would be livid. The structure had survived nearly two hundred years of Smiths and Katy would manage to raze it in less than two months.

"Okay, whoever you are," Katy called out, giving her words force to hide the tremor in her throat. Supermom, that was she. "My husband's on his way."

If the trespasser was familiar with Gordon, which was likely, he might not be intimidated by the pudgy professor's wrath. But the jerk might know Gordon's habits, too, and that he rarely arrived home before dark. He would know Katy and Jett were by themselves and the nearest neighbor was a quarter mile away. So Katy added, "I called the sheriff's office."

Something thumped, the sound muffled by the piles of hay. A

patch of lesser gray shifted against the darkness. Katy swallowed hard.

The boots drummed, or maybe it was Katy's heart.

The shape charged her in a shower of dust and straw.

Katy raised the knife, her scream reverberating off the tin roofing like stage thunder in a theater.

The goat stopped in front of her, head lifted, the oblique eyes gathering the faint light and reflecting it in emerald streaks.

A goat.

A goddamned goat had been walking around up here, scaring the stuffing out of her. It must have smelled the hay, climbed up the stairs, and gotten itself locked in.

But who had locked the door?

Katy was on her way to the stairs again when she heard the moan. A barn owl?

No. It came from inside one of the wooden grain barrels that stood near a feed chute. What sort of animal would she find in there? A wounded possum or a feral cat giving birth?

How could she *not* look?

Jett was curled inside, arms folded over her face.

"Jett, honey," Katy said. She sniffed for dope but it could have been something taken internally. Jett's eyes were bloodshot but, even in the weak light, her pupils appeared normal. "Honey, what happened?"

The girl's mouth moved soundlessly for a moment, her face like a ghost's in the blackness of the barrel. She blinked and looked around as if she'd fallen asleep on a car trip. "Where am I?"

"The barn."

"Where am I?"

Drugs. Katy thought they'd left all that behind, and that drugs would be impossible for Jett to find in the rural mountains.

"You're in the barn, Jett." She would save the mother-daughter talk for later, maybe bring Gordon into the act. Gordon wasn't yet a potent father figure, but he knew how to lecture. Right now, she wanted to get Jett in the house so she could check her pulse.

"There was a man . . ." Jett said.

"No, there's nobody up here. Just a goat. I looked. How did you get in the barrel?"

"I don't remember."

The nanny goat, its belly swollen with pregnancy, came over and watched as Katy pulled Jett from the barrel and helped her down the stairs.

Chapter Five

Mouse doodie.

Sarah Jeffers ran her broom along the baseboard of the counter. The counter stood by the front door of Solom General Store and was dark maple, the top scarred by two million transactions. Most of the lights were turned off for closing time, and the dolls, tools, mountain crafts, and just plain junk that hung from the ceiling beams threw long shadows against the walls. After all her years as proprietor, the aroma of tobacco, woodstove smoke, Dr Pepper, and shoe polish had seeped into her skin like balm.

The store had been built during the town's heyday just before World War I, when the timber industry made its assault on the local hardwoods. The train station had been a bustling place, bringing Sarah's grandparents to the mountains from Pennsylvania. The Jeffers, who had once gone by the family name of Jaffe, built the store from the ground up, collecting the creek stones for the foundation, trading and bartering for stock, even breeding their own workforce. They were Jewish but no one paid that any mind, because they kept closed services in their living room and the store remained open on both Saturdays and Sundays.

When the forest slopes were nothing but stumps and the timber cutters moved on, the sawmill shut down. After that, it was like the hands ran backward on the clock. The earthen dam slowly eroded on Blackburn River, and the little housing settlement that sprang up around the mill began succumbing to the gray and ceaseless weight of gravity. Though the first Fords had made occasional visits over the dusty mountain roads, mostly driven by lumber barons who wanted to check on their investments, the town's slow exodus was almost entirely via horse-and-wagon. By the Great Depression, Solom was little more than a whistle stop on the Virginia Creeper railroad line. Then came the great 1940 flood, sweeping away the station and a third of the remaining houses, killing a dozen people in the process.

Sarah's grandparents died within weeks of one another, and the three children fought over who had to stay and run the store. The short straw belonged to Sarah's father, Elisha, who promptly took on a Primitive Baptist wife, Laurel Lee, because she knew addition and subtraction and silence. Through it all the general store stood on its little rise above the river, the stock changing with the times. Chesterfield tobacco pouches and Bugler papers gave way to Marlboro tailor-mades, horehound stick candy disappeared from the shelves in favor of Baby Ruths. A Sears & Roebuck catalog by the register once allowed a mountain family to order practically anything a New York city slicker could buy, but that had been replaced by a computer during the Clinton era. Sarah didn't trust it, had even named it "Slick Willy" and suspected it of swallowing a dollar once in a while, and the screen stayed black unless Gretta, the thick-ankled college student who worked part-time, was on the clock.

The computer was one of the few modern touches, besides the sheer volume of cheap imported crafts designed to look folksy. The wall adornments—rusty advertising signs, farm implements, and shelves of old ripple glass bottles—furthered the illusion that the general store was lost in time, a nostalgic reminder of more carefree days. Sarah didn't buy the illusion, but she sold it. Times were better raking in leisure dollars than dunning the local folks for nickels.

Sarah had grown up in the store, dusting the shelves and tallying pickled eggs in her plain cotton shift. She remembered when the store's first indoor toilet was installed, and though as a four-year-old she'd had a great fear of the roaring flush of water, she'd had an even greater fear of hanging her bare bottom over that stinky black hole in the outhouse. Even back then, she'd pushed a broom, and had asked her mother about the numerous little black needles amid the stray hair, spilled sugar, dried grass, and dirt.

"Mouse doodie," Laurel Lee had said. "A mouse goes to heaven in a country store."

Sarah had always thought of those mice as happy, blessed creatures, scurrying under the floorboards, worrying their way through sacks of feed grain, chewing into the corners of cornflake boxes. But after nearly seventy years of sweeping up their damned doodie, she was about ready to wish them to a Baptist hell.

But at least the mice gave her something to blame when strange sounds echoed through the aisles. She didn't like being in the store alone, but she could barely afford her two part-time helpers. So she'd spent the past decades running the broom, ignoring the evidence of her ears, and not thinking about the scarecrow man.

The bell over the screen door rang. It was ten minutes after seven, past closing time, but she hadn't locked the door. The porch light bathed the deck in yellow light, and Sarah squinted against it at the bulky shadow.

"Howdy," she said. It was still tourist season in the mountains, though the Floridians and New Yorkers were usually tucked away in their Titusville hotel rooms by now, afraid of getting a mosquito bite, or else squirreled away in their Happy Hollow rental cabins at $150 a night. The kayak and rafting trade from Sue Norwood's little shop had boomed a little along the river, helping the general store keep its head above water. Seemed like every time the business wanted to sink down to the sandy bottom and take a nice, long nap, some moneymaking scheme came along and dragged it back to the surface for another gasp.

The shadow stood in the door, hands in pockets, the head obscured by an outdated hat with a wide brim. All Sarah wanted was to get a little of his money and send him on his way in time for the latest rerun of *Seinfeld*, delivered via her little satellite dish.

"Can I get you something?" she said, glad to be shut of mouse doodie for the moment. Her voice had developed a mountain twang over the years, partly unconsciously and partly to help sell the illusion.

The figure shuffled forward. People in these parts, even the visitors, usually answered when addressed. But occasionally a creep came through looking for the best place in the neighborhood for fast money. She did a mental calculation, figured she had maybe eighty bucks in the register. Worth killing somebody over, these days.

Sarah leaned her broom against the counter, flicking her eyes toward the shotgun she kept on the second shelf beneath the register. The shotgun was well oiled but hadn't been fired in twenty years. Currently it was covered by stacks of the *High Country News*, a free weekly that was such wretched oatmeal she couldn't give it away. She'd hidden the newspapers, not wanting to disappoint the friendly young man with the crew cut who delivered them early Thursday mornings. She figured there were at least two months of bad copy between her and the firearm.

She'd have to talk her way out of this one. "Got a special on canned ham," she said. "Nine dollars. Let the missus take an evening off from the kitchen."

Nothing, not even a grunt. The man was three steps inside. She wished she'd left more lights on. It was the electrical cooperative's fault. In her father's day, the Blackburn dam had a generator, cranking out enough juice to light up the store and two dozen homes. Then the co-op came in and hooked five counties together, and you had to be on the grid or off, no in between. After that, the power bill had gotten higher every month.

Sarah could make out the man's form now, the collar of his coat turned up even though the fall had yet to turn chilly. The front brim of the hat was angled down, keeping the face in shadows.

The stranger stood there, his breath like the whistle of a distant train. Something creaked in the hardware section, in the back corner of the store that Sarah avoided after sundown. Things went wrong in that corner: alakaline batteries leaked, boxes of nails busted open for no good reason, the fingers of work gloves somehow grew holes. Her father had sold guns, and the ammunition used to be locked away in that corner, but one afternoon some of the bullets somehow got hot and exploded, sending lead fragments whizzing over the heads of the customers. Sarah wished for a magic bullet right now, one that would knock the stranger's hat off his head.

Because the hat didn't belong.

"Your first trip to Solom?" Sarah said, keeping her voice steady. She eased toward the counter, closer to the register and the shotgun. She'd been driving some tacks into the shelf so she could hang her metal signs, the ones that said A BAD DAY OF FISHING BEATS A GOOD DAY OF WORK and I AIN'T OLD, I'M JUST EXPERIENCED. She leaned on the counter with one elbow, her other arm reaching for the hammer. It felt good in her hand.

"You staying up at the Tester B-and-B?" she asked the mute man. "Or the Happy Hollow cabins?"

Sarah brought the hammer closer to her hip, imagining its arc as she brought it into the dark, unseen face. Her lips creased into the tired, welcoming smile she gave to first-time customers, an expression meant to elicit pity and a desire to help out a little old lady by giving her money. "You ain't from around here, are you?"

The stranger stepped into the light, lifted his hat, and smiled. "Once I was," he said, in a voice as patient as a river and as deep as a subterranean cavern. "But that was a while back."

Sarah dropped the hammer, nearly breaking her big toe.

Jett didn't have an appetite, so Katy put her to bed early after checking for signs of drug use. Her daughter's respiration and pulse were slightly elevated, but that could have been from the fright. Jett's eyes weren't bloodshot but were wild and frantic, and they kept flicking toward the corners of her room and the closet door.

"He was tall," Jett said. "Wearing black, with an old hat."

"Let's talk about this after supper, honey."

"Can I leave my light on? Please?"

"Sure."

Jett had never been afraid of the dark, not since the age of three. Katy felt guilty for leaving her upstairs, but she had to salvage dinner before Gordon arrived. She was reluctant to tell Gordon about

the incident. As conservative as he was, he would want to search
Jett's room. It was a showdown in which everybody would lose.
Besides, Jett said she had quit drugs, and Katy gave her daughter
the benefit of a doubt. People changed, and they changed a lot
faster when they were new and still learning to be people.

Suppose there had been a man dressed in black? Katy had heard
the boots walking on the loft floor, and they'd sounded much
louder than goat's hooves. She didn't want to think about it. A goat
made more sense than a stranger in black. Odus Hampton wouldn't
have skulked around, he would have called out in his friendly but
deferential voice.

"Why don't you read something?" Katy said, going to the book-
shelf. "How about a comic book? 'Sandman.' That sounds like it
could put you to sleep."

"Mom, you're so out of it."

"Music, then?" She scanned the row of CDs. Jett had raided
Katy's collection and plucked some of the most rebellious titles.
Here was Patti Smith, the manic street preacher warning people
away from the golden stairs of heaven. Kate Bush, a reclusive genius whose voice could seduce and excoriate in the same breath.
Siouxsie and her Banshees, who smothered you with sonic layers
that were as sweet as funeral flowers. The Psychedelic Furs with
their manic saxes and dismal lyrics. Jett had some newer music that
Katy was unfamiliar with, Angelfish and Bella Morte.

Katy knew what it was like to be twelve. She'd been there once,
and not so long ago. Decadence and doom seemed like perfectly
reasonable pursuits for a girl on the verge of becoming a woman,
as long as it was confined to the realm of rock 'n' roll. But, in a
quirk that secretly pleased Katy, her daughter had also sneaked a
lot of upbeat guitar pop out of Katy's collection: the Replacements,
dBs, Let's Active, Tommy Keene, and Robyn Hitchcock.

"I just want to lay here and think," Jett said.

" 'Lie here,' " Katy corrected.

"Yeah, I was going to say that, but I'm not lying. I really saw
him."

Katy sat down on the edge of the bed and felt Jett's forehead.
Clammy, no sign of a fever. "Okay, we'll see about whether you're
up to school tomorrow."

"I *want* to go to school."

"New friends, huh? A guy?"

Jett twisted her lips into a "yuck," but her eyes narrowed into a secretive expression. Without her dramatic eyeliner and face powder, Jett looked innocent and girlish. Her careworn teddy bear, Captain Boo, was tucked against her chin. If only those who judged her by her boots and chains and dyed hair with the purple streak could see her like this, Katy thought, maybe they'd give her a break.

Like that would ever happen. Katy had a hard enough time keeping Gordon off Jett's case, which had nearly been a dealbreaker after his sudden proposal. It was only after Gordon agreed to give it some time and let Jett deal with the transition in her own way that Katy accepted. Jett even admitted she wasn't a serious Goth. Hers was more an act, a Goth Lite traveling show that would have been tiresome to her if it didn't upset some people so much.

That was the part Katy understood and supported. Despite her former career as a loan officer, very little else about her was ordinary. She'd always had an unhealthy self-image, the scrawny redhead with freckles, and she'd compensated by going out of her way to be a "somebody" in school. Sometimes that meant beating out a girl on the volleyball or cheerleading squad, and a couple of times she'd resorted to stealing one of the more popular girls' boyfriends. Because she considered herself unattractive, she had to engage in behavior that was a little more extreme than that of her competitors.

So she could cut her daughter some slack. Besides, Katy wasn't exactly jumping into her new role as farm wife as if it were a second skin, despite a newfound fondness for Smith family recipes.

She pulled the blankets up and kissed Jett's forehead. She thought about asking if Jett wanted to say a prayer, then realized how phony that would sound. Jett would shoot her down by asking how come they never prayed in Charlotte. And, she'd add, what was so freaking great about Solom that deserved special thanks?

"I'll come up after supper and check on you," Katy said. "Or you can come down if you feel up to it."

Jett turned to face the window, hugging Captain Boo tightly. "I'll be here. Unless he comes to get me again."

"Honey."

"Never mind."

Katy rose from the bed. If she had the guts, she would tell her daughter about the mysterious figure she'd seen in the kitchen, the wispy form that had vanished in the pantry. But Katy wasn't ready to admit that the vision was real. No footsteps had sounded on the stairs when she was home alone, and the sudden scent of lilacs hadn't drifted across the kitchen whenever she performed a domestic task. This was an old house, that was all, settling wood and seeped-in aromas. Maybe she'd leave her own mark for the next generation: blackened cabbage and funky salmon.

"If it really was a man, Gordon will probably know him," Katy said, not quite believing her own words. "He'll know what to do."

"Sure, Mom." Jett didn't believe her at all.

"I love you."

"Love you too." Sounded like she almost meant it.

Katy went downstairs into the kitchen, where she scraped the cabbage into the garbage. Perhaps she should dump the mess outside, but she wanted to get something on the table before Gordon showed up. She rummaged in the fridge, then with a sigh retreated to the safety of the freezer and a microwave TV dinner. Gordon's first wife, Rebecca, had never used a microwave, and Katy suspected the one she brought from her Charlotte apartment was the first to ever emit radiation in this house. Perhaps this meal was an affront to the generations of Smiths who had gone before.

"Get used to it," Katy said.

Something crashed in the pantry.

"Wonderful." She punched up the proper cook time on the keypad of the microwave. She couldn't handle cabbage but she was magic with instant meals.

With the microwave whirring behind her, she went to the pantry and pulled back the curtain. The aroma of lilacs was so strong it was like a slap in the face. Rows and rows of Mason jars lined the shelves, containing raspberry preserves, chow chow, sauerkraut, and a dozen other goods all expertly canned by Gordon's first wife. Enough to last a nuclear winter.

On the floor, juice leaking from shards of curved and gleaming glass, was a jar of pickles. Broken like the spaghetti sauce. As Katy knelt to pick up the largest pieces, she felt the curtain stir behind her, as if someone was through with business in the pantry and had chores elsewhere.

Jett listened to Mom banging around in the kitchen. She tried to muster a little sympathy, because Mom was trying to be some kind of trophy wife and didn't have the sense to recognize it just wasn't in her blood. Mom had just been plain uncool lately, a slave to the kitchen, fussing over the house, keeping dirty laundry off the floor. All to please Gordon, a man who wouldn't notice his slippers were on fire unless somebody turned a hose on him.

She tugged her Walkman from the lower shelf of her bedside table. She almost wished she had a joint. That would go over well with the Cure whispering through the headphones, Robert Smith going on about how he couldn't find himself even when he was in love with someone happy and young. No wonder, he should ditch the "happy" part and find a real woman. Jett would gladly volunteer.

After all, Jett was a drug-addict loser who had finally gone so far over the edge she was imagining mystical encounters with giant scarecrow men. If she had been stoned, she could have laughed it off. But she had promised Mom that drugs were a thing of the past, a habit left in Charlotte, and she was determined to keep the promise. If Mom could change, so could Jett. Though it looked like neither of them were changing for the better.

The front door closed downstairs, and over the guitar solo she heard Gordon's belly-deep professor's voice delivering his standard catch phrase. "Where are my favorite girls?"

Jett wormed deeper beneath the blankets. Gordon never entered her room after she was in bed, thank goodness. That was one advantage of his being a religious guy. He had some weird Old Testament code that kept women in their place but also placed them on an altar. Mom had swallowed it hook, line, and sinker. After Dad's neglect, any sort of attention was a cause of mindless joy for her. Not that Dad was a bad guy. He just had his own fucking shit to deal with, truckloads of it, and Jett wished she could call him right now. She needed somebody real to talk to, somebody who would understand about stupid scarecrow men.

But what would she tell him? She couldn't really remember. The whole thing in the barn seemed like a bad acid trip, and Jett knew about acid because she'd dropped it a second time at Melissa Sanderson's fourteenth birthday party. She'd spent the whole night hiding under Melissa's bed, talking to the dust bunnies. The weirdest thing was that the dust bunnies had talked back, and they even *acted* like bunnies, hopping around, frolicking, twitching their little whiskers. But that was a lifetime ago and a whole other person. That had been a stupid, skinny kid trying to fit in with the crowd.

Now she was trying to fit *out* of the crowd.

She cranked the Cure up to full volume and put the blanket over her head so Mom would think she was asleep. She wouldn't sleep. She didn't dare. Because, if she closed her eyes, she might see the tall, dark man with the sickle.

Somehow, morning came just the same.

Chapter Six

Ray Tester pressed the lever beneath the fuel control of his Massey Ferguson, raising the hydraulic arms at the rear of the tractor. The arms held a bush hog, an oversize lawn mower attachment that hacked meadows into hay. Ray only had ten acres, the smallest of the parcels that had been divided among the family when Zachariah Tester died. Old Zack had been the preacher at Rush Branch Primitive Baptist Church, a position now held by David Tester, Ray's oldest brother. David had gotten sixty acres in the will and Ray's attendance at the church had been spotty ever since, mostly funerals, weddings, and whenever some good home-baked pies were being served.

Ray surveyed the slain grass behind him. The signs called for dry weather, and if the rain held off for five days, Ray could get the hay rolled and stacked safely in the shed. He had a dozen head of cattle, but the way people were breeding goats up here, he might be better off culling his herd and paying his property tax bill by selling hay. He could understand the temptation to raise goats over cows: goats preferred to browse instead of graze, so you could turn them loose in the woods and they did gangbusters. They didn't mind a steep slope, either.

On the downside, and Ray had learned there was always a

downside when it came to farming, goat meat was like a gamier version of venison and you'd never find it served up at McDonald's. Some of the organic farmers that had settled in Solom over the last decade had taken to milking goats. A nanny raised holy hell if you didn't tug her teats twice a day, the yield wasn't all that hot, and unless you were squeezing the milk into cheese, you had to hustle it off to market in Asheville or Charlotte. Both of those cities were full of queers and Asheville in particular was known to harbor witches, so as far as Ray was concerned, the organic hippies could keep that little business.

Ray wiped the sweat from his bald head. A Cadillac passed on the road, white as a virgin, with tinted windows and tires wide enough to roll out pizza dough. Damned tourist. Ray thought about flipping a finger, but Sarah down at the general store had lectured him on how outside money was good stuff. Yankees with summer homes paid the county plenty in taxes but didn't require many services, since they were only down here two or three months a year. Still, a Yankee was a fucking Yankee, and the invasion that had started in the War Between the States with General Bill Stoneman and finished up with Sherman had never really ended, just changed tactics. Instead of cavalry and carpetbaggers, New York sent its developers and architects and their scrawny, pale wives.

But the driver of that heavy-assed hunk of steel was probably spending money down at Sarah's, and she was as sweet as sugarcane, so Ray lifted his hand in a halfhearted wave. Tourists liked that sort of thing, the farmer in his field, a simple picture hearkening back to a simpler time. Wasn't nothing simple about it. You couldn't barter for what you needed anymore, and the government had gotten bigger every year, despite the Republican takeover of the South. Ray could sell down at the farmers' market in Boone and pocket some tax-free income, but he also had to be on the Agricultural Extension Office books so he could get his handout when the government decided to subsidize some crop or another.

The Cadillac disappeared around the curve and Ray turned the tractor for another pass. He lowered the bush hog and the thick blade cut into the clover, dandelion, rye, and sour grass. The green scent filled his nostrils. A horsefly landed on the back of his neck and he swiped at it. The fly lifted and settled again just above his ear. Ray slapped again, twisting his neck, so he wasn't watching as his tractor hit a hump, causing the front tires to bounce. Ray's left foot reached for the clutch but the back tires had already rolled over the same hump. The bush hog blade made a whining noise, and Ray looked back to see a stream of dark liquid spew from beneath the protective metal shield.

"Shit fire," he said, disengaging the tractor's transmission and throwing the PTO into neutral, stopping the blade. He set the hand brake and got down from the seat. Sometimes you hit a nest of rabbits in a hayfield. Once, Ray had accidentally chopped up a fawn. If a doe left her fawn, the fawn would remain at that spot until the mother came back, no matter what, even if a giant, smoke-spitting mountain of steel was heading for it. But this was no bunny and no fawn.

Four goats, their heads gone, their carcasses ripped with red gashes.

Somebody had slaughtered them and tossed their bodies into the knee-high grass. Somebody who wasn't interested in goat burger or rank cheese.

Ray killed the Massey Ferguson's engine and leaned against a rear tire, watching the flies swarm around their decaying feast. The first buzzard appeared in the sky, its black wings buffeted by the high September wind.

Hippies. Had to be. Or Yankees, maybe. Who else would kill a damned goat for no good reason? Though Ray saw no use in the stubborn critters, he wouldn't kill them on purpose. He was raised to kill only for food, anyway.

This was the work of somebody with no respect for the mountains, for the ways of the farm, for life. A person who pulled something like this didn't belong in the valley. Solom had always taken care of itself, even if outsiders had started buying up the land. And Ray was sure that, one way or another, Solom would take care of whatever disrespectful trash had done this messy deed.

Maters.
Those blessed maters were going to be the death of her.
Betsy Ward had canned, stewed, frozen, and dried about thirty

pounds of those red, ugly things. The blight had hit hard because of the wet summer, and the first frosts had killed the plants, but her husband, Arvel, had brought in a double armload just before the big autumn die-off. Now tomatoes sat in rows across the windowsill, along the counter, and on the pantry shelves, turning from green to pink to full sinful red, with the occasional leaking black spot. The thing about tomatoes was that no bug or cutworm would attack them. The plants were as poison as belladonna, and bugs were smart enough to know that maters would kill you. But people were a lot dumber than bugs.

Betsy wiped the sweat away with a dirty towel. She had been born in Solom, and had even gone off the mountain for a year to attend community college. She'd wanted to be a typist then, maybe get on with Westridge University and draw vacation and retirement. But Arvel had come along with his pickup and Doc Watson tapes and rusty mufflers and he'd seemed like the Truth for a nineteen-year-old mountain girl, and then one night he forgot the rubber and nine months later they were married and the baby came out with the cord wrapped around its neck and they had tried a few times after that, but now all they had was a long piece of property and a garden and so many tomatoes that Betsy wanted to grab Arvel's shotgun and blow them all into puree.

She looked out the window and saw Gordon Smith's new wife checking the mailbox. The woman had that big-city, washed-out look, as if she couldn't wander into daylight without a full plate of makeup. Still, she seemed harmless enough, and not as standoffish as the other outsiders who had flooded the valley since Betsy's knee-high days. And Betsy was sick to death of her kitchen, anyway. She flicked the seeds from her fingers and headed for the door, determined to greet her new neighbor.

Four mailboxes stood at the mouth of the gravel drive. Arvel's place was the closest to the highway, followed by Gordon's, then by a fellow Betsy had never met, though she'd peeked in his mailbox once and learned that his name was Alex Eakins. A young woman drove by to visit him about once a week or so, probably up to fornication and other sins.

"Howdy," Betsy called from the porch.

The redhead looked up from the box where she had been

thumbing through a stack of envelopes. Her eyes were bloodshot. Betsy wondered if she was a drinker, then decided a God-fearing man like Gordon would never stand for the stuff in his house. Even if she was kind of good-looking, in an off-the-mountain kind of way. Her ankles were way too skinny and would probably snap plumb in half if she ever had to hitch a mule to a plow and cut a straight furrow. Still, she looked a little tough, like a piece of rawhide that had been licked and stuck out in the sun. And she'd walked the quarter mile to the mailbox instead of jumping in a car.

"Hi, Mrs. Ward," the redhead said. "Gordon told me about the tomatoes."

Betsy wondered just what Gordon *had* told, because there wasn't a lot to tell. She'd known Gordon since he was dragging stained diapers across the floor of the Smith house. Sure, he'd gone off and gotten educated, but he was still the same little boy who'd once pegged her cat with a rotten apple. Plus he had the tainted blood of all the Solom Smiths. "How you liking Solom so far?"

"I like it here. A little different from what I'm used to, though."

Betsy wasn't so sure the redhead meant that first part, since the corners of her mouth were turned down and her eyes twitched like she hadn't got a wink of sleep. "How did your garden do this year?"

"Well, Gordon keeps up with that," the redhead said, fanning herself with the envelopes. "We had some cruciform vegetables, cabbage, broccoli, some corn. Gordon said I should take up canning."

Betsy wanted to ask about the Smith tomatoes, because tomatoes were how you judged a mountain garden. Any two-bit, chicken-stealing farmer could grow a cabbage. But if you could fight off the blight, you either knew what you were doing or your garden had been plain blessed by the Lord. But this skinny thing had come in during late summer and wouldn't know a thing about blight.

And probably didn't know a thing about Gordon's ancestor the Circuit Rider.

Betsy couldn't say whether that was a good or a bad thing. Ignorance was bliss, they said, but stupidity got you killed.

"Where you from?" Betsy asked. The new woman didn't seem

Yankee, or of that species from Florida that had lately become the ruin of the valley.

"I was born in Atlanta, but I settled in Charlotte."

"Charlotte, huh? I seen about that on the news." Betsy was about to bring up all the niggers that shot each other down there. But even with the Confederate battle flags that flew up and down the highway near the tabernacle, she didn't think "nigger" was a Christian term. Besides, those Rebel flags usually flew just beneath the Stars and Stripes, so she reckoned that Lincoln's law was probably just a mite superior, though of course far short of the Lord's own.

Arvel's border collie, Digger, had dragged itself from under the shade of the porch and stood by the steps, giving a bark to show he'd been on duty all along.

"It's quite a change," the redhead said. She turned her face to the sun and breathed deeply. "All these mountains and fresh air. It's a little strange at night to fall asleep without lights burning everywhere."

"Oh, we got lights," Betsy said. "God's lights. Them little specks in the sky."

The redhead stopped by Betsy's gate. Digger sniffed and growled.

"Hold back, Digger," Betsy said. "It's neighbors."

"The constellations," the redhead said, her face flushing a little. "You can see them all the way down to the horizon. In my old neighborhood, you saw maybe four stars at night."

"What else you seen? That's a little strange, I mean?"

"Strange? Well, it's all new, of course. Gordon's family has such a rich history here."

History just means you lived too long, Betsy thought. *Valley families have made their peace with the past. And with the Circuit Rider. The families that are still around, anyhow.*

"How's Gordon doing?" she asked.

"He's working on a new book. About Appalachian foot-washing practices."

"If he spent half as much time in church as he did writing about it, he'd be in the Lord's bosom a hundred times over."

The redhead gave a smile, but it looked as if she were chewing glass behind it. "Gordon has a passion for Baptist religion."

"Not the right kind of passion."

"Sorry, Mrs. Ward. I respect his work, and so do a number of anthropologists and sociologists who study this region."

"He ain't dealt with the proper side of things." Digger barked beside her in punctuation.

"I'll share your opinions with him," the redhead said. "My name's Katy, by the way. Katy Logan."

"Logan? I thought you was married."

"We are. I kept my maiden name. Long story."

No story could be long enough if it defied the Old Testament creed that kept a woman subject to her husband. Why, if Betsy so much as opened her mouth in anger to Arvel, he would slap her across the cheek and send her to the floor. In the Free Will church, she kept her mouth shut except for the occasional hymn or moan of praise, and she sat to the left with the other wives and the children. It was important to know your place in God's scheme of things. First there was God, then the Circuit Rider, and then the husband.

Digger growled again, sensing Betsy's unease.

"That girl of yours," Betsy said. "Seen her waiting for the school bus. What's her name?"

"Jessica," the redhead said, avoiding the question that Betsy had really asked: *Who was the evil child's father? Because we all know it ain't Gordon. With all that makeup, it's obvious the little tart came straight from fornicating with Satan. Or maybe a Solom billy goat, which amounts to the same thing.*

"How's she like school?"

"Okay so far. You know how kids are."

Betsy knew, despite never having raised one. "Well, I'd best get back to my canning."

"Could you show me how to do it someday?"

"Sure thing." Though Betsy had no intention of giving away any information that was useful.

"By the way, do you know anything about the scarecrow? Gordon said it's a local legend."

"Scarecrow? Not heard tell of anything like that."

Unless you have it confused with the Circuit Rider. But Gordon knows better than that.

"Well, no big deal." Katy waved and added a "Good doggie" for Digger's sake, though Digger was having none of it.

Betsy left the dog on the porch to encourage Katy on her way. She watched between the kitchen curtains as the bony woman made her way up the gravel road, grabbing at the goldenrod that bloomed along the ditch.

"Trouble," Betsy muttered to herself. "A skinny woman ain't never been nothing but trouble."

Odus Hampton pulled his battered Chevy Blazer into the general store's rutted parking lot. It was a quarter till nine, which almost guaranteed he'd be Sarah's first customer of the day. He figured on buying a cup of coffee and a honey bun, something to kick the hangover out of his head before he went up to Bethel Springs. In addition to odd jobs, he worked part-time for Crystal Mountain Bottlers, a Greensboro company that siphoned off fresh mountain spring water, shipped it to a factory for treatment, then charged idiots over a buck a bottle. Even with all those tricks the Arabs were pulling, gas was still cheaper per gallon than the stuff Odus pumped through a hose into Crystal Mountain's tankers.

He stepped from the Blazer with a silent groan, his ligaments tight. Maybe if he stuck to spring water instead of Old Crow bourbon, he wouldn't feel like a sixty-year-old twenty years too soon. He stabbed a Marlboro into his mouth and fired it up, counting the number of steps to the front door to see if he could get half the smoke finished. Even good old Sarah had given in to the "no smoking" bullshit, and though she sold two dozen brands of cigarettes, pipe tobacco, and snuff, she wouldn't let her customers use the products in her store. That whole tobacco thing was as bad as the Arabs and their gas, only this time it was the federal government turning the screw. Did away with price support so cigarette companies had farmers by the balls, then taxed the devil out of the stuff on the back end.

Odus coughed and spat as he climbed the porch steps. The general store wasn't as grand as it had been in his childhood, when he'd bounced up those steps with a quarter in his pocket and all

manner of choices. A quarter could buy you a Batman comic book
and a candy bar, or a Pepsi-Cola and a Moon Pie, or a pack of baseball cards and a bubblegum cigar. Now all a quarter did was weigh
down your pants. And Odus's pants needed all the help they could
get, what with his belly pushing down on his belt like a water-
melon balanced on a clothesline.

The front door was open. That was funny. Sarah always kept it
closed until nine on the dot, even though if you were a regular, you
could knock and go on in if you showed up a little early. Odus took
a final tug of his cigarette and threw it into the sand-filled bucket
with all the other unfinished butts. He peered through the screen
door, looking for signs of movement.

"Sarah?"

Maybe she was in back, checking on inventory or stacking up
some canned preserves that bore the Solom General Store label but
were actually contracted to a police auxiliary group over in
Westmoreland County. Odus called again. Maybe Sarah had gone
over to her house, which sat just beside the store. Decided she'd
need a helping of prunes to move things along, maybe. At her age,
nature needed a little push now and then.

Odus went to the deli counter at the rear of the store. The coffeepot sat on top in a little blue tray so customers could help themselves. Nondairy creamer (which was about like non-cow
hamburger if you stopped to think about it), straws, white packets
of sugar, and pink packets of artificial sweetener were scattered
across the tray. The coffeemaker was turned off, and the pot was
empty and as cold as a witch's heart in December. Sarah always
made coffee first thing.

A twinge rippled through Odus's colon, as if a tiny salamander
were turning flips down there. It might have been a cheap whiskey
fart gathering steam, or it might have been the first stirring of unease. Either way, Odus felt it was time for some fresh morning air.
As he passed the register on the way out, he saw Sarah's frail body
curled across a couple of sacks of feed corn. Her eyes were partially open, her mouth slack, a thick strand of drool hanging from
one corner of her gray lips.

Odus went around the counter and knelt on the buckled hardwood floor, feeling for her pulse. All he felt was his own, the hang-

over beating through his thumb. He turned her face up and put his cheek near her mouth. A stagnant breeze stirred, with that peculiar old-person's smell of pine and decay. She was alive.

"Sarah," Odus said, patting her cheek, trying to remember what those emergency techs did in the television shows. All he ever watched was the crime scene shows, and those dealt with people who were already dead. He turned back to the counter and was searching among the candy wrappers, invoices, and business cards for the phone when he heard a soft moan.

Sarah blinked once, a film over her eyes like spiderwebs. She tried to sit up, but Odus eased her back down.

"Sarah, what happened?"

Her mouth opened, and with her wrinkled neck and glazed eyes, she looked like a fledging robin trying to suck a digested worm from its mother's beak.

"Easy, now," Odus said, his mouth parched, wishing Solom wasn't in the dry part of the county and a cold beer was in the cooler alongside the seventeen kinds of cola.

"*Hat*," Sarah said.

"Yes, ma'am, it's sure hot for September," Odus said. "You must have worked up an early sweat. Overdid it a little. But you just sit and rest now."

Sarah slapped at his chest with a bony hand. "*Haaaat*."

"I know. I'll get you some water."

Sarah grabbed his forearm, her fingers like the talons of a red hawk. She sat up, her face rigid. "You damned drunken fool," she said, spittle flying from her mouth. "The man in the hat. He's back."

Sarah's eyes closed and she collapsed onto the gray, coarse sacks, her breathing shallow but steady.

Odus renewed his search for the phone. Going on about a hat, of all things. She must have had a stroke and blown her senses. Most males in these parts wore a hat, and it wasn't unknown for them to come back now and again.

Chapter Seven

Total suck city.

Mrs. McNeeley was outlining on the chalkboard, lecturing like she usually did with her back to the class. To the sixth grade English teacher, instruction meant breathing chalk dust and turning her pupils' brains to sawdust. Who the hell cared what a direct object was, or a plural nominative? Like anybody was ever going to need to know that stuff in real life.

But teachers like Mrs. McNeeley were great for those kids who were logging their time and sopping up free lunches while waiting until they could legally drop out. Like Grady Eggers and Tommy Williamson on the back row. If McNeeley had the sense to seat the kids in alphabetical order, the problem would cut itself in half. As it was, the two goons kept up a spitball barrage and a constant taunting of everyone around them. Like all successful goons, and most of that species had been gifted by God, Grady and Tommy knew when it was time to play the angel, to let their faces go soft and wounded whenever another student made an accusation or complaint.

Like this morning when Tommy had made a grab for Jett's ass in the hall.

That kind of thing was flattering in the fifth grade, when you didn't have any ass worth grabbing, but now she was on the verge of becoming a lady, and as freaky as that was, she thought her body had some value. She had whirled and tried to kick him in that mysterious region between his legs, where all manner of lumpy, disgusting things dangled, but at the last second he had twisted away and her foot bounced harmlessly off his thigh. Worse, he caught her leg while she was off-balance, tilted her over like DiCaprio going for Winslet in *Titanic*, or maybe Gable doing Leigh if you were lame enough to have watched *Gone With the Wind*, as she had. Tommy put his mouth close to hers, braces and all, and whispered, "Not a bad move for a headless chicken."

Then he spun her in spastic imitation of a Spanish dance, the other kids laughing as she fell to her knees, and a nuclear orange anger had erupted behind her eyelids. She must have screamed, because when the dust cleared, the beefy assistant principal Richard Bell, known to the kids as Dicky Dumbbell, had sequestered Tommy away for a private counsel. Apparently sexual harassment wasn't a serious offense at Cross Valley Elementary, because Tommy had been right on time for first-period geography, and since Cross Valley was a small school, Jett was in the same class. Tommy had winked at her and given a twisted smile that held the promise of future humiliation.

The worst thing of all was that part of her had flushed, some secret and forbidden woman region that craved attention but didn't know quite what to do with it.

And so the day had gone. Now, with McNeeley's sentence diagrams covering the chalkboard and the hands of the clock reaching wearily toward two, Jett was calculating how fast she could reach the door when the final bell rang. She closed her eyes and must have dozed, because she saw a man in a black hat at McNeeley's desk, seven feet tall, moth holes in his frayed suit. He held a thick Bible in his left hand, his pale right hand raised and miles beyond the sleeve of his too-small jacket.

"The possessive of a name ending in *s* is followed by apostrophe *s*, except, strangely enough, in the case of Jesus," he intoned, with a voice as dark and loud as Revelation's thunder. "In that case, it's just an apostrophe by itself. That's according to *The Chicago Manual of Style*, brothers and sisters. Special rule for Jesus. Amen."

Jett's eyes snapped open and she found her head had almost banged against the top of her desk, the one with the greasy pencil slot and *Suck Big Donky Dix* carved into the surface.

McNeeley was finishing some monotone declaration or another, and the class had long since given in to fidgeting. Tommy made a bleating, goatish sound from the back of the class, causing McNeeley to turn. She stood with the piece of chalk in her hand, her eyes like milk.

"Did someone have a question?" she asked.

"Yeah," Grady Eggers said, raising his hand and lifting himself out of his seat. He was already five-ten and had the first signs of stubble, the kind of kid who was headed for either gridiron glory or the oily pits of auto shop.

McNeeley tugged at her cardigan and pushed her cat's-eye glasses up her long nose. "Mr. Eggers?"

"Does Jesus really get no *s*?"

"Excuse me?"

"I mean, why does he get treated any different? You said every rule applies to everybody the same."

Jett was wide awake now, no matter how drowsy she had been before.

"I don't understand," Mrs. McNeeley said, putting on her teacher's smile, the automatic response to anything that cast doubt on the textbook.

"You said Jesus was the exception to the rule."

The class grew silent. Even Tommy Williamson looked pensive, a rare expression for him.

"I'm sorry, Mr. Eggers. I didn't say a thing about Jesus."

"You said he don't get no apostrophe *s*, just an apostrophe." Grady sounded uneasy, on the edge of rage. "I heard it plain as day. Why come is that?"

"We were discussing when to use 'who' or 'whom' in the objective case," McNeeley said. "I don't see how our dear Lord and Savior could enter into it."

The bell gave its brittle cry of release, and the tension in the class dropped like a wet rope.

Jett gathered her books, hoping to make it to the next class before Tommy caught up with her. She felt faint, partly due to the vision she'd had of the man in the black hat. But Grady had apparently heard the man's words, though from McNeeley's mouth. Did it really count as a vision if two people experienced it, or did you chalk it up to the beginnings of mass hysteria?

In fifth grade health class in Charlotte, Jett had been subjected to the ever-popular drug scare videos. While most of the kids had snickered as somber narrators expounded on the dangers of evil weed, Jett had actually paid attention. Unlike the others, who wouldn't know a yellow jacket from a roach, Jett saw it as an opportunity to educate herself. She'd paid attention when the talking head launched into a tirade on acid flashbacks, in which a bad trip could come on weeks, months, or even years after the initial "exposure." Come right out of the blue, the narrator had said. Totally unexpected and without warning. Flashback sufferers often went to the hospital because they thought they were having a nervous breakdown.

The whole thing was starting to freak her out. It was possible that Grady, too, had dropped LSD. But that still didn't mean they would have the same flashback. And how could you "flash back" to something that had never happened before?

Gordon would probably know, but she'd rather eat a hot popsicle in hell than talk with him about anything in her personal life.

But which one was the hallucination, the scarecrow man she'd seen in the barn or the man in the black hat?

She negotiated the halls, weaving through kids in denim jackets with rolled-up sleeves, low-hanging pants, the girls wearing wide belts. Even here in the sticks, it seemed everybody knew about Old Navy and Gap. A bunch of brainless trendoids. Some of the redneck boys wore flannel, but they stuck to their own kind, stomping their boots as if to knock the cow shit out of the treads, sneaking pinches of Skoal between their cheeks and gums.

"What's the hurry?" came a girl's voice behind her.

Jett wheeled to face Bethany, who was as cool as Mentos in her short skirt and blue halter top with bra straps showing. "No hurry, I just have to do my homework before math class."

"But class starts in four minutes."

"That's what I mean. I don't want to disappoint Mrs. Stansberry. She's the only cool teacher I have."

"Did you sleep okay? You look like you're late for your own funeral. Or maybe your eye shadow's a little thick today."

"Thanks for the compliment."

"No, you're good. This Goth thing looks bitching. I wish my parents would let me get away with it."

"See, that's just it. You don't *ask* your parents, you tell them. Have to show them who is boss right from diapers."

"I'll bet yours were black."

"Well, not while they were clean."

"Ooh, yuck." Bethany crinkled her overly pert nose.

"What are you doing after school?"

"Feeding the goats."

"I hate those cloven-hoofed little monsters. They scare me."

Bethany laughed. "They're okay. The males, the billy goats, stink unless you cut their balls off. My dad has a metal band that you put around them, then leave it for a few weeks. The balls swell up and turn black and gross, and then they fall off. Problem solved."

Jett shuddered. She wasn't an expert in male anatomy, but she was under the impression that the testicles were the most vulnerable spot on their bodies. Which is why you tried to kick there in an emergency. But causing their balls to rot seemed like the sort of punishment that should be reserved for the very worst of them. Creatures like Tommy Williamson.

Jett decided she wouldn't complain about her own chores for a while. Sweeping the living room didn't seem so bad when compared to forking hay to a goat. "Well, I've got to get to that homework. Say hi to Chuck for me."

Bethany's eyes narrowed. "What do you mean?"

"Your boyfriend. The Chuckster."

"You don't even know him."

"You told me all about him. Chuck steak, one hundred percent lean."

"And don't forget he's mine." Bethany frowned and turned, then was swept away in the tide of students. Jett looked at the clock on the wall. Two minutes to solve six math problems. And the rest of her life to solve all the rest of her problems.

September was a melancholy month for Alex Eakins. It was the month his childhood mutt rolled himself under the wheels of a FedEx van, the month he'd lost his virginity after a high school football game to a girl who later ditched him for a married man, the month his dad and mom separated, the month he'd been kicked out of Duke for lousy grades and attendance. Since he'd moved to the mountains and spent his trust fund on a little piece of south-facing land on the mountain above Solom, September had been a time of dying.

He sniffed the air, which was sweet with the sugar of red maples and crab apples. The stench of decay should have been there, but the only rot came from the black innards of his composting toilet, where bacteria performed its thankless job of turning shit to dirt. Nature was just beginning to accept that winter was on the way, that every living thing would soon be asleep or dead. He wondered which of those he would be.

Alex had embraced organic gardening as a lifestyle, earning enough by selling produce at the county farmers' market to pay his property taxes. He had studied all the latest sustainable building techniques, and his own house was a mix of technologies both primitive and new. Since he lived off-grid and wasn't beholden to the building inspection and permitting process, Alex had used cob and straw bale construction for part of his house, which was cut partly into the bank. From the outside, the structure looked as much like an aboriginal mud hut as anything, but it was incredibly energy efficient. A small cluster of solar panels on the roof ran a dorm-sized refrigerator, and a woodstove system circulated hot water through the house. Alex had fixed a generator to a paddle wheel in the creek that gushed along one side of his property. The generator, along with a miniature wind turbine, fed a bank of alternating-current batteries, so he was covered no matter what the weather.

The system was put together in the aftermath of Y2K, when all the doomsayers had realized the world wasn't going to end after all and had sold their survival gear. Well, the world may have ended already, for all Alex knew. Because it was autumn again, and the tomatoes were turning to mush on the vines and the corn was getting hard. The cool-weather greens like collards, spinach, and turnips still had a few weeks to go, but soon enough the market would close for the season. Alex had a truckload of pumpkins to sell for Halloween, and one more good haul of organic broccoli, but after that, he would have to go back to work. Or else sell a little of the marijuana he cultivated.

But that meant dealing with people.

The same idiotic people who had driven him to the isolation of his mountain retreat. Despite the added pleasure of end-running the government and the lure of the world's last free-market economy, selling dope was almost as much trouble as having a square job.

Alex dumped a bucket of table scraps onto his garden compost heap and looked over the valley below. The trees were just starting to turn color along the highway, where the roots were stressed by construction and carbon monoxide. A gravel road ran past the Ward and Smith houses before disappearing into the thicket and winding up to Alex's house. The road got a lot bumpier and rutted past Gordon Smith's, because Alex believed in inhibiting curiosity-seekers. Not because he was antisocial as his mom had claimed, or a stubborn asshole as his dad had believed, but because he didn't have the patience to deal with accidental tourists and uninvited guests. Plus, the government might have an interest in finding him.

Besides, he wasn't antisocial. Just ask Meredith, the earth chick he'd met at the farmers' market who had occupied half of his bed on and off since April. But April was a green month and October was red and golden, so he expected her to light out before the first killing frost.

Her voice came from the wooden deck. "Honey?"

Honey. That reminded him, next year he planned on setting up a honeybee hive. With all the pests that attacked honeybees, the real stuff was getting more and more valuable. Alex was sure he could do it right, and have the fringe benefit of his own tiny, winged army of blossom pollinators—

"Alex?"

He put down the scrap bucket and picked up the heavy hoe. "Yes, dear?"

"Are you mad at me about something?"

"Of course not." Down below, through the trees, a thread of gray smoke rose from the Ward chimney.

"You only call me 'dear' when you're mad at me."

"That's not so."

"And you say it out the side of your mouth, like you're talking on automatic or something. Like you're miles away."

Gasoline was pushing two-fifty a gallon, thanks to the military-industrial complex that ruled the country, and that had to be factored against the profit from a load of pumpkins. Maybe he'd drive the load to Westridge. The college kids had plenty of money. He should know, as much grass as he'd peddled to them over the last couple of years. "Everything's fine, dear."

"See? There you go again."

"Huh?"

"You said 'dear' again."

He turned and squinted up at the deck. The day was bright, though cool. Meredith stood in a gray terry-cloth robe, her blond hair wet and steaming. No doubt she was nude beneath, and Alex thought of those nipples that were the color and consistency of pencil erasers. He could almost smell her shampoo, the hippie-dippy expensive stuff she bought at the health food store. He tightened his grip on the hoe.

"Sorry," he said. "I was thinking about autumn."

"Like, fall?"

"Yeah. Everything's dying but there's a promise of rebirth. It's metaphorical."

"Alex, have you been in the stash?"

"Did you know that most leaves aren't really green? The chlorophyll in the leaves masks their true color, and when the growing process slows down for autumn, the chlorophyll fades and the true color emerges. It's the process of dying that finally reveals the leaf. So all that green, happy horseshit is a lie."

"Alex? Are you okay?"

Sure, he was okay. He had been okay for years. Marijuana was his antidepressant, and his crop kept him supplied year-round. He also traded on the black market to support his other little hobby—the one locked in the walk-in closet downstairs—but figured he'd probably get caught one day and the cops would seize his land. All because he liked to smoke a little weed, which was none of the government's business besides the fact that it kept Republicans in office. At least weed was honest, though the system wasn't. Weed stayed green, even after it was dead, even after you smoked it and it grew a bouquet of blossoms in your head. True colors, for real.

Meredith smoked it, too, but only before bed, because it made her terribly horny. In fact, Alex often wondered if that was the sole reason she had stayed over that night in April, and then the next night, and before the end of the week she'd begun leaving her clothes in his dresser. And that, as any guy knows, had been the time to say he wasn't sure they were ready for such a commitment, but another joint and Alex had his head between her thighs and, well, he supposed it could be worse. At least she could cook vegan meals.

He smiled up at her, or maybe he was grimacing from dawn's glare in his eyes. "I'm fine," he said. "I was just wondering whether to take the pumpkins down to the college or try my luck at the market."

"The market's been a little slow, and some of the other vendors will probably undercut you. Better to go where there's no competition."

"Makes sense." Meredith had been a business major, graduating cum laude the year before with a degree in marketing. Alex had majored in botany, but all he'd learned was how to grow some high-class, kick-ass grass. And how to flunk out and disappoint his parents.

"Are you going into town?" Meredith asked. "Town" meant Windshake, the Pickett county seat, which was fifteen miles away. No one thought of Solom as a town, though it had a zip code and post office. Windshake was where people did their serious shopping, and the Solom General Store was a place to pop in for vegetable seeds, or a bag of Fritos corn chips and a Snickers bar when the munchies got extreme.

"Maybe later," he said. He never wore a watch, and if he had to get a part-time gig for the winter, that meant showing up according to some corporate master's rigid timetable. Time was flexible and shouldn't be tied down to numbers. Like, this was now and later was later, and yesterday was like the ashes and grunge in the bottom of the bong. And tomorrow was, like, maybe a pot seed or something.

"Well then, what do you want to do this fine Saturday morning?" Meredith leaned over the deck, letting her robe fall open and offering a generous view that rivaled the glory of the Blue Ridge Mountains.

He grinned, or maybe a gnat was flitting near his eyes. "Roll one and I'll come up in a minute."

She smiled. "Breakfast in bed?"

"Sure—" He started to add "dear," but caught himself.

Meredith padded across the deck Alex had built with his own two hands using wormy chestnut planks he'd taken from an abandoned barn. Maybe Meredith belonged here. She was organic in her way, wasn't spoiled by modern conveniences, and had grown on him over the months. He just couldn't understand why, as she'd talked to him, his grip on the hoe had tightened. He looked down and saw that his knuckles were white.

"Yes, dear," he whispered, chopping at a plantain that had taken root by the garden. Plantains carried the same blight that killed tomatoes in wet weather. They were evil weeds if God had ever made such a thing.

Alex had lifted the hoe for a second blow when he saw a skewed stand of stalks at the end of his garden. Something had been in his corn. He stepped over the rows of broccoli and walked past the beds of young collards, his blood rising to a boil. The corn had been trampled and the tops were bitten off a number of the plants. Deer sometimes came through the woods to feast on the garden, though their visits had dwindled after Alex had picked up a tip from a fellow organic gardener. A little human piss around the garden's perimeter kept deer away, because as dumb as the dark-eyed creatures were, they'd been around long enough to associate people with murder.

This wasn't deer damage. Because a slew of stalks were littered along the fence that separated his property line from the Smiths'.

Alex was ambivalent about fences, since Starship Earth belonged to everybody, though he'd made sure he knew his property boundaries after the survey was complete. He believed in the laws of Nature, but that didn't mean the rest of his nasty, grab-ass species did. They believed in pieces of paper in the courthouse, or pieces of paper in banks, or pieces of paper in Washington, D.C.

But, piece of paper or not, one thing was for sure: goats couldn't read, and even if they could, Alex would bet a half kilo of homegrown that they would ignore what was written on the deed anyway. He kept a tight grip on the hoe just in case one of the weird-eyed bastards was still around.

The wire fence was bent just a little, as if something heavy had leaned on it. Heavier than a goat, by the looks of it. Alex hesitated. He tried to live in harmony with the world, even if six and a half billion hairless apes threatened to make the place uninhabitable. He could either go down and have a talk with Gordon Smith or he could crawl over into enemy territory and administer some mountain justice.

"Alexxxxxx!" From the purr in Meredith's voice, Alex guessed she'd already fired up the joint. He dropped the hoe.

"I'll be back," he said to the woods beyond the fence.

Gordon sat by the cold fireplace, a book in his lap called *The Airwaves of Zion* by Howard Dorgan. Gordon had explained the significance of backwoods gospel radio shows on tiny AM stations, but Katy had nodded enthusiastically while her mind wandered to the fresh asparagus and dill weed in the refrigerator. She'd left the room at the earliest opportunity, and she'd returned to find him dozing. His head was tilted back on the Barcalounger, a delicate snore rising from his open mouth. Katy had never noticed how pale his neck was beneath his closely trimmed beard. His hands were soft, with the fingers of an academician, not a farmer. He had the drawn and wrinkled cheeks of a smoker, though he owned a pipe merely as an affectation. He'd only smoked it a half dozen times since they had been married, which was good, because the smell of the rich tobacco made Katy's head spin.

It was rare that she had a chance to study him in daylight. When they were together, his eyes dominated her, and she felt herself paying attention to his every word. That same power had brought Katy under his spell when he'd delivered his presentation on Appalachian religion at that Asheville seminar.

Looking back on it, she realized she'd been lectured, not conversed with. And she had been the student eager to please, sitting on the edge of her seat, face warm at the prospect of proving her worth as a listener. She found herself flushing now, standing over his sleeping form, bothered that she was only on equal footing when Gordon was unconscious. Even in bed . . .

She didn't want to think about *bed*. Their sheets were way too clean and smooth, each spouse's side clearly marked. A stack of hardcovers on Gordon's dresser, a water glass, and a case for his eyeglasses. A box of Kleenex on Katy's side, along with a bottle of lotion, a candle, and a pack of throat lozenges. In her drawer lay birth control pills, clothing catalogs, Tylenol PM, Barbara Michaels paperbacks, lip balm, and beneath all that feminine detritus, Katy's vibrator, her longtime romantic partner in Charlotte. A monogamous and loyal lover, always attentive, considerate, and sober. Everything that Mark wasn't.

Katy was afraid Gordon would find the vibrator, but Gordon hadn't exactly set the marital bed on fire, either. In fact, he'd not even struck a match.

Maybe professors of religion had to take a vow of celibacy. Though Katy had no moral qualms on the issue, she wondered if premarital sex should perhaps become a legal requirement. After all, you might say "I do" even when the person standing with you before the priest might be thinking "I never will." Mark had been a real believer in premarital sex, to the tune of two or three rounds per day. He called it the "Protestant sex ethic," though Mark had been about as Protestant as a pope. His ardor hadn't dampened once they had tied the knot and the beautiful miracle named Jett had slid down her vaginal canal. Still, the years had left a growing gap between them, and late-night whispered secrets had given way to accusations and aloofness.

But that's not why you divorced him.

Katy walked away from the fireplace. She had more pressing matters at hand than a good wallow in the swamp of regret. Like the butternut squash in the oven.

She found herself thinking of it as the "fucking butternut." Katy made a conscious effort to quit cursing when Jett was a toddler, after the first time she'd heard Jett burp, sit propped up on her wadded diaper, and say, "Fuck." With a toothless grin that melted matronly hearts all the way back to Mesopotamia, Jett had declared her intelligence and the simultaneous importance of surroundings on her upbringing. But Jett was on her way home from school, either by bus or with the trustworthy Mrs. Stansberry up the road.

So Katy felt comfortable saying it aloud, but not too loudly. "Fucking butternut," she said, as she grabbed her pot holder and reached for the oven door.

The whisper that skirled from the pantry was probably nothing more than the September breeze bouncing off the curtains and playing around the room, carrying the autumnal scent of Queen Anne's lace, goldenrod, and pumpkin. But it sounded like a word. Or a name.

"*Kaaaay.*"

Katy grabbed a spatula between the thumb and mitt of the pot holder and spun like a ballet dancer after three shots of whiskey. "Who said that?"

She was annoyed, both at herself and at whatever trick of physics had made her panic.

Her heart fluttered, and an uneven rhythm pounded in her ears, like when the natives were asking King Kong to step up to the altar and accept their drugged sacrifice. Fay Wray in the original, Jessica Lange in the De Laurentiis version, and Naomi Watts as the hot blonde du jour in the Peter Jackson remake.

"*Kaaaaaaaaay.*"

"Go away." Katy held up the spatula like a hatchet, hoping to ward off the invisible thing in the corner of the kitchen. Gordon's first wife didn't belong here anymore. She was dead. Rebecca didn't exist.

This was Katy's house now.

And Solom was her home.

Something stirred in the attic. Damned mice. She'd have to speak to Gordon about them.

Later. First, she had a meal to prepare.

Chapter Eight

Rush Branch Primitive Baptist Church was a one-room wooden building that sat on a crooked row of concrete blocks. The white paint had curled away in places, and the thickness of the chips showed the age of the church. The grounds were well tended, and the waterway that gave the church its name ran barely twenty feet from the front door. A deep pool at the base of a short waterfall made for convenient dipping when baptisms were performed.

David Tester ran a Weed Eater around the wooden steps. Like most rural mountain preachers, he had a real job during the week. David owned a landscaping business, which never would have made it had it not been for the seasonal home owners who had neither the time nor the inclination to do their own yard work. David saw it as a sign from the Lord that outsiders belonged in Solom. Since the Primitives believed in predestination, David didn't have to worry about converting anyone. Their names were either listed in the Big Book or they weren't, simple as that.

Gordon Smith, the college professor, had asked him why his denomination still held services when there seemed to be no ultimate goal. To David, the goal was to live right and to get along, and regular church services couldn't hurt. Besides, this was a community church, and though families could now pile up in a car and drive to one of the fancy churches in Windshake or Titusville, most of the locals preferred to go to the church where they had been raised. The congregation was aging, but that was true of all the old Baptist subdenominations. Seemed the kids didn't take to the Bible the way they used to, and David could hardly blame them.

The Weed Eater's thick fishing line plowed through the ragweed and saw briars that sprouted along the building's foundation. The buzz of the gas-powered engine echoed over the hillside and a veil of blue smoke lifted into the cloudless sky. The rotating line hit gravel and a rock spun free, bouncing off the plank siding of the church. Shredded vegetation stuck to the shins of David's jeans.

David was about to trim around the old cemetery stones when he noticed a small dark hole in the ground by the first grave. He killed the engine and his ears rang in the sudden silence. He knelt by the hole. The grave was that of Harmon Smith, a horseback preacher from the 1800s. Horseback preachers traveled from community to community in all kinds of weather, staying with a host family for a week or two at a time. David admired the sacrifice of such men of God, though Smith had been a little scattershot in his beliefs. He preached to all denominations and, according to legend, had managed to fit his message to each without ever slipping up by trying to save a Primitive or letting a woman wash a man's feet during the annual Old Regular Baptist foot-washing ceremonies. Then he'd gotten what the old folks called "a mite touched" and had become devoted to the idea of sacrifice, even breeding his own livestock to serve as Old Testament–style offerings.

The grave hole was probably made by a mouse. David looked around for a rock so he could plug it. A mouse's den probably had a back door, but David didn't think it was proper for a creature to be crawling all around in the preacher's bones. Harmon Smith had earned his rest.

David went to the parking lot and found a fist-sized chunk of granite. He tossed it up, enjoying its weight. David had been a pitcher on the Titusville High School nine and still liked to play church league softball. He was approaching the grave again when he saw the twitch of a dark tail as it disappeared down the hole. Too big to be a mouse. And it was scaly.

Sort of like a . . .

David told himself that no snake would burrow into the ground on such a sunny day. It would be on a rock somewhere, absorbing the heat. David ran across snakes all the time in his landscaping work. They were mostly harmless, though copperheads and rattlers lived in these mountains and water moccasins could be found along the rivers and streams. David held the rock by his ear as he approached, ready to hurl it if a serpent's head poked out of the hole.

A truck passed on the highway, slowed, and honked. David lifted his left hand in greeting without taking his gaze from the hole. The truck pulled into the parking lot. David knew how silly he looked, standing in the little cemetery with its worn gray stones, holding a rock like some kid who was afraid of ghosts.

He tossed the rock toward the creek. The truck door opened and James Greene, one of the church elders, climbed down from the seat. He wore denim overalls and a plaid shirt, his sleeves rolled up to reveal thin forearms with silver, wiry hairs. Greene pushed his Atlanta Braves baseball cap off his balding head, wiped at the sweat, then returned the cap to its usual skewed resting place.

"Hi, Elder David," James said.

"Elder James," David said in welcome.

"You tending to the grounds?"

"Even Eden needed a little clip job now and then."

"Hmm." James looked at Harmon Smith's grave, which had a depression in the earth at the foot of the stone. "The grass grows best over him that sleeps with a clear heart."

"The joyous day is coming soon," David said. "The elected shall rise up and walk with the Lord."

James noticed the dark hole. "Hey, look at that," he said.

"Figured it was a mouse. It's about time of year for them to start laying winter plans."

"No mouse. That's a copperhead tunnel."

"I never saw a copperhead in a hole before."

"Of course you ain't. Smart, ain't they? A lot of people think snakes are pure, dumb evil, but they know how to sneak. Do you know if you cut off a snake's head, the snake won't die till sundown?"

"I've killed one or two in my time."

"Some of them churches in Kentucky handle snakes during worship service," James said. "Pretty damn stupid if you ask me."

"There's a verse in the Gospel According to Mark that says if your faith is true, you can take up serpents and they will not harm you."

"Still sounds pretty damn dumb to me. Pardon my language, Elder David."

David kept his eye on the opening to the hole. He was trying not to think of the snake twisting through the moldy rib cage of the itinerant preacher. That seemed like a blasphemy that God would never allow. Maybe David could set some kind of trap for it, restore things to their proper order. If it be God's will, of course.

"I hear the Carters left the congregation," James said. "Took up with the Free Willers."

David wiped the sweat and stray bits of grass from his face. "Yeah. I talked to Benjamin Carter about it. He said with all the trouble going on in the world, he needed extra reassurance. Said it wasn't enough to just sit back and hope you were one of the saved. Said he felt better if he took matters into his own hands a little. Of course, Rosie went along with him, like a good wife will."

"We're down to two dozen members, Elder David."

David nodded. Since the Primitives didn't believe in missionary work, there was no call to go out among the people and recruit new members. The younger generation had drifted away from all the churches, not just the Primitive subdenomination. Sometimes David watched those showy evangelists on television with their silk neckties and stiff hair and felt a little jealous. He wondered how he would fare out there onstage, where you felt the Spirit work in you as you exhorted others to take Jesus Christ into their hearts and be born again.

The Primitives had already been born into grace, according to their statement of beliefs, so believers had little to do besides wait around for the Rapture. Of course, the rituals at church helped soothe worldly troubles. And services offered fellowship, too, something still a little rare in the mountains, with the closest Wal-Mart over fifty miles away. The Solom General Store had a potbellied stove and a little dining area, but loud tourists with their cell phones and cologne had altered the store's atmosphere, and in some ways, their money had taken it out of the hands of the community.

"The Lord will take care of it," David said. The collection plate had yielded more metal than paper over the last few months. David didn't preach for money, though he did accept reimbursement for the gas and equipment he used to maintain the church grounds.

"Folks around here could use a good miracle or two," James said.

"Amen to that." David fixed his gaze on the hole, which glared right back like a cold, ebony eye.

Sarah Jeffers came to her senses in a dimly lighted room. At first, she thought she was in her bed on the second floor of the old family home by the store, because the light through the window had a late-Sunday-morning quality. Sunday was her sleep-in day, and her headache might have been caused by a couple of tall after-dinner sherries. Her eyelids were heavy, so she listened for the ticking of the antique grandfather clock downstairs. She heard nothing but a faint, irregular beeping.

And the smell was all wrong. Instead of aged wood, musty quilts, and cats, the room had the crisp tang of antiseptic. She opened her eyes and blinked her vision into focus. The walls were white, unlike the maple paneling of her bedroom. The pillows were encased in vinyl and the bed was angled up like a lounge chair at the side of a swimming pool.

"Back among the waking," a young woman said. "How do you feel?"

"Get me a doctor," Sarah said.

The woman smiled. "I *am* a doctor. Dr. Hyatt. You're in Tri-Cities Regional Hospital."

Sarah closed her eyes. Doctors were supposed to be male and gray-haired. How could this urchin know the least little thing about the workings of the human body? She didn't look old enough to have ever dissected a frog, much less gone through medical school.

"One of your friends found you at your store," Dr. Hyatt said. "You were unconscious."

"And that's a bad thing, right?"

"A sense of humor. Good. 'Laughter is the best medicine' is not just a section in *Reader's Digest*. The claim also has some research backing it up."

"Then tell me a good one so I can laugh my way out of this hundred-dollar-an-hour prison cell. Let me out of here."

"It's not that simple, Miss Jeffers. It *is* 'miss,' isn't it?"

"I can't lay around here during store hours. I got customers to see to."

"We ran some tests while you were unconscious. You had symptoms of a stroke, but your EEG and CAT were fine and your blood pressure is that of somebody thirty years younger."

"Tests? Who signed for them? And why are these wires sticking in me?"

"The gentleman who called 9-1-1 said you had no next of kin. We followed the usual procedures for treating an apparent stroke victim."

"But I ain't been stroked, have I?"

"Not that we can tell. We thought you might have suffered a blow to the head, maybe by a can falling from a top shelf. Or a robbery. But the register was untouched and the store appeared to be intact. Your friend called the sheriff's department and they checked it out. And you have no visible marks."

Sarah struggled to sit up, saw black spots before her eyes, and decided to try again a little later. "I hope somebody locked up. Half the merchandise will walk off otherwise."

"The deputies will take care of that. Your job is to get better."

The black spots coalesced behind her eyelids, turning into a shadow, a man in a black, wide-brimmed hat. She reached out for the doctor's arm and clutched it, afraid the image would still be there if she opened her eyes. The beeping accelerated.

"Are you okay, Miss Jeffers?"

"I seen him," she said.

"Your friend? He said you were unconscious, but you might have been partially aware of what was going on. It's not unusual during a fainting spell."

"No, before that. I seen him." Suddenly she wasn't in such a big hurry to leave Titusville and go back to Solom.

"Just breathe regularly," Dr. Hyatt said, patting Sarah's hand until the beep marking her pulse became steady again. "Rest up. You're not going anywhere for a little while."

That sounded good to Sarah. She closed her eyes and tried to block the recurring image of the man tilting up his chin until the wide brim no longer hid his face.

Or what was *left* of his face.

Odus had stayed with Sarah for a couple of hours, but when the doctor reported that she was awake and alert, yet refusing visitors, he'd driven his Blazer back to Solom and the Smith farm. He had agreed to help Gordon put up some corn, though it hadn't quite gotten frozen enough to harden for feed. Now, ripping and twisting the brown ears from their stalks, he decided that Gordon's crops were Gordon's business, as long as the man paid cash. Odus was thirsty after the fright Sarah had thrown into him, and he'd picked up a quart of sipping whiskey from the Titusville liquor store. A few hours of September sweat and he'd have earned a sip or two.

Gordon usually left the grunt work to Odus, but today the professor was pitching in, working the rows right alongside him. They filled bushel baskets and carried them to the end of the row where Gordon had parked his riding lawn mower. Gordon didn't own a tractor, though a metal relic from the horse-drawn days gathered rust between the barn and garden. Odus was thinking about what Sarah had said, about the man in the hat, when Gordon spoke.

"Guess it's time to take down the scarecrow," Gordon said.

Odus looked up at the form on the wooden crossbar whose head stood a good two feet above the dried blooms of the corn. It wore an old straw-reed hat that had been bleached by the sun and mottled gray by the rain, tied with twine to the feed-sack face. People in Solom were peculiar about their scarecrows, treating them like family members, using the same one from year to year. Odus had always thought it was some sort of good-luck ritual. The habit was to store the scarecrow in the barn, where it would hang on the wall and watch over the livestock during the long winter. Odus had been working for Gordon three years, and knew the usual time to tuck the straw man away was in late October, when the nights grew short and the wind rattled strange syllables in the leaves.

"A little early yet, ain't it?" Odus asked.

Gordon put a gloved hand over his eyes and scanned the clear sky. "There's a storm coming."

"Don't believe so. The birds aren't quiet and the mice are no busier than usual."

Gordon pulled off his glove, fished a handkerchief from his jeans pocket, and wiped his glasses. His eyes were glittery and unfocused, and he looked lost. "I'm talking about a different kind of storm, Odus."

Odus plucked another ear and twisted it free with a crackle of ripped vegetation. He tossed it in the basket, then moved the basket a few feet forward.

"I don't know anything about that," Odus said.

"Do you know the scarecrow is more than just a trick to keep birds away?"

Odus didn't like the way Gordon's soft eyes looked past him to the pastures beyond. "Well, I'm not so sure they even do that worth a darn," he said. "I had to replant three times this spring. The little thieves just swooped on in here like nobody's business."

Gordon kept on as if he'd not heard Odus, who imagined that this was how the professor got when he was lecturing in the classroom to a bunch of stoned-out rich kids. "The scarecrow is as old as domesticated crops. Way back to Babylonia, which many scholars believe is the Garden of Eden of the Bible."

"I'm not much on history books *or* the Bible." Odus tore a couple of ears of corn free, reveling in the sweet starchy smell. "The first tells you what went wrong and the second tells you why. I prefer to stay uninformed, myself."

Gordon put his glasses back, which eased Odus's worry a little. Odus realized what Gordon's naked eyes had reminded him of: the goats. They had that same heavy-lidded, unfocused stare.

"The scarecrow wasn't always an outfit of clothing stuffed with straw," Gordon said, returning to work. "In the old days, a live man was tied in the garden."

Odus glanced at the professor, figuring the man was putting him on. Gordon's face was as steady as always. Come to think of it, Gordon had never cracked a joke. He seemed unable to laugh and even a smile looked like it hurt him some. "To keep birds away?"

"Well, that it did. Except other animals came, especially at night. A helpless man in the wilderness drew a lot of predators."

"Why did they do that? Punishment?"

"More than punishment. Sacrifice. A gift to the harvest gods."

"Sounds like something a heathen would do."

"It was widely practiced in many cultures. Germanic tribes used to spike their victims to a tree. In the South Seas, witch priests claimed their island deities called for sacrifices to appease their wrath. African kings killed those magicians who failed to bring the rain. The ancient Greeks had all manner of sacrificial victims, both to Diana, goddess of the hunt, and Ceres, the harvest goddess."

"Did they really believe it?"

"Blood makes the best fertilizer," Gordon said.

They were closer to the scarecrow now, and the coarse fabric of its face suggested a scowl. Odus couldn't be sure, but it looked to have changed position on the crossbar, its arms hanging down a little lower. Ragged gloves had been attached to the flannel shirt-sleeves with baling wire, and Odus thought he saw one of the gloves lift in a beckoning motion.

"The scarecrow is dry," Gordon said. "And it thirsts."

Odus swallowed hard. He thirsted, too, and hoped the quart of bourbon would be enough to wash down the vision of the scarecrow's wave.

"Well, I think we got enough to tide the goats over for a few days," he said. "Maybe we should leave the rest of it to cure a little more."

"The goats shall multiply if the blood is pure," Gordon said, as if reciting the words to some bizarre sermon. The man had a houseful of books, and being a descendant of Harmon Smith was plenty enough excuse for being a little *off*.

"Looks like they've done plenty enough multiplying already. You'll need to cull the herd before winter, or you'll be spending a hundred bucks a week on grain. The does have been pretty much in rut nonstop. And you know how the bucks are, they start trying to stick it in anything that moves from the time they're three weeks old."

"The herd is a blessing," Gordon said, ripping down ears of corn with both hands and tossing them toward the basket. One ear missed and bounced against the hilled furrow. Odus bent to pick it up, and when he stood, he saw the scarecrow lift its head.

The afternoon sun glinted off the ivory eyes. Before, the head had sagged, as if its owner was weary from a season on the spike, and its eyes had been hidden in the shade of the straw hat's brim.

"Really, Mr. Smith, I think we got plenty."

"What do you think of my new family?" Gordon asked, continuing to harvest ears as if hordes of locusts were swarming.

"Miss Katy seems right nice," Odus said. "And your daughter— I mean, your stepdaughter—"

"She's my daughter now," Gordon said. "She's part of this place."

"Well, she seems nice, too. She stands out a little, but she don't seem a bit of trouble to me. You know how kids are, they just need to find their own way in the world."

"They shall be shown the way," Gordon said, lapsing into that sermon-voice of his, but Odus wasn't paying attention. He was watching the scarecrow, expecting it to loosen the ropes that held it to the crossbar, wriggle to the ground, and drag itself off to quench its thirst.

The bushel basket was full again, and Gordon stooped and picked it up by its wire handles. "Know them by their works, not by their words," he said.

"Sure, Mr. Smith. Whatever you say."

"I think we've picked enough for today."

Odus hoped his sigh of relief passed for a tired gasp. Gordon would slip him a tax-free twenty and Odus would be doing some slipping of his own, first down the snake-belly road to his caretaker apartment, then down the soft and hazy river of eighty-proof Old Mill Stream.

"But we still need to take down the scarecrow," Gordon said.

The scarecrow's form had slackened again, as if it were made of cloth and silage after all. Odus wasn't in the mood to touch it. This had been Harmon Smith's land, after all, and though the Circuit Rider hadn't been seen in a decade or so, sometimes bad air lingered long after a dark cloud had drifted away.

"I've got to be off to Titusville," he lied. "Sarah Jeffers took a spell and she's up in the hospital. I ought to check in on her, seeing as how she got no kin."

"Sorry to hear she's not well." Gordon dumped the bushel basket into the wheelbarrow, which was overflowing with green-wrapped ears of corn, the tassels and tips of the shucks burned brown with frost. "Come back tomorrow and we'll take care of the scarecrow."

"Sure thing, Mr. Smith. Can you pay cash today instead of saving up my time until Friday?"

"Of course." Gordon removed his gloves and laid them across the staves of the wheelbarrow. He thumbed a twenty from his wallet and handed it to Odus. As Odus's fingers closed on the money, Gordon grabbed his wrist and pulled him off-balance. Though Odus weighed two hundred pounds, Gordon had leverage and an advantage in both height and weight. Odus found himself looking through the distorted left lens of Gordon's eyeglasses. Again Odus was reminded of the goats, and the professor's pupils seemed to take on that same narrowed and flattened aspect.

"Know them by their fruits," he said, his breath rank with pipe tobacco and garlic.

Odus nodded as Gordon released him, then tucked the money in his pocket and headed toward the gate. He took one last look to make sure the scarecrow still hung on its stake. It did, though the ragged brim of its hat was angled even lower, as if the stuffed head had dipped in a prayer of resignation.

He climbed in his Blazer and drove away as the goats came down from the pasture to see what Gordon was serving for lunch.

Chapter Nine

Eggs over easy.

That was what Katy was thinking as she went down to the barn, just as the dust from Odus's Blazer settled over the driveway. Gordon had a half dozen guinea hens and they laid little brown eggs almost every day. The nesting boxes were arrayed across the front of the barn, screened with chicken wire tied in a series of hexagons. The nests had little holes carved in the front and were covered with rubber flaps so the gatherer, in this case Katy, could reach an arm into the dark box and feel around in the straw for eggs. Gordon had explained the design discouraged possums, foxes, and other lazy ovum-stealing predators.

But that didn't make Katy feel any better about reaching through those black little curtains that looked all the world like sharp, rotted teeth. At least she didn't have to go *inside* the barn, where the goats had spooked her and Jett had suffered some sort of delusion.

The farm was too quiet. She'd expected a big change from the city, but she had imagined barking dogs, crowing roosters, badly tuned tractors, and the rattle and clank of distant, rusty machinery. This was autumn. Where were all the chain saws turning hardwood forests into firewood?

The guineas were strangely hushed in their boxes and the goats watched her as they usually did, standing stiff-legged in the field, their beards drifting slightly in the breeze, ears flapping at the flies. In her mind, she imagined them skinned for meat, their oblong pupils regarding her from the slope of their skinned skulls.

She shook the woven basket farther up her left elbow and reached into the first nest. Gordon didn't have names for the hens, so Katy thought of them collectively as "Martha." The first one was M, the second one A, and so on. If they were fryers instead of laying hens, she couldn't bear to name them. It was bad enough just eating their eggs. Even though they were unfertilized, it was hard not to think of the yolks as little abortion victims. She had never considered such a thing before, despite being a lifelong omelet lover. Funny how being on a farm made you more aware of and connected to the food, whether it was the seeds that grew into turnips or the steers that turned into ground round.

"My, M, you must be feeling your oats today," Katy said, finding two eggs in the first nest. She laid them gently in the basket as M clucked in either motherly anguish or pea-brained hunger. Katy peered through the chicken-wired slot at A in the next box. All she could see was the serrated, black-and-gray pattern of the hen's feathers. A's head was tucked under one wing, making her look like a soft wad of thrift-shop rags.

"Okay, girl, here I come." Katy reached her arm into the curtained slot. She felt around in the straw, finding nothing. Maybe A was sitting on her egg. The hens sometimes did that, driven by an instinct stronger than the memory of all the previous unhatched eggs that had gone before. Katy felt the soft downy feathers of A's chest, then slid her hand underneath.

She nearly broke her wrist snatching her hand free. Something cool and scaly had writhed away from her touch.

It wasn't a chicken leg. This thing had rippled.

Did snakes eat eggs? Could one have crawled through the curtain, or dropped onto the wire from above and slithered into A's nest?

Katy didn't know, but she wasn't about to stick her hand in to find out.

But what would Gordon say when he saw only two eggs in the

refrigerator? He would ask why, and Katy would have to say "Chickenshit." Because she was too chickenshit to stick her hand into the nests. And Gordon's forehead would furrow slightly, accompanied by a gratuitous, understanding, demeaning smile, all the while his eyes saying, "I thought I'd found a replacement for Rebecca, but all I got was this skinny Irish redhead who can't even pluck an egg, much less a whole chicken."

"Chickenshit, chickenshit, chickenshit," she said to herself. She had placed a moratorium on cussing because she didn't want Jessie picking up the habit, but she was alone and who gave a good goddamn what the goats thought?

She looked around for something to poke into the nest. Maybe if she could get A to move, she would be able to see the snake. Or whatever it was.

God, please let it be a snake, because, sure, they are scary as seven hells, but at least snakes live and breathe and are listed in zoology catalogs.

Katy was about to give up, to go out into the cornfield to find Gordon, when she remembered the pitchfork inside the barn. She hadn't mentioned the scarecrow to Gordon, because he would have laughed. And she had been scared out of her wits by Jett's strange bout of amnesia. And then there was the goat that had somehow locked itself in the loft. The barn was a place to avoid. Nothing good seemed to happen there. Just ask all the livestock that had been slaughtered over that straw-scattered floor, that had been decapitated and strung up on chains and turned from livestock into *deadstock*.

But the pitchfork was a weapon. If she could hoist a skewered snake before Gordon, show off her grit and determination, then perhaps Gordon would at last accept her as a suitable replacement and draw her into his arms at midnight, accept her and take her and finally make her his wife.

Besides, next to a confrontation with a snake, a little trip inside the barn was nothing. The pitchfork was hanging twenty feet from the front sliding doors. She could be in and out with barely enough time to smell the trampled manure. And once she had the pitchfork, even a goat wouldn't scare her.

She set the basket on top of R's nesting box and went to the sliding doors. The oaken, crudely planked doors were suspended on rusty wheels that rolled across a steel track overhead. The left one was partially pulled back, and cool air wafted from the opening. The midmorning sun cut an orange sliver into the darkness, but the great, hulking black beyond gave off an almost palpable weight, like oily water held back by a dam.

Twenty feet. Ten steps max, each way.

She leaned against the edge of the left door and shoved. It slid across its track with a metal scream. The sun poured in at her back like a sacred ally. She was sweating, though the temperature was in the fifties. She looked into the pasture. The goats seemed curious and faintly amused.

"Chickenshit, chickenshit, chickenshit."

Katy squinted into the barn, trying to locate the pitchfork on its wooden-pegged resting place.

Twenty feet. She could be there and back before you could say "Children of the Corn, Part Thirteen."

Now she saw it, hanging among some coils of rope, a thick length of rusted chain, a strange set of clamps that looked like a medieval torture device, and a crooked-handled scythe whose blade was brown with age. She didn't remember the scythe from before, but it didn't look like an effective weapon against a snake.

She stepped into the barn, breath held. Eighteen feet to go. No biggie. Six yards. Not even as far as a first down in football, and she didn't have eleven steroid-inflated males trying to stop her. All she had was her fear.

Another big step and she was on the dividing line between sun and shadow. One of the goats bleated behind her, and it sounded terribly like laughter. Another joined in, and another, and Katy screamed as she ran, "Chickenshit, *chickenshit, CHICKENSHIT!*" Then she had her hands around the rough, grainy handle of the pitchfork and she was pulling it from the wall and it felt good and right and powerful and she could take on any damned snake in the world and she was already halfway back to the bright square of the barn door when she happened to look up at the wall above the loft stairs.

There hung the scarecrow, fully articulated, its straw planter's hat resting on the gunnysack head, the bone-button eyes catching and reflecting the sun, burning like autumn bonfires, staring bold and red and hellish, and Katy didn't know what she screamed, it may have been "Chickenshiiiiiiiit," but the sound was swallowed by the dry timber of the walls and the hay bales above and the packed dirt below and the pitchfork bounced to the ground and Katy was running across the yard toward the house where Gordon's dead wife might be drifting around the kitchen and tears were streaming down Katy's face, the goats were joined in a chorus of gleeful laughter, a snake was in the henhouse, but all she could think of was the two eggs in the basket, those sad orange yolks and twin chicks that would never be born.

Mrs. Stansberry had to stay after school for a meeting, so Jett rode the lame-o school bus home. She sat near the front with the first graders because she didn't want to be teased by Tommy Williamson and Grady Eggers, who sat in the back and ruled their keep like warlords. Grady had toned down a bit since yesterday, when he and Jett had suffered their mutual acid flashback in English class. But Tommy was still Tommy, and he tried to play grab-ass with her whenever she wasn't paying attention and drifted within reach.

The bus was half-empty when it reached her road. She wrestled her book bag down the steps and the bus was pulling away when Tommy called from the rear window, "Hey, shake it for me, Plucky Duck."

She flipped a middle finger without looking back, then checked the mail. Phone bill, Mom's October issue of *Better Homes & Gardens*, a seed catalog, a Honda dealership circular. At the bottom of the pile lay a crisp white envelope. She recognized the handwriting right away. Dad's.

Jett slipped the letter into a pouch of her backpack, her heart racing. The sun felt brighter and warmer somehow, and the wildflowers along the ditch were more colorful. She skipped a few steps, scuffing the toes of her black boots on the gravel. The Wards' dog barked at her, and she resumed walking, albeit at a faster pace. She didn't want creepy old Betsy Ward to call to her through the kitchen window.

Betsy wasn't inside the house this time. She was down by the little garden shed, holding a pair of hedge clippers. The shed was by the ditch and Jett would have to walk right by her. She kept her eyes on the rocks in the rutted road, wishing she could will herself into invisibility like Sue Storm of the Fantastic Four comics.

"Good news?" Betsy said.

"No, just some magazines," Jett said, figuring she could stop for twenty seconds and go on her way without seeming rude.

"A pretty girl like you shouldn't wear makeup."

Jett had been raised to respect her elders. Except, as Mom had said, when they were obviously full of crap. "Mom says it's okay."

"You come from Charlotte, I hear."

The old woman said it in a knowing manner, as if Charlotte were the only place you could buy black eyeliner and purple hair dye. "I was born there."

"What do you think about Solom?"

Jett shrugged. She saw little point in telling the truth. Betsy probably saw the world beyond the county borders as a strange and unholy land, fraught with terrorists, gangland shootings, adult bookstores, and kids dressed in black. "It's not so bad," she said. "Kind of quiet."

"Be glad of the quiet."

"Well, I'd better get home. My mom's expecting me. Been nice talking to you, Mrs. Ward." *Like hell*.

Jett was already on her way again when Betsy's next words stopped her. "See the horseback preacher yet?"

"Preacher?"

Betsy was grinning like a possum that had just eaten a dozen hen's eggs. "About the time of year for it. He comes galloping into town to grab mean little girls and boys and drag them off to the jangling hole up on Lost Ridge."

"Sorry, Mrs. Ward. I don't go in for spook stories."

"You will."

Jett hurried on up the road, Betsy Ward's cackle behind her. She couldn't help eyeing the barn on her way to the house. She didn't believe in spooks. She only believed in hallucinations.

If she had a joint, she would have sneaked into the bushes and fired it up, despite her promise to Mom. Solom was making her uptight, and she didn't like it. And why be uptight when nature offered several substances that served no other purpose but providing artificial relaxation? And where nature came up short, chemists had picked up the slack and come up with a whole alphabet soup of drugs. She had never tried ecstasy or angel dust, but those substances had floated around the big consolidated schools of Charlotte.

Good one, birdbrain. Try to kill the anxiety of a drug-induced hallucination by taking more drugs. Sort of like drinking yourself sober. Sounds like something Dad would dream up.

Instead of running from her problems, she could face them head-on. March right into the barn and up those stairs into the loft, hammering the hell out of her boot heels so the monster or the seven-foot-tall creep or the carniverous goat would know she was coming and—

Actually, the joint was starting to sound better and better. But she didn't know how to score in this backwoods tractor graveyard. She'd probably have to be friends with rednecks like Tommy Williamson if she ever wanted any connections. The thought made her shudder.

Mom's Subaru was in the driveway, as usual. Mom was becoming a real homebody, a turn for the weird. "We don't have to change who we are," Mom had said, when convincing Jett that marriage would be a positive move for both of them.

Except the drugs would have to go. That was part of the deal, and the part Jett felt responsible for. She wondered how much of Mom's hasty decision to marry was fueled by a desire to whisk her daughter away from the big-city lifestyle and the accompanying bad influences she had collected. Jett was surprised she didn't miss most of her friends, but instead of seeing her dad every weekend, she had only seen him once since the move.

But she had the letter . . .

Jett was starting up the flagstone walk when a bleat erupted behind her. A goat stood by the wire fence, gnawing on a locust post. The green irises glittered in the afternoon sun, the boxy pupils fixed on her. Like it was sizing her up. Inviting her into the loft.

"No way, Joshua boy," she said, louder than she wanted.

She backed the rest of the way up the walk and onto the porch, not letting the goat out of her sight. Just before she opened the door, she glanced at the barn. A figure stood in the upper window, in tattered clothes, face lost in the shadow of a wide-brimmed hat. Jett slipped inside the house and slammed the door closed, then leaned against it, trying to catch her breath.

"Honey?" Katy called from the kitchen. "Is that you?"

Jett didn't trust her voice enough to answer. Instead, she eased the backpack off her shoulder and peeked through the curtains at the barn. Nothing. Even the goat had turned away and ambled up to a tangle of blackberry vines.

A for-Christ's-sake flashback. Acid bouncing back like a cosmic boomerang to whack her on the ass.

"Jett?" Katy appeared in the kitchen doorway, wet dough nearly up to her elbows.

"Hi. What are you making?" Jett forced a smile, an expression she'd avoided since getting braces. A grimace went well with her glum Goth look.

Katy looked down at her hands as if surprised to find them coated in white goo. "Chicken and dumplings, I think. And scratch biscuits."

"Cookbook?"

Katy shrugged. "An old family recipe. I found it in the pantry."

Jett nodded. When they first moved, she and Mom had a long talk about Rebecca, Gordon's first wife. Mom insisted she wouldn't try to replace Rebecca. Mom was sure Gordon would appreciate her for who she was, and she might not be the world's greatest homemaker, but she was willing to try. "I'll never be the next Rebecca Smith, but I'll be the first Katy Logan, and that's the best Gordon could hope for," Mom had said.

Except a little of the sparkle had faded from Mom's eyes, and she seemed a little shaken today. Jett felt a pang of guilt for even thinking of breaking her promise to stay clean. Katy had enough to worry about. Like whatever was causing that smoke in the kitchen.

"I think your biscuits are done," Jett said.

Chapter Ten

The dinner table was made of ancient oak, the legs hand-carved by some distant Smith ancestor. It wobbled slightly when Katy put her elbows on it. She caught Jett's eye and frowned. Jett was staring off into space, right in the middle of Gordon's blessing. Then Katy realized her own eyes were open, and she turned her attention back to the lump of mashed potatoes. The potatoes were a bad choice with the dumplings. The meal appeared gray and bland, even with the pink meat of the chicken stirred among the dumpling juice. At least they had fresh broccoli, and Katy was grateful for the hardy crop that continued growing through the early frosts.

". . . and may the Lord bless this bounty placed before us, and the hands that prepared it," Gordon said, in a voice Katy imagined he used when delivering a lecture to half-asleep sophomores. "Amen."

"Amen," Katy said.

Gordon flipped out his cloth napkin with a flourish. Katy had never used cloth napkins in Charlotte, considering them an extravagance, the kind of thing that led to a premium charge at a fancy restaurant. But Gordon had showed her the drawer that held the table linens, and explained how Rebecca had always kept three clean sets of the same off-white color. He didn't exactly *order* Katy to lay out cloth napkins with each dinner, but if Rebecca was able to do it, then why shouldn't Katy? So what if it meant extra laundry and another three minutes of her day wasted?

"These dumplings look plumb delicious," Gordon said. He speared a lump of cooked dough with his fork, brought it to his nose, and sniffed. He took a bite.

Jett picked up a sprig of broccoli with her fingers, tossed it into her mouth, and began chewing noisily. Katy didn't even think to ask Jett to mind her manners because she was so intent on Gordon's reaction.

"Mmm," Gordon said. "Acceptable. Most acceptable indeed."

Acceptable? What in the hell did that mean? That Rebecca's were better? But all she said was, "I'm glad you like them, dear."

"Maybe we should tell him about the scarecrow now," Jett said.

"Scarecrow?" Gordon reached for the white wine. Katy would never have dared select a suitable wine. She was a gin girl, at least on her infrequent opportunities to imbibe. Since Jett's drug problems began, though, she had denied herself the dubious pleasure of alcohol. Gordon didn't seem to care about intoxication. He rarely drank more than a glass or two. To him, it was an affectation, like his pipe, the requisite habit of a tenured scholar.

"The scarecrow in the barn," Katy said.

"Oh, that old thing? What about it?"

"Yesterday, it was out in the cornfield. Now it's hanging on the wall."

"Maybe Odus Hampton brought it in. He was doing some work for me a few days ago, while you guys were shopping in Windshake."

"It was on the wall, then it was gone yesterday. And it was back again today." Katy didn't want to tell the other part, about how the goat had dragged it away, about how she thought it had moved under its own power. And how it must have put itself together, climbed the wall, and snagged itself on the hook again.

"Just like the story you told us," Jett said. She didn't seem as enamored of Katy's dumplings as Gordon was. She worked on the broccoli and her milk, then dipped into the bowl of cinnamon apple slices that Katy had prepared as a side dish.

"The scarecrow boy," Gordon said, breaking into a grin. His cheeks were flushed from the wine.

"I saw it, too," Jett said. "The night I"—she shot a glance at Katy—"freaked out in the barn."

Gordon's eyes narrowed, and Katy saw a hint of cruelty in his face. "You haven't been messing with drugs, have you? I thought I made it clear to your mother that I wouldn't tolerate that business in my house. It's bad enough you have to go around dressed like a prostitute at a funeral."

Jett slumped in her chair, jaw tightening. She fingered the studded leather band around her throat as if it were cutting off her oxygen.

"Gordon, please," Katy said.

Gordon sipped his wine. "Rebecca would never have allowed such foolishness, God rest her soul."

"Jett's not doing drugs anymore," Katy said. "She promised. We both promised."

Gordon patted his lips with the cloth napkin, and Katy wondered if she'd have to spray Spot Shot on it later. "Sorry. That wasn't fair. I did accept you for better or worse, after all."

Katy flashed a pained smile at Jett as if to say, *See, I told you he's not so bad. We all just have to get used to each other.* Except part of her was thinking, *If Rebecca was so wonderful, why didn't she bear Gordon a perfect child, one who wasn't individual and human and as achingly beautiful as Jett?*

She squeezed her own napkin under the table until her fingers hurt. Jett said, "It's okay, Gordon. No sweat."

Gordon didn't know Jett well enough to detect the sullen defeat in her voice. Gordon raised one eyebrow at Katy in a *When is she going to start calling me Dad?* expression. Katy wondered when they were going to quit communicating in unspoken words and actually talk to one another. But that was silly, because Gordon wouldn't even talk to her in bed when the lights were out and her heart was beating hard with expectation. Perhaps Rebecca had suffered the same neglect. The thought brought a sudden smirk to her face.

Jett pushed her plate away. "I've got homework, folks."

"You didn't finish," Gordon said.

"I'm not hungry."

Jett stood, her chair scraping across the floor. The sound cut the silence like a scythe through a tin can. Katy waited to see how the power struggle would play out, praying she wouldn't have to take sides, mentally exploring a way to broker a peace settlement.

"You shouldn't waste what God's blessing has brought to our table," Gordon said.

"I'll put it in the fridge and she can have it for a snack after school tomorrow," Katy said.

"I don't want it tomorrow," Jett said.

"Honey, we've all had a long day," Katy said. "Why don't you go do your homework and we'll be up to talk about it later?"

She knew Gordon wouldn't join in on the talk. He had rarely been in Jett's room, apparently considering it some sort of den of iniquity. Rock posters, a black light, a tarantula in a small aquarium, melancholy music playing constantly, at least while Gordon was home. No, Gordon hadn't yet reached out to his stepdaughter, though he expected automatic respect by sole virtue of Jett's residence under his roof.

"Sure, Mom." Jett left the room and Katy took her first taste of the chicken and dumplings. Too salty. Rebecca's recipe had called for two tablespoons. Or was it teaspoons? The recipes were handwritten, and Katy could easily have made a mistake.

"Do you really like them?" Katy asked.

Gordon was staring out the window at the darkness that had settled on the farm as they ate. The crickets chirped, katydids rubbed their wings together, and moths fluttered against the window screen.

"They were fine," Gordon said absently.

"Can we get rid of the scarecrow?"

"The scarecrow?"

"The one in the barn."

"What about it?"

"I don't like it hanging in the barn. It spooks me."

Gordon laughed. "That's been in the family for years. I put it up for the winter so it doesn't rot."

"I thought you said Odus Hampton put it up."

"Yeah. I guess he did."

"It's out there now. I saw it."

Gordon reached across the table and took her hand. He smiled, his eyes bright, cheeks crinkling in the manner that had first attracted her. "Let's forget about the silly scarecrow."

"You shouldn't be so hard on Jett."

Gordon drew his hand away. "It's just that I care about her. About *both* of you. I want you to be happy here."

Katy was about to say she would be a lot happier if she didn't feel the invisible presence of his first wife. But as she opened her mouth, a brittle clatter arose from the kitchen and something broke on the floor.

"Sounds like you have some work to do," Gordon said.

David Tester cut over Lost Ridge, taking the shortest route from his house to the church. Though it was dark, David knew the path well and carried a flashlight. An owl hooted in the unseen treetops and other nocturnal animals scurried on their way to put up winter supplies. The leaves were still crisp underfoot, though dew was starting to settle on the ground. A sodden wedge of moon tried to break through the canopy overhead.

He was on the upper edge of the Smith property, a forested hilltop that Harmon Smith had owned and that now belonged to Gordon Smith. Rush Branch started as a trickle between some worn granite boulders near the peak, but gathered momentum and a few stray springs before churning into a frothing waterway by the church. Harmon Smith had deeded property for the church, though the original log building had been torn down and replaced after the turn of the last century. Harmon had ridden his horse over this very trail, had slid off the saddle for a sermon many times before mounting up and heading to neighboring counties. This walk had become something of a pilgrimage for David, as if he expected to find an answer to the mysteries of the Circuit Rider, faith, and love lying along the trail.

Too bad Gordon took only Smith's surname and none of the fervid, passionate blood. Primitive Baptists didn't have the duty of saving souls, but the preacher had to tend his flock all the same. David knew the weight of that responsibility. His brother Ray had disowned him because of it and had taken up with the Free Willers. Maybe Ray needed the little extra comfort that came from bringing the Lord into your heart. But Ray was born to believe he already had a place waiting in heaven, whether he forgot it or not.

David played the flashlight over the trail, dodging the snakelike roots of oak and buckeye. Walking this trail had always soothed him and rejuvenated him, as if he were drawing on the spirit of those who had served before him. Walking right, that was the ticket. Following the path.

Occasionally an acorn or nut slapped through the leaves and bounced silently on the ground near him. The woods had the earthy scent of loam and the salamander smell of muddy springs. David came to a strand of hog wire and knew he had reached the corner of Gordon's pasture. The professor's flock was made up entirely of goats. That said plenty about the current state of the Harmon Smith legacy.

"Don't be bitter, now," David said to himself. "Gordon likely has a place in heaven the same as everybody else."

That was one of the things that bothered David about predestination. If the Lord already knew you were going to be worthy of eternal reward, why did he make you go through the whole works? Why didn't he just beam your soul straight up to heaven from your mother's belly? But that would make God little more than a parody of Scotty from the old *Star Trek* show.

So God had to want something more. He laid out tests for you. David wondered if even thinking about God's plan was somehow wrong, the kind of sin that wasn't written about in the Bible.

David climbed across the fence. His boot hung in a bottom strand of wire as he planted it on the far side, causing him to lose his balance. The flashlight fell to the ground and the beam flickered and died. David hung on top of the waist-high fence, the top wire digging into his upper leg. He righted himself and tried to free his boot. A wetness trickled down his left hand, and he felt the first burning of a cut.

Something scuffed the leaves twenty yards to his right, inside the pasture.

The moon glinted off the flashlight's metal switch. David reached down from the top of the fence for the flashlight, but it was just beyond his fingertips. He stood up again, the wire yawing back and forth between the support posts. He yanked his stuck boot, but one of the eye hooks must have been caught on a stray sprig of rusted steel.

Crackling leaves heralded the approach of something big. There was little to fear in the mountains except rabid animals. All the large predators like mountain lions had died out along with the buffalo and elk that had fed them. Black bears might attack if threatened, but David didn't feel very threatening with his foot stuck and his crotch riding the thin line of the fence top. He swung his free leg over and planted it on the ground, giving a painful twist to the ankle of the trapped foot.

Now his back was turned to the approaching creature. David twisted his neck and almost laughed.

"What in tarnation are you doing out here?" David said. "Trying to figure out who's trespassing?"

The goat stood ten feet away, head lowered, the bottom half of the face lost in shadows. Its emerald eyes glittered in the muted moonlight.

"The Lord's Prayer says forgive us our trespasses as we forgive those who trespass against us."

The goat lifted its nose and sniffed at the air as if it couldn't care less about the Lord's Prayer. The wicked curves of its horns suggested it was a billy buck. Though the horns were angled flat against the slope of the animal's skull, they had the look of serious business. Goats butted heads as a mating ritual, or used their horns to drive away predators like foxes, bobcats, or wild dogs. But they didn't attack people.

David put his free foot beside the stuck one and tried to jimmy the wire. He was sweating from the exertion. After a few seconds of struggling, he sat down, scooted himself close to the boot, and began unlacing it. Maybe once his foot was free, he could work the boot loose. Now he could see the cut on his hand, the blood black in the weak light. It would need a heavy bandage, maybe stitches.

Served him right, walking in the dark like that. Even though he thought of the trail as a sacred path, that didn't mean it wasn't treacherous. Rattlesnakes lived in the granite crevices along the ridge, and it was easy to trip over a root or stone and break a leg. Out here, he might not be found for days if he became immobilized. And it wasn't like the Lord cast down a holy beacon to show the way.

No, this wasn't a test. Just too much tread on a Timberland workman's boot.

As his fingers loosened the square knot, he looked back at the goat. It was three feet away now, and its strong musky scent filled his nostrils. Goats were such nasty, stubborn animals. David didn't understand their growing popularity among local farmers, no matter how exotic goat cheese and goat meat sounded to people raised on beef and beans.

"Just be glad the Lord doesn't require sacrifices like he used to," David said. "Abraham would have you up on a rock altar right now, a blade against that stringy neck of yours."

The goat bent its head down and stepped forward, the dark cloven hoof landing right next to David's thigh. The animal panted, its breath rank with half-digested goldenrod and maple leaves. The elongated face swung near David's cheek, the tangled beard whisking across his shoulder. The goat sniffed, the black nostrils flaring, the queer, oblong pupils fixed on David.

"Go away, boy. Aren't you supposed to be in the barn or something?"

The animal sniffed the length of David's arm.

"Get," David said, louder now, almost angry.

And, if he dared to admit it, a little scared.

The goat drew back a step. Saliva sparkled on the protruding lips.

David tore at the bootlaces, sweat stinging his eyes. The goat moved in again, this time going lower on his arm. The animal's tongue darted out and licked at his hand.

The cut hand.

The rough tongue slid out again, this time lingering on the flesh below the pad of his thumb where the cut was deepest.

It was drinking his blood.

It's sweet, David told himself. *And the goat's thirsty. That's all.*

Nonetheless, David jerked the two sides of his boot apart, yanked his foot free, and scrambled back over the fence.

He studied the goat, which licked at the leaves, searching for spilled drops of David's juice. The animal glanced up and let its tongue loll, as if inviting David back over to its side of the fence.

David turned and ran, the sock on one foot flopping out beyond his toes. Branches tore at his face as he plunged through the dark woods. The church visit could wait until sunrise. And, Harmon Smith's sacred path or not, next time David would make the trip over gravel and asphalt, in the cab of a Chevy pickup truck.

Chapter Eleven

The doctor must have dosed her with some sort of horse pill, because Sarah Jeffers woke up with a mild headache. The sun was already streaming low through the window, so it must have been midmorning. She hadn't dreamed at all, and her tongue was thick and sticky in her mouth. It took her a moment to remember where she was.

She peeled the sheet off her chest. She was dressed in a baby-poop-green gown tied loosely behind her back. Her clothes were folded in a chair at the foot of the steel-railed bed. So somebody had seen her naked, something that hadn't happened in at least twenty years. Served them right. They had no business poking around in her innards anyway.

She lay there, calculating yesterday's lost profits. She should have called in one of the Hancocks, or the boy who swept up after school. Even paying somebody a full day's wages, she would have netted fifty bucks at the least. And you never knew when a tourist bus was going to pull up, or a pack of Christian Harley riders. This time of year, with the fall colors starting to come on, the general store needed to bank enough to get her through the winter. Which meant she couldn't lie there another day, not while customers turned away with full pockets.

A new doctor came in, a man with a mustache that looked penciled over his lip, who looked more like a game-show host than somebody in the medical field. It was getting so you couldn't peg people anymore.

"Morning, Miss Jeffers. I'm Dr. Vincent." The doctor put a wrist to her forehead and checked the tension on the clip attached to her finger. Apparently that little clip fed a lot of information to the video monitor on the wall. All the signs appeared to be jagging up and down in some kind of steady pattern.

"Am I fit to go?" Sarah was going to ask for a cup of orange juice, but figured that would probably run her five bucks. She was on Medicare but she'd still be stuck with her 20 percent of the bill, meaning the juice would cost her a buck out-of-pocket. She wasn't that thirsty.

"Everything looks good," the doctor said. "You had a rough patch for a little bit, but all your signs are stable. We've diagnosed exhaustion."

"I took on a spell," Sarah said. "I'm all better now, like you said."

"I'll sign your discharge papers, but I urge you to get some extra rest in the next few weeks. I wouldn't want you coming back in with something more serious."

"Don't you worry. I haven't spent so much time in bed since my honeymoon, and that was before you were born."

The doctor almost grinned. "One thing . . . while you were out, you were muttering 'Harm me,' over and over again. Did you think somebody was going to hurt you?"

Sarah let her face slip into a mask of cool stone. "Nobody's going to hurt me. I can take care of myself."

"Of that, I have no doubt." He patted her hand. "I'll have the nurse help you get your things together. Do you have someone to drive you home?"

"I'll call somebody."

"Good. Extra sleep for a while. Promise?"

"Sure, Doc."

He left the room, and Sarah lay there in the stink of antiseptic. The beeping of the monitor accelerated and the jaggedy lines on the screen became erratic. Sarah removed the clip from her trembling finger. She must have been dreaming of him, to have called out his name like that.

Not "harm me."

Harmon.

Harmon Smith, the man in the black hat.

When the bus picked Jett up, she walked straight down the aisle, her gaze fixed on the emergency release latch for the back door. Tommy Williamson let out a wolf whistle, and one of the third graders was opening his lunch box, filling the air with peanut butter smell. She bit her lip and slid into the empty seat on the second row from the rear. Right in front of Tommy and Grady. She expected Tommy to make a grab as she sat, but he must have been too shocked by her abrupt approach.

Tommy said, "Hey, Grady, I think she likes me."

"In your dreams, man."

"No, really. She knows when she's licked . . . *all over*." Tommy snickered. Jett could smell it on them, the reason she had ventured into the goonie zone.

"Why don't you ask her, then?" Grady taunted. "If you're so hot, why ain't she sitting in your lap?"

Jett didn't turn. Compared to the inner-city school she had once attended, where fourth graders sometimes carried switchblades, a Cross Valley Elementary bus offered little to fear. Tommy in his Carhartt jacket with the scuffed elbows was about as threatening as Fonzie from *Happy Days*, in that warm-and-fuzzy era after the likeable hoodlum had jumped the shark.

"Yeah? Just watch a stud in action." Tommy leaned over the seat. Jett could feel his breath on her neck, and the smell of pot was thick and potent. "Hey, sweet thing. I dig chicks in black."

She waited. Maybe he had been practicing his lines on his sister or something, because they sure were lame. He could have done better reading books like *How to Talk to Girls (And Don't Call Them "Chicks")* or hanging out in Internet chat rooms.

"What do you say?" Tommy's voice fell into a low, murmuring rhythm. "You know you want it. Can't keep away, can you?"

"I'm fine, thanks," she said without turning.

"She talked to you, dude," Grady said.

"Shut up." Tommy moved closer, and now his breath was on her ear. "Want some of what I got?"

"As a matter of fact, I do."

Tommy was silent, though he was panting audibly now.

"Seven grams will do," she said. Her father had mailed her fifty dollars, telling her it was for her personal use. This was about as personal as she could get.

"Grams? Do what?"

"Or do you sell it by the quarter ounce up here? I don't know if the metric system has hit the sticks yet."

"You ain't right, girl."

"Come on, let's not play games. You've reeked of marijuana since the first day I walked into school. The only reason the teachers can't smell it is because they're probably smoking it themselves."

"Hey, big-city bitch, don't get so high and mighty. Just because you talk all fancy and got black stockings don't mean you can—"

Jett turned and put her face close to his, their noses almost touching. "Listen, redneck. Next time you lay a hand on me, I'll take your fingers and shove them one by one up your asshole until you're tickling your own tonsils."

Grady shrank into the corner, shooting a glance at the driver twenty rows up. Tommy blinked but didn't back away. A kindergartner was crying in the front of the bus. Trees whizzed by beyond the windows, and leaves skirled along the gravel road in the draft of the bus's wake.

"I've got money and I need grass," she said. "You've got grass and you need money."

"I don't mess with that shit."

"Like hell. What's that you were smoking this morning, goat turds?"

Grady giggled and Tommy elbowed him in the ribs. "What if I *could* get some? I want something more than money."

"Like what?"

Tommy ran his tongue over his lips like a poisoned rat at a water puddle. "Some of your sweet stuff."

Jett tucked a strand of dyed hair behind her ear. "Fine. Bring it on. But there's something you ought to know."

Tommy's eyes widened, and Grady leaned toward her, too, not believing his good buddy was going to score. "What's that?" Tommy said, in a dry croak.

"I've got AIDS. So any time."

Tommy went pale. Jett faced the front, smiling to herself. The rumor would make the rounds, and by Christmas break some teacher or other would probably call her mom. It might even get as far as the school board. She'd probably be asked to take a blood test by next semester. With any luck, it would lead to an indefinite suspension until the matter was cleared up.

But by tomorrow, she would have a bag of pot, even if Tommy delivered it wearing rubber gloves and a surgical mask. The good times would roll, and all her problems would go up in smoke.

Katy had gone back to bed after seeing off Jett. She lay under the covers, half asleep, trying to free the stolen sheet from Gordon's clutches. This was Friday, and Gordon's only class was in the afternoon. They had taken to sleeping late that day, especially as the mornings had grown chillier. Katy felt a bit decadent, having been a chronic early riser during her banking career. She still wasn't sure if she missed working or not.

Gordon snorted and rolled over against her. His body warmth was comforting and she let herself roll against him into the curved middle of the mattress. Rebecca's weight had helped make the depression in the mattress, from her two thousand nights of lying here. But Rebecca was gone and now this space was hers.

Katy wriggled her rear against his thigh, hoping to elicit a response. She was rewarded when one of his hands slid across her waist. It was the most intimate he had been in weeks. She wriggled some more and his hand slid up to her breast. She wished she had removed her bra. She'd always slept in the buff but Gordon had acted like that was a dirty habit. He wore pajamas, rumpled cotton that didn't flatter him. The pajamas made him look like a nursing home inmate.

Gordon squeezed her breast and her nipple hardened. She snuggled closer, hoping he would turn so she could feel his arousal. She twisted her neck and kissed his cheek. He smelled masculine, like wood smoke and metal. His hand worked her flesh in small circles.

"Gordon," she whispered, and then a moan escaped her lips.

She didn't want to move away from his hand, but a tiny spark had taken hold in the center of her body. She raised herself up on her elbow so that she was nearly over him. Even asleep, his body revealed evidence of his lust. His erection tented the blankets.

Katy moaned and let her fingers slide between the buttons of his pajama top. Gordon grunted in his sleep and put his hand over hers. Katy nuzzled his neck and Gordon's eyes flickered.

"Rebecca," he said in a hoarse, low whisper.

Katy froze. Maybe he was dreaming that she was Rebecca, and that was the reason for his response. He'd barely touched Katy, had not even slipped her some tongue when they kissed, had left her to masturbate on their wedding night. But here he was as hard as Pittsburgh steel and as hot as Costa Rica, and it was his dead wife that was doing it for him.

Not Katy.

But Katy was so desperate for affection and contact that a cynical part of her took over. She would screw him no matter who she had to be. There was more than one way to consummate a marriage.

"Yes, darling," Katy said, not knowing where the endearment came from. She'd never said "darling" in her life. But she was slipping into a role, and the deception fueled her lust. If Rebecca was what Gordon wanted, then Katy would give her to him, and fulfill her own desires in the bargain.

She pressed her lips to his and Gordon's tongue probed her mouth. She was fully on him now, kicking the blankets away, pressing her chest against his. Gordon's arms went around her back and stroked her hair. She raised one leg and straddled him, settling so that her vagina was over the straining bulge of his pajama bottoms. She rocked gently back and forth, savoring his saliva, breathing wildly through her nose.

Gordon lifted himself, thrusting against her. He pulled his mouth free and gasped. "Yes," he said.

His hands came down to her bra strap and he deftly unhooked it. He peeled the bra away and flung it off the bed. She reached between their bodies for the waistband of his pajamas, wanting to unbutton them. Instead, her fingers found the fly and slid into the little pocket toward the heat beneath. She had seen his penis, of course, he hadn't been that strange. But she had yet to see it in all its glory, pumped full of blood and quivering for release.

"Oh, honey," he whispered, and Katy no longer cared if he was talking to her or to Rebecca. The ache in her loins was taking over, and she probably would have ridden him if he had called her Catherine the Great.

"Mmmm," she said, not sure what sort of language to use. Mark liked dirty talk, and they'd often ranted themselves into a frenzy as they worked toward what were almost always simultaneous orgasms. She blushed for thinking of Mark, but her cheeks were already warm and pink and she decided that was no worse than Gordon's little fantasy. Besides, her brain wasn't the organ doing her thinking at the moment.

Her fingers slipped into his pajamas and found the rigid flesh of his penis. There was still another layer of fabric over it, and she fumbled for the waistband of his briefs. Gordon's hands enclosed her breasts, kneading them with a gentle firmness that suggested experience. While he'd been chaste with Katy, he certainly was no virgin.

She was panting, her heart galloping, and a strand of drool hung from her lower lip. Her hand worked down his underwear and at last she had him. His penis was like a smooth piece of wood encased in warm velvet. She worked it free of the confines of cloth and stroked it, bringing tiny grunts of approval from Gordon.

One of Gordon's hands slid down her panties and she bit her lip as his middle finger slid between her labia. She was soaking wet and could smell her own juices. Gordon's other hand continued to work her breasts; then his mouth enveloped her left nipple. She opened her eyes and saw the dark tangles of his hair and the slight bald spot at the top of his skull. Gordon's throbbing heat nudged against her panties, and then he eased one of the leg bands aside and slid the head against her moist outer folds.

Katy fought an urge to mash herself down onto him. This was

their first time, and it should be slow. As much as she hated to break the contact of his tongue on her nipple, she tilted his head back to look him in the eyes.

"Gordon," she said, and the word came from low in her throat, like the growl of an animal.

His eyes remained closed, though his eyelids fluttered as if he were asleep and experiencing the rapid eye movements associated with dreaming.

She rubbed his penis against her, making his skin damp and slick. She stroked down until she felt his coarse pubic hair, then squeezed the base of his turgid stalk. Her hips quivered of their own accord, and she knew she couldn't hold out much longer. Gordon's finger returned to the sheath inside her and caressed her clitoris. He was definitely no virgin.

"Rebecca," he said, lifting his hips off the bed and pushing the head of his penis inside her.

Katy almost hesitated. This was too weird. The only way she could get laid was to pretend to be dead. Or, more precisely, be someone who had died. Her rival. The woman she hated.

But another part of her saw it as revenge, as if she were seducing Gordon into cheating on Rebecca. She knew how crazy that sounded, but lust made people crazy anyway, and if she was going off the deep end she wanted to go with a bang.

Katy impaled herself on his hardness and felt the burning length of it drive inside her. She raised herself again and settled, letting it slide even more deeply.

"Rebecca," he repeated.

"Yes, darling, I'm here," she said, shivering in anticipation and an odd sensation that she might have recognized as fear if she weren't so far gone. She scarcely recognized her own voice.

Gordon's hands went around her waist and lifted her, then let her fall back down. They gained speed, working toward a frantic pace, Gordon grunting, his lips peeled back and teeth clenched, his eyes still closed.

Katy flung her head back, hair flailing across her shoulders. She put her hands on his chest and caught his rhythm, pushing herself down as he released her waist at each apex. His penis filled her, and a glow built from inside her belly, a tiny spark expanding into a golden fire.

"Yes, darling, yes," she said, words interrupted by thrusts. "Give it to me."

She started to scream, "Fuck me harder," but something held her back. After all, Gordon wasn't Mark and she'd have to adjust her sexual habits. And it didn't seem like the kind of thing Rebecca would say.

She smelled lilacs, but before she could comprehend the scent the fire expanded and electricity jumped the wires in her arms and legs and this was way better than another lonely bout with the vibrator as the flood of his passion erupted inside her and their hips slammed together and she may have shouted something and she hoped to God it wasn't Mark's name, not that Gordon would have heard her anyway because he gave a loud, shuddering groan and thrust up against her, lifting her nearly a foot off the bed. They collapsed with a squeak of bedsprings and Gordon thrust again, less vigorously this time, but she was finishing her own orgasm and so pressed down enough for both of them.

Their bodies writhed together several more times before slowing. Katy relaxed onto Gordon's chest, her hair flowing over his neck and shoulders, chest heaving from effort. The area below her waist was a warm taffy and she couldn't tell where she ended and Gordon began. His arms went around her and he squeezed more tightly than he ever had before, even when the minister David Tester had pronounced them man and wife in the little church on the other side of the mountain.

"That was worth the wait, darling," she said into the dark, curly hairs on his chest.

"As good as the first time," he said.

She lifted herself, arms trembling in postcoital weakness. "What?"

His eyes, which had remained closed throughout the intercourse, now flicked open, then widened. "Rebecca?"

Gordon sounded dismayed. Had he carried the fantasy all the way through to the end and not even allowed himself to give anything to his new wife? As horny as she had been, was the physical release worth this feeling of rejection?

She rolled off him, or perhaps Gordon had raised himself on one hip and eased her to the side. They separated with a slight sticky smack.

"Gordon, what's wrong?" she said, drawing the sheet over her breasts in an attempt to hide from his shocked stare.

He rubbed a hand over his face and closed his eyes. "Nothing, it was just . . . that was wonderful, honey."

Gordon bent and kissed her lightly on the forehead, then sat on the edge of the bed. He buttoned his pajama top, fussed with the alarm clock, and stood and stretched. Without a word, he went into the bathroom and closed the door.

Katy lay there, the heat fading between her thighs until it felt as if someone had driven an icicle inside her. She couldn't escape the feeling that she had just been cheated on by her husband's late wife. Gordon turned on the shower, and the hissing spray sounded almost like a mirthful and devious giggle.

Chapter Twelve

The cornstalks were streaked with brown from the early frosts, the tassels stiff and dry. Ray Tester worked his way between the rows, checking the ears. He'd grown Silver Queen, which produced sweet but short ears with small, white kernels. By this time of year, what hadn't been harvested or nibbled down by cutworms was left to freeze and harden. The crows, who hadn't been around since first planting, when they'd go down the rows like mechanical chickens and pluck seeds from the ground, were now back for fall.

Some farmers laced loose kernels with battery acid and spread the tainted bait around the edges of their fields. Others would duck down in the rows with double-barrel shotguns, the shells loaded with small pellets to give the most scattering power. Ray figured both of those methods were useless. Crows were too stupid to learn a lesson, and if you killed one, then four-and-fucking-twenty would swoop down in its place. No, the best way to handle the black, thieving bastards was to head them off at the pass.

Which meant a scarecrow.

Not just any old scarecrow, either. Crows were dumb but they had eyes, and if you propped up something that looked like a sack of Salvation Army rags, then the crows would just sit on its head and shit on its shoulders, laughing in that cracked caw of theirs, a sound that taunted farmers everywhere. No, what you needed was something so close to flesh-and-blood that even *humans* did a double take.

Ray was a champion scarecrow maker. He'd entered his best creation, named "Buck Owens" after the star on the old *Hee-Haw* television show, in a contest at the Pickett County Fair three years ago and had taken home the blue ribbon and fifty bucks. Buck had an ugly striped shirt and frayed overalls and a head that was sack-cloth stuffed with old linen scraps. The judges had especially liked the straw boater that was perched atop its head, dented and torn and weathered. Ray had been proud of his handiwork, especially since he'd dropped out of school in the ninth grade and had never been mistaken for a genius. But while the scarecrow was on exhibit for the better part of that harvest week, the crows had ravaged his fields and taken up residence in the trees above the farm. His late wife, Merlie, had a little bird feeder built in the shape of a church that hung from a wire on the porch. The crows had streaked the church with green-and-yellow runs, proof that the winged rats had no respect for neither God nor man.

Since then, Ray had never entered another agricultural contest. He kept his scarecrow out in the field where it belonged, a good soldier on sentry duty who didn't complain and would give its life to defend its home ground. But even a soldier needed an overhaul every now and then, just to keep its spirits up. So Ray was bringing a moth-eaten scarf he'd found tangled in the briars at a county Dumpster site. The scarf had the extra advantage of being plaid, something that would spook even those nearsighted crows.

He could hear the crows in the forest at the edge of the pasture, cawing from throats that seemed way too long for their bodies. In case some of them had witnessed another farmer scattering their kind with buckshot, he'd tucked a gun in his scarecrow's arms. It was a rusty old air rifle scrounged from the flea market for a dollar. That helped with the soldier idea, too, even though that didn't square with the "Buck Owens" name. But a banjo wouldn't have done a damn thing against those miniature buzzards, unless the scarecrow started twanging it as off-key as did those Christian bluegrass bands.

The corn was about two feet over Ray's head. It had been a good year, rainy in the spring and sunny in the summer, and fall had been pretty slow and mellow. From between the rows, he couldn't see the scarecrow where it hung on a tall oak stake in the center of the field. But he could almost feel its gaze sweeping across the rows, alert for the slightest flicker of black feathers. Ray grinned, his feet crunching in the high weeds and dirt clods. The air smelled of that sweetness the grass and trees only gave off just before winter, when the sugar was breaking down inside.

At the center of the field was a rusty fifty-five-gallon drum that caught rainwater. Ray didn't have an irrigation system, but the barrel would provide some backup in case of a dry spell, especially when the seedlings were young and tender. That was also when the crows liked to swoop down, when the green shoots were easy to spot from above. The birds would tug the nubs out of the ground and eat the just-split kernels, sprouting roots and all. A few tools leaned against the barrel, and the scarecrow stood sentinel beside it.

Ray eased back the cluster of stalks that separated him from the clearing. The first thing he noticed was the empty pole and crosspiece. He thought at first old Buck had slipped to the ground, blown by a strong wind, even though the scarecrow had been tied in place with baling wire. But there were no rags on the ground beneath the pole. The dirt was scuffed as if someone had been dragging away a heavy load. Ray dropped the scarf and ran to the pole.

Not a scrap remained of the scarecrow. Ray squinted over the rows of corn to the edges of the field. Some kid was probably playing a prank. One of those Halloween trick-or-treat deals. But whoever had stolen his award-winning scarecrow didn't know that some tricks weren't worth playing.

Ray looked in the weeds surrounding the barrel, figuring he'd at least find the air rifle or the battered straw boater. He studied the dragging marks for footprints. That's when he realized that something hadn't been dragged *away*, it had been dragged *to*. There were no footprints, just fine squiggles that looked as if someone had swept the dirt to erase tracks.

The marks led to the water drum. The stagnant water gave off the scent of rust and something ranker.

Ray looked in the water. At first all he saw was a reflection of the sky in the greasy surface, the frayed strips of cirrus clouds and a sun the color of a rotten egg yolk. But a shape hung suspended beneath the surface. Ray thought of one of those carnival sideshows he'd seen as a kid, back before polite society decided freaks couldn't earn an honest dollar with their talents. He'd seen the conjoined fetus of Siamese twins floating in a milky jar of formaldehyde, two tiny arms complete down to the fingernails, two legs curved like those of a frog. The two heads hung at different angles, one leaning forward with a single bleary eye open. Ray got in plenty more than his fifty cents' worth of looking before the crowd nudged him along.

This shape was almost like that, except indistinct. Somehow, the extremities didn't quite add up. Ray took the hoe from beside the barrel and dipped it into the tainted water. He hooked and lifted, straining from the weight. The odor hit him before his eyes could make sense of what they were seeing.

It was a goat, at least a week dead, its meat beginning to turn to pink soap. The animal had been gutted and a few ribs glinted in the afternoon light. The head hung by a narrow scrap of skin and the horns had been sawed down to blunt stumps. One leg was missing, and in the lower part of the goat's body cavity was a furry lump. Ray lifted the hoe higher to get a good look, and the head broke free and plopped into the barrel, splashing stinky water onto Ray. The head bobbed in the surface, the lips puffed into a grin.

Ray twisted the hoe handle so he could see what was inside the body cavity. He'd slaughtered plenty of livestock in his time, and he knew that guts were gray and pink and most major organs were ruby red. Nothing grew inside that was furry. He shook the corpse, expecting pieces of it to slough off and slide back into the water. It held together long enough for him to see what was lurking where the stomach, kidneys, and liver should have been.

It was another goat head, that of a billy, the horns long and slick. One of the horns had perforated the animal's skin. Ray let loose of the hoe and it slid into the barrel along with thirty pounds of scrambled goat parts. The stench was stronger now, and Ray wiped at the front of his soaked shirt. He forgot all about Buck Owens as he made his way into the sanity of the long, straight rows.

The Circuit Rider might have come riding through, but he wouldn't have any business with scarecrows. He'd never been known to slaughter livestock, either, at least not since he'd passed from the mortal coil. This business was different. As mysterious as the Circuit Rider was, at least he was a part of Solom, regular, reliable, not given to trickery.

"Better the devil you know," Ray figured. But some new devilry was afoot, and he didn't want to be caught out alone if that particular devil came calling.

Ray glanced back once as he entered the corn. A murder of crows had settled onto the crosspiece. One of them fluttered down and gripped the rim of the barrel, dipping its head to drink at the sickening soup.

Jett tuned out the monotone of Jerry Bennington, her earth sciences teacher. That was no challenge, because Bennington was lecturing about gravity and, even though gravity tied all the stars and planets into place, he managed to make it sound as simple and boring as a math problem. Like there was no magic or mystery in it at all. Public school teachers weren't allowed to address religion in the classroom, and explaining how heaven stayed in place might have made the subject a little more colorful.

The boy sitting in front of her, Harold Something-or-Other, must have raided his dad's medicine chest, because he reeked of Old Spice or Brut or one of those stinky-sweet colognes. She could endure it as long as Harold didn't bend forward to pick up a pencil or something and flash his sweaty crack over the belt loops of his low-riding blue jeans. She slipped Dad's letter from her backpack and read it for the fourth time since yesterday.

Dear Punkin,

I miss you so much mucher than all the chocolate donuts in the world. Right now I'm looking at the picture of us from the Outer Banks trip we took the summer you were seven. You look a lot like your mother in that one, more than you do now. I guess you were getting ready to be your own self.

How do you like the mountains? I'll bet they're not as

strange as you thought they would be, but I wish you were down here right now so we could go to Discovery Place or a Panthers game, or anywhere that sold cotton candy and root beer. You'll have to tell me all about your school and teachers. I would e-mail you but your mom told me her new husband (I don't like to say his name, I guess that's small of me but that's the way it is) put a password on the computer so you can't use it without his permission. Plus ink and paper give you something real to hold on to, and you can keep a letter nearby for when you want it.

Are you making new friends? I finally went out with that poodle woman but I don't think any sparks flew. If they did, I didn't get burned. I guess it's taking me longer to get over the breakup than it did your mom. But she's a great woman and a great mother. I tried my best but things happen, and I'll still always try my best for you no matter what. Listen to your old man going on like this. A good parent leaves the kids out of it, they say. I wish I could have left you out of my other problems, too.

It's not that long until Thanksgiving and I'm so much mucher looking forward to having you down for a few days. You know I'm not a cook but even turkey cold cuts will taste fine with you at the table. Work's going great, I'm designing some new wrought-iron furniture, wine racks and chandeliers, fancy stuff. They pay me for all the designs they use and then I get a royalty on each piece cast from my design. I hope that will allow me more free time in the next few years so I can get up and see you whenever I want. Maybe I can even move near you, since there's nothing keeping me in Charlotte now except the manufacturing plant. All I would need is a small house and a workshop, and maybe we can work it out so you're with me on weekends.

I was not going to mention the drugs, but it seems like part of the problem that caused the Big Problem. I'm sorry if I was a bad influence on you. I let that stuff take me over and steal part of my soul away, and things might have been different if I had given that bit to my family instead. The reason I bring it up is this: You're going to be a big girl soon and *have to make your own decisions about your life. I know better than anybody that you can't change your heart just by changing your scenery. Because my heart still belongs to you even though we're two hundred miles apart.*

So tell me all about Solom and send me some pictures when you write back. I've enclosed some stamps and a money order. The money is for you and you don't have to tell any grown-ups about it. I miss you all the world and love you all the stars in the sky and think of you all the fish in the sea. See you in November.

Giant hugs and supersize kisses,
Dad

Heavy shit, Dad.

"Miss Draper?"

Jett slid the letter into the papers on her desk. She wondered how many times Bennington had called her name before she'd noticed. Harold turned in his seat with a faint farting noise and smirked at her. She was used to the stares by now. Solom's first genuine artificial Goth girl, and the attention was half the fun. "Yes, Mr. Bennington?"

"We were discussing Sir Isaac Newton."

"The guy who invited the delicious fig cookies?"

That got a muffled laugh out of a couple of the kids. She had to admit, it was a pretty lame comeback, but she was off her game. Maybe when Tommy came through with the pot, she'd sharpen her wit a little and really wow the crowd.

Bennington wasn't amused, his Grinchish frown seeming to stretch longer in defiance of physics as his lips receded deeper into his mouth. "We were discussing Newton's Third Law of Motion."

"Oh yeah, that one. How does it go again?"

This drew a few more laughs. Bennington glanced above the chalkboard at the clock. Two minutes away from the bell. "It seems not everyone benefited from today's lecture, so perhaps the entire class should read chapter four in your textbooks and write a two-page report on Isaac Newton's laws."

Bennington's frown lifted a little as the class let out a collective groan. "Good going, witch," Harold whispered.

After the bell sounded, Jett hurried from the room. She was to meet Tommy just before sixth period in the boiler room behind the gym. Tommy had skipped English class, so Jett assumed he'd gone off the school grounds to score. She didn't feel the least bit guilty for her part in his truancy. His attendance record was his problem. It wasn't like the goon was going to last past the legal dropout age of sixteen anyway.

The gym was set apart from the school, with a walkway that led to the bus parking lot. Phys ed classes weren't held during the last period, so it was the perfect place for a little privacy. Jett passed a necking couple who were tucked behind a screened Dumpster. The boy wore dark boots and a stained baseball cap, the girl wore cheap jewelry and an outdated *Friends* hairstyle. From their downscale Kmart fashion wear, she pegged them for trailer trash. The girl would probably be pregnant by ninth grade and the boy would do the honorable thing and marry her, at least until he realized that diapers didn't change themselves and three people could never live as cheaply as one.

Not that you're any great shakes, Jett, but at least you're aware of your flaws. Like criticizing others.

She hefted her backpack higher on her shoulder and cut around the gym entrance, where cigarette butts and old ticket stubs littered the gravel. The dirt around the boiler room was stained black from spilled fuel oil. A large rusty tank was half-submerged in the ground, the cap locked to prevent sabotage or theft.

The door to the boiler room was ajar. The custodian must have been performing maintenance earlier in the morning. She'd expected the door to be locked and for the deal to go down in the shadows of the little brick outbuilding. The building had no windows. Now they would have decent concealment, and if she and Tommy were caught, they could always pretend they were just another couple sneaking off to swap a little saliva.

She took a look around before easing into the boiler room. It was dark and smelled of oil, musty pasteboard, and old pipes. Something rustled behind the giant steel-plated, pipe-entangled contraption in the center of the room.

"Tommy?"

She reached into her hand purse for the money. She usually didn't carry a purse but had gone with a black, ruffled skirt today, with white knee hose, figuring cold weather would come soon enough so she might as well log some leg time while she could.

The noise came again, and the room grew darker. The door slammed shut behind her. A ventilation grille in the wall allowed some light, but it took her eyes a few seconds to adjust. Tommy must be playing some stupid stoner game. Or maybe he was dick-headed enough to try and get laid even under threat of death from AIDS.

"That's not funny, Tommy," she said, trying the doorknob. Stuck tight.

"It's not funny," came a voice from behind the boiler. It wasn't Tommy's. It was deep and raspy and evoked a tingling familiarity.

Jett turned with her back to the door. The custodian? Maybe he hung out in here with his girlie mags in the afternoon, waiting for the last bus to leave so he could run a buffer over the hallway tiles. Except how had he closed the door when he was on the opposite side of the building?

A pipe reverberated as if someone had bumped into it. Though the boiler wasn't running, the room was stuffy. Jett tried the door again, wondering if her screams would carry to the couple by the Dumpster.

"It's not funny, it's serious," said the voice, and a blacker shadow moved in the darkness.

The brim of the hat lifted and the moon-white face gave a grin. Except it wasn't a grin, Jett saw, just an illusion caused by the man's missing upper lip. She decided it was a man though she had little evidence that it had once been human. A stench flooded the room, and Jett recognized the musky aroma of a male goat.

"You're not real," Jett said, moving her backpack to her chest as if to add a protective layer between her and the nightmare.

"Judge not, that you be not judged," the man said. The head turned and dull silver flashed where the eyes might be. "I just wanted to tell you something while you were away from home, be-cause home clouds your judgment."

"It's not my home," Jett said, throat dry, sure she was having a nervous breakdown spiced with a bad acid flashback and a panic attack thrown in for good measure. Each breath felt like swallowing a handful of sand. She worked the knob with all her strength, chafing her palm.

"It will be your home soon enough." The man waited, as if reluctant to leave the safety of the shadows.

"What do you want?"

"To warn you about false prophets."

"I don't know any prophets." She wondered if acid flashbacks had a time limit, or if she was likely to keep on retro-tripping until her brain was a puddle of ooze.

"Yes, you do."

"Okay, whatever. I'll watch out for them, just let me go."

"Beware of false prophets, who come to you in sheep's clothing, but inwardly they are ravenous wolves."

Jett nodded toward the dark figure.

"You will know them by their fruits," the voice said, as the shadows merged into an unbroken darkness.

The knob turned in her hand. She staggered blinking into the sunlight.

Tommy Williamson sat on the oil barrel, legs crossed, cigarette trailing smoke into the cloudless autumn sky. "What the hell were you doing in there?"

She didn't want to blow her cool in front of this ass clown. "Waiting for you."

Tommy inhaled, blew out a long snake of smoke as if he were sighing, then flicked his butt onto the gravel. "Who were you talking to?"

"Nobody."

"You're as crazy as you look."

"No wonder the girls flock to you, with lines like that."

"Whatever." Tommy slid down from the barrel and reached into his NASCAR windbreaker. He pulled out a paper bag that had been twisted into the size of a hammer handle. "Here's your quarter ounce. Fifty bucks."

Jett peeled off the bills with a trembling hand, hoping Tommy would think she was nervous instead of insane. She put the paper bag in her backpack without looking at its contents. "Thanks. I've got to get to class."

"Sure. Plenty more where that came from, just say the word."

She left him lighting another cigarette, her heart throbbing, wondering how she would make it through math with the man in the black hat's voice buzzing through her skull.

Chapter Thirteen

Katy lay on the bed, listening to the ticking of the tin roof as the sun warmed it. The afterglow of sex had faded, and only a faint stickiness remained. Her toes were cold. Her robe was tangled around her. She must have fallen asleep because the alarm clock on the bedside table read almost ten. She forced herself out of bed, legs heavy, head feeling as if it were stuffed with wet rags.

On the way to the bathroom, she paused at the linen closet to get a clean towel. The closet was still a mess from moving, strewn with garbage bags full of winter clothes, boxes of shoes, and bundled-up coats. The door bulged open, with mufflers, pajamas, and dish towels oozing from the crack. Had Rebecca been this messy? She kicked the clothing away and opened the door, and a shoe box fell from the shelf and bounced off her shoulder. As she put it back, she noticed a string running down the inside of one wall. She thought it might be a light switch and gave it a tug, peering into the darkness above. There was a slight metallic rasp and the squeak of a spring. Katy pulled harder and saw a small wooden door descending. It must be an attic access.

Curious, she took a flashlight from the bedside table and carried one of Gordon's heirloom rockers to the closet. Climbing unsteadily onto the rocker seat, she grabbed the lip of the door and pulled it down until it bumped the shelf. Rough pine rungs had been hammered onto a set of steel bars, making a folded ladder. She shone the light into the opening and saw the ribs of the ceiling joists and the dull galvanized tin of the roof. Cobwebs hung in large dusty beards and the air was stale and humid. Katy shucked her robe so she could climb more easily and grabbed the highest rung she could reach and pulled herself up. She held the flashlight in her left hand, keeping two of her fingers free for gripping. She nearly lost her balance, but managed to get a bare foot on the shelf for purchase, knocking off the shoe box again in the process.

With one more heave, she got her other foot on the lowest rung and stood, poking her head into the attic. Louvered grilles were set at each end of the attic to allow air circulation, with wire covering the openings. The old house must have once been insulated with shredded paper, because bits of gray fluff hung to the wooden support posts. Pale fiberglass had been rolled out in places, though a large section had been floored around the opening as a storage space. Katy focused the beam on the boxes, old lamp shades, and small pieces of furniture that were stacked around the floored area. A fuzzy orange ball bounced among the clutter; then she realized it was the flashlight's beam reflected in a dusty mirror.

Katy climbed through the access hole and crawled on her hands and knees to the mirror. A space had been cleared away in front of it. Two rolls of lipstick, a makeup kit with several peach shades of face blush, and a silver-handled hairbrush were arranged before the mirror as if some woman had tended her appearance here. A small glass spray bottle lay on its side, and it took Katy a second to realize what was out of place: the bottle was free of dust, as if it had been recently used. One of the cardboard boxes was open and a cotton dress hung over the edge, bearing an autumnal print with a frilly white collar.

Behind the mirror was a long, wooden box covered with books. The box appeared too large to have fit through the access hole. Katy wondered if someone had carried the boards up one at a time and assembled the box in the attic. If the box were meant for book storage, it would have been simpler to nail shelving boards between the joists.

So something was inside the box.

Maybe books, maybe air.

Maybe a piece of Smith family history, something that would help her better understand Gordon.

Or understand Rebecca.

As Katy crawled past the clutter, she regarded her reflection in the mirror. Because of the dust, her reflection was fuzzy. Katy tried to grin at her double that was crawling closer. In the dim light, the reflection became distorted and for a moment, Katy's face was narrow and pinched and snarling. But was it *her* face? The fragrance of lilacs rose over the odor of dry wood and blown insulation.

She closed her eyes and forced herself forward, knocking over a stack of Mason jars filled with a dark substance. One of the jars broke, emitting a fetid smell and spilling a tarry liquid on the plywood floor. Katy brushed the shards of glass away and eased her way beside the box. She carefully removed the books from its top. The lid was hinged, with one end held in place by a hasp that was hooked with an open, rusty padlock. Katy removed the padlock and laid it to the side, propping the flashlight so that its cone of light swept over the box.

The lid lifted with a groan, and Katy broke a fingernail as the lid banged back against the floor. She gathered the flashlight and brought its beam to bear on the box's contents.

Katy nearly bumped her head as she drew back from the sight.

A prone figure was laid out in the bottom of the box. Its suit was faded black, spotted gray with dry rot. The arms were crossed over the chest, a straw boater hat resting on them, and straw spilled from the stained sleeves. The face was made of cheesecloth, with white buttons sewn for eyes. A gash in the cheesecloth represented the mouth, and filthy cotton wadding bulged from the opening. The scarecrow was almost a replica of the one in the barn, except this one had never been in a field.

What had she expected to find? Rebecca's body?

She wouldn't have looked otherwise.

Katy was about to close the lid when the flashlight glinted off something tucked in the scarecrow's jacket. She reached toward the dusty figure and pulled the object into the light, a small chain trailing behind. It was a locket, its gold plate peeling away in spots, the alloy beneath smudged and worn. Katy opened it and played the light over the portrait that was set in the locket's base and covered with glass.

The woman in the black-and-white photograph was beautiful. Though the hairstyle was not of any identifiable era and she'd seen no other photographs of her, Katy knew it was Rebecca. No wonder Gordon still thought of her and fantasized about her. She was ethereal, cheekbones fine and thin, eyes dark between soft lashes. She wore a dress with a frilly collar, and Katy recognized it as the dress with the autumnal print.

Gordon must have placed the locket here. But why go to all the trouble of making a scarecrow, an oversize fetish doll? Looking at the objects stored in the attic with new interest, she realized that none of these things were Gordon's. The books were mostly romantic suspense, Mary Higgins Clark, Daphne du Maurier, and Anne Rivers Siddons. The few pieces of furniture might have come from a college girl's sorority room, thrift shop junk made of cheap wood. Perhaps Gordon had set up the attic as a shrine to Rebecca's memory, though there was certainly no loving arrangement to the clutter.

Gordon studied religion and probably saw symbolism in ordinary objects. The locket was more than just a picture memory; it must have been an aged heirloom, and Katy found it hard to believe that Gordon would banish it to the attic. Maybe Rebecca's loss had been so devastating that he'd put her things out of sight and out of mind, though he hadn't the heart to throw them away. Katy played the light over the scarecrow once more.

Had the mouth twitched?

Perhaps mice nested in the wadding. She let the lid drop with a wooden bang and backed away to the mirror, propping the flashlight on a ceiling joist so that it shone down like a stage spotlight. She hooked the clasp on the locket's chain and placed it around her neck. Her reflection seemed pleased, smiling back at her through the snowy film that covered the glass. Katy picked up the tiny spray bottle and sniffed.

Lilacs.

This was Rebecca's scent, the one that drifted across the kitchen or rose from the bed in sudden urgency. Katy sprayed a little on her neck, the mist tickling and chilling her flesh.

She then picked up the lipstick tube, pulled off the cap, and regarded the rose shade. This might have been the lipstick Rebecca wore when the portrait was made. Katy sniffed it. She rarely wore makeup, though as a business professional she'd had to dress in pantsuits. Her hand lifted as though of its own accord, the lipstick sliding across the grinning lips in the mirror. Next she applied the blush to her cheeks. Her reflection startled her. In the yellow circle of the flashlight, she looked deathly pale. Too deathly.

She stood and removed her robe. The attic was warm but her nipples swelled inside the cups of her bra. This was dirty and exciting, the putting on of a mask. She thought of the morning's intercourse with Gordon and his calling Rebecca's name. The memory of her own orgasm came back and she was tempted to slide her finger into her panties.

Instead, she tried on the dress.

It fit perfectly.

Alex Eakins parked his pickup at the edge of the woods, below an embankment where the road had been cut to his property. He finished the last of his joint and doused the roach. He almost tossed it in the ashtray for later, but if a cop found it there, that would probably constitute grounds for a search warrant. The fucking pigs were just that way, and they'd gotten a lot porkier under the nouveau Stalinism of the Bush II regime.

Fuck them all. Fuck big-budget Bush and his totalitarian ways. Fuck the spineless Democrats who curled up in a ball as they were kicked, and fuck even his own chosen Libertarian Party for lacking in ability to capture the popular imagination. When it really counted, political action was up close and personal.

He got his Pearson Freedom compound bow and arrows out of the backseat and wandered to the fence. Gordon Smith's goats grazed and browsed among the scrub vegetation, eating blackberry vines, pine trees, locusts, and pokeweed, not caring what entered their mouths as long as it was green or brown. Alex considered having a neighborly talk with Smith, but that might lead to unexpected visits and snooping around, and then maybe a peek into the little shed behind Alex's mud house. Gordon was a professor, which almost certainly meant he'd smoked some weed in his day, but when it came down to it, someone on a university payroll was part of the Establishment and couldn't be trusted.

Besides, it was the *goats* that had fucked with his garden, not their owner. So it was the goats that had to pay. Alex notched an arrow and tilted the bow, then pinched and stretched the string back, muscles straining against the taut arc. It was power, primitive and raw and heady. Or maybe he was stoned.

The flock of a half dozen had paused and given him a speculative appraisal when he'd parked, but the animals now returned to their chewing. The nearest goat was thirty yards away, peeling the bark from a bare sapling. It was tan and white, ears long and funneled, horns curved and short. The age of goats was hard to figure, since they got plump and grew beards before they were a year old, but Alex figured this one for middle age. Probably was bound for the meat locker this winter.

Alex sighted down the arrow, aiming just a little high to compensate for the natural pull of gravity. He was about to let fly when he saw movement in a prickly grove of crab apples behind the flock. Somebody was walking toward him. Shit. Must be that redneck goon Odus Hampton, the odd-jobber who hung around down at the general store. Odus did chores around the Smith place in exchange for liquor money and crops, and probably had some sort of inbred devotion to his master. Mountain folk like Odus seemed to cling to the ideals their Irish and Scots ancestors had brought to the mountains as they fled to the freedom of the Southern Appalachians. They were driven by a rebel streak, but still measured themselves against the value systems of their oppressive overlords and would do anything for a dollar.

Or maybe Odus was just drunk and rambling.

And maybe the Scots-Irish who wanted to be left alone had a lot in common with antigovernment stoners.

Alex was shielded by a stand of small poplars, so Odus wouldn't be able to see him right away. Alex eased the tension on the string and leaned against the camouflage to wait for Odus to move on. The goats didn't turn toward Odus's approach, which didn't make sense. If Odus was the one who regularly fed them, they should have gone running at the first sniff of his bourbon-sweet stench.

Alex peeked from his cover. It wasn't Odus coming down the dirt path.

It was a man in a hat and an ill-cut suit that was too short for his arms. He wore a ragged black tie that was cut in the shape of a cross, and his white linen shirt looked like a stained tooth against the grimy topcoat. His bony wrists were exposed, along with a couple of inches of pale forearm. He wore square-toed leather boots and his woolen pants were riddled with tiny rips and moth holes. His face was hidden in the shade of the hat's oversize brim.

Fucking Twilight Zone *material, weird dude walking*.

Alex debated getting back into his truck and driving away, but the man would probably see him carrying the bow and arrow. The stranger wouldn't know that Alex had been about to kill a goat, but he might tell Gordon about the encounter. And Gordon might get suspicious, drive up the dirt road, and knock on Alex's door, or take a look around the property. Worse, Gordon might report Alex to the sheriff's department as a trespasser, and they would come with a warrant whether Alex was guilty or not. That's just the way the fucking cops were, they made up a stupid reason to investigate you so they could find something serious to bust you over. It was the same whether your broken taillight led to a drunk-driving arrest or a bogus trespassing claim got you busted for illegal manufacture of a Schedule I narcotic.

Alex decided to wait it out. Maybe the stranger was trespassing, too, and would walk amid the flock and head on down to the road. Weird Dude Walking could just walk the fuck right on off the stage.

But the stranger didn't keep walking. He stopped in the middle of the flock, in a cleared area of trampled goldenrod and tickseed. He tilted his head forward so that even the shadow of his face was hidden by the hat's brim. He folded his hands in front of him and stood as still as a scarecrow. The goats stopped their ruminating and turned to him, one by one. The only sounds were the September breeze skirling dead leaves and the ticking of the Jeep's engine as it cooled. Even the crows had grown hushed in the high treetops.

The goat closest to Alex, the one he had planned to murder, took a few steps toward the man in the hat. It emitted a soft bleat. Another of the goats, farther up the hill, echoed the bleat, and then others joined in. It wasn't the yearning bleat that hungry goats often made. These calls were gentle and almost tender, like the sound a kid would make as it neared its mother's teats.

Weird Dude Walking kept his head tilted down but slowly lifted his arms until they were suspended straight out from the sides of his body. It looked as if he were imitating a giant bird and would at any moment start flapping for takeoff. But his movements were slow and graceful, like those of someone at peace. The goats all moved forward at the same time, headed for the stranger. The largest, a fat old billy with a long, filthy beard, reached him first and sniffed at the wool suit. The man remained perfectly still, though his body seemed to relax a little, his limp hands dangling from the ends of his raised arms. Other goats crowded around, their nostrils flaring as they checked the air.

The nearest goat put its nose against the man's coat, then opened its jaws and took the cloth in its mouth. The man kept his head tilted and made no sign of movement. The goats squeezed closer, and now others put their snouts against his skin. The big billy tugged on the coat, first gently and then harder, until a lower button popped free. The other goats nipped at the fabric, yanking their heads back with the clothing clenched between their jaws, their bleats growing more frantic.

Alex wondered if Weird Dude had worn some sort of scent that attracted the goats. Deer hunters would splash their coveralls with buck urine, hoping to entice does from the woods. Maybe there was a special scent to attract goats, though goats were tame enough that they didn't need to be stalked. Alex fell back on the theory that the man had fed the goats before and they associated his scent with grain or sugar. Or maybe homegrown sinsemilla bud dulled Alex's thought process. Alex liked that theory better, because then he could take the credit for growing mythical motherlode mind-fuck instead of the possibility that something fucked up was happening that might be happening whether or not the observer was stoned. Like Einstein on acid or something, or an Escher drawing where you were on the inside looking out.

Whatever, man, because it's happening no matter which theory fits. . . .

Desperate goat mouths ripped open Weird Dude Walking's coat, the bone buttons sparkling in the sun as they arced to the ground. The man had on a flannel long john shirt underneath, but it was shredded in places and deathly pale skin showed through the openings. The goats tugged on the man but he kept his balance. Alex wondered why Weird Dude didn't push the animals away.

Because this is only happening in your mind. Yeah. Okay.

The man's arms were pulled down, and one of the sleeves was yanked free. Two goats played tug-of-war with the wool coat, and then jerked it off the man's back. The coat settled on a patch of dried goldenrod. Weird Dude finally lifted his face and Alex expected either the awe-inspiring expression of a Mushroom God or else a Carlos Castaneda smirk. From fifty yards away, all Alex could tell was that Weird Dude looked sick, his skin unhealthy and sallow. But a smile creased his doughy face as he looked at the sky and endured the hircine assault.

The goats grew frantic, their teeth tearing the man's clothes, and Alex almost left his hidden vantage point and went to the rescue. If Weird Dude had acted in any way alarmed, Alex would have emptied his quiver of arrows into the goats. But his unnatural serenity caused Alex to watch and wait.

The stoner stereotype called for an indecisive and befuddled reaction. Alex was no fucking stereotype. He knew he was a stoner and that put him several rungs above the people who bought his dope. For all Alex knew, this was some elaborate trick of the Drug Enforcement Agency, because the spooks would spare no expense in bringing down a single freethinking, tax-exempt American. Because from such men revolutions were sparked.

The goats ripped until Weird Dude's flannel underwear gave way, and then one of the goats bit deep into the man's side. The man should have screamed, but the smile didn't waver as the goat worked its head back and forth, trying to pull the piece of flesh free. Another goat went for the soft portion of the stomach just below the navel and backed away, a string of meat dangling from its mouth.

Alex gripped the tree in front of him, the bark scraping his cheek and his breath so loud he was sure the goats could hear it above their own noise. A mantra came to him, in a dull throb that mirrored his accelerated pulse: Not Real, Not Real, Not Real. And then came the syncopated accent beat: Not-Fucking-Real.

Instead of blood spilling from Weird Dude's wounds, a milky substance oozed out, thick as cottage cheese. The goats bit into the man, and one butted him in the left thigh, causing him to lean to one side. A dirty brown goat grabbed the outstretched arm as the man tried to regain his balance. Its teeth clamped on the wrist and dragged the man toward the ground, the black hat flying from the man's head and landing in the trampled vegetation. Once the man was on his knees, the goats clambered over him, rending the flesh of his neck and back. Not once did the man cry out.

The goats' bleats grew muffled as their mouths filled. They fed on the clabbered juice that leaked from the man's torn flesh.

Weird Dude Walking ain't fucking walking anymore.

Alex broke from the trance that seemed to have fallen over him as he watched the bizarre spectacle. This was no psychedelic vision, this was an ass-end-up slab of reality. He gripped his bow and arrows and stepped from his cover. "Hey," he shouted.

The goats kept feeding. Weird Dude was buried beneath the goats, hidden by the mass of dirty, furry animals that were now in a feeding frenzy. The bearded billy backed out of the herd with a prize, a swinging slab of gristle that looked like the man's cheek. No blood leaked from the ripped skin, only a few dribbles of moon-white liquid. Another goat tottered away, dragging what looked to be the strip of a forearm. A third dipped its head into the downed man's belly and came up with a swollen rope of intestines decorating its blunt horns like a satanic Christmas trimming.

Alex fought an urge to vomit. The vestiges of the morning's bong hits faded, and even the high from the seedless, resin-sticky buds he'd crammed into the recent joint had deserted him. He grew kick-ass weed by any standard, but no buzz was deep enough to mask the insane scene that played out before him. Fuckers didn't just crawl out of the weeds and get eaten by goats. Didn't happen. Maybe in a video game, maybe in a shitty direct-to-video horror movie, but certainly not here on the slopes above Solom, where the Bible thumpers said God was closer than ever and the sky weighed three thousand pounds and the government didn't meddle too much and his girlfriend Meredith was sleeping off the effects of a bottle of wine and three orgasms and *no fucking way in the world is Weird Dude getting reamed by goats!*

Alex debated his options. He could charge into the midst of the herd and scatter them, but as much meat as they had stripped from Weird Dude, Alex didn't see any way the man could still be alive. Alex had four arrows, so he could thin the flock a little, except then they might turn their eye to fresh prey. And he knew how goats were—once they got a taste for something, they gobbled it until it was extinct. The third option made the most sense: back the hell away, get in the truck, and pretend this had all been a hallucination. Forget reporting the incident to the authorities, because authority equaled government equaled search warrants.

When he started the truck, one of the goats looked up from the corpse and stared in the direction of the noise. A couple of maggot-white fingers protruded between the twisting lips. The goat looked right through the windshield and met his eyes. Alex was probably just stoned—yeah, that *had* to be it—because there was no way the goat could have been grinning. Either he was stoned or else he had cracked, and he was too rational to crack.

As the pickup bounced up the pitted mountain road, Alex realized that Weird Dude Walking, even while the goats were eviscerating him, had not uttered a single sound.

Chapter Fourteen

"The goats is riled," Betsy Ward said. She dried her hands on her apron, wincing because her skin was chapped and the cool weather hadn't helped a bit. She had a sweet potato pie in the oven. It was a point of pride with her, because sweet potatoes didn't grow worth a darn in the mountains. Yet Arvel's crop always turned out fine. You'd think God was a tater man, judging how he blessed the Ward household.

"Goats?" Arvel was watching a reality show on TV. Betsy couldn't tell the shows apart, but one thing most had in common was they got women into tank tops and tight shorts at some point. Which was all the reason Arvel needed, whether he admitted it or not. Betsy's tight-shorts days had passed some twenty years ago, but she didn't hold that against the skinny things that paraded around before the cameras. No, what she held against them was the makeup, the hairstyles, and all the nipping and tucking that went on these days. Any woman could look good with a little cheating.

"Goats," Betsy said. "Over at the Smiths. Except the new wife ain't named Smith."

Arvel had put in a hard day at Drummond Construction, driving a concrete mixer over the twisting mountain roads. Concrete mixers were the most contrary vehicles on earth, according to Arvel.

The weight could shift in two directions without warning, and once in a while the slooshing mix of sand, gravel, and mortar coincided with the deepest cut of a sharp curve, and nothing had a mortality rate like the rump-over-clutch-pedal tumble of twenty tons' worth of cement and steel. Or so he said.

"What are you worrying about goats for?" Arvel didn't turn from the flickering light of the screen. "They've not got in the garden in two years or so. Leave them be."

"They ain't right. They come down to the edge of the fence and stare at me when I'm hanging out laundry."

"Maybe you ought to lose some of that fat ass of yourn and then they'd quit staring."

Arvel had never made a mention of her weight until he'd taken up watching TV every weeknight, some five years back. Since then, he'd scarcely shut up about it. She wished she could shrink inside her gingham dress, but she was here and this was all of her. "They started about time the new wife moved in. Been breeding like rabbits, too."

"You know how them billy bucks are," Arvel said. "They'll stick it in anything that wiggles, and some that don't."

A commercial came on for some kind of erectile dysfunction product, and a wattled old guy was in a hot tub with a woman young enough to be his daughter. Arvel thumbed down the sound with his remote. "You keep going on about this new wife. If you want to know what I think, I bet you're mad as a pissant because she's skinnier than you."

Betsy was double upset. Arvel had no business looking at the neighbor's wife. Even though Betsy did, every chance she got.

"She ain't no skinnier than Gordon's first wife, and you never said a thing about her," Betsy said.

"Rebecca was different," Arvel said, eyes flicking back to the TV to make sure the commercials were still going. "She's from here."

"She was," Betsy corrected. "*Was.*"

"Let's not get into that."

"She drove too fast for these twisty roads. Heck, Arvel, I know she turned a few heads, probably even yours, but the stone truth of it is she got what was coming to her."

"Like *you* know what happened to her?"

"I ain't saying a thing. The sheriff and the rescue team called it an accident, and they know better than me."

"Solom's took more than a few through the years," Arvel said. "Forget it."

"I *can't* forget it."

"You think it was the Circuit Rider?"

"I don't know."

The commercials were over and Arvel punched a button. The sound burst from the speaker, and a dark-skinned boy with greasy hair was explaining why somebody was kicked off the show. "I smell something," Arvel said.

The pie. The crust must have burned. Betsy had forgotten to set the timer. She was getting more absentminded every day, but she blamed it on worrying about the neighbors. With a possible wife-killer next door, not to mention his witchy-eyed stepdaughter, your train of thought was liable to get derailed now and then. When you threw the Circuit Rider into the mix, it's a wonder anybody in Solom ever got a wink of sleep.

She hurried from the living room and went into the kitchen, where the goat was waiting for her.

Shit. Jett couldn't take another second of reality. She probably should have hidden in the woods, but needed to be close to the house in case Mom called. Jett could always claim to be feeding the chickens or something. The barn door was nearly closed, allowing just enough light to take care of business. Her back was against the wall, and from her sitting position, she could see the back door that led to the kitchen.

She laid out her world history book and pinched some of the pot from the plastic Baggie. In Charlotte, she'd owned an alabaster pipe carved in the shape of a lizard, but she'd left it with her best friend. It was time to improvise. She took the piece of aluminum foil from her pocket, twisted it into a narrow tube, and used her pinky to make a hollow depression in one end. A piece of baling wire hanging on the wall of the barn served to prick three tiny holes in the curved end of the makeshift pipe.

Smoking in the barn was dangerous. During his Great Barn Tour of July, Gordon had made a big deal about how dry the place was. Apparently one of his grandparents' barns had burned to the ground in the 1940s, but that had been the fault of lightning. This barn had been built on the same foundation, and lightning never struck twice in the same place, did it?

She sprinkled some of the dark green leaves into the depression and set the pipe on her book. She'd taken some matches from the tin box on the mantelpiece. She snapped one of the sulfur-tipped stems free from its folded-over cardboard sleeve. *Get a degree at home*, the matchbox read, along with an 800 number, and beneath that, in smaller letters, *Close cover before striking.*

"Fuck it." She scratched the match head across the rough strike pad and the flame bobbed to life. She tucked the pipe between her lips, aplied the flame, and inhaled. The first hit tasted like hot metal, like braces, and she nearly coughed. The harsh smoke settled in her lungs; then she blew out gently. The match had burned down to her fingers, so she held the pipe in her mouth while she used her other hand to grab the burnt end of the match. She then turned the match upside down so it would burn the unused portion of the paper.

The Kid knows all the tricks.

The next hit was a little smoother. She held the flame just above the grass so that it toasted rather than scorched. Yep. That was the ticket. Her throat was dry and she wished she'd brought a Sprite from the fridge. The smoke filled her nostrils, weakening the smell of old dust and animal manure.

She let the buzz work its way through her nervous system, feeling her pulse accelerate. Tears collected in her eyes. Good shit. Tommy Williamson might be a world-class jerk, but he had good connections. A smile crept across her face, and it felt good. Why did the cops and Jesus freaks get so uptight about something that was so natural? She hadn't smiled in weeks, and now here she was with her cheeks stretching and her head feeling light.

The fucking weight of the world temporarily lifted.

Fucking. What a weird word, when you think about it. I mean, fuck, what's the big deal? Mom said I was able to have babies now and maybe that has something to do with the tingling I feel down

*there sometimes. I don't understand how a boy's weenie can fit in
there, as little and floppy as they are. At least Mom didn't give me
the jazz about safe sex. Guess she trusts me.*

Trust. Jett looked down at the pipe and the bag of dope, the
crumbled marijuana scattered across her book.

*I don't have a drug problem. "Drug problem" is what the
English teacher would call an "oxymoron." Well, the teacher's a
plain old fucking moron.*

Jett's stoned leap of logic seemed like the most hilarious thing
since Beavis and Butthead did America, and she giggled. The
sound was like blue bubbles in her brain. She closed her eyes and
listened to them pop.

Blop-bloop-blooooop.

Beh-eh-eh-eh-eh.

Beh-eh?

That wasn't right.

She opened her eyes to find the goat standing right in front of
her, its head at eye level with hers. She rolled away with a start. The
goat lowered its neck and sniffed at the marijuana, then licked at it.

"Get away, you ugly fucker," Jett said, picking up a dry, dark
clod that was probably a goat turd. She flung it at the goat, but it
swabbed its tongue across her stash again.

Damn it, this is war. She gave the goat a kick in the side, not too
hard but loud enough for a *thunk* to fill the barn. The goat turned
toward her. For the first time, she noticed the pale brown horns.
Though they lay nearly flat against the animal's skull, the tips
curled back under and out above the ears like oversize, twisted
fishhooks.

"Easy, there, Fred," she said. Gordon had names for the goats
but she hadn't bothered to learn them. He'd taken them all from the
Old Testament. She wondered whether it was Adam, Seth, or Ruth.
Couldn't be Ruth, because it had a tube of loose flesh hanging from
its loins. She figured the goat didn't know its name, either, so
"Fred" would work just as well.

She backed away and the goat stepped closer. At least she'd distracted it from her expensive cash crop. Now if it would only go
out the door and act like the brainless sack of fur and manure it
was.

But it didn't go for the door. It backed her to the foot of the stairs that led to the loft. And the loft was where she'd blanked out the day before yesterday. Freaked Mom out but good. The bitch of it was, the blackout hadn't been drug-related. She'd let Mom suspect drug use because the alternative was just a little too weird, even for her.

Jett didn't want to go up those stairs. Because the image of a man flashed across the inside of her forehead, like a still from an out-of-focus slide projector. The man with the out-of-fashion hat with the low crown and wide brim, the one who had warned her to "Know them by their fruits." She had a feeling he was waiting up there in the silence and dust of the hay bales.

The goat snorted a little and bobbed its head as if threatening her. Or else commanding her to climb the stairs.

Whoa the fuck down. Goats don't boss humans around. They're stupid Fred-faced, squid-eyed, dumb-as-dirt pieces of meat on the hoof.

The goat grinned, revealing a five-dollar chunk of marijuana bud that was stuck between two upper teeth. Jett almost laughed. This was the kind of stoner story she'd tell at the next party, if she ever made any friends in Solom: "Yeah, a goat came up while I was smoking and gobbled down my stash."

She'd leave out the part about the goat scaring her, and the man in the black hat, and the voice she'd heard in the boiler room behind the school. Because those were things that could get you locked up in the nuthouse, where the drugs were no fun at all, according to her friend Patty from Charlotte. Nuthouse drugs were designed to perform chemical lobotomies, eliminating the problems by stripping away any desire to suffer a thought or feeling. As tempting as oblivion was, Jett liked hers in small and controlled doses.

Besides, who could be bored when a goat was after you?

The wall was covered with garden tools, ropes, and harness. She picked out a hoe, figuring she could use the blunt end of the handle to drive the goat away. The animal clambered forward as she leveled the handle and pointed it like a jousting lance. In the distance, the Wards' dog barked, followed by the sound of tires on gravel. Gordon must be home.

Great.

Gord the Wonder Nerd.

She waited for his SUV engine to die and for the vehicle's door to open. Then she could yell for help. Except the goat had paused, too, and lifted its head as if listening. Like maybe Gordon had a treat.

If Gordon came to the barn, he would see the pot and bust her. She'd probably be grounded for the rest of the school year, or maybe even until high school. Gordon was one of those uptight people who made a big deal about morals without being religious. Because, despite all his blowhard lecturing at the dinner table about this and that denomination, and the fact that he was the great-great-grandson of a circuit-riding preacher, Gordon wore a sneer on his face when he talked about people going to church. Jett wasn't sure what she believed yet, but one thing was for sure, she thought Jesus Christ was the kind of guy who wouldn't put you down for a little bit of weed. True, he probably wouldn't inhale, but he also wouldn't hit you over the head with a Bible because of it.

So calling for Gordon was out of the question. She had to make a decision on whether to try for the loft and wait it out, or scoot past the goat, collect her stash, and sneak around the backyard and into the house before anyone noticed she was missing. Mom had been a real space cadet lately, so Gordon would probably make the obligatory room check. She planned to be at her desk with a text-book open, so she could bat her eyelashes at him in a "What do *you* want?" look. Pop an Altoid mint, drop in some Visine, and she was bulletproof. The only symptom would be goofiness, and all twelve-year-old girls were goofy.

She prodded at the goat with the hoe handle. It turned and trot-ted to the barn door, standing just beyond the reach of daylight, as if it were afraid the sun would burn its skin and turn its carcass to dust. Jett dropped the hoe and scooped up her Baggie of marijuana. She tucked it in the pocket of her sleeveless jean jacket. Though she was craving another hit to cap off the buzz, the whole scene was getting to be like a psychedelic, fluorescent-colored episode of *The Twilight Zone.* She expected the ghost of Rod Serling to step from one of the stalls at any second, wearing a tie-died T-shirt and a ponytail, a pencil-sized joint replacing his ever-present cigarette.

The rear of the barn had another large wooden door, suspended on rollers that slid in a steel track overhead. It was latched from the inside with a dead bolt, but Jett thought she'd be able to maneuver the heavy door open enough to slip around the back way. Gordon's SUV door slammed. That meant he'd go through the front door in about fifteen seconds if he followed his usual routine. Unless he saw the goat in the barn.

Jett wrestled with the dead bolt. It was rusty, as if it hadn't been operated in years. She banged her knuckles trying to work the bolt free, scraping the skin. She put her knuckles in her mouth and sucked at the blood. Something nudged her hip, and she looked down to see the goat's face turned up to hers, its nostrils dilating, eyes glinting in the dim light. The animal emitted a low moan, as if a hunger had been awakened by the scent of fresh fruit.

"Back off, Fred," she said.

Jett threw back the bolt and leaned against the edge of the door, hoping to get some momentum. The door opened six inches. The goat jumped up and put its front hooves on the door, raising itself up to the height of her shoulder. It was bleating deep in its throat, and raised one hoof and banged it against the wood. Frightened now, almost forgetting her buzz, Jett flung her shoulder against the edge of the door, sending a fat spark of pain down her arm. The goat hammered on the door with both hooves as it creaked open another half a foot. Jett turned sideways and squeezed her body into the gap, squinting against the early evening sun.

As she worked her way free, she felt a rough tongue against the back of her hand.

Great. Goat cooties on her wounded knuckles. She'd probably get a staph infection.

She struggled through the door and moved away from the barn. The goat was too plump to get through the door. An absurd wave of relief washed over Jett. Getting stoned had been almost more trouble than it was worth.

As she went down the path that led between the barn and the garden to the apple trees near the house, she glanced back. In the loft opening was a dark shadow that looked a lot like a man in a black suit, arms spread, a wide-brimmed hat on his head. Jett blinked and hurried under the trees. She wanted her drug-induced visions to stay inside her head where they belonged, not out wandering around in the real world.

But the world hadn't been very real ever since she had moved to Solom. Thank God for dope.

Evening fell like a bag of hammers, and Odus decided there was no better place to let the sun die on you than the cold bank of Blackburn River. He had two rainbow trout on the stringer and half a six-pack of Miller High Life floating in the water, the plastic ring tethered to a stick. The mosquitoes had quit biting weeks ago, and even if they were sorry enough to try to suck his blood, they would be drawing nothing but high-octane, eighty proof out of his veins. The bottle of Old Crow was nearly gone, and that meant another long haul into Windshake to replenish his supply. He cussed God and the virgin whore Mary for making Pickett a dry county.

He was below the old remnants of the dam. Part of the earthworks was still in place, funneling water past in a series of tiny falls. The trout loved to lie among the rocks beneath the white water, where the oxygen level was rich and food dropped down like earthworms from heaven. Odus's hook dropped in, too, though he had to work the reel with a steady hand because the bait washed downstream in the blink of an eye.

The general store up on the hill was dark. That was contrary, because Odus had never known it to be closed for a full day. He'd called up to the hospital to check on Sarah, and the receptionist had hemmed and hawed about federal privacy rules until Odus claimed to be her son. Then the receptionist declared Sarah to be in stable condition and scheduled to be kept overnight for observation.

A few tracks from the old Virginia Creeper line, some that hadn't been washed away in the 1940 flood, lay in weed-infested gravel across the river. The creosote cross ties had long since rotted, and the steel rails themselves would have long been overgrown if the tourists hadn't made a walking trail out of the line. Tourists were the damnedest creatures: they took the ugliest eyesores of Solom, such as fallen-down barns and lightning-scarred apple trees, and proclaimed them a glory of Creation. Took pictures and bought postcards, put their Florida-fat asses onto the narrow seats of expensive ten-speeds, and pedaled down the river road as if they were going nowhere and had all day to do it. Beat all, if you asked Odus, but nobody asked, because he was just a drunken river rat and didn't even own any property. He lived in the bottom floor of a summer house and kept the grounds in trade for rent.

But, by God, he knew how to troll for trout, and he could take a ten-point buck in October, and when spring came he could pick twelve kinds of native salad greens, and in summer he knew where the best ginseng could be poached, and then it was fall again and he could make a buck or two putting up hay or helping somebody get a few head of cattle to the stockyards. All in all, it was a king's life, and he wasn't beholden to anybody. If you didn't count the Pennsylvania couple that owned the house where he boarded, and Gordon Smith, and the people who had loaned him money.

The sun slipped a notch lower in the sky, spreading orange light across the ribbed clouds like marmalade on waffles. Fish often bit more at dusk, just as they did at the break of dawn, because the insects they fed on were more active then. A lot of the tourists went in for fly-fishing, and all the gear, complete with hip waders, LL Bean jacket, floppy hat, woven basket and all, would run you upwards of three hundred dollars at River Ventures, the little place up the road that rented out kayaks, canoes, bicycles, inner tubes, and every other useless means of transportation known to man. Odus figured the tourists must be bad at math, no matter how many zeroes they had in their bank accounts, because three hundred dollars would buy you more store trout than you could eat in a year.

But that wasn't his worry. Odus wanted one more rainbow on the trotline before he headed home for a late supper. He planned on stopping by Lucas Eggers's cornfield on the way home and snagging a few roasting ears. That and some turnip greens he grew in the Pennsylvania folks' flower garden were plenty enough to keep the ache out of his belly.

He hit the Old Crow and was about to draw in one of the Millers for a chaser when he saw weeds moving on the far side of the river. The rusted-iron tops of the Joe Pye weed shook back and forth as something made its way to the water. Probably deer, because, like the fish, they got more active at sundown. But deer were likely to stick to a trail, not tromp on through briars and all. Odus played out some slack in his line and waited to see what came out on the river-bank. Odus didn't have a gun, so he couldn't kill the deer, and so didn't care if it was a deer or a man from outer space. As long as it wasn't a state wildlife officer ready to write him up for fishing without a license.

At first, Odus thought it *was* a wildlife officer, because of the hat that bobbed among the tops of the weeds. But the hat was dirty and ragged like that of—

The Smith scarecrow.

Then the weeds parted at the edge of the river.

The sight caused him to drop his pole in the mud, back up onto the slick rocks skirting the riverbank, and wind between the hemlocks and black locust that separated the water from the river road. His heart jumped like a frog trapped in a bucket. The orange light of sunset had gone purple, and the clouds somehow seemed sharper and meaner. A bright yellow light shone above the general store's front entrance, the one Sarah claimed kept bugs away, though Odus could see them cutting crazy circles around the bulb. He broke into a jog, sweat under his flabby breasts and in the crease where his belly lay quivering over his belt. He didn't once look back, and even though the river was between it and him, he didn't feel any safer when he reached his truck.

Odus was fumbling the key into the ignition when he remembered the Miller, and for just a moment, he hesitated. He would definitely need a good buzz later. But three beers wouldn't be nearly enough to wash away the image that kept floating before his eyes. The best thing now was to put some distance between him and what he'd seen. Maybe some tourist would be out for a walk, or a bicyclist would get a flat tire, and it could take *them* instead.

As he drove away, his chest was tight and he could barely breathe. He wondered if he could get a hospital bed in Sarah's room, because now he knew what she'd been going on about as she lay on the sacks with her eyelids fluttering.

It hadn't been the scarecrow he'd seen. It had been much worse than that. The man in the black hat, face white as goat cheese, as if he'd been in the water way too long.

And he had, if you believed the stories.

About two hundred years too long.

Chapter Fifteen

Betsy Ward didn't scream when she encountered the goat. She'd milked plenty of the critters, and the teats were tiny and tough, a workout for her hands. But they usually kept to the field, even when they were riled. Occasionally one slipped through a gap in the fence or squeezed between two gateposts, but when they did that, they usually made a beeline for the garden or the flower beds. Goats had a nose for heading where they could do the most damage.

But she'd never had one come in the house before. The back door was ajar, as if the goat had nudged it open with its nose. The mesh on the screen door had been ripped. Maybe the goat had put one sharp hoof on the wire and sliced it down the middle. Goats weren't that smart, even if they smelled something good in the kitchen. In this case, the only thing going was the sweet potato pie. No doubt the goat had smelled that and come in for a closer look, though Betsy had no idea how in the world the creature had worked the doorknob. Why hadn't Digger run the goat off, or at least raised the alarm with his deep barks?

"Shoo," she said, waving her apron at it. "Get on back the way you come."

The goat stared at her as if she were a carrot with a spinach top.

"Arvel," Betsy called, trying not to raise her voice too much.

Arvel didn't like her hollering from the kitchen. He thought that amounted to pestering and henpecking. Arvel always said a wife should come up to the man where he was sitting and talk to him like a human being instead of woofing at him like an old bitch hound.

Arvel must not have heard her over the television. The goat's nostrils wiggled as they sniffed the air. The oven was a Kenmore Hotpoint, the second of the marriage. In the red glow of the heating element, she could see the pie through the glass window in the oven door. It had bubbled a little and the tan filling was oozing over the crust in one spot.

The goat lowered its head and took two steps toward the oven. It had small stumps of horns and was probably a yearling. Sometimes goats would get ornery and butt you, but in general they avoided interaction with humans, except when food was at stake. It seemed this goat had its heart set on that sweet potato pie.

Betsy shooed with her apron again, then moved so that she was standing between the oven and the goat. She didn't think the goat could figure out how to work the oven door, but some sense of propriety had overtaken her. After all, this was *her* kitchen. "Get along now."

The goat regarded her, eyes cold and strange. She didn't like the look of them. They had the usual hunger that was bred into the goat all the way back to Eden, but behind that was something sinister. Like the goat had a mean streak and was waiting for the right excuse.

"Arvel!" By now Betsy didn't care if her husband thought she was henpecking or not. You don't have a goat walk into your kitchen and expect to take it in stride. She'd gone through three miscarriages, the drought of 1989, the blizzard of 1960, and the floods of 2004. She knew hard times, and she knew how to keep a clear head. But those things were different. Those were natural disasters, and this one seemed a little *un*-natural. Like maybe the goat had something more in mind than just ruining a decent homemade pie.

Betsy put her hands out, hoping to calm the animal, but its cloven hooves thundered across the vinyl flooring as it closed the ten feet separating them. Betsy saw twin images of herself reflected in the goat's oddly shaped pupils. Her mouth was open, and she may have been screaming, and her hair hung in wild, slick ropes around her face. She didn't have time to step away even if she could have made her legs move.

The goat hit her low, its head just above her womanly region, driving into her abdomen. The nubs of the horns pierced her like fat, dull nails, not sharp enough to penetrate but packing plenty of hurt. The unexpected force of the assault threw her off-balance, and she felt herself falling backward. The kitchen ceiling spun crazily for half a heartbeat, and she saw the flickering fluorescent light, the copper bottoms of pans arranged on pegs over the sink, the swirling patterns in the gypsum finish above.

Then she was falling and the world exploded in sparks, and she thought maybe the pie filling had leaked onto the element. As she slid into the inky, charred darkness, the smell of warm sweet potatoes settled around her like the breath of a well-fed baby.

"Pie's done," she said. Her eyelids fluttered and then fell still.

"Honey, what are you doing?"

Katy turned away from the squash casserole she was making. Her hands stank of onions. Little jars and bags of spices were strewn across the counter: basil, pepper, dill weed, cumin. Eggshells lay in the bottom of the sink, slick and jagged. The clock on the wall read ten after six.

"I'm making dinner," she said.

"I hate casseroles." Gordon took off his tweed jacket and folded it over his arm.

"I found the recipe in the cabinet. I thought . . ." Katy brushed a strand of hair from her forehead. Her face was flushed.

"Where did you get that dress?"

She looked down and found herself in a dress she'd never seen before. It had an autumnal print and was a little more frilly and feminine than the austere styles Katy preferred. The dress was dusty but it fit her body as if it had been tailored. Why was she wearing it to cook?

"It was in the closet, I think. Must have been something I packed years ago and came across while I was cleaning."

"You look nice." Gordon went to the refrigerator and took out a bottle of Merlot. He didn't stop to kiss her as he passed. He poured himself a glass of wine and sat at the butcher block table that stood in one corner and served as a stand for several houseplants.

"About this morning," Katy said. She focused on slicing a red onion. Any excuse for tears was welcome.

"Let's not talk about it."

"We *have* to, honey. We're married."

"I lost control. It won't happen again."

Katy slammed down the knife. "I *want* it to happen again. But I don't want it to be cold and strange."

If only Gordon would stand up and come to her, take her in his arms, nuzzle her neck, and make stupid promises, she would have accepted his earlier behavior. She even would have defended it. After all, Katy had her own problems. She wasn't exactly coming into the marriage as a virgin.

"Where's Jett?" Gordon asked.

"Jett?" Katy looked down at the raw food and spices. Jett was probably in her room studying. She had walked through the front door hours ago. Katy should have checked on her, or at least called up the stairs to make sure her daughter knew she was around. That was Katy's part of the deal. She would be an involved parent while trusting Jett to stay away from drugs and giving her daughter some breathing room.

"She's in her room," Katy said.

"I have a job for her."

"About the eggs," Katy said.

"Forget it. I'll have Odus do the farm chores from now on. It wasn't fair for me to expect you to take on extra work. You have enough to do here in the house."

In this house that seemed more like a prison. Katy had to think back to remember the last time she'd left the house. Grocery shopping, three days ago. Most of her time in the house was spent in the kitchen, and she'd never liked cooking before. Now she was making casseroles.

"How was your day at the college?" It was the kind of thing a normal wife would ask, and she wanted very much to be a normal wife.

"Long," he said, then finished his glass of wine. "Try telling that idiot Graybeal that Methodists weren't the only denomination to use circuit-riding preachers."

"Graybeal? He's the dean, isn't he?"

"Yes, but you would think he's lord of the fiefdom to see him swagger around, whipping out his shriveled intellectual dingus."

"He's probably just jealous because of your book."

"No, he thinks foot washing belongs to the realm of human sacrifice and snake handling. Anything that's not Hindu, Buddhist, or Taoist is all lumped together under 'God worship.' "

Katy stared down at the yellow grue of the casserole. Should she add an extra quarter of a stick of butter? "I thought 'God worship' was the point."

"Graybeal thinks Christianity is a cult. A popular one, to be sure, but a cult nonetheless." He was falling into lecture mode. His voice rose slightly in pitch, the words carefully enunciated.

Katy was pleased that he was spending time with her instead of hiding away in the study, but she wanted to move the subject over to something a little closer to home. "What job did you have for Jett?"

"I want her to feed the goats."

"I thought Odus was going to do the farm chores."

"I mean tonight. Odus doesn't have a phone. I'll probably have to drive over to his place tomorrow, or catch up with him at the general store."

Katy wiped her hands on the dish towel that hung from the oven handle. "I'll go get her."

"No, you're busy." His upper lip curled a little, as if he had smelled an unpleasant odor.

"I thought you'd like this," Katy said. "It's your family recipe."

"I hate onions," he said. "They give me indigestion."

Such was marriage. You didn't learn the important things until after the knot was already tied. If you tried to be respectful and cautious, you didn't jump into the sack with the guy you were going to marry until the vows were made. At least not the second time around. You figured there would be kinks and quirks to sort out, but older people were wiser and more experienced. Or maybe just slower to admit mistakes.

Gordon rinsed his wineglass and left the room. "I'll talk to her."

"Be polite," Katy said. "She's trying, you know."

Gordon didn't answer. Katy opened the refrigerator and took out a pint of heavy cream. She had never bought cream in her life, though she had picked some up at the grocery store Tuesday. It was almost as if she knew she would need it for the recipe she'd found this afternoon.

Odus eased his truck into the gravel lot of Solom Free Will Baptist Church, parking beside the Ford F-150 driven by Mose Eldreth. Most likely the preacher was taking on an inside chore, mending a loose rail or patching the metal flue that carried away smoke from the woodstove. A dim glow leaked from the open door, framing the church's windows against the night sky. Odus cast an uneasy glance in the direction of Harmon Smith's grave, but the white marker looked no different from the others that gleamed under the starlight.

Odus didn't hold much stock with Free Will preachers, but at least Preacher Mose was local. Preacher Mose knew the area history and, like most of the people who grew up in Solom, he'd heard about Harmon Smith. After all, Harmon had a headstone in the Free Will cemetery. That didn't mean the preacher would talk to Odus about it. Like Sarah Jeffers, most people in those parts didn't want to know too much about the past.

Odus went up the steps and knocked on the door. "You in, Preacher?"

A scraping sound died away and there was the metallic echo of a tool being placed on the floor. "Come in," Preacher Mose said.

It was the first time Odus had been in a church in a couple of years. He'd attended the Free Will church in his youth, but the congregation didn't think much of his drinking so he'd been shunned out. He didn't carry a grudge. He figured they had their principles and he had his, and on Judgement Day maybe him and the Lord would sit down and crack the seal on some of the finest single-malt Scotch that heaven had to offer. Then Odus could lay out his pitch, and the Lord could take it or leave it. Though hopefully not until the bottle was dry.

The Primitives were different, though. A little drink here and there didn't matter to them, because the saved were born that way and the blessed would stay blessed no matter how awful they acted. Odus could almost see attending that type of church, but he liked to sleep late on Sundays. As for the True Lighters, they took religion like a whore took sex: five times a day whether you needed it or not.

Preacher Mose was kneeling before the crude pulpit up front. He wasn't praying, though; he was laying baseboard molding along the little riser that housed the pulpit and the piano. A hand drill, miter saw, hammer, and finish nails were scattered around the preacher like sacraments about to be piled on an altar. Preacher Mose was wearing green overalls, and sweat caused his unseemly long hair to cling to his forehead. "Well, if it isn't Brother Hampton."

"Sorry to barge in," Odus said. "I wouldn't bother you if it wasn't important."

"You're welcome here any time. Even on a Sunday, if you ever want to sit through one of my sermons."

"Need a hand? I got some tools in the truck."

"We can't afford to pay. Why do you think they let me carpenter? I'm better at running my mouth than driving nails."

The church had no electricity, and even with scant light leaking through the windows Odus could tell the preacher's molding joints were almost wide enough to tuck a thumb between. "This one's on the house. A little love offering."

"Know him by his fruits and not by his words," Preacher Mose said.

"Good, because my words wouldn't fill the back page of a dictionary and half of those ain't fit for a house of worship."

Odus got his tool kit from the bed of the pickup and showed the preacher how to use a coping saw to cut a dovetail joint. After the preacher had knicked his knuckles a couple of times, he got the hang of it, and left Odus to run the miter saw and tape measure.

The preacher bored holes with the hand drill so the wood wouldn't split, then blew the fine sawdust away. "So what's troubling you?"

"Harmon Smith."

The preacher sat back on his haunches. "You don't need to worry about Harmon Smith. His soul's gone on to the reward and what's left of his bones are out there in the yard."

"That's not the way the stories have it."

"I'm a man of faith, Odus. You might say I believe in the supernatural, because God certainly is above all we see and feel and touch. But I don't believe in any sort of ghost but the Holy Ghost."

"Do you believe what you see?"

"I'm a man of faith."

"Guess that settles that." Odus laid an eight-foot strip of molding, saw that it was a smidge too long. "Always cut long because you can always take off more, but you sure can't grow it back once it's gone."

"I'll remember that. Maybe I can work it into a sermon." Preacher Mose drove a nail with steady strokes, then took the nail set and sank the head into the wood so the hole could be puttied.

"What I'm trying to get around to is, I seen him."

"Seen who?"

"Harmon Smith."

The preacher paused halfway through the second nail. Then he spoke, each word falling between a hammer stroke. "Sure"—*bang*—"don't"—*bang*—"know"—*bang*—"what . . ."—*bang*. He paused, then wound up with a flourish. "In heaven's name you're talking about"—*bang, bang, bang, BANG.*

"He come down by the river while I was fishing. Face like goat's cheese and eyes as dark as the back end of a rat hole. He had on that same preachin' hat you see in the pictures."

Preacher Mose drilled another hole and positioned the nail. Odus noticed his hands were shaking.

"Sarah Jeffers saw him, too, only she won't admit to it."

The preacher swallowed hard and swung at the nail. The hammer glanced off the nail head and punched a half-moon scar in the wood.

"A little putty will hide it," Odus said. "That's the mark of a good carpenter. It's all in the final job."

Preacher Mose swung the hammer again, this time the head glancing off his thumb. "God d—" He stuffed his thumb in his mouth and sucked it before he could finish the cussword.

"Don't be so nervous. It's just a finish nail."

"Harmon Smith died of illness. He caught a fever running a mission trip to Parson's Ford. He had a flock to tend, and his sheep were scattered over two hundred square miles of rocky slopes."

"That's the way the history books tell it. But some people say different, especially in Solom."

"And they probably say there's a grudge between us and the Primitives."

"No, they don't say that."

"We all serve the same Lord, and on the Lord's Earth, the dead don't walk. Not till the Rapture, anyway."

"Maybe you ought to tell that to *him*." Odus lifted his hammer and pointed the handle to the church door. Framed in silhouette was the tall, gangly preacher, the one who was nearly two hundred years dead.

Preacher Mose knelt at the foot of the pulpit and stared at the black-suited reverend. He put his bruised thumb back in his mouth and tightened his grip on the hammer until his knuckles were white. Harmon Smith's shadow started to move into the church, but dissolved as it entered the vestibule. The last thing to flicker and fade was the wide brim of the hat.

Chapter Sixteen

Arvel remained calm when he found his wife sprawled on the kitchen floor. He'd been a volunteer firefighter for over a decade, ever since a liquored-up cousin had set one of his outbuildings on fire by dropping a cigarette in a crate of greasy auto parts. Arvel didn't know all the fancy techniques used by the Rescue Squad folks, but he'd watched them in action plenty of times. His favorite emergency tech was Henrietta Coggins, who was built like a cross between Arnold Schwartzenegger and Julia Roberts, except unfortunately Henrietta had Arnie's chin and hairline and the Pretty Woman's nose and muscle tone. Despite this unsettling mix, she was cool as a September salamander when the pressure was on, and it was her voice that Arvel now heard in his head. He repeated the imagined lines to his wife as he knelt beside her and felt for her pulse.

"Hey, honey, looks like you had you a little mishap." *Check pulse, don't know a damned thing about how fast it's supposed to be, maybe it's* mine *that's thumping like a rat trapped in a bucket, but yours feels mighty shallow.* "But don't you worry none, 'cause old Arvel's right here beside you. We'll get through this and have you baking lemon cakes again in no time."

When Arvel had heard the noise from the kitchen, his first reaction had been annoyance, because one of the guys on TV was about to get voted off the show. It was the guy with the bandanna who hadn't shaved; there was one on every reality show. Arvel could always tell which asshole was going to get cut loose, though it never happened in the first few episodes. No, they had to string the audience along and let all the viewers build up a real hate for the guy, which was made worse by the fact that he just might have a chance of winning. Which would mean another asshole millionaire in the world while folks like Arvel still had to get up at 6:00 a.m. and put in ten hard hours. Well, seven if he could help it. So he'd been working up a decent dose of spite for the asshole in the bandanna when the floor shook and thunder boomed in the kitchen, as if his wife had dropped four sacks of cornmeal. But since she couldn't lift even *one* sack of corn meal, that meant something else had dropped.

His wife, all 195 pounds of her.

Arvel put a cheek near her lips, making sure she was still breathing. He looked at the back door, where he'd seen the flicker of movement as he'd entered the room. He was almost sure it was some kind of animal, and he had been getting ready for a closer look when he saw Betsy laid out like Sly Stallone in *Rocky*, only Sly had managed to climb up the ropes and lose on his feet and Betsy appeared down for the count.

She was still drawing air, but her eyes were hollow and sunken. He lifted one eyelid, just the way Henrietta would do. Betsy's pupil was as tight as a BB. Her long skirt bunched around her knees, showing the purple road map of her varicose veins. Arvel felt the back of her head and found a raised place the size of a banty egg.

"You just got a little concussion, is all," Henrietta would say. She spoke in that slow, reassuring way even when the patients were unconscious. Once Arvel had heard her waltz a car crash victim through death's door with that same kind of talk.

Arvel didn't think he could pretend to be Henrietta anymore, because he wondered what would happen if his wife stopped breathing. "Don't die on me, now," he said, a line Henrietta would never use in a hundred years.

He went for the phone and dialed 911 with no problem, then

found himself talking to the communications officer in Henrietta's words. "Is this Francine?"

Of course it was Francine, because Arvel knew all the communications folks from the scanner he kept in his truck. When Francine said, "Yes, go ahead," Arvel took a deep breath and said, "Sorry to bother you, but I was wondering if you could have the squad come down to 12 Hogwood Road in Solom. I've got a patient down."

"What's the emergency, sir?"

"I'm not no sir. I'm Henrietta. I mean, this is Arvel Ward." Somewhere in his glove box, he had a sheet with all the emergency response codes, but since his job was putting out fires or occasionally directing traffic, he'd never bothered to memorize the list. All he knew was that, in car wrecks, "PI" meant "personal injury" and "PD" meant "property damage," and you hurried with the red light and siren for the first but not the second. So he said, "We got a PI here, weak pulse, possible head injury. Plus something's burning in the oven."

"Hold on, Arvel, we'll get somebody right there. Are you with the patient?"

"Not right now. I'm on the phone."

"I meant, is the patient in the house with you?"

"Yeah. She lives here."

"Okay, stay on the phone and let me give you some instructions."

"I can't leave her alone, and the cord won't reach. Tell them to hurry, and send Henrietta."

Arvel hung up. When he got back to the kitchen, he knelt over her again to check her pulse. The hand he placed on the opposite side of her body touched a wet place on the floor. He lifted his hand and saw it was blood, leaking from somewhere just above her waist.

Arvel wondered if maybe Betsy had landed on a butcher knife when she fell, because it surely wasn't her head giving off that much blood. He tried to roll her over but she was too heavy. Finally, he lifted her enough to see a rip in her dress and the burgundy maw of a wound in her side, a few inches below her rib cage. It looked like some kind of bite mark, because the edges of the wound were stringy and jagged.

He looked once more at the back door, wondering what kind of beast had wandered in and taken a chunk out of his wife. And wondering why Digger hadn't raised holy hell, and if Henrietta would know how to handle something like this. Because, right now, with Henrietta's voice in his head or not, he couldn't think of a single comforting thing to say.

Jett dropped her book bag on the floor and dove onto her bed. Her heart was racing, as it always did when she was stoned. Pot was a stimulant, and the textbooks classified it somewhere between a narcotic and a hallucinogenic. It didn't make you hallucinate like acid did, but she'd never known acid to trick you into thinking you'd had a battle of wits with a goat. She swore to herself she wouldn't get stoned ever again. At least not until after Mom and Gordon went to sleep.

She was just kicking off her shoes when she heard the pounding on her door. "Jett?"

Great. It was Gordon. Just the thing to kill a good buzz. "Yeah?"

The door handle turned. Gordon must have decided to treat her with some respect, though, because he let go of the handle and said, "Can I come in?"

"Just a sec. Let me get dressed." She got up, threw a book and some paper on her desk, and slouched into her chair. She hooked headphones around her neck and punched up some Nine Inch Nails, just to piss off Gordon, though she preferred Robyn Hitchcock when she was stoned. No time for the Visine in her desk drawer. She'd just have to bluff it out.

"Come on in, it's unlocked," she said, deciding not to call him on his turning of the knob before she'd invited him in.

Gordon walked in as if he were a professor and Jett's bedroom were the classroom. Lecture time. "Why aren't you helping your mom with supper?"

"I have homework." She nodded at the book on her desk.

"Oh." He looked around, as if he'd never seen the room before.

His eyes stopped on the movie poster of a gaunt and pale Brandon Lee from *The Crow.* "We haven't had time to get to know each other, Jett. It's important for me that we get along. Important for both of us, I think. It will make things easier on your mother."

"Mom's been kind of weird lately."

"She's trying hard to make this work." Gordon acted like he wanted to sit down, but her bed was the only suitable surface in the room besides the floor, and Jett couldn't picture him sitting on either of those. He fingered the knot of his tie. "I think we ought to have a father-to-daughter talk."

She opened her mouth but he held up his hand to cut her off. "I meant that as a figure of speech. I don't want to replace your real father. But we do live under the same roof and we need to lay out some ground rules."

"Besides the 'no drugs' thing."

"That's for everybody's peace of mind, especially yours. We have high aspirations for you, Jett. I never thought I'd have somebody to carry on the Smith tradition."

"But I'm not a Smith." Jett wondered if Gordon was stoned on something himself, because he was making less sense than she was. From the way he hovered over her, she could see straight up his nose to the black, wiry hairs inside.

"We're still a family. I know things have been a little rough on you, having to make new friends and acclimate yourself to this old farmhouse. It's a major transition from Charlotte to Solom."

"Yeah, they don't have no goats grazing along Independence Boulevard."

Gordon's lips quavered as if he were trying to smile and failing. "That's 'any' goats."

"Any goats. Like, what's their deal?"

"Deal?"

"Your goats act like they own the place. I know they're supposed to be stubborn, but they're kind of creepy."

"They're more pets than anything. They won't hurt you."

Maybe they won't hurt you. *But you're part of this place. Maybe they think I'm some kind of alien freak, come in from the outside world to threaten their way of life.*

As soon as the thought arose, Jett dismissed it as silly. The goats were weird, that was for sure, but they were just shaggy, cloven-hoofed, goofy-eyed animals when you got right down to it. Nothing to be afraid of. Even if they ate your dope and looked at you as if you were a germ under a microscope.

"Your eyes are bloodshot," Gordon said, sniffing the air and causing his nostril hairs to quiver.

"Yeah. I'm not sleeping very well."

"I thought you'd be settled in by now."

"Bad dreams. There's this man in a black hat who—"

Gordon took an abrupt step backward and accidentally kicked her backpack with his heel. The zippered section was open, revealing the dull glint of her pot Baggie. She expected Gordon to give it a once-over, but he regained his balance and said in a near whisper, "A man in a black hat?"

"Yeah, and an old-timey suit that's all black and worn out, like it had been picked over. I can't really see his face, it's like the brim of the hat throws a shadow over it." Jett didn't mention that she'd seen him three times: in the barn loft, in English class, and in the boiler room at school. If the man *was* real, then Gordon might know something about him. But if Jett's acid trips had eaten a permanent hole in her brain, she didn't want to arouse any suspicions or she might end up in lockdown at a psychiatric ward. Not that a vacation would be all bad, but Mom was already a basket case and that might send her over the edge. And good old Dad would probably drop his job and his new girlfriend and make a beeline to Solom to straighten things out, fucking everything up in his usual bumbling way.

"I won't lecture you on the chemical changes caused by substance abuse," Gordon said. "Drugs can do permanent damage. Hallucinations, confusion, memory loss."

Jett nodded absently, focusing on the brittle grind of Trent Reznor's voice leaking from the headphones. *And don't forget that good old side effect of fun. So quit fucking lecturing already.*

"Okay, Gordon. I promised you and Mom I'd stay clean. No sweat."

Gordon reached out and put a hand on her shoulder, as if he'd been studying parental techniques in a textbook. "Hang in there, Jett. We'll make this family work."

"I know. But I'd better get back to this homework."

"The satisfaction of academic achievement is the best drug of all."

Whatever.

He paused at the door. "Dinner in fifteen minutes."

After he left the room, Jett locked the door and popped the Nine Inch Nails out of the Walkman. Hitchcock's "Element of Light" was the ticket now. She retrieved the Baggie from her backpack, sprinkled a pinch of grass in her aluminum-foil pipe, and carried it with the lighter to her window. She eased the window up and the evening chill sliced its way into the room. If she took small puffs and exhaled through the gap, then even Gordon's big hairy nose couldn't detect the scent.

Beyond the glass, the world was dark and still. Even the insects were tucked away, as if hungry predators roamed the night. The stars were scattered like grains of salt on a blue blanket, the quarter moon sharp as a scythe. The mountains made sweeping black waves along the horizon. She had to give it to Solom on that count: it had Charlotte beat all to hell on scenery.

She was about to thumb her lighter when she saw movement out in the cornfield. The tops of the dead stalks stirred. She expected a wayward goat to walk out from the rows. The animals were renowned for breaking through their fences. The Fred-faced fuckers never seemed to get enough to eat. They probably chewed in their sleep.

But it wasn't a goat. It was a man. In the scant moonlight, she could just make out the brim of his hat. The brim lifted in her direction, as if the man were staring at the window.

She looked down at the dried leaves in the curled bowl of the pipe. "Hallucination, my ass," she said.

Jett sparked the lighter and touched the flame to the weed, inhaling deeply. She planned on losing her mind, at least for a little while. Because if her mind was gone, then she wouldn't have to remember. And if she didn't remember, then the man in the black hat didn't exist.

Drug problem.

Oxymoron.

Drug problem equals no problem.

She closed her eyes and let the smoke seep out her mouth into the Solom sky.

Odus took a drink of Old Crow, the best four-dollar bourbon around. Preacher Mose didn't bat an eye as the man pulled the bottle from the hip pocket of his overalls, though it was the first time anyone had ever brought liquor into the church during his tenure. Mose almost reached for the bottle himself, but figured now wasn't a good time to let his principles slide. They sat side by side in a front pew of the church, staring straight ahead as if expecting a sermon from the silent pulpit.

"Now do you believe me?" Odus asked.

"I believe in the Lord, and just at the moment, that's the only thing I believe in."

"That was him. Harmon Smith."

"People don't come back from the dead."

"I thought that was what the Bible was all about. Hell, if you don't get resurrected, then why miss out on all the fun of sinning?"

"That happened in the Bible," Mose said. "This is real life."

"Fine words, coming from a preacher."

Mose still had the hammer in his hand. He hadn't relaxed his grip since the mysterious figure had appeared at the church door. The man in the black hat stood there for the space of three heartbeats, his head tilted down, face hidden. There were holes in his dark wool suit, and the cuffs were frayed. The flesh of his hands was the color of a peeled cucumber. He turned up one palm, like a beggar seeking alms. Neither Mose nor Odus had spoken, and the man finally lowered his hand and stepped out of the church without turning.

Or moving his feet, Odus thought. Except now he couldn't be sure what he'd seen or if he had merely imagined the whole scene. By the time he'd finally unlocked his muscles and run to the door, the strange man was nowhere to be seen. Despite his poor church attendance and his fondness for illicit activities, Odus was true to his word, which was why his reputation was good among the people who hired him for odd jobs.

"What are you going to do about it?" Odus asked.

"Do? Why does anything have to be done?"

"You know the stories."

"That's just a folktale, Brother. I can't give it any credence. I'm an educated man."

"Well, a preacher has to believe in miracles, so what's to say a *bad* miracle can't happen now and again?" Odus sipped the bourbon again as if he'd been giving the matter a great deal of thought over the course of many pints.

"Okay, then," Mose said. "Just supposing—and I'm doing this like maybe I was writing a spooky movie or something—supposing Harmon Smith did come back to life after two hundred years? What would he want? What would be the point? Because he'd have been swept right up to Glory when he died, and wouldn't have any reason to come back."

"Except for the oldest reason ever."

"What's that?"

"Revenge."

"The church records say he died in an accident. He had no reason not to rest in peace."

"What else would you expect them to say, Preacher? That he got conked on the head and thrown in the river because he was doing missionary work?"

"A folktale, I told you."

"The Primitive Baptists didn't cotton to Harmon Smith's ideas. Neither did the Free Willers."

"We believe in salvation. Why would our people want to kill him?"

"Ask Gordon Smith. He'll tell you all about it."

Mose ran his thumb over the head of the hammer and stared at the wooden cross that hung on the wall behind the pulpit. "If I told you something, would you think I was crazy?"

"No crazier than you think *I* am."

"I saw the Circuit Rider when I was a kid. He snuck up behind me like a shadow one afternoon while I was skipping stones down at the trout pond. I thought he was going to grab me, but he just shook those long fingers at me. I ran all the way home and didn't go outside for a week. That was about the time that Janie Bessemer took infection from a cut foot and died from blood poisoning. I always thought it was the Circuit Rider's doing."

Odus took a deep gulp of the Old Crow and coughed. "I was wrong. You *are* crazier than me."

Mose stood up. "I'd better get this molding nailed down before dark so it will be ready for services tomorrow."

Odus grabbed Mose's arm. "Didn't one of the disciples deny Jesus Christ after the Last Supper?"

"Peter. Jesus predicted Peter would deny him three times before the cock crowed."

"Maybe you're like Peter. You believe in Harmon Smith, but you're not going to admit it to anybody."

Before Odus could answer, the air of the church sanctuary stirred. A crow swooped down the aisle and landed on the pulpit, where the black bird shook its wings and regarded them both with eyes like dirty motor oil.

"Know them by their fruits, Preacher Mose," Odus said, tilting the bottle once more. "You never know which one of them's going to turn rotten."

Chapter Seventeen

Sue Norwood turned around the sign in her window to inform any late-night cyclists that she was CLOSED—GONE FISHING. Not that she'd ever cared for sportfishing, even though she sold Orvis rods and reels, hip waders, hand-tied flies, coolers, Henry Fonda hats, and everything the genteel fisherman needed except for alcohol. Solom was unincorporated, which precluded a vote on local alcohol sales, and Sue figured in maybe five years the seasonal home owners from Florida would own enough property to push for a referendum. For now, she was content to bide her time on that front. The pickings were easy enough as it was.

In 1995, Sue had purchased a small outbuilding that had belonged to the Little Tennessee Railroad, one of the few structures in Solom to survive the 1940 flood. It sat within spitting distance of the Blackburn River, but was on ground just high enough to survive the calamities that Solom seemed to call down upon itself. Ice storms and blizzards were biannual events, high water hit every spring and fall, hellacious thunderstorms rumbled in from March through July, and the winter wind rattled the siding boards as if they were the bones of a scarecrow. But all the outbuilding needed was a green coat of paint, a twenty-thousand-dollar commercial

174   *Scott Nicholson*

loan at Clinton-era rates, and sixty hours of Sue's time each week to hang in there despite Solom's lack of a true business climate.

Sue had converted an upstairs storage room into an apartment, and it was to this space she retired after closing. She passed the racks of kayaks that stood like whales' ribs on each side of the aisle, making sure the back door was locked. As an all-season outfitter, she'd packed the place with every profitable item she could order, from North Face sleeping bags to compasses to Coleman gas stoves. Ten-speed bicycles were lined against the front wall, with rentals bringing in more than enough to keep her wheels greased. Ever since Lance Armstrong had trained along the old river road before his third run at the Tour de France (a little factoid that Sue always managed to slip into her advertising copy, when she couldn't get the local media to mention it for free), out-of-shape amateurs had been flocking to the area to rest their sweaty cracks on her bicycle seats. At twenty dollars a day, they could hump it all they wanted. She was even willing to sponsor a community fundraising ride for the Red Cross each summer, a nice little tax writeoff that paid back in spades.

Sue counted the bikes before she went upstairs, her last official chore for the day. Two were still out. She checked her registration records at the desk and found the bikes were rented by a Mr. and Mrs. Elliott Everhart of White Plains, New York. Fellow Yankees. Sue was from Connecticut herself, but she'd graduated from the University of Georgia with a degree in exercise science, spent three extra years in Athens as an assistant coach for the women's field hockey team, pretty much flattening her vowels and slowing down her speech enough to pass for southern if she was drunk. At the age of twenty-five, she had written down the names of all her favorite rock-climbing spots, clipped them apart with scissors, and randomly pulled one out of a hat. Solom wasn't on the list, but it had been the closest to the Pisgah National Forest, which featured Table Rock and Wiseman's View. Since Solom was near a river, and rock climbing wasn't exactly a major source of commercial recreation income, as it required little more than a rock and an attitude, she'd launched Back2Nature Outfitters and had been expanding ever since. Funny thing was, she'd been so busy these past few years with her business that she rarely was outdoors herself.

The Everharts. Sue could remember them because the husband, Elliott, had detected her up-coast accent and made conversation about it. Sue couldn't remember the wife's name, but she was a quiet, willowy blonde who spoke little and didn't seem all that thrilled with the idea of human-powered transportation. They had rented the bikes at 2:00 p.m. and had estimated their return at 6:00 p.m. Elliott told her they had rented a cabin on the hill above Solom General Store and had walked down so as not to take up a parking space in the small gravel lot. Sue had said, "Thank you kindly," an artificial southern response that had come more and more easily over the years, then sent the couple on their way with bottled mineral water (two dollars a pint) and a map free with any purchase. Sue now checked the clock above the front door, the one that elicited native birdcalls with each stroke of the hour. It was ten minutes away from Verio, nearly two hours later than the Everharts' anticipated return.

People who rented bicycles sometimes got flats. That was rare, because she kept the equipment in good condition. All those who rented equipment, whether it was a propane lantern or a kayak or a ten-speed, were required to sign release forms absolving Back2Nature Outfitters of any responsibility. That didn't mean that people didn't screw up, especially the types of deep-pocketed but shallow-skulled clients to which Sue usually catered. Even if the Everharts had gotten lost or had a breakdown, they most likely could have walked back to Solom, flagged a ride, or called for assistance on their cell phones.

Except Sue could see three problems with that scenario, because she'd experienced each of them. Sometimes bikers got lost when they tried to walk back, because the going was so much slower that the maps became deceptive. Flagging a ride was no guarantee because there simply wasn't that much traffic after sundown in Solom, and outsiders were loathe to pick up anyone wearing fluorescent spandex and alien-looking crash helmets. And cell phones were almost universally useless in Solom because the valleys were deep and the old families owning the high mountains had yet to lease space for transmitting towers.

Sue considered a fourth alternative. The Everharts appeared to be in their thirties and were presumably childless, at least for the length of their vacation. Maybe good old Elliott had gotten a boner for nature and coaxed his wife into the weeds for a little of the world's oldest and greatest recreational sport. Or maybe the willowy blonde had been the one to turn into a ravening maw of wild lust. Either way, Sue couldn't blame them. Some of the locals had whispered that she was a lesbian, and, sure, like many girls she'd sampled that particular ware in college, but she was pretty much married to her business these days.

As far as Sue could tell, there was no reason to call out the search-and-rescue team just yet. Besides, she earned an extra thirty dollars for late fees and the Everharts had put a five-hundred-dollar deposit on their credit cards to cover much of the value of the bikes. With depreciation, subsequent tax write-off, and the tip they'd probably give when they rolled in red-faced tomorrow morning, Sue figured the old saying "Better late than never" wasn't quite as good as "Better late and *then* never."

She left on a small light above the desk, went up the stairs at the back of the store, and made herself a dinner of canned salmon, creamed rice, and fresh collard greens, all heated over a Coleman gas stove. The stove was a legitimate business expense. She'd checked with her accountant boyfriend, Walter, whom she'd met on a white-water rafting expedition.

Though the relationship had launched on class-four rapids, it had drifted into shallow eddies by summer's end. That was okay, too. The money she'd spent on condoms and Korbel champagne was a valid tax write-off. Sue had a warm meal ahead and a vibrator waiting under her pillow, the famous Wascally Wabbit that was never too "hare-triggered" and didn't lie or cheat. If the Everharts came knocking in the middle of the night, she planned to sleep right through it.

Odus had first heard about the Circuit Rider when he was eight years old. His grandmother, a thick, dough-faced woman who survived the Great Depression and hoarded canned foods because of it, would often gather the grandkids around the front porch on Saturday nights. The older kids complained because they would rather watch television, but, to Odus, it was a way to stay up after bedtime without getting in trouble. He knew even then that stories were a way of passing along the truth, even when they walked on the legs of lies.

Granny Hampton was the matriarch of a half dozen kids, and three of those had seen fit to breed. Odus was an only child, but he had five cousins, and that was before they all moved away from Solom, so Granny's front porch was a lively and crowded place during the summer. Granny would settle in her rocker, the smaller kids gathered on the cool boards at her feet, the bigger ones slouched against the railing. A Mason jar at Granny's feet served as her spitoon, and she wouldn't talk before she'd placed a large pinch of Scotch-colored snuff behind her lower lip. As if on cue, the dusk grew a shade darker, the crickets launched their brittle screams, and fireflies blanketed the black silhouettes of the trees. The stars twinkled over the bowl of the valley, and the rest of the world may as well have broken off and drifted past the moon for all it mattered. It was as if Granny were a witch who conjured up a magical stage for her tales and Solom were the only solid ground in the universe.

"The Circuit Rider was one of the first horseback preachers to come through these parts," Granny said on that July night of 1966. "There had been a couple of Methodists and an Episcopalian, but Harmon Smith was a converted Primitive Baptist. The Baptists weren't all over the place like they are now, and most of the white settlers kept their religion to themselves. The thing about Primitives is they don't believe in salvation—"

Lonnie, who was a year older than Odus, cut in and said, "Does that mean they don't believe in Jesus?"

"They believe in Jesus, but he ain't the only way to heaven. Primitives believe you're born saved."

"I don't want to hear no sermon," said Walter Buck, Odus's oldest cousin and the one probably most in need of a sermon. "Get on to the ghost."

Granny paused to let a tawny strand of saliva leak into the Mason jar, her eyes like onyx marbles in the weak light of the porch's bare bulb. "I'll get to the ghost soon enough, but if I was you, I'd make sure the ghost don't get on to *you*."

Walter Buck snickered, but there was a little catch in his breath when he finished.

"Harmon Smith decided he liked the look of the land, because it reminded him of his homeland in the Pennsylvania high country. He aimed to settle down and build a little church here. Problem was, a couple of other preachers had been riding through the region, and they were all hell-bent for saving souls in those days. The Methodists were the worst, or the best, depending on how you looked at it. They would ride themselves ragged, cross mountains in the dead of winter, sleep on hard ground, and generally run themselves to the bone in order to bring a single person into the fold. They tended to wear down and get ill, and it was common for them to die before the age of thirty. This all happened two hundred years ago, so people didn't live all that long back then anyway."

"Was Daniel Boone here then?" Lonnie asked.

"Boone never was here, much. He'd come up and hunt, maybe spend a few weeks in the winter. He kept a little cabin over on Kettle Knob, but he never had much claim on this place. Besides, this story ain't about Daniel Boone, it's about Harmon Smith."

All the cousins had watched Fess Parker wearing his coonskin cap on television, starring as Daniel Boone, the fightin'est man the frontier ever knew. But Odus was more interested in the Circuit Rider, and looked at the Three Top Mountain range, imagining Harmon Smith guiding his horse along the rocky trails.

"Harmon Smith was based in Roanoke, Virginia, at the time, and his territory went into Tennessee and Kentucky. He had used up three horses by the time he first set eyes on Solom. In them days, there was probably two dozen families in the valley, and most of them are still here."

"Was there any Hamptons?" Lonnie asked.

"Quit interrupting or we'll never get through," Walter said.

Granny lowered one eyelid and gave Walter a stare that shut him up for the rest of the story. The bugs had found the porch light by that time, and a mosquito bite on Odus's ear had swollen up and begun to itch, but he could put up with a hundred bites to learn about the Circuit Rider.

"The Hamptons were here, Robert and Dolly, they'd be your great, let me see, great-great-great-grandparents, if I'm figuring right. They were one of the first to invite Harmon Smith in for a bite of supper, which is why I know so much about him. The story's been passed down all these years, but I'm sure there's some parts that have been beefed up a bit along the way. Wouldn't be a good folktale otherwise.

"Harmon Smith told Robert and Dolly that he wanted to buy some land up here. Preachers in those days never had any money, figuring they'd get their reward in heaven, not like them slick-haired weasels you'll find behind a pulpit these days. But Harmon had a young coon dog with him, and one of the Hicks boys took a cotton to the hound and ended up trading ten acres for it. By that time, Harmon had persuaded Dolly and Robert to join the Primitives, mostly because joining didn't seem to require any kind of obligation. You didn't have to give up dancing or corn liquor, not that any Hamptons ever liked to take a drink."

Odus knew that was one family trait that hadn't made it into his branch, because his dad rarely went through a day without a drink. But Odus didn't think liquor was bad, because it made his dad sleepy and talkative. When he wasn't drinking, he was prone to cussing and stomping around, so Odus's gut always unclenched when his dad twisted the cap on a pint bottle.

"Harmon ended up building his church, but it took him five long years. In the meantime, he was still making his circuit on his horse, Old Saint, taking collections where he could, preaching the Primitive line as he went. Harmon took a wife but she must have wandered off and left him, because she was never heard from again. The preacher turned peculiar after that. He took up farming, but his soil was too thin and rocky. One autumn, Harmon stacked up some stones and covered them with dead locust branches. He knelt before them and prayed, then took one of his chickens and *chopped*"—here spit flew from Granny's mouth as she made a chopping motion with her hand and Lonnie jumped a foot in the air even though he was sitting on his rump—"and its head flew off and dribbled blood all over the wood. He set the branches on fire and tossed the chicken on it, like the way they used to offer up lambs in the Old Testament. People whispered about that, but figured Harmon knew how such things were done. The next year, Harmon's crops were busting open they were so thick, corn and cabbage and squash and even things that don't take hold too well here like melons and strawberries. In his church he said God had smiled down on a humble servant, but that October he sacrificed a goat on his stack of killing stones. Garden got even better, so the autumn after that it was a cow, and the wood had to be stacked as high as man's head in order to do the job proper."

"Didn't anybody think he was crazy?" Debbie asked, who was the weird cousin who had once tried to show Odus her panties. The night had settled down more heavily than ever, a thick, black blanket held in place by the glittering nail heads of the stars.

"Sure, some did, but they figured if burnt offerings was good enough for Abraham, it was good enough for Harmon Smith. Other horseback preachers came through, though, and talk went around that they weren't happy with the way old Harmon had set up shop. These were 'enlightened minds,' and they didn't hold with old-fashioned ways. The Methodist man in particular felt the strong hand of God pushing him into this territory as if there was only one right way to put us mountain people on the path to Glory."

Granny Hampton paused on that word "glory," and let them chew it over as she relieved her mouth of brown saliva. The way she said it, getting to heaven sounded almost like a scary thing, because you'd find a cavalry of nasty horseback preachers guarding the Pearly Gates.

"One November Sunday morning, when Harmon was due back for a service, Old Saint came clopping down Snakeberry Trail with an empty saddle." Here Granny Hampton gave a vague wave to Three Top, and Odus could almost hear those iron horseshoes knocking off of granite and maple roots. "Some of the menfolk went up to hunt for him, and they saw what looked like signs of a struggle near the creek. Never found his body. Your ancestor Robert figured he got took by a mountain lion. Some said Harmon went in the water and got tugged down into a sinkhole and turned to soap."

"Yuck," Lonnie said.

"Others said he never did die. They say he still comes back every decade or so to toss a body on his killing stones. And it ain't animals no more."

"What is it, then?" Walter Buck said, and his voice was low and reverent and maybe just a little bit spooked.

"Now nothing will do for Harmon Smith's garden but a bad little young'un."

Granny Hampton lifted herself up with a groan of both breath and chair wood, took up her cane, and headed for the screen door. She paused and looked out at the mountains once more and said, "Praise the Lord, I'm mighty glad I'm old. Not much left to be scared of anymore."

She went inside, her chair still rocking, the runners whispering against the night like a language two hundred years lost.

Odus never forgot that story, and more than once he'd found himself alone at night on a dark trail or stretch of pasture and recall that image of Old Saint prancing down off Three Top. Except, in the image, a soapy, pale figure was perched on the horse's back, the head beneath the black hat swaying back and forth with the horse's motion. For those who had ever heard Granny Hampton tell the story, it was easy to believe Harmon Smith was still riding the circuit.

"Do you want to talk about it?" Katy asked.

"What?"

"The thing you don't want to talk about."

Katy turned her back to him and shimmied out of the dress with the autumnal print. She hung it in the closet, though she'd spilled some butter sauce on it during dinner. She felt oddly exposed in front of her husband, though she was in her bra and panties and he'd certainly viewed the marital merchandise on at least one occasion.

Gordon was in his pajamas, in bed, pretending to be engrossed in a Dostoyevsky novel. He had changed in the bathroom, locking the door so she couldn't enter while he was taking a shower and brushing his teeth.

"You mean Jett?"

That wasn't what she meant, and she approached the dresser for the sole purpose of glancing in the mirror to see if he was looking at her body. His gaze never left the book. "What about Jett?" she asked.

"I know a counselor. He teaches part-time at Westridge, and I'm sure he'll give me a discount if insurance doesn't cover it."

She removed her earrings, a set of sterling silver crescent moons, and put them in the cedar jewelry box on the dresser. Only after she closed the lid did she realize she'd never seen either the earrings or the box before. "What?" she said, too loudly for bedtime.

"For her problems. The drugs, the wild stories, the way she dresses to intentionally offend. She's making a classic ploy for attention."

Like mother, like daughter.

Katy removed her bra and let it slip to the floor, still looking into the mirror. Her freckled breasts were high and firm, even though she had breast-fed Jett. Katy picked up the silver-handled brush on the dresser and began running it through her red hair, flipping her head so the sheen would reflect in the bedside lamplight. Gordon was reading the Dostoyevsky.

"Do you think I'm prettier than Rebecca?" she asked.

Gordon closed the novel with a slap of pulp. "That's a hell of a thing to ask a man. It's like asking if I think you're fat."

"I've seen her picture. She's not like me at all. Brown hair, dark eyes, fuller lips. They say some men have a 'type' and go for it time after time, even when it's bad for them."

"We were talking about Jett."

She turned to face him, her nipples hard in the cool September air. "You keep changing the subject."

"The subject is us. All of us." His eyes stayed fixed on hers, resisting any temptation he might have had to let his gaze crawl over her figure. Perhaps he had no desire and nothing to hide. Maybe this morning's sex had been his version of a personality warp. Jett might not be the only one in the house who had hallucinations. Then again, Katy had been the one to wear a dead woman's dress without a moment's consideration of how strange that was, especially when the dress belonged to Gordon's first wife. Even stranger, Gordon had not commented on it.

Were they all going insane? What if Jett was spiking their food, slipping LSD or some other brain-scrambling substance into the recipes she'd found scattered about the kitchen? No. Jett was off drugs. She had promised.

"We're trying, Gordon," she said. "You knew we came with strings attached."

"You look cold. Why don't you put on a robe?"

"I'm fine."

"I'm worried about you."

"Maybe you should save your worry for what's happening between us. We screwed each other's brains out this morning, and it was the first time you ever touched me in any way that mattered. I thought I'd finally broken through. Now you act like nothing happened."

Gordon never looked embarrassed, but his cheeks turned a shade rosier. "It's complicated."

"Not really. Either I'm prettier than Rebecca or I'm not. Either you want to screw me or you don't. Either we're married or just people who sleep in the same bed. Sounds pretty damned simple to me."

"You're not from Solom."

"I am now. I *moved* here, remember. I said 'I do' and I gave up my stable if unspectacular career in Charlotte and yanked my daughter's roots out of the Piedmont dirt and dragged both of us up here because I thought we had a future with *you*. Only it turns out I'm second on your 'honey-do' list behind your dead wife."

Gordon exploded out of the blankets, rising from the bed with an angry squeak of springs. His pajamas were askew, one tail of his shirt dangling across his groin. "Leave Rebecca out of this."

"How can I? I thought you wanted me to *be* her."

"You'll never be Rebecca."

Katy stormed out of the room, tears blurring her vision. She slammed the bedroom door as punctuation to her unspoken comeback. Her curled right fist ached, and she looked down to see the silver-handled hairbrush with the initials R.L.S.

Rebecca Leigh Smith.

Katy flung the hairbrush down the hall and ran to the top of the stairs. The air coming up from the landing was cool and drafty, moving around her flesh like soft hands. The smell of lilacs wrapped her, carrying a faintly sweet undercurrent of corruption. She leaned against the top post, the landing spread below her like still and dark water.

Maybe if she died, Gordon would love her as well.

"*Do you love him?*"

The words crawled from the hidden corners of the kitchen, out from the cluttered pantry shelves, beneath the plush leather couch, off the mantel with its dusty pictures and Gordon's collection of religious relics, up from the dank swell of the crawl space. Katy thought she had imagined the words, that the voice was the whisk of a late autumn wind, or the settling of a centuries-old farmhouse. Better that than to accept she was losing her mind. Because, however briefly and innocently, she had just contemplated suicide.

The realization brought fresh tears, and behind them, a surge of anger. She had always thought herself strong. After her divorce, she had maintained a household, provided for her daughter, and resisted any temptation to reconcile with Mark, who would occasionally make overtures that seemed more like the pat chatter of a horny male than the sincere revelations of a man suffering regrets. She had moved on, moved up, and though this new marriage hadn't been the stuff of dreams, she was determined—

"*DO YOU LOVE HIM?*"

This time the breeze was staccato, deep, the sounds rounded off into syllables. The voice was female, as frigid and calm and dead as the lost echo from a forgotten grave.

"Who's there?" Katy said, not really thinking anyone was there. The house was locked. Only crazy people heard voices when no one was there. And she wasn't crazy.

"Mom?"

The voice was behind her now. Younger, higher . . .

"Jett?" She turned. Her daughter stood in the shadows of the hall, her silhouette visible against the slice of light leaking from her room. Katy was aware of her exposed body and wrapped her arms around her chest.

"Are you okay, Mom?"

"Sure, honey. I was just checking on something in the kitchen."

"I thought I heard you talking to somebody."

Had Katy spoken? She couldn't be sure. A horrified part of herself wondered if she had actually answered the Voice's bare and bald question. But the Voice wasn't real and the house was quiet and it was always easy to lie to yourself when you didn't like the truth. What she couldn't avoid was her daughter's stare. Katy had never been a prude about nakedness, but there was an unwritten rule that you didn't go starkers around your kids once they passed the toddler stage.

"It's okay, sweetie," Katy said. "Go on back to bed. You have school tomorrow."

"It's not even ten yet, Mom. That's pretty lame even for Solom."

"Well, go read or study or something. Listen to some music."

"Are you sure you're okay?"

"I'm fine."

Jett stepped back into the light of her doorway. Her dyed-black hair was tied back in a ponytail, her face bare of makeup, braces glinting silver. A sweet, round-eyed child. Not a drugged-out potential menace to society, as Gordon saw her, and not a disruption to learning, as her teachers claimed. Just a sweet little girl. Her baby.

"Whatever," Jett said. "It's not like we get through problems together or anything. That's just a line we use for the counselors, right?"

Jett was about to close the door, but then stuck her head back out and said, "By the way, what's that smell? Like somebody farted flowers or something."

The door closed with a click and the hallway went black and Katy slid down the newel post and sat on the top stair until her tears had dried.

Chapter Eighteen

Elliott was being a total dick. Carolyn Everhart didn't like to think of her husband in such bald, crude terms, but he'd taken the whole vacation as a measure of his testosterone levels. From booking the rental car ("Let's go with the guys who try harder") to deciding on restaurant stops on the trip down, Elliott always had a snappy answer for her every question, and a good reason why he knew best. As they'd followed the Appalachian foothills south, Elliott seemed to have grown wax in his ears and a fur pelt that hadn't graced humans since they'd started shaking their Neanderthal origins.

Solom had been picked almost at random. Elliott worked at PAMCO Engineering with a guy who'd attended Westridge University and said the North Carolina mountains were relatively unspoiled ("A perfect place to get away from it all while still having it all"). An Internet search and credit card reservation later, and they were booked in the Happy Hollow retreat for a week, and since September was leaf season, the cabins cost a premium. A two-day drive from White Plains, with a Holiday Inn Express layover ("Complete with a 'lay,' what do you think, honey?") in Scranton, Pennsylvania, and they had arrived with not a single argument over road maps.

But here in the failing light, she couldn't get Elliott to even look at the map, much less admit they were lost. The pocket map they'd picked up from the outfitters' had been fine as long as they stuck to the river road, which was flat and gently curving. But Elliott had insisted on what he called "a little off-roading," though after two hours her legs had begun to cramp and the air temperature dipped into the low forties. Instead of complaining, she pointed out that the bikes were geared for road racing and not mountain climbing. Too late. The name "Switchback Trail" had intrigued him. Besides, he'd complimented her on how the biking shorts snugged her ass, and that had bought him a little slack. Elliott chased down a forest trail barely wide enough for a fox run, and that trail branched off twice, crossed a narrow creek, and cut around a cluster of granite boulders that had risen like a backwoods Stonehenge from the swells of the earth. Two forks later ("The road less traveled or the road not taken, what do you say, you liberal arts major, you?") and he'd juddered over a root in the gathering darkness and been thrown over the handlebars. No bones broken, but some serious scrapes that would require antibiotic ointment.

Now they stood in a cluster of hardwood trees whose branches were nearly devoid of foliage. If any houses were around, their lights didn't show. Small, unseen animals skirled up leaves around them and darkness was falling harder and faster than a Democratic presidential hopeful's poll numbers. Carolyn, a homemaker, Humane Society volunteer, member of the Sands Creek subdivision bridge club, and devout Republican, resisted the urge to say, "Well, we really got away from it all, didn't we?"

Elliott pulled a penlight from his fanny pack and played it over the bicycle. "I think the front wheel's warped. We'll have to pay for the damage when we get back."

"You mean 'if' we get back."

"I know exactly where we are."

"Show me, then." She pulled out her copy of the fourfold pocket map. It was bordered with ads for area tourist attractions, fine dining establishments, and investment Realtors. The river road was marked by a series of arrows, and the Solom General Store and Back2Nature Outfitters were marked with red X marks. State Highway 292 leading from Windshake was clearly delineated in thick black ink. Tester Community Park, about five miles from the outfitters' judging from the scale of the map, was the last recognizable landmark they'd passed.

"We're right about here," Elliott said, running the beam of the penlight over a printed area that represented two square miles.

"There aren't any lines there," Carolyn pointed out.

"Sure. But we were headed east, remember? The sun was sinking behind us."

Actually, Carolyn recalled only vague glimpses of the sun once they'd left the relatively familiar flatness of the pavement. What bits of scattered light did break through the gnarled and scaly branches seemed to originate from a different position with each new slope or fork. When the sun had settled on the rim of the mountains, the entire sky had taken on the shade of a bruised plum, and Carolyn was thinking by then that even a trail of bread crumbs out of "Hansel and Gretel" wouldn't have led them home before midnight.

"Can the bike roll?" she asked.

"Sure, honey." Elliott lifted the bike by its handlebars and spun the wheel with one hand. The wheel made three revolutions, the rubber sloughing erratically against the tines, before it came to a complete stop. "Well, it can work in an emergency."

"At what point does this become an emergency?"

"Take it easy, Carolyn. We can walk out of here in no time. Once we find the river, we'll be home free."

"Do you know where the river is?"

"Sure, honey." He took the map from her, and fixed the penlight on the place he'd decided as their present location. With the beam, he traced a line to Blackburn River on the map, which was conveniently marked with a sinuous swath of blue. "We're here and the river's there. A half-hour's hike, tops."

"I see the river on the map, but where's the river out here?" Her voice took on the tiniest bit of sarcasm despite her best efforts.

"Water runs downhill. Ergo, we walk downhill, and there will be the river."

"Ergo" was one of those annoying, know-it-all, engineering-type words Elliott occasionally sprang on her when he was feeling defensive.

"I'm glad we wore athletic shoes and not moccasins," Carolyn said. Elliott had stopped at a little souvenir stand when they crossed the North Carolina border, one with a fake moonshine still by the front door and a wooden bear that had been sculpted with a chain saw. She'd talked him out of buying the Rebel flag window decal and the Aunt Jemima figurine-and-syrup decanter ("Just wait till the guys at PAMCO get a load of these!"), but he'd gone for the jen-u-wine hand-stitched leather Cherokee mocs at $29.95 a pair.

"Do you have any water left?" He'd used up the last of his water rinsing his wounds.

"A little," she said. Though she was under no illusions that they'd be back in the comfort of their rental cabin within the hour, she didn't think they were at the point where they'd need to conserve water to survive. She handed him her bottle and he dashed some in his mouth and swallowed.

"Okay, let's rock and roll," he said, walking his bike back down the hill. There was just enough daylight left to see the darker cut of the trail against the thick tangles of low-lying rhododendron. She tucked the map in the tight pocket of her biking shorts and followed, the bike leaning against her hip.

They had gone fifteen minutes before the invisible sun slipped down whatever horizon led to morning on another side of the world. Elliott switched on the penlight and its weak glimmer barely made a dent against the walls of the forest.

"Remember those big rocks we passed?" Carolyn asked, the first time she'd spoken since they'd started their descent.

"Yeah."

"We should have come to them by now."

"They're probably uphill from us. We're at a lower elevation now."

"'Probably'?"

He flicked the beam vaguely to his right. "Sure, honey. Up there. We'll come to that creek soon, and then we can decide whether to follow it down to the river or stick with the trail."

It was the first time he'd hinted that any decision would be mutual. That should have given her a cheap glow of victory, but it actually made her more nervous than she wanted to admit. She looked behind her, hoping to recognize the trail from their earlier passage, but all she could see were hickory and oak trees, which stood like witches with multiple deranged arms.

"Let's hurry," she said. "I'm getting cold."

The colorful nylon biking outfits gave a pleasant squeeze to the physique, but they were designed to let the skin breathe so sweat could dry. Breathing worked both ways, though, and the soft wind that came on with dusk made intimate entry through the material.

"I think I remember this stand of pines," her husband said. He gripped the penlight against one of the handlebars as he walked, so the circle of light bobbed ahead of them like on one of those "follow the bouncing ball" sing-along songs on television. Carolyn thought the perfect tune for their situation would be AC/DC's "Highway to Hell."

It was maybe a minute later, though time was rapidly losing its meaning during the interminable trek, that Carolyn heard the sounds behind her. At first she assumed they were the echo of her own footsteps, or maybe a whisper generated from the bike's sprockets. She breathed lightly through her mouth, or as lightly as she could, given the fact that she was bone tired, a little bit pissed, and more than a little scared. Leaves rustled. Something was moving, larger than squirrel-sized, churning up dead loam and breaking branches.

She edged her bike closer to Elliott's, until her front tire hit his rear.

"Jesus, Carolyn. Are you trying to run me down?"

"I heard something."

"I hear lots of somethings. Didn't you read the guidebook? The Southern Appalachians are home to a number of nocturnal creatures. Don't worry, all of the large predators are extinct, thanks to European settlers. Ergo, nothing to fear."

"Can we stop and listen for a minute?"

"Every minute we stop is another minute we're lost."

"I thought we weren't lost."

"We're not. We're just reorienting with our intended destination."

"Try the cell phone again?"

"No bars. Signal's deader than a mule's dick."

Ten minutes later and they reached the creek. The gurgling of the water and the cold, moist air alerted them to its presence before they blundered into it, because the penlight's beam had begun to fade. Carolyn welcomed the discovery not because it was the first definite landmark (if, in fact, it was the same creek they had crossed earlier), but because the white noise of the rushing water masked the sounds of the footsteps that followed their tracks a short distance behind.

"The creek, just like I said." Elliott pointed the light into Carolyn's face. It was barely bright enough to make her squint. "The question is, do we follow the water or stick with the trail?"

Carolyn was tempted to remark that he was finally asking her opinion, now that the situation had reached the south side of hopeless. Instead, she allowed him to retain a sliver of his pride. After all, there *would* be a later, and the politics of marriage, just like the politics of a republic, were constantly swinging from one party to another. And the pendulum was going to be weighted to her side big time for the rest of the vacation.

People didn't wander off and die in the Appalachian Mountains. There was just too much development. Maybe in Yellowstone, where grizzly bears still roamed, or the Arctic Wildlife Refuge with its sudden snowstorms and subzero temperatures. Here, the worst that could happen was a miserable night in the woods, with granola bars for supper and a surly husband.

Except something had been following them. No matter what Elliott said.

"We shouldn't follow the creek," she said. "It looks like the rhododendron get thick down there, and all those rocks are probably slippery. One of us might fall and break an ankle. Then we'd be in real trouble."

"Good point."

Another blow for girl power, but Carolyn didn't think the creek was that dangerous. She was afraid she wouldn't be able to hear the footsteps over the rushing water. "Why don't we leave the bikes here? We can't ride them, and they're slowing us down."

"We paid a deposit."

"We can come back and get them tomorrow, once we figure out where we are."

"I know where we are. I'm an engineer, remember?"

"Ergo." Carolyn didn't mean for the response to sound so bitter, but she was cold, her rump was sore from the ten-speed's narrow seat, her calves ached, and branches had scratched at her face and arms. "In case you haven't noticed, this isn't a goddamned circuit board or something you can solve with quadratic equations."

Elliott's widened eyes doubly reflected the penlight, as if she had slapped his face. She savored the victory for a mere second, then decided to finish the coup. She grabbed the light from his hand and swept the beam against the surrounding trees and underbrush, like Luke Skywalker slashing down Empire storm troopers.

"I heard something out there following us, and I'm good and goddamned scared." She hadn't used two expletives in the same conversation since her days at Brown, and it gave her a sense of what the feminists called "empowerment." It was frightening. She would give up power for security any day. But she had a feeling she needed the adrenaline and anger if she was going to get them out of this mess.

"Okay, okay, calm down," Elliott said, and the patronizing tone was suppressed but audible. "You're right. We should leave the bikes and stick with the trail. Let's cross here and hide the bikes in that thicket, then keep walking."

"Fine." She trembled, and she didn't know whether it was from the chill mist of the creek or her anxiety. She held the light while Elliott guided his damaged bike through the water, carefully choosing his steps on the mossy stones so his shoes would stay dry. He slogged through the mushy black mud of the opposite bank and stood above her, lost in the dark web of wood and vines.

"Come on, Carolyn. I can't see anything."

She took one look behind her, half expecting to see a crazed black bear or a red wolf or even a mountain lion, then navigated the rocks and headed up the embankment. She slipped once, going to her knee in the lizard-smelling mud, but Elliott grabbed her upper arm and tugged her to solid ground. Then he dragged the bike up and wheeled it into the bushes.

"Do you want to have a snack?" he asked. "An energy bar or something?"

"I want to get out of here."

"Let's look at the map one more time."

Carolyn nodded and gave the penlight back to her husband. She recognized that she had literally and figuratively passed the torch, but she didn't care. Truth be told, she was nearly in tears. So much for her run as Margaret Thatcher or the Republican Hillary Clinton.

They moved a little away from the water and gathered around the penlight as if it were a battery-powered campfire. Somewhere above them, the moon had risen, but its reassuring glow was filtered into a teasing gauze by the treetops. Elliott was studying the map when Carolyn heard the scrape and rustle of leaves.

"Did you hear that?" she asked, her heart a wooden knot in her chest.

"Just the wind. Or maybe a raccoon."

"The wind's not blowing. And raccoons don't get that big." Carolyn was struck by the image of a mutant, man-sized raccoon, reared up on its hind legs, crazed yellow eyes blazing from a bandit mask. The image should have made her chuckle, at least on the inside. Instead, the tension increased its grip on her internal organs. And, goddamn, she suddenly had to pee.

She didn't relish peeling down her nylon shorts and squatting in the darkness, further exposing herself to whatever was out there.

"Okay, if we're right here, and can make three miles an hour, we should make it to the main road by eleven o'clock. Then we can find a house and call for a cab or something."

The idea of walking up on a stranger's porch and knocking was almost as scary as the thing that was or wasn't following them. "I don't think they have cabs out here."

"Maybe the police. Or the Happy Hollow office."

Elliott must be scared, too. Otherwise, he'd never admit to others that he'd made a mistake. Carolyn's knowledge of his failure was one thing, he could gloss that over in the coming week and eventually have her believe getting lost had somehow been *her* fault. But here he was, ready to tell the local sheriff's department or the rental cabin management that he'd wandered off with no respect for the wilderness, that his modern-day James Fenimore Cooper act had gone bust, that a Yankee engineer with a wristwatch calculator couldn't navigate the ancient hills. Carolyn couldn't wait, even if it meant he'd be surly until they made it back to White Plains.

Mostly, she couldn't wait to see a streetlight.

Because the noise was back, closer, to the right now.

"You heard *that*?"

"No." He said it so firmly that it sounded like self-denial.

"It's closer."

His face contorted in the dying orange orb of light. "Listen, Carolyn. This is the twenty-first century, not the goddamned *Blair Witch Project*. In real life, people don't get stalked by cannibalistic hillbillies or eaten by wild animals. And, last I heard, aliens don't have secret landing sites in the Appalachians. That's the Southwest desert, remember? Ergo, there is nothing following us and I'm trying to solve this little problem you created and get us safely back to civilization."

Leaves rustled ten feet ahead of them, behind a gnarled evergreen. Despite herself, Carolyn moved closer to Elliott and clung to his arm. He stiffened and smirked.

"I'll get us out of here," he said. "Have I ever let you—"

The penlight died and darkness rushed in like water flooding a ruptured bathysphere. It was almost as if the light had warded off the other sounds of the night, because the still air was filled with chirring, scratching, and creaking. Beneath those came the ragged whisper of breathing.

Caroyln's eyes adjusted to the dim moonlight just in time to see a large black shadow hover beyond Elliott, and then her husband was ripped from her grasp. He gave a wet gurgle, as if a freshet had erupted between the granite stones of his face. One of his legs flailed out and struck her kneecap, and he gave a bleat of pain. Drops of liquid spattered on Carolyn and she screamed. The air stirred above her head and she looked up to see a curved and dripping grin of metal catch the distant eye of the moon. The grin descended and bit with a meaty *thunk*, and all Carolyn could think was that the meat must have been her husband, that arrogant engineer with a fondness for college football, the Bush clan, plasma television, and pharmaceutical stocks.

The scream jumped the wires from her brain to the ganglia low in her spinal cord, a place encoded during the Paleozoic Era when flight meant survival and the higher thinking processes shut their useless yammerings.

She ran blindly, branches tearing at her hair, heedless of the trail's direction. The moist hacking continued behind her, but she scarcely heard, because her eardrums protected her high-order brain. She was an animal, scrambling through the leaves, guided by instinct as she ducked under branches and dodged between scaly oaks and beech. She couldn't see but she didn't need to see, because her eyes were jiggling orbs of deadweight in her skull and a more primitive sight led her onward. All knowledge was in her skin, mind given over to flesh, she was aware of nothing but the roar of wind through her throat and the pulse in her temples and the dark sharp thing at her back and—

She didn't see the maple with the low branch, because her eyes had shut down, but she did see the bright yellow and green sparks that exploded like fireworks on the movie screen of her forehead.

Carolyn was unconscious as the goats gathered around her, and her useless, high-order brain stayed mercifully absent as her true-blue Republican blood leaked into the land of legends.

Chapter Nineteen

The general store was crowded with a mix of locals and tourists. Odus, his ball cap tipped low and a toothpick between his teeth, stood by the sandwich counter and waited as Sarah rang up the purchases of a chubby boy in too-tight nylon biking shorts and tank top. The customer's shoulders were pink and peeling, the sign of a spoiled city boy getting too much sun on vacation. The boy's dad stood beside him in a red sweatsuit that was meant to portray athleticism but instead gave the impression of a sausage that was about to bust out of its skin. Sarah bagged the boy's mound of candy bars, pork rinds, and lollipops.

A bluegrass band was tuning up in the park across the road. A Solom community group had bought four acres along the river that were now cleared and grassed, with a band shell at one end. From early summer until the end of October, weekly shows were held in the park. The music was either bluegrass or traditional old-timey, though the general store hosted occasional debates about the difference between the two labels. Odus picked some mandolin himself and even sat in on some local recording sessions, but he didn't like performing in front of people.

Sarah looked away from the register and frowned at him. He

gave a small nod that said, "We need to talk after you take care of business."

Sarah paid rapt attention to the customers, smiling as if she appreciated them for more than just their money. A six-pack of Mountain Dew, two cups of overpriced coffee, a microwave burrito, a honey bun, a bottle of sunblock, a rustic birdhouse, a basket made of entwined jack vine, a stack of Doc Watson CDs, and two bags of Twizzlers changed hands before Sarah got a break. She picked up a dusting cloth, came to the sandwich counter, and began wiping down the dewy glass.

"You had me worried," he said.

"Don't waste a good worry on me."

Normally Odus wouldn't. Sarah Jeffers was tougher than beef jerky and had the backbone of a mountain lion. But toughness and spine didn't matter when you were standing up against something that ought not be. Odus ground the end of his toothpick to splinters as he spoke around it. "I seen him."

"Seen who?" Sarah said, suddenly taking a great interest in the chub of gray liverwurst. Odus didn't see how anybody could eat that stuff. Bologna was okay, but he preferred good and honest meat, like ham, that looked the way it did when it came from the animal.

"We both know who," he said.

A tan, Florida-thin blonde approached the cash register, pigtails tied with pink ribbons. She wore a T-shirt that read *This dog don't hunt*. In her hands were a gaudy dried flower arrangement and a miniature wooden church, no doubt decorations for a seasonal second home. Sarah's face uncreased in relief as she went to ring up the sale.

"Are you the storyteller?" a voice behind him asked.

He turned and faced a man wearing sunglasses who held a cassette tape as if filming a commercial. Odus was on the cover, dressed in his folksy garb of denim overalls and checked flannel shirt. He'd even borrowed a ragged-edged straw hat for the photo because the university woman who had recorded it said the package needed what she called a "hook." Odus didn't know a damned thing about marketing, but he knew stories from eight generations back.

The Hampton family had passed along the Jack tales, in which Jack usually put one over on the old King. "Jack and the Beanstalk" was the best-known of the stories, but that one didn't have a king in it. The university woman said they were parables in which the Scots-Irish who settled the Southern Appalachians were able to get proxy revenge on their English oppressors. Odus didn't feel particularly oppressed by anybody in England, except maybe when Princess Diana got all that attention for getting killed, but he figured the university woman was a lot smarter than he was about such things.

"I did some telling on that one," Odus said. The tape was called *The Mouth of the Mountain*.

"So you're a celebrity." The man was eating a Nutty Buddy ice-cream cone, and a string of white melt rolled down the back of his hand. He licked it up.

"Not really. I just talked. The woman who made the tape did all the work." Odus looked over at Sarah, who was busy taking money for a gee haw whimmy-diddle, a folk toy that basically consisted of three sticks and a tiny nail. Retail value: $6.99 plus tax.

"Do you tell them in public? We're going to be up for two weeks and would love to hear some authentic Appalachian stories."

"They ain't authentic," Odus said. "They're all lies."

The man laughed, ejecting a tiny peanut crumble that arced to the floor at Odus's feet. "That's good. I'm buying this one, and I'm sure I'll be pleased. If you're not holding any performances, can I hire you to come down and tell some stories around the campfire in our backyard?"

Sweat pooled in Odus's armpits. He didn't mind telling the stories to family or his few close friends, and he could even put up with talking them into a microphone, but the idea of spinning out some Jack yarns while a bunch of tourists yucked it up and sipped martinis was more than he could stand. "I don't do tellings in a crowd," Odus said.

"This won't be a crowd. Just us and the neighbors. Maybe ten people."

"Ten's a crowd."

The man looked at the tape. "Fifteen dollars for this, huh? I'll pay a hundred dollars for one hour."

Odus thought of the wallet in his back pocket, the leather folds so bare a fiddleback spider wouldn't hide in them. A hundred bucks would buy a case of decent whiskey, and decent whiskey would maybe drown out those dreams of the cheese-faced man in the black hat. From the park, the sounds of the string band blared from the PA speakers. "Fox on the Run," complete with three-part harmony.

The man was mouthing the waffle cone now, running his thick, pink tongue around the cone's rim.

"I'll have to think on it a spell."

The sunglasses hid the man's expression, which could have been disbelief or impatience. Odus didn't much care. It wasn't like losing a steady job or anything. If he'd even wanted a steady job, that was.

"I'll listen to the tape and get back to you," the man said. "What's the best way to reach you?"

Odus took the toothpick from his mouth and pressed the tip into his callused thumb. "I don't have no phone. Usually you can find me here at the store or around."

The man smiled, vanilla cream on his upper lip. "Okay, 'Mouth of the Mountain.' Have it your way."

He went to pay for the tape. He left the store, and Odus watched through the screen door as the man made his way to the park.

"Sold a tape," Sarah said. "There's another buck-fifty for you."

"Except I don't get it for six more months," Odus said. "That royalty thing."

Sarah took a five out of the cash register and held it out to him. "I'll report that one as damaged. Call it an advance."

Odus swallowed hard and went to the counter. The store was quiet. An elderly couple was browsing in the knickknacks, and a kid faced tough choices at the candy rack. Odus reached out and took the bill, but as he pulled his hand away, Sarah grabbed his wrist with all the strength of a possum's jaws.

"Take it and buy you a bottle, and forget about it," Sarah said. "You ain't seen nothing, and I ain't seen nothing."

Their eyes met. Odus, at six feet two and 240, somehow seemed to be looking up at Sarah, who stood all of five feet and weighed in at a hundred soaking wet.

"He's back, and getting drunk won't change that."

"Getting drunk never changed anything, but that never stopped you before." Sarah let go of his wrist. "Don't go blabbing it or people will think your brain finally pickled and they'll throw you in Crazeville to dry out."

"The people I tell it to will believe me, because they'll know."

"I heard what you told that man. Your stories ain't authentic, they're lies." Sarah began fussing with the cigarette packs and cans of smokeless tobacco behind the counter.

"The biggest lies are the easiest to swallow," Odus said. "But they burn like hell when you puke them back up."

He went out into the sunshine and the last chorus of "Fox on the Run."

Jett stood by the pay phone in the school lobby, fumbling in her pocket-sized purse. Many of her classmates, especially the girls, had their own cell phones, but Gordon thought they were a "distraction to learning." As if she couldn't get Brittany to text-message her the answer to a quiz question. Phones were tools and were here to stay, so why couldn't Gordon get with the future already?

Because he was lame, that's why. She pulled out the phone card her dad had given her as a present when she and Mom left Charlotte. "Five hundred minutes, call any time," he'd said. Actually, he probably didn't mean *any* time, since he'd started dating the blond librarian. Mandy, Mindy, Bambi, something like that. Lots of checking out going on there, probably.

Noise leaked from the lunch room, typical middle-school jokes, flirting, the rattle of silverware on hard vinyl trays. She pressed her ear to the phone and punched in her card digits, waded through the operator's asking if she wanted to donate minutes to the troops, then entered the numbers for Dad's work.

"Draper Woodworking and Design," the female voice said.

"Could I get Mark Draper, please?"

"May I ask who is calling?"

"Jett. Jett Draper."

"Oh." Uttered with a tone of sympathy.

After thirty seconds, Dad came on the line, bluff and hearty and probably stoned. "What's up, pumpkin? Aren't you in school?"

"Yeah. It's lunchtime. I have five minutes before the bell rings."

"How's it going? Did you get my letter?"

"Yeah. Thanks for the money. It really saved my sanity."

"I'll send some more soon."

"No, I'm fine. Really."

"Are you liking Solom any better now that you've had some time to get settled?"

"It's all right. A little slow, but you get used to it."

"Made any friends?"

She thought of her drug connection, the goats, the man in the black suit, the kids on the bus, creepy old Betsy Ward. "Yeah. I'm fitting right in."

Her dad's tone turned serious. "And your mom? Is she okay?"

"Actually, that's what I called about."

"Talk to me, sweetheart."

"I'm afraid she's starting to lose it."

"Lose it?"

"Yeah. She's, like, not Mom. Like some alien came down and took over her brain. She's changed so much in the last few weeks. Sometimes I can't believe it's the same person who told me that life sends messages in invisible balloons."

"She's going through an adjustment period. She'll be fine once—"

"Don't give me that counselor babble horseshit, Dad."

"Jett."

"Sorry. It just blurted out."

"I can tell you're upset. Calm down and tell me what she's up to."

"She stares off into space. I'll walk into a room and it's like she's forgotten what she was doing, or like she'd been in the middle of a daydream and I woke her up. She's totally changed her wardrobe and—this might be weirdest of all—she's started *cooking*. And I don't mean beanie weenies and frozen waffles. I'm talking honest-to-God *recipes*."

"Well, if you'll forgive the counselor babble, I'd guess she's trying hard to make things work with her new husband."

"You sound sad about it, Dad."

"We had our chance and blew it. Things just didn't work out. But—"

"I know, I know, it's not my fault and it had nothing to do with me."

"I know it's tough on you, honey. Getting along with Gordon okay?"

She didn't know whether to lie or not. Dad shouldn't have asked, or maybe it was his way of showing he cared about her. It was an uncomfortable subject. Gordon had wanted her to take the Smith name, but she'd balked. Mom had sided with her, of course, but not too vocally. "He's been a hard case but Mom says he just wants what's best for me. But I don't think him and Mom are getting along too well."

"I'm sorry to hear that."

She could tell he wasn't. She didn't understand much about boy-girl stuff, except she was smart enough to know that you wanted to forever own the one you loved, even if it was bad for both of you. "He's not mean or anything, just cold. Not to get too personal, but he never kisses her."

"They'll work it out. I'm more worried about you. I hate to ask, but how are things going with the drugs?"

"Fine." She realized she'd snapped at him, and that was the worst possible thing to do, because it would make him suspicious. "They haven't even invented drugs up here yet. It's like the 1800s. Plowing with mules, no electricity, a church down every dirt road. Nothing but clean air and sunshine."

"Good for you, pumpkin. I don't mean to pry, but I'm your dad. It's still my job, even if we're two hundred miles apart."

The bell rang, its brittle, metallic echo bouncing off the concrete block walls. The traffic in the hall picked up, a few of the guys giving her the eye, no doubt because of her black lipstick. "Got to go to math," she said.

"Love you. Keep in touch, and tell your mom I said hello."

For a moment, Jett almost told about the man in the black hat, but Dad would think she was either cracking up or in serious need of some counselor babble horseshit. Ditto with the menacing goats. Just thinking of them made her a little light-headed, as if such things were never real unless you spoke of them. Better to just ignore them, pen them up behind the walls of Stoner City. "I love you, too, Dad. 'Bye."

She wiped her eyes, careful not to smudge the liner, and waded into the hallway crowd. —

Carnivorous goats.

Sounded the fuck like a cheesy zombie movie to Alex Eakins. He could dig zombies, even cheer for them in a way, because when you got down to it, those gut-munching things from beyond the grave were about the most libertarian creatures around. Talk about your free-market economies. But goats were another matter.

Alex was smart enough to be aware of his eccentric nature. His parents were afraid he was turning into a survivalist who would one day construct an armed bunker and have a standoff with federal agents. But the true survivalist didn't want to be noticed by the government, much less stage a confrontation. And a true survivalist didn't go around ranting about man-eating goats, because that was a surefire way to *get* noticed.

So Alex would have to figure out how to handle this on his own. The first order of business was a trip to the general store to get a few reels of barbed wire. He could add another couple of runs around the perimeter of his property as a first line of defense. His gun rack held a .30-30, a sixteen-gauge Remington shotgun, and a .22 so his girlfriends could participate in target practice. He had his bow and arrows, a slingshot, and a couple of sticks of dynamite he'd bought under the table at the last Great Tennessee Border Gun Show. Plus there was the contraband arsenal in his secret room. So goats, even a herd of them, were not something to lose sleep over.

Weird Dude Walking was another story altogether.

Because Alex had returned to the scene of the slaughter yesterday afternoon, and not even a stitch of clothing remained. No blood on the ground, either, and not a goat in sight (Alex had the Remington with him just in case). Goats would eat any old thing, especially natural-fiber clothing, but surely a few scraps would be scattered around, or a bone button from the coat. Strangest of all, though the ground was pocked with cloven hoofprints, there was not a single mark from the boots the man had been wearing.

Which meant Weird Dude Walking must have risen up and floated away like Christ gone to heaven.

Even if Alex wanted to report what he'd witnessed, he had no evidence. He never doubted his sanity, though his own family had called him "crazy" any number of times. But only a crazy person would witness a man feeding himself alive to a bunch of goats.

Maybe not crazy, though.

Maybe special.

If a thing like that happened in the old days, the people called you a prophet and let you boss them around.

"Alex?"

Alex looked up, not realizing he'd been staring at his palms as if expecting them to start bleeding. "I thought you were at work."

"It's my day off."

"Oh yeah."

"Something wrong?"

"No, babe. Just thinking about the state of the world. It's a guy thing."

"I've got a guy thing for you." Meredith nuzzled her breasts against his back and put her arms around his chest.

"Not now. I've got some things to work out."

"Don't you want to smoke some?"

"I need to keep a clear head. Dope is the opium of the masses."

"Huh?"

"Hemingway. He said dope is the opium of the masses. But that's pretty fried, because opium is what they make heroin out of, and not many people can hook up with some H. I guess they didn't smoke much weed back in Hemingway's time."

"I thought he said *religion* was the opium of the masses. Or was that Karl Marx?"

"Same thing. Religion is for dopes, so it all works out." He gave a stoned snicker, though he'd not had any marijuana since the night before.

"You want some lunch? I could cook one of your acorn squashes and some wild rice."

"I'm not hungry. I think I'll go check the babies and meditate."

He got up from the table and went outside. He had a small green-house, but he didn't grow his dope in it. The surveillance planes might see it and that would be the first place the snooper troopers would train their little spy cameras. His marijuana was in a little shed by the garden. He used a wind turbine and water wheel to generate electricity for the full-spectrum lights, because one of the ways cops got a warrant was by checking the electric company's records for a jump in kilowatt hours. The jump was "evidence" that a citizen might be using grow lights. Since he was off-grid, he was outside the system, in more ways than one.

He unlocked the shed, checked the sky for bogies, then went in. The main room was filled with a blue glow thrown off by the bank of grow lights. Marijuana plants, spawned from Kona Gold seeds a friend had mailed from Hawaii, stood as tall as Alex, and the room was sweet with the fully flowering buds. The three dozen plants were grown in five-gallon buckets, and the soil was ripe with the best compost Mother Nature could produce. Alex sat cross-legged before the plants in a yoga position. He was at peace in this place, this shrine to the sacred buzz.

Too bad he had to hide it away. In a righteous world, he could grow it out there in the garden, right in front of God and every-body. Even Weird Dude Walking. If grass were legal, maybe the country's farmers wouldn't need crop subsidies. Get them off wel-fare and stifle the feds' war on drugs at the same time. Damn, why couldn't the Libertarians come up with any good candidates?

He let his anger at social injustices slip away as he breathed deeply of the *Cannabis sativa*. A spider had spun a web at the base of one of the plants. The spider was yellow with black streaks across its back, and it worked its way toward the center of the web where a struggling fly was tangled in the silken threads. Alex real-ized it was life in a microcosm, a symbolic play. You buzz around minding your own business, and then suddenly your ass is snared and along comes Reality to suck out your juices.

Just like the goats had sucked the life out of the man in the black hat.

Heavy.

Too heavy to contemplate with a straight head, despite what

he'd told Meredith. He just didn't want to smoke with her, because then he'd have to either talk or silence her in bed. The only way to shut up a woman was to stick part of yourself in her. He needed to be alone. He pulled a joint out of his sock and fired it up, not shifting from his yoga seating as he puffed. He began a game of situation-problem-solution.

Situation: You had a vision. Nobody else will believe you, because you don't belong to any religion of the masses. Well, Meredith will probably believe you, but she believes in Atlantis and UFOs and even Dunkin' Fucking Donuts.

Problem: You either keep it to yourself and forget it, or you have to admit that miracles happen.

Solution: Smoke more dope.

He took a deep draw off the joint and held the smoke in his lungs. In his mind's eye, the blue smoke seeped into his bloodstream and sent its tendrils into his brain. The drug stimulated him and relaxed him at the same time, one of its contradictions that appealed to him and suited his worldview.

Been a long time since you were in Methodist Bible school, but miracles in the Bible sort of had a point to them. Like Jesus with the loaves and fishes so everybody could eat, and Jesus turning water into wine so everybody could get wasted. Far as I can remember, nowhere in the Bible did some dude feed his own ass to the goats.

Alex took another puff. The spider had reached the fly, which must have worn itself out, because it had stopped struggling. Or maybe the fly had sensed the jig was up and could see two dozen copies of the approaching spider through its compound eyes. Alex considered rescuing the fly, playing God, releasing it to go off and eat shit and hatch maggots. But it wasn't right to fuck with Nature. Besides, that would have meant standing up, and his legs had a nice tingle going.

Situation: Weird Dude Walking had to come from somewhere. Miracles don't just crawl down off the top of the mountain in the middle of the Blue Ridge, half a world away from the Red Sea and Egypt and Jerusalem.

Problem: That means Weird Dude was an emissary of some sort. Sent by God or the devil or what the movie trailers call the "dark imagination of M. Night Shyamalan." An emissary sent specifically for you, *Alexander Lane Eakins, and for you alone.*

Solution: *Just because an emissary drags ass to your castle door doesn't mean you have to open up and let him in. Pretend it never happened. Denial is a Good Thing.*

The joint was down to an orange roach, and Alex hot-boxed it until it burned his fingertips. He exhaled the smoke so that a blue cloud swept over the spider and the fly. One could get the munchies and the other could die with a shit-eating grin. Seemed to be some sort of circular cosmic justice in that.

He sat until the sparkling edges of his buzz wore off; then he went into the house to ignore Meredith.

Chapter Twenty

Katy's back ached. She'd ended up sleeping on the couch, unable to face Gordon, much less lie in the same bed. She'd cooked oatmeal for Jett, then walked to the end of the road and waited for the bus with her. Gordon must have arrived late and headed out early. He hadn't even made his usual pot of coffee.

After Jett rode away on the bus, sitting at a rear window and refusing to wave, Katy went back up the gravel drive. As she passed the neighbor's house, she hurried, afraid that Betsy Ward would come out on the porch and try to engage her in conversation. She'd always picked up on a distinct coldness emanating from the woman, as if Katy's big-city accent were somehow alien and even infectious. Plus the Smiths appeared to have a bit of a bad reputation, and Gordon's distant and antisocial manner certainly didn't help. Gordon had warned her that Solom was a little clannish, at least among the families that had owned land here for generations. He assured her attitudes were changing as more outsiders moved in, but she sensed resentment rather than acceptance was the more common response.

No one seemed home at the Wards', so she continued up the long gravel road to the Smith house. As she mounted the steps, she realized with alarm that she still thought of it as the "Smith house," even though by legal rights it was half hers. She put away the blankets from the couch, cleaned the bedroom, then found herself in the kitchen. It was only ten o'clock, too early for lunch. Besides, with no one else to cook for, she often resorted to an alfalfa-sprout-and-cheese sandwich or a can of vegetable soup. She was digging for a can opener in one of the drawers when she found a handwritten recipe on a dog-eared index card. She recognized the writing; it was done in the same elegant penmanship of the other recipes she'd found tucked in books, on the pantry shelves, or amid stacks of dishes. Rebecca's recipe for sweet potato pie.

It sounded like a nice treat to draw the family together over the dinner table. She checked off the items she would need. She had cinnamon, nutmeg, brown sugar, and even whipped cream, but she had no evaporated milk. She could call Gordon at his office and ask him to stop by the grocery store, but she wasn't in the mood to ask a favor, even if the favor was for his benefit too. She would pick it up herself at the general store. That meant she had a four-mile round trip. Might be a nice day to walk, because the weather was clear and fortyish, with the barest whisper of wind. Besides, the house had started to become oppressive. She thought she'd get used to being a housewife again, the way she had been the first two years of Jett's life. But back then, she'd been busy with an infant. With the house to herself all day, she'd become increasingly bored, despite her newly discovered culinary adventures.

She changed into stone-washed jeans, blouse, jacket, and tennis shoes. At the last minute, she decided on a scarf in case the weather changed suddenly, and rummaged around upstairs until she found a green silk scarf that happened to match her eyes. She couldn't remember buying it; perhaps someone had given it to her as a gift and it had been packed away and forgotten. Outside, she made a cursory check of the hens' nests, spying several eggs she would collect for the pie when she got back, assuming she was brave enough. The goats weren't around the barn. They must have been up in the forest, working the underbrush.

She passed the Wards' house again, and this time Arvel's pickup truck was in the driveway. The man himself was checking the fluids in his tractor, which was parked by the barn up behind the house. She waved in what she considered a neighborly fashion. Arvel flipped a grease rag at her, then motioned for her to come to him.

He met her in the driveway. "How ya doing, Mrs. Smith?"

"It's Logan. Katy Logan."

"Oh yeah, that's right." He gave her a one-eyed squint. "Things going good?"

"Fine. A lovely day."

"Sure enough. Taking a walk, are you?"

"Yes. I'm going to the general store."

Arvel rubbed his hands on the grease rag. "Shame Gordon won't set you up with a better car. Him being a professor and all, he's bound to have the money."

"We decided we'd save up for a while and wait for things to settle down a little." She didn't want to tell her neighbor that Gordon was turning out to be a control freak. She'd always kept her personal life to herself, which might have contributed to the failure of her first marriage. Katy recognized the irony of requiring Jett to undergo drug counseling while she and Mark had never sought marriage counseling. "How's Mrs. Ward?"

"She's in the hospital."

From his tone, he could have been talking about a leaky radiator. "What's wrong?" Katy asked, hoping she didn't sound snoopy.

"Slipped in the kitchen yesterday and busted her skull. Had a few stitches and a concussion, but the doc said she ought to be home in a few days." He gave an uneven grin. "I always said she was a hardheaded woman."

"I didn't hear any sirens."

"You're a good piece up the road, and there's a stand of pines between our houses. Most neighbors in these parts are kind of on their own."

"I'll have some flowers sent to her room."

"She'd like that. Except no Queen Anne's lace. Betsy's allergic to that."

"Is there anything I can do to help?"

"Nothing can mend her but time. And I'll get along fine myself. I learned to cook on camping trips, and the laundry will keep until she's back on her feet."

"Okay. But come knocking if you need anything."

"I'll do that. Say, I'm driving the tractor up the river road. I have a job tilling up an old burley tobacco field. Want to catch a ride?"

She smiled despite herself. "It might be faster to walk."

"No, really, just climb up here and straddle the P.T.O. box. If you're going to be a mountain woman, you might as well learn the basics. Plus the goats are riled."

"Riled?"

Arvel hesitated, then looked out across the pastures that ran alongside the gravel road. "Uppity. They usually rut in the spring, but for some reason they're tangling here on the front door to winter. They get mighty strange when they're in the fever."

Katy started to chuckle, but something about the man's expression stopped her. She remembered her own encounter with Gordon's goat. "Mighty strange" seemed like a good catchall phrase for the odd occurrences that had plagued her over the past few weeks. "Maybe a ride wouldn't be so bad after all," she said.

David Tester sought to live his life according to the words of the Bible. Primitive Baptists didn't hold with the cross, the crucifix, or even pictorial representations of the Lord. Such things were graven images, and therefore false idols. It was God's decision alone to decide which souls were taken to Glory, and God might choose all or none. To leave that choice up to the sinner was an insult to God's power over all things. The best course of a sinner was to live according to the gospel here in this life and assume God had ample room in the next. As the church elder, David served as an example, and even though he avoided temptation when possible, he knew he suffered the sin of pride.

Primitives chose their elders from among the congregation. The position required no formal training. Basically, anyone who heard the call of the Lord would stand up and give it a go, and sometimes would preach for years before being officially selected to lead the church. In the meantime, other elders sought the same position, depending upon the passion in their hearts. David's own brother Ray had delivered a few sermons, but Ray didn't have the gift of oration that his older brother did. David's biggest regret was that Ray had subsequently left the church, and David's biggest failure was the pride he had felt at being named elder. Ray's chances of reaching heaven were just the same as they had been before, but David sometimes wondered if weakness ran in the Tester blood.

Because Harmon Smith was back, and the only way that could have happened was if the Lord so willed it. David had no magic spells he could invoke, no special dust he could sprinkle, no prayers for strength against enemies. The plain, bald truth of it was God had brought Harmon to Solom for a reason. He almost wished he were a Southern Baptist, so he could believe Harmon was of the devil and therefore had arrived to work against the Lord's purpose. The only comfort David could draw was that God's ways were known to God and should be accepted. Even if you didn't have such faith, God was going to do as he pleased anyway, so it was best to be prepared for the worst.

The question now was whether or not David should try to do anything about Harmon. If the answer was no, then David would go about his business, keep his head down, and let his congregation deal with the situation as the Lord so chose. If the answer was yes, then maybe the little valley community of Solom had been chosen as the final showdown, the battleground depicted by the apostle John in the book of Revelation. Maybe the signs had already shown themselves, the seven seals broken, the red dragon risen up from the sea, and all that, and the farmers of Solom had been just plain too busy to notice. The charismatic Baptist sects had made a lot of hay over the signs, and it seemed like, growing up, David had heard almost daily that the end was nigh and the Lord's return was just around the corner. What David could never understand was the fear in the voices of the doomsayers. The Lord's return was a thing to be welcomed, no matter if it rode in on fire, famine, and spilled blood.

But what if the Lord had sent Harmon Smith back as some kind of test? The Old Testament was practically one long test, what with Abraham being ordered to offer up his son on the altar and Job undergoing terrible trials. Even Jesus Christ had to stand on a plateau and turn down the devil's offer of a shining city laid out before Him, and if God couldn't trust His very own Son to do the right thing, then what chance did David have?

David paused in his work forking mulch over Lillian Rominger's strawberry bed. After the killing frosts, David's landscaping business slowed down, and besides some tree pruning and a side business growing poinsettas in a small greenhouse, he would be scraping by the next few months. Lillian was one of his best customers and kept him busy through November doing odd jobs. She was a Methodist widow, stocky and brusque, but for all that she was attractive and only a decade or so older than David. During the summer, whenever the heat drove him to remove his shirt, she always seemed to pop up with a glass of iced tea. In the autumn, she often worked alongside him, not afraid to get her knees dirty.

Today she was busy feeding the two goats she kept in a pen on her two-acre property. Her place was bordered by two large stretches of pasture but couldn't rightly be considered a farm, though she had numerous flower gardens, with strawberries, blueberries, gooseberries, and a couple of dozen apple trees. She was a postal carrier in the next county and had to work most Saturdays, though she claimed the federal holidays made up for the aggravation. David rested against his pitchfork and watched her sprinkling hay into the pen.

The animals mashed their faces against the wire fencing, greedy for food. One of the goats reared up on its hind legs and nipped her hand.

"Ouch," Lillian said, yanking her hand back. David could see the blood even from fifty feet away. He jammed his pitchfork into the remaining heap of mulch in his truck bed and jogged to her side. Lillian's blue eyes were wide and startled.

"You okay?" David asked. He pulled a bandanna from his pocket, thinking he would wrap her wound, but the cloth was sweaty and stiff.

"Blamed creature about took my whole hand off," she said. The skin was broken on three of her knuckles, blood dripping onto her canvas sneakers.

"We'd better get that inside and washed," David said. The goat that had bitten Lillian stood by the fence, chewing hay with a twist of its bearded jaw.

"I'll be okay," she said. "I think he's just worked up because he knows I'm going to geld him."

"Geld him?"

She pulled a circular iron band from her back pocket. There was a clip at one end of the hinged band that allowed it to be opened and closed. "You reach under the billy boy and grab that sack and yank down like this"—Lillian gave a demonstration that looked as if she was plucking grapes from an ornery vine—"and snap this little puppy up above the twins. The sack rots off in a few weeks, and that musky odor gets a lot more bearable."

David blanched at the thought of having that band clamped on his own testicles. He'd been raised in the ways of farm life, but somehow castration seemed far crueler than slaughtering for meat. Back in his youth, there had been few goats in Solom. It seemed the past few years either the goats had been breeding like rabbits or everyone had simultaneously developed an affinity for the stubborn creatures.

"Well, I can see why he got a little testy," David said.

"Odus Hampton told me you can't trust goats this time of year."

David wondered what else Odus had told her and if he should mention his own encounter on the trail above the Smith place. "They've been acting strange lately. Tell me, why did you get yours?"

The goats pressed against the sides of the pen, stomping the dirt with their hooves, as if they were trying to bust out. Lillian wiped her hand on her jeans, then inspected the ragged skin. "Gordon Smith gave them to me. Said I could eat them, milk them, or breed them. Said goats made good pets and that everybody in Solom should have some."

"I don't guess they carry rabies."

"Probably could, if they got bit by a bat or bobcat that was infected."

The goats retreated to the center of the pen, where Lillian had constructed a makeshift shelter. The billy that Lillian planned to geld lowered its head and ran full-tilt at the fence, denting the wire and jiggling the fence posts. The other goat, the female, which looked pregnant with its swollen belly and dangling teats, bleated frantically. The billy backed up a few steps and hurled itself at the fence again.

"Jesus," Lillian said. "He's gone crazy."

David put an arm around her and pulled her away from the pen. David felt silly fleeing a goat, but something about the mad shine of its eldritch eyes gave him the creeps. Lillian's house was two hundred feet away, so they retreated to David's pickup as the goat continued to batter the fence. They slid into the cab just as the fence gave way and the billy came staggering over the tangled mesh. David expected it to make a direct line to the truck and ram its horns into the sheet metal. Instead, it stopped where Lillian's blood had dripped and began licking at the ground.

"It wanted my *blood*?" Lillian said, examining the gash on her hand. "What the hell's going on here, David?"

"I've been wondering that myself." He looked in the rearview mirror. He could probably grab the pitchfork before the goat reached him. But then what would he do? Stick it in the creature's ribs? The billy lifted its head from the ground and sniffed the air, then looked directly at David.

"David?" Lillian's tone chilled him.

"He's staying where he is."

"That's not what I mean." She nudged his elbow and he looked through the front windshield. A dozen goats from the neighboring pasture had come down to the barbed-wire boundary and were watching the encounter. David wondered if they had smelled the blood, too, and thought of sharks in the water being thrown into a frenzy.

But these were *goats*, for God's sake. Livestock. Food. They were technically herbivores but had a reputation for eating tin cans, wool blankets, newsprint, anything they could squeeze down their gullets. As far as David knew, they had never been carnivorous. Then why was he so afraid that the goats would break through the barbed wire and surround the truck?

"Do you have a gun?" he asked Lillian.

"In the house. A little twenty-two pistol to scare off burglars."

"I suggest we head for the house, then."

He turned the ignition key, half expecting the engine to grind over and over without firing, like a scene in a B-grade horror movie. Instead the engine roared to life, he jammed the gearshift into first, and peeled up two strips of mud as he popped out the clutch and spun the rear wheels. David fought an urge to plow over the billy, which stared at him with those oblate pupils boring holes in David's face, as if marking him for later revenge. David brought the truck to a halt beside the porch, and then he and Lillian scrambled inside and slammed the door.

David peeked through the curtains while Lillian retrieved the pistol from her bedroom. The goats in the neighboring pasture had lost interest and scattered across the grass, grazing as before. The billy took a tentative nibble at an apple sapling, then went back to the pen where its mate waited by the shelter. They lay together in the afternoon sunlight, shaking their ears to drive away flies.

"Did what I think happened really happen, or am I going crazy?" Lillian said.

David suddenly felt foolish. Looking out, he found the scene almost pastoral, with the dark green grass, the beds of plants and hibernating flowers, the far mountains stippled with gray trees. He imagined himself picking up the phone and calling the sheriff's department to report a wild animal attack. He could almost hear the dispatcher's voice: "What kind of animal? Bear? Dog? Treed raccoon?" He would bet his truck that "goat" wouldn't make the list.

"Let's get your hand patched up," he said, dropping the curtain on the bizarre world outside, wondering what the book of Revelation had to say about the role of goats in the Apocalypse.

Jett managed to stay straight most of the day. She didn't like stoning at school, especially alone. She wasn't close to any of the other kids, and getting totally roped wasn't as much fun with nobody else in class giggling along. But home had gotten so weird, she couldn't imagine trying to get through the evenings without sneaking a puff or two. Gordon must have had an argument with Mom, because she had slept on the couch. When Mom and Dad were together, Dad was always the one who got thrown out of the bedroom. That must mean Gordon had some sort of power over Mom.

When Jett got off the bus and walked the quarter mile up the gravel road, neither Mom nor Gordon was home. That was strange, because Mom had been practically glued to the kitchen for the past couple of weeks. But having the house to herself meant she could light up without worrying about getting caught. She went to her room, put her books away, and took a couple of tokes. Then she put on some tunes—Tommy Keene, *Songs from the Film,* from her mother's eighties collection—and lay back on her bed, grooving to Keene's harmonious and jangling guitar pop. At school, she was all about hard-core Goth glam, but secretly she'd decided songs that basically said "Let's fuck and die" could only get you so far. In fact, the whole Goth thing was getting a little old, and she would probably have outgrown it already if they were still in Charlotte. Here in Solom, though, the look was still an aberration that drew sidelong glances consigning her to an eternity in hell. Plus, it really rammed sand up Gordon's ass, and that was worth a little extra time applying black eyeliner.

Keene was just reaching one of Jett's favorites, "My Mother Looked Like Marilyn Monroe," and her stoned mind adapted it into "My Mother Looked Like Marilyn Manson." Maybe Weird Al Yankovich could do that one sometime.

She reached over to turn the CD player up a notch when she saw the man in the black hat through her window, standing by the barn. He motioned to her, his waxy fingers stiff. The hat shaded his face, but the lower part of his chin showed over the collar of his wool jacket. His skin was the color of clabbered milk.

Jett thought the best plan of action was to get in bed and hide her head under the pillows. If Gordon were here, she could point out the man and say, "See, I told you I wasn't losing it." Except part of her was afraid that Gordon, like the kids in her class, wouldn't be able to see him. That would serve as proof to Gordon that Jett needed a good, long stretch in the nutter wing of Faith Hospital in Boone. Lockdown wouldn't keep away the man in the black hat, though; hallucinations had a way of ignoring doors and windows.

Jett was about to turn away when the man tilted his head to look up at the window. More of the face was revealed, a dark line of lips, sunken cheeks. The fingers moved again, beckoning. Jett shook her head.

The man began walking toward the house, moving with brittle steps. The grass wilted where his shadow fell. When he reached the fence, he didn't climb over or slow down. Instead, he seemed to pass *through* the wire, though at no time did he appear transparent.

Jett turned over her racing thoughts, trying to find something important. She hadn't locked the front door. But who was she kidding? If it passed through wire, a door would be no problem. She could dial 911, but then what would she say? A cheese-faced dude in creepy clothes was breaking into the house?

She could hide. But where? The house was old and rambling, but it didn't have any hidden passageways or bookcases disguising secret rooms. She could hide in the linen closet, but that would be the first place he would look.

The attic. When they'd moved in, Gordon had asked her to put some of her summer clothes away. She and Mom had sorted them, stuck a few stinky mothballs in the boxes, and tucked them into the dusty space above the linen closet. Jett hadn't gone into the attic, just set the boxes around the edges of the access hole. But she'd gotten the vauge impression of a large, cluttered space, with old furniture and stacks of boxes. If the man went up there and found her, she'd be trapped, but she was trapped now, unless she made a run for the back door. The man moved like an arthritic puppet, but that didn't mean he couldn't make his boots drum if necessary.

She hurried down the hall to the closet, the energetic pop music providing an incongruous soundtrack. She climbed the shelves and tugged the string that led to the access, and a little folded ladder appeared as the small door swung open. Jett straightened the ladder and scrambled up, closing the ladder behind her as she went. The access door slammed shut with a creak of springs. The attic was dark, with the only light leaking from ventilation slats at each gabled end of the house.

Jett's heart thudded in her chest, and the marijuana made her aware of the blood pulsing through her body. She paused and listened, wondering if the man had reached the front door yet, and if he was going to enter. All she could hear was the muffled backbeat of the music. She crept deeper into the attic, ducking under the ceiling joists until she came to a cluster of furniture. There she found a pine box that was nearly the size of a coffin, but was obviously a shipping crate of some kind. She lifted the lid, then scooted it to the side, taking care not to make scraping sounds. Any noise she made would likely be audible to the man if he was on the second floor.

When the gap in the lid was wide enough, she felt through the opening to see if the box was empty. Her hand brushed against coarse cloth. There appeared to be room inside, so she climbed in, then slid the lid back into place, hoping the stirred dust didn't make her sneeze. In the blackness of the crate, she could hear the rasping of her breath. It sounded as if she had emphysema, but that must have been an acoustic trick of the confined space. She closed her mouth, forcing stale air through her nose. Still the rasping continued. In her bedroom, the CD ended, and the house was quiet. She wondered if the man's boots would make footsteps, or if he somehow floated over the floor in the same way he drifted through the fence.

Despite her fear, she was still buzzed, and her brain raced frantically. Pot sometimes gave her anxiety, and she thought this would be a real bad time to get claustrophobic. She was wondering how long she would have to hide before the man would give up. He didn't look like the giving-up kind.

Something wriggled beside her, in the pile of clothes. It was probably just the cloth settling from her moving it. Probably. Certainly it wasn't rats.

It wriggled again.

She held her breath, but the rasping went on. A hand touched her arm, or what felt like a hand, though the surface was abrasive. Like a scratchy piece of wool. Her heart jumped against her rib cage and she kicked the lid off.

Jett scrambled out of the crate as the hand grabbed at her leg. She kicked backward in the darkness, and the rasping changed pitch into a low chuckle. A chest of drawers with a mirror was beside her, reflecting the scant light. In the mirror, she saw a shape rising out of the crate. She screamed and ran for the access door, banging her shoulder hard against one of the joists. When she reached the access, she climbed onto it, and the door swung open under her weight, pitching her into the closet. Sparks of pain shot up from her ankle, but she rose to her feet and opened the closet door, fully expecting to come face-to-face with the man in the black hat. But he couldn't be as scary as that chuckling creature in the attic.

The hallway was clear, and Jett made a run for it, hobbling on her gimpy leg.

"Jett?"

Mom was downstairs. Jett ran to the head of the stairs. Mom stood below her, a paper grocery bag in her hand.

"What's going on?" Mom asked.

"Nothing, I was just . . ."

Hiding from a hallucination.

"Your face is pale. Are you running a fever?"

Sure, Mom. Bogeyman fever. "No, I'm okay."

"Did you know you left the front door open?"

I didn't. He did. "Sorry."

"Come on down and help me make dinner. I got a new recipe to try."

Jett descended the stairs, using the banister to keep the weight off her injured ankle. She checked rooms as she passed, wondering if the man in the black hat was going to get two people for the price of one. But he wasn't in the house. Assuming he'd even existed in the first place.

Chapter Twenty-one

Sue Norwood had spent the morning doing inventory. Winter was not a big merchandise deal in Solom, and the kayak rentals all but died as the weather got colder. She normally took December off, though she'd thought about starting up a cross-country skiing racket and see if she could get the Floridians to bite. Trouble was, most of them took off at the first frost. Besides, the end of the year was a time to start lining up tax deductions.

Today she'd only had three customers: a scruffy college kid who purchased a North Face sleeping bag, a housewife who popped in for a two-dollar tube of Wounded Warrior all-purpose healing salve, and a big-boobed blonde with a flat tire on her ten-speed. Sue noted that the Everharts hadn't turned in their rental bikes during the night.

She was patching a split seam in a kayak with fiberglass and epoxy when the bell over the door rang. She figured it was the Everharts, limping in sore and tired. "Hello?" she called from her work area in the corner of the shop.

"Miss Norwood?"

"Odus? Come on back, I've got a mess on my hands."

Odus Hampton wasn't really a regular, though he occasionally bought some fishing hooks or monofilament line. She sometimes hired him for heavy work if big shipments came in, and he was happy to work for store credit. He had taught her a lot about the river, and she'd taken him out in a canoe a few times so he could show her the currents, falls, and rough patches. She had offered to hire him as a river guide, but he wasn't interested in steady work, though he'd filled in a few times when Sue was under the weather. She trusted his outdoor experience, partly because he camped out for most of the summer, even though he did it on the cheap, without a Coleman lantern, mosquito netting, or a pair of steel-toed Herman Survivor boots.

"Busted a boat?" Odus said. "You ain't been crazy enough to take that out on the river? The water's probably forty degrees."

"I'm getting it ready for spring. This is the only time I have to catch up. Did you go fishing today?"

Odus shook his head, his full beard brushing the tops of his overalls. "The fish won't be biting."

"I thought they always bit for you." The fumes from the epoxy were giving her a headache.

"Not when the water's tainted."

"What's wrong with the water? Did it get contaminated?" The Blackburn River had been designated a national scenic river, and President Clinton had even given a speech there. No factories or major commercial farms lay along its banks, and the headwaters sluiced down from largely undeveloped mountains. If Sue had suspected problems with water quality, she'd have screamed for Greenpeace, the Southern Environmental Defense League, the local branch of the Democrat Party, such as it was, and the North Carolina Department of Environment and Natural Resources. Clean water was money, just like scenic beauty was money. A lot of mountain communities were selling out their slopes to millionaires who built garish houses, and change was inevitable, but Sue planned on Solom's not going to hell until she was ready to retire.

"It ain't what's *in* the water. It's what's *got* the water," Odus said.

"Don't scrunch up your eyes that way. Makes me worry."

"Maybe you ought to."

"Talk to me plain. This isn't one of your legends, is it? The kind you tell for money?"

"You're not from Solom, so you won't understand."

"I'm as much a part of this place as I'll ever be."

"All right, then." Odus's eyes roamed over the store and settled on the bike rack. "You got two bikes out."

"Yeah, a couple rented them yesterday and hasn't turned them back in yet. I figure they pulled a few muscles and are lying in bed trying to recuperate."

"Where were they going?"

"They didn't say, but they headed east up the river road."

"I think I'll run my truck up that way and have a look."

"Do I need to call them? They left their cell phone number on the deposit slip."

"It's probably nothing. Just some odd goings-on got me a little spooked."

Sue looked up the number and punched it in on her phone. A monotone female voice came on the line and informed her that service to the number was unavailable. "This valley's got more dead spots than a cemetery," Sue said.

"You got that right," Odus said. "If you see any strangers, keep a close eye on them."

"I like strangers. They usually have money in their pockets."

"Not the one I'm talking about."

"Damn it, Odus, why do you have to be so mysterious? Why don't you just come out and say it?"

"Because you'll think I'm drunk. Or worse."

Sue nodded in agreement. "You got me on that one."

"We're having a meeting at the general store after closing time. Come over and you'll find out more than you want to know."

"Sure. It's not like I got anything better to do."

Sue followed Odus to his truck, checking out the river where it made a gentle bend below the store. She'd built a small ramp leading into the water to serve as a launch for canoes and kayaks. A patch of brambles, stalks of Joe Pye weed, and tangled polkweed stirred along the riverbank. The yellowed vegetation parted, and a goat's head emerged. The animal's horns caught the autumn afternoon light and gleamed like a couple of bad teeth.

"Hell of a lot of goats around here lately," Odus said through his open window. The engine wheezed to diseased life, throwing a clot of blue smoke into the air.

"Should I call the police about the bikers?"

"Solom likes to take care of its own."

That's the trouble, Sue thought, as Odus guided the truck down the road between the post office and the general store.

Sarah watched Odus drive by in his Blazer. If only he didn't have to stir things up. Just like a Hampton. Back in her father's day, a branch of the Hamptons had operated a gristmill and feed store on the back side of the mountain. When the state paved the roads in the 1930s, people found it was easier to drive into Titusville and buy their cornmeal and flour than to pay to have their own crops ground. The general store had lost some business as well, but her father had expanded with the times, going for cigars, candy, and pulp magazines. The Hamptons stuck to tradition and tradition left them busted. The gristmill still stood by a silver creek, like the bones of a dinosaur that had died standing up and was too dumb to fall over. The Hamptons had retreated back up into the hills, selling off their land, and generally ending up like Odus, either drunk or living hand-to-mouth.

Sarah changed with the times, too, and times lately had gone deep into the contrary. She had convinced herself she hadn't seen the Circuit Rider, but Odus wouldn't let her hold on to that pleasant deception. And Gordon Smith's wife had been in today, buying the oddest assortment of goods the shelves could conjure. The last person to shop so impulsively had been Gordon's first wife, Rebecca, that pretty, black-haired gal with dimples. Rebecca was magic in the kitchen, and every fund-raiser in the park or volunteer fire department potluck brought out a few of her finest offerings. It was a terrible tragedy for her to run off the road like that. The emergency responders had stopped in the next day for Dr Peppers and a pack of Camels and told Sarah all the gruesome details. The car had rolled, and Rebecca's head had been sliced clean off, her body bruised as if she'd been beaten with hammers. It was a closed-casket funeral. Sarah thought at the time the Jews had it right by burying their dead on the same day, the better to get it over with and move on.

A stack of cans fell over in the back corner of the store. It was the area where she kept the number 10 cans of vegetables, product that moved so slowly the cans often had flecks of rust before someone bought them. She grabbed the broom, determined to addle the brains of any mouse that might be causing trouble. The store was empty of customers, not that unusual for midmorning.

She moved past the black metal woodstove in the center of the store and through a few mismatched tables where the lunch crowd could enjoy their deli sandwiches. A sprinkle of black spots appeared before her eyes, but she told herself she wouldn't pass out again. She'd rather go down with a stroke than have Odus Hampton haul her to the hospital again. Shelves on each side of her were packed with jelly jars, mountain crafts, floral arrangements, mass-produced folk art, motor oil, tire chains, boxes of cookies, assorted screws, Thanksgiving table settings, dinner candles, rubber gloves, and mousetraps. She figured her store was as general as they came, and she held to a pet theory that customers were more apt to buy things they didn't want if they had to hunt hard for the things they did.

She turned the corner between the Coca-Cola cooler and a rack of picture postcards and came face-to-face with a goat. It must have been a wether, because she hadn't smelled it. Billies liked to piss all over themselves when they were in rut, and they didn't smell too good any other time, either. She'd never owned goats, though she sold stakes, chains, and collars for people who liked to use them as cheap lawn mowers. Sarah didn't have any particular grudge against goats, but she didn't want one messing around in her store.

"How did you get in here, you knothead?" she said. Good question, one the goat didn't answer. The back door was locked and Sarah had been standing by the front door for at least the last half hour.

The goat's mouth worked in that peculiar sideways twist, and Sarah looked around to see if it had chewed into any of the birdseed sacks. The floor was clean, but the billy was busy cudding up *something*. Sarah knelt and peered, not trusting her ancient eyes. She owned glasses but always left them by the register. Red specks dotted the animal's lips, and a pink strand of drool ran down the crusty beard.

"I can't tell what you're eating, but it damn well better not be my pickled beets." Sarah swept the broom around and gently swatted the goat on the shoulder. "Now get on out of here."

The goat continued chewing as if relishing a palmful of artichoke hearts. Avoiding the curled horns, Sarah moved beside the animal and slammed the straw end of the broom against the goat's rump. The billy looked at her out of its nearest eye, and Sarah saw a small version of herself in the rectangular pupil. The reflection looked scared.

"Get on, get on," she said, her voice nearly breaking. Because now something was crunching inside the animal's mouth, like peanut shells. She delivered one more blow, and the goat took a few steps down the aisle, hooves scruffing over the hardwood floor. It looked back at her and seemed to grin before it headed to the front of the store, pushed open the door with its horns, and sauntered off the porch.

Odus had scheduled a little meeting here tonight to discuss the strange carryings-on, and Sarah wondered if she would tell what she had just seen. Dangling between the goat's ochre teeth had been a dark, wet string that looked for all the world like a mouse's tail.

Jett wasn't hungry, despite the lingering effect of the munchies that pot usually caused. Mom had laid out quite a spread, with a casserole, roast beef, butternut squash, and a coconut cream pie for dessert. Mom had never made a pie in Jett's whole life, if you didn't count those that came out of a Sara Lee package. Gordon ate with hardly a word, stuffing his face and washing the food down with goblets of red wine.

"How was your day?" Mom finally asked him, like a zombie mom out of some dippy sitcom.

"Departmental meeting," Gordon said. "The dean's pressuring us to get more articles published."

"Isn't your book good enough to satisfy him?"

Gordon set down his wineglass hard enough to clink. "Nobody cares about Appalachian religion anymore. The old churches are dying out. Foot washings, tent revivals, creek baptisms, it just seems like a bunch of superstitious nonsense to my peers. But why should they think any differently? The faculty's from Boston, Berkeley, Tallahassee, and Detroit. They know more about the thousand Hindu gods than they know about their own backyard."

"Now, dear, I'm sure your work is appreciated."

Jett was freaking. Mom had never called her dad "dear." Jett had to shove some pie in her mouth to keep from gasping in disbelief. She had to admit, the pie was pretty awesome.

"They don't understand the importance of the church in Solom's history." Gordon pushed away his dinner plate and started on the pie. He raised one eyebrow in pleasure. "I'm impressed."

"Just an old family recipe," Mom said.

"I didn't know we *had* any old family recipes," Jett said.

"Sure, honey. It's about time you started taking on a bigger share of the kitchen work. After all, you'll be a woman soon."

"More chores," Gordon said. "That's what builds character. Hard work will keep you out of trouble. Speaking of which, you'll need to feed the goats after dinner."

"In the barn?" Jett looked at mom. Mom wore a faint smile, her lips stiff like those of someone sitting for a painting.

Gordon focused on the last of his pie, shoveling it down in gooey white lumps. He scraped his fork across the plate and licked it clean. "Sure. Just throw down a couple of bales from the loft. The grass isn't growing as fast with winter coming on."

"But it's almost dark."

"There's a flashlight in the hall closet."

"What about the man—"

Gordon looked at her, his eyes like lumps of cold coal behind his lenses. "What man?"

"Never mind."

"It's a rite of passage," Gordon said. "If you're going to live on the farm, you're part of the farm. Persephone's about to go back to Hades and winter's on its way."

"Who is Persephone?" Jett didn't really want to sit through a lecture, but figured she might as well stall for time.

"Persephone was the daughter of Demeter and Zeus in Greek mythology. Hades, the king of the Underworld, fell in love with her and dragged her to his realm. Demeter, who was goddess of the harvest, was angered and hurt. She punished the world through cold winds and freezing weather."

"Sounds like a bummer for all concerned."

"Especially the poor humans, who thought they had lost Demeter's favor. Hades eventually agreed to let Persephone come up to the world for half the year, giving us spring and summer."

"Why didn't Persephone just run away?"

"Because she had fallen in love with Hades."

"Some people just fall in love with the wrong person," Jett said, giving Mom a bloodshot stare. Mom smiled.

"Okay, chores now," Gordon said. "Just don't try to sneak a puff of drugs while you're out there. I know what that stuff smells like. Those hippies in East Dorm crank it out like a steam train."

"Mom?" Jett looked to her mom for any sign of concern, but Mom could just as easily have been watching television on the dining room wall. Jett had almost blurted out to Mom about seeing the man in the black hat, or being touched by the scarecrow guy in the attic, but she hadn't, and now it would sound like the ultimate case of crying wolf. Or else the rantings of a deranged dope fiend. Besides, she didn't want Gordon to get one over on her. She'd show the bastard, even if it killed her.

Well, maybe that was a little extreme. Stoner paranoia. She pushed her pie away and went to the closet, finding the flashlight and shrugging into her favorite studded jean jacket. "If I'm not back in fifteen minutes, tell them my merry-go-round broke down," she said.

Gordon paused with his goblet to his lips. "Some kind of drug slang?"

"A Tommy Keene reference. Get it, Mom?"

Mom gave a Stepford grin. "No, dear. Who is Tommy Keene?"

Freaky.

Before Jett could dwell on the shadowy man who no doubt awaited her, she burst out the front door, gripping the flashlight as if it were a billy club. "Don't let Hades come up and grab you," Gordon hollered after her.

She should have told Gordon to go take a flying fuck at his precious goats. Maybe a good, old-fashioned blowup would shatter the creepy little drama stage that the Smith house had become, maybe even yank Mom out of Stepford mode. If Jett and Gordon got into a knock-down, drag-out, surely Mom would take her side. Wouldn't she?

Dusk was settling in the east as she made her way to the barn, the sky gone as purple as a Goth's eyeliner. Crickets chirruped in the cool night air, but the forests were still. The lights of a few houses cast solid sparks against the darkening slopes, but they seemed miles away. The creek gurgled like a hundred men with cut throats.

I can do this, she thought as she opened the gate. *I can feed Shadrach and Nebuchednezzer and whatever the fuck else Gordon named them, then walk back in the house whistling. That way I can score points on Gordon. I won't let that fucker win.*

She shuddered as she walked through the spot where she'd seen the man in the black hat earlier, when he'd lifted his hand and waved those cheese-colored, stiff fingers. She thumbed on the light and played the beam in front of her, watching for piles of goat goodies. She reached the barn without incident, and took a last, longing look at the lights of the Smith house before she entered. Part of her expected to see Mom at the kitchen window, watching after her, but all the curtains were drawn.

Figured. Mom was Gordon's now, for whatever reason. This seemed like something Jett was supposed to do alone. So much for getting through things together.

She had to throw all her weight against the barn door to slide it open, the little wheels creaking in their metal track. Her ankle throbbed like a sore tooth. The inside of the barn was nearly pitch-black, the chicken-wired windows leaking the last of the dying daylight. The odor of manure, animal hair, and straw filled her nose and nearly made her sneeze. The goats must still have been in the fields, because the bottom floor appeared empty. She played the cone of light over the stairs. The scarecrow was in its usual place, hanging from a wire tied to a fat nail. Straw bulged from the seams in the clothes, and the cheesecloth face was expressionless. As the flashlight beam swept slowly over the wall, Jett paused. The wicked-looking sickle was gone.

Something stirred just outside the barn, and Jett told herself the goats had decided it was feeding time. She went up the stairs, carefully adjusting her weight with each step to protect her sprained ankle. The wood groaned and squeaked like a beast with an arthritic spine. The door leading to the loft was shut, with the hasp in place, but the lock hadn't been snapped. Just like the first time she'd seen the man in the black hat. Or the scarecrow creature. Or the abominable fucking snowman.

If she'd even seen anything at all.

To hell with it, just get it over with.

She could hear the goats milling below, calling out in anxious voices with their peculiar bleats. They must have been out in the barnyard the whole time, as if expecting her. It seemed crazy, but it sounded like there were lots more of them. They had somehow multiplied in number in the last couple of days.

What was it the Bible said? Be fruitful and multiply? Did that apply to goats or just to people? I'll have to ask Gordon. Strike that. I could never ask Gordon anything that would make him even more fucking smug than he already is.

Jett eased into the loft, her footfalls hushed by the scattered hay. The air was as thick as snuff, and golden motes spun lazily in the flashlight's beam. The bales were on the far end of the loft, and even dry, they weighed about forty pounds each. She couldn't lift them, especially not while holding the flashlight. She rested the light in the crotch of an angled support beam so that it cast a spotlight on the area in which she would be working. She grabbed a bale by the twin strands of twine and yanked it toward the hole in the floor of the loft. She should have worn gloves. The twine gave her rope burns and cut into her palms. By the time she'd dragged the first bale over the square hole and shoved it to the nattering creatures below, her palms were wet with blood.

The animals drummed their hooves on the packed earthen floor of the barn, thumping against each other in their lust for hay. She wondered if Fred was down there, the one who had eaten her stash the day before. Maybe the next bale would fall on him and break his frigging neck. She had dragged the next bale halfway to the hole when the flashlight fell to the floor, bounced, and went out.

Shit damn almighty Jesus on a toothpick.

Jett was so pissed off, she forgot to be afraid. For at least three seconds. Then she heard the soft shuffling of rag feet on the floorboards, and a whispering rush that was too small to be the wind, though it was loud enough to carry over the bleating goats. She backed away, toward the opening on the far end through which the bales were loaded into the loft. She tripped and fell into a suffocating stack of hay, kicking and choking until she scrambled to her feet, awaiting the embrace of flannel arms, the crush of a cheesecloth face against her cheek, the singing of a grinning sickle as it swept in a grim harvest.

She felt nothing, though, only the sickening pull of gravity as she slammed against the loading bay door. It gave way before her, spitting her out into the moist darkness with its faint dusting of stars. She fell, spinning as awkwardly as a merry-go-round broke down, and, even if she had thought to scream, she wouldn't have had time.

Nothing like dying to kill a good buzz, she thought, then had no thoughts at all.

Chapter Twenty-two

Sarah didn't know what to make of this little get-together. She'd locked the front door, but didn't rightly know whether she was more afraid of whatever was outside or the people inside and of what they might tell her. Odus had made the invites, so he had pretty much staked a claim to being the leader of the bunch. The Chesterfield clock above the door showed a quarter till ten, nearly her bedtime, but she had a feeling she wouldn't be sleeping tonight.

She brought a full coffeepot to the table as Odus laid a fire in the woodstove. The general store had no insulation in the floor, and the weather had turned colder with sunset, an arctic air mass making an early entry from the Northwest. Ray Tester slouched on a bench, his brother David sitting erect, his elbows on the table as if he were about to pray. Lillian Rominger dealt cheese crackers from a cellophane pack and crunched them, the only sound in the room besides the crackling fire. Lillian's right hand was swathed in gauze and tape. Sue Norwood stood to one side, playing with a wind chime, not far from where the mouse-munching goat had passed not more than four hours ago.

"Come have a seat, Miss Norwood," Sarah said. "Got some drip grind right here."

"Half off?" Odus asked with a crooked grin.

"I'll take half off your head if you keep talking like this. We're supposed to be serious."

Sue sat beside David, in one of the wooden-slatted chairs with uneven legs. The preacher nodded to her. Sarah set a Styrofoam cup in front of her and filled it before Sue could say whether or not she wanted some. When all the cups were full, she put the coffeepot on top of the woodstove and sat at the table with the others. Odus tossed a splintery chunk of locust into the stove and closed the cast-iron mouth, then stood and looked around the dining area.

"I reckon we all know each other," Odus said. "So let's just get right to it. The plain truth of it is Harmon's come back to Solom and all hell's about to break loose."

Ray shook his head. "You've been in the bourbon. Only a drunk would talk like that."

"He's here."

"Harmon Smith is dead and planted, long gone to dust. That's just an old wives' tale."

"Speaking of wives, then, where's yours?"

Ray shut up at that, but Sue cut in with, "Who is Harmon Smith?"

"The Circuit Rider," David said. "Some call him the man in the black hat or the horseback preacher. He rode these mountains in the early 1800s as a Methodist, set him up a homestead and a garden. He was a little touched in the head, though, and started bucking the Methodist beliefs, turned to sacrificing animals in the Old Testament fashion. They say he was murdered on a mountain trail one night. Some believe it was fellow Methodists who did him in, others say it was the ones who began to follow his ways."

"I reckon they figured if animal sacrifice made God happy, then offering up a human ought to do wonders," Odus said. "But he didn't stay dead."

"Sounds like so much horseshit to me," Ray said.

"There are ladies present," David said. Ray turned away.

"Don't hold back on my account," Sarah said. She ought to jump in and confess that she'd seen the Circuit Rider. After all, David was a preacher, even if he believed a messiah had already come and gone in this world, and Catholics said confession was good for the soul. But the words wouldn't leave her lips. She'd heard the local legends all her life, but had never put too much stock in them. Jews had their dybbuks and golems, but nowhere did men of God ever come back from the dead to bring suffering to the living.

But *had* the Circuit Rider brought suffering? In all the stories she'd heard, the man had done nothing more than appear, like the Virgin Mary on a grilled cheese sandwich, or the devil in the clouds of those mocked-up photos that graced the cover of the *Weekly World News*. Sure, some claimed he caused calamity and death, but plain bad luck could account for a lot of the mishaps.

What had the man said to her? *I'm back*. Like it was neither a brag nor a threat, just a plain fact.

"It's one of those things where you need to make believers out of people," Odus said. "No offense, Elder David, but your branch of Baptists don't go in for conversion."

Sue raised her hand, like the new student in a grade school class. "Sorry, folks, but I don't get any of this, and I'm not sure why I'm here."

Odus nodded, went around the middle aisle to the dry goods section, and returned stooped over, rolling a battered ten-speed. The wheels wobbled, the chain dragged the floor, and the seat cushion was gouged and pocked. It looked as if it had been trampled by a herd of elephants. "Recognize this?"

"That's one the Everharts rented."

"Found it on Switchback Trail, off in the laurels. No sign of the couple, just a bunch of scuffed leaves by the creek. But there was *this*." Odus held up a small flashlight that appeared to have dried blood on the handle.

"I told you we should have called the cops," Sue said.

"What for?" Odus said. "This is Solom's problem. It's our job to take care of it. Besides, what would we tell them? That a man two hundred years dead has come back to square things with them that did him in?"

"Hold on," Lillian said. "You don't think this is supernatural, do you?"

"I just know what I seen. What about you, Elder David?"

David lowered his eyes. The stove popped in the gap of silence, and the long stovepipe ticked with rising heat. Hickory smoke that had escaped during the igniting of the fire now settled in a blue-gray layer five feet off the floor. Sarah wished she had a chore, another pot of coffee, or a round of sandwiches to give out on the house.

"Sarah?" Odus challenged her, his blue eyes piercing hers, somehow harder to meet since they weren't bloodshot. "You saw him, didn't you?"

Sarah looked at the counter, and the glass pickle jar by the register with the change in it. The jar held donations for Rupert Walpole, a retired postal carrier who had developed cancer of the larynx. As if a few dollars could make any difference once the cancer dug its claws into you. Just like the Circuit Rider had wormed his way back into Solom's heart. "He came in, all right," she said. "Walked right to the cash register like he was born here and knew every inch of this community. How can that be, if he's been dead all this time?"

Ray gave a rat-squeak of laughter. "Tell us, Brother David. I bet you got it all figured out, with your Bible and your big words. You're the one who's big on believing things you can't see."

"I haven't seen him," David said. "But something strange is going on here."

Lillian stood up. "I'm sorry, David. This is getting too wacky for me. I need to get home."

"And do what, Lillian?" David said. "Tend to your goats?" He nodded at her wounded hand. "*Feed* them?"

Lillian sat. Sarah felt sorry for her. She was one of the imports, an alien invader, but they were all tourists when you got right down to it, even the ones who were born here. First came the buffalo, then the Cherokee came after the buffalo, then the Virginia hunters came after the buffalo, then the buffalo were gone and the Cherokee were gone and the hunters were driven off by the settlers who squatted in these hills. Then came people like Harmon Smith to save them, and he was driven into his grave, and came the wagon trains and the railroad and the Model T and Jewish merchants and a post office, then a bed-and-breakfast, a rental-cabin retreat, a bunch of summer people, and it seemed like everything just kept pushing and pushing until the place called Solom was ripe for something like Harmon Smith. Something that would make the whole crazy cycle complete, knock this little Appalachian valley back to the way God intended from the beginning. "I guess that brings us to the goats," Sarah said.

"I saw one," Sue said. "Down by the river. It must have got out of its fence."

"One of them bit Lillian, then chased us into her house," David said. "It would be funny if it wasn't so gosh-darned creepy."

"They been breeding like rabbits this year," Odus said, letting the bike rest against a chain-saw sculpture. "Seems like everybody's got a herd, and they're acting more ornery than usual."

"Found four goat heads in my hayfield," Ray said. "Figured it was kids playing tricks, or else some pissed-off neighbor trying to gum up my bush hog."

"Speaking of neighbors, why ain't Gordon Smith here?" Sarah said, determined not to mention the goat she'd found in the store earlier.

"Gordon don't take kindly to talk about the Circuit Rider," Odus said. "It's his kin, after all."

"Well, he's got the biggest goat herd on this side of the county. If anything funny's going on with the animals, he'd probably know about it."

"I was over mending fence for him last week." Odus moved over by the woodstove. "He told me a few of his nannies would go into rut this week. His eyes got all faraway when he said it, like there was a mountain somewhere that needed climbing. And his scarecrow . . . well, never mind about that."

"His wife was in today, looking like she'd swallowed a happy pill," Sarah said.

"Remember the last time the goats got uppity?" Ray said.

"Yeah," Odus said. "Right before Gordon's first wife got killed in that car wreck."

"Shit," Ray said. "You don't reckon Gordon Smith has gone wacko and decided to take up Harmon's old ways, do you?"

"No matter what they say about Harmon Smith, he was a man of God," David said. "I just can't believe God would send anything to his earth unless there was a good reason."

"God don't need no devil, does He?" Ray taunted. "He's done

decided who's going to heaven, so what's the point? Ain't that what you're preaching to the flock, Brother?"

"You ought to come to a service once in a while," David said. "Might do you good to get down on your knees and wash somebody's feet."

"Save the family feud for later and let's worry about the Circuit Rider," Odus said. "I ain't ever been sure whether Jesus Christ is going to return or not, but I know for a fact that Harmon Smith has."

"Do you think he—or it, whatever *it* is—killed the Everharts?" Sue asked.

"I don't know." Odus stroked his beard, picked something from the hairs, and stared at it. "Might be he's setting things right, as he sees it. The Everharts ain't from Solom. Or it might have something to do with the goats."

Lillian took her coffee cup away from her lips. The white rim was ragged, and the perfect imprint of her teeth showed where she'd been biting into the Styrofoam. "Well, even if we accept what you're saying, and we've got a vengeful preacher in our midst, what in the world are we supposed to do about it?"

"That's what this meeting's about," Odus said. "Any ideas?" He looked around the room.

Sarah shook her head. She was determined not to get dragged into this mess. Who cared if goats wandered her aisles and a stranger in black stopped by once in a while? As long as her routine didn't change, and the Circuit Rider didn't do away with her best customers, she was willing to live and let live. If such a thing applied to dead people.

"I guess this isn't a garlic-and-crucifix kind of thing, is it?" Sue asked. "I mean, nobody's come up with a mythology. I'd almost rather have a vampire or werewolf, something that had rules."

"You're the Bible guy," Odus said to David. "What do you make of it?"

"Harmon Smith seemed to follow some of the Celtic ideas of harvest sacrifice," David said. "Gordon probably knows more about that than anybody, since he teaches it at the college."

"Well, you work for him," Ray said. "Anything peculiar going on at the Smith place?"

"He's been mighty riled up about his scarecrow," Odus said. "Muttering strange stuff under his breath and tending to his goats."

"Every religious figure needs a flock," Lillian said. "Without Moonies, Sun Myung Moon would be just another businessman."

"Moon do what?" Ray said.

"The leader of the Unification Church," she said. "He has a church in Washington, D.C., and owns a ton of real estate and international newspapers. The conspiracy theorists believe Moon has his mouth whispering in the ear of our politicians while his fingers are slipping cash into their back pockets. Some say even the president is an ally."

"Now don't you be knocking George Dubya," Ray said. "The worst thing that ever happened to Solom was letting Democrats come in. If Clinton was a Jew, he'd have been the Antichrist."

Sarah didn't rise to the bait, though she made a mental note of his remark. Her father had changed the family name from Jaffe to Jeffers before moving to Solom. She'd never made a big deal about being Jewish, though she was the only one in the valley, though so many summer people had built homes here that some were bound to be Jewish. She wasn't all that religious, anyway, and she sold plenty of knickknacks that featured Bible verses or pictures of a snow-white Christ.

All she knew about the Moonies was from the *Guinness Book of World Records*, where they set the record for the number of people married at one time. Out of the thousands, most of them were strangers. Well, she supposed your odds of getting divorced were about the same as whether you thought you were in love. She'd been in love a couple of times, and in something close enough to it a few other times, and they'd all ended up the same.

"Maybe the goats tie in with fertility and harvest," David said. "The more you sacrifice, the more they multiply. The Old Testament sacrifices were all about pleasing God. It's the same with most religions, whether you're lighting candles, taking communion, shaving your head, or offering food."

"All I know is the billy goats don't like it when you talk about gelding them," Lillian said, holding up her injured hand.

"Hold on a minute, folks," Sue said. "I can accept that the Circuit Rider is real. After all, every legend has a basis in fact. And

I'll even buy that goats are evil. I mean, with those creepy eyes and cloven hooves, how could anybody think otherwise? And let's assume 'its hour come round,' as the Yeats poem goes, and Solom is our backwoods Bethlehem. After all, the battle of Armageddon has to start somewhere. The question is, what do we do about it?"

They all looked at each other, except Lillian, who was staring into the bottom of her coffee cup as if the answer were spelled out there. "I reckon we have to find a way to take down the Circuit Rider," Odus said. "We have to figure out what he wants, then give it to him and make him go away."

"What if he wants us all to suffer like starving dogs on a slow trip to hell?" Ray said.

"Revenge," David said. "He might hold the people of Solom responsible for his death, and his spirit can't rest in peace."

"Maybe he's looking for his horse," Lillian offered.

"What I think," Odus said, "and I can't blame him because I kind of feel the same way, and I've only been here thirty-eight years instead of two hundred, is he's come to clean house. If he's really been around all this time, he's probably sick of flatlanders coming up here and building on our ridgetops, crowding the valley with their SUVs and bluegrass festivals, flushing their shit in the river. I'd bet he's just homesick, and since it looks like God won't let him into heaven and the devil doesn't have the room to spare, old Harmon's stuck here and decided to take on Solom as a fixer-upper."

"And he's doing it by killing tourists?" Sue said.

"Well, he's been killing us for years and years," Odus said. "Maybe he's decided he needs to hurry things along now, because of all the growth. So he goes after the rest of us, probably trimming back to the handful of families that were around when he first came to Solom."

"The only problem with that theory is he's a tourist just like the rest of us," David said. "You can't turn back the clock."

"You can't come back from the dead, either."

Sarah suddenly felt all alone, even in the presence of company. She imagined the general store under the great, crushing weight of night. Despite the ticking woodstove, a chill settled into her brittle bones. Darkness pressed against the window, and the porch light did little to scare it off. Black was every color rolled into one, they said, and when everything bled together it made just the one color, the absence of light. And it looked like there was going to be plenty of bleeding going on.

A clatter arose from the front of the store, near the register. She'd turned off the lights as she usually did at closing time, and the corners of the store were cloaked in shadows.

"Who's there?" she said. Nobody could have broken in without her hearing. But somehow the goat had passed through these walls, and a man who could command goats and defy the grave probably wouldn't be considerate enough to knock. Besides, he'd already paid her a visit once.

The Circuit Rider stepped into the light. He held a pack of Beechnut chewing tobacco in his hand, and as they watched, he slowly peeled the foil pack open and shoved a moist wad into his mouth, shreds of the dark tobacco dribbling down his chin to the floor. The brim of his hat was turned low, but the bottom half of his face was waxen and milk-colored, not as ghostly as when Sarah had first seen him. His mouth was filled with broad, blunt teeth, like those of a grazing animal.

"Put it on my tab, Sarah," he said, grinding the tobacco with his jaws, his voice cob-rough and deep.

"What business you got here in Solom?" said Odus, the first of them to recover.

"No business, just pleasure," he said.

A whinny came from outside, near the front of the store. The Circuit Rider plucked a Macintosh apple out of a bushel basket. He polished it against the sleeve of his black wool jacket. "There's pleasure in the fruits of your labors."

Lillian spilled her coffee and Odus backed up until he bumped into the woodstove. David had risen half out of his chair and stood there, bent over as if he'd been flash-frozen. Sarah thought about the shotgun under the cash register, but it was still covered by newspapers.

"Nice of you folks to hold this little get-together for my sake," he said.

"We don't want nothing from you," Odus said. "We just want to be left alone. We're willing to let you rest in peace."

"Love your enemies, right, Elder David? Bless those who curse you, do good to those who hate you." The Circuit Rider gave a laugh that held no humor, with just the hint of a hell wind behind it. He shot a thick stream of tobacco onto the pine floorboards, causing Sarah to wince. Touching the brim of his hat, he dipped his head slightly, as if nodding to the ladies.

"Sorry to rush off, but I have work waiting in the orchards of life," he said. He went to the door, his boots loud on the wood, then opened it and went outside, merging into the darkness from which he'd come. From which they all had come, and to which they were inevitably bound.

Hooves thundered down the asphalt road, and the six people sat in silence, afraid to give words to their fear. Eventually, Sarah went to get a rag and mop up the tobacco juice. By the time she reached the spot by the register, the dark stain had vanished, as elusive as the creature that had left its mark.

Chapter Twenty-three

Katy was elbow-deep in dirty dishes when the back door swung open. Gordon must have forgotten to lock it, and the wind was picking up, skating leaves against the side of the house, sending cold air against her bare legs. She realized with a start that she wasn't wearing panties, and she must have changed into the autumnal-print dress sometime after dinner. She put a soapy hand to her forehead. What was happening to her memory?

The wind skirled the pantry curtains. The pantry. What about it? Something had happened in there. Not just broken pickle jars and hidden recipes, but a secret as old as the Smiths.

Yeah, sure, sounds pretty melodramatic.

But she was attuned to melodrama. After all, she'd married a man on what amounted to a whim, she'd tossed away her past and her career and settled for a housewife role in a mountain community where the women were valued as good cooks and compliant bed partners. Not that the bed part had been much of a challenge, with Gordon content to fall asleep reading research books while she waited for him to doze so she could masturbate. Something was wrong, a deep part of herself knew, but she was caught up in the small rhythms of daily life and had surrendered herself to them.

Surrender was good, surrender was easy. A man to provide, leaving her free to focus on raising a family . . .

Jett.

She flung the suds from her fingers and went to the back door. Jett should be upstairs studying. Had Gordon sent her out to do chores? Surely not on a night like this, not when Jett was acting so strangely.

She stepped out on the back porch and looked around the farm. The barn made black angles against the purple sunset. A white shape moved beyond the fence, then another. Goats. Gordon's damned goats. She shuddered and stepped inside, drawing the door tight and fastening the dead bolt.

"*Katy.*"

She spun, looking toward the foyer, which was the only other entrance to the kitchen. "Gordon?"

But it couldn't have been Gordon. This was a female. And the voice was near.

Coming from the pantry.

Katy yanked the curtains, nearly pulling down the bar that held the checkered fabric. The smell of crushed lilacs overwhelmed her, intoxicating enough to make her head spin. "Who's there?"

"*Come inside.*" The whisper was an Arctic breeze, a frozen scalpel, a long, cold fingernail down the nape of her neck.

The pantry was empty. Katy wasn't sure whether she was imagining voices or whether a ghost lived in her kitchen. The imaginary voice sounded like a more practical, though possibly more unnerving, option. Because how would a ghost know her name?

A pint jar of stewed tomatoes fell on its side on one of the waist-high shelves, rolling with gritty purpose. Katy reached to catch it, but it slipped between her fingers, shattering on the floor, throwing the seasoned smell of basil and oregano in the air to join the lilac. The sprayed viscera of tomato pulp glistened against the broken glass. Among the wreckage was a metal object, smeared red by the juice.

Katy knelt, careful not to cut herself on the glass, and fished out the object. It was a bronze key, pocked by the acid from the tomato juice. She could imagine a ring, or perhaps a measuring spoon, being accidentally dropped into a jar during high-pressure canning, but a key?

"Katy?" This time the voice was Gordon's, booming from the living room. For some reason, Katy felt the key held a secret meant only for her. It was such an obvious metaphor, and she had come to think of the pantry as her domain, part of the kitchen she'd come to love.

"Yes?" She clutched the key in her fist so that it was hidden.

"Where's that daughter of yours?"

"Isn't she upstairs in her room?"

"I didn't hear her come in from feeding the goats. She's probably out there shooting up heroin."

God, how long had it been? She tried to remember Jett going out the front door, but her mind was blank. Considering the stack of dirty dishes and the leftovers being put away, Jett must have been gone at least half an hour. "Will you go check on her?"

"I've got a faculty report to get to the dean tomorrow. Departmental politics."

Katy wiped her hands, opened the odds-and-ends drawer, and slid the key into an envelope of pumpkin seeds. She pulled out a penlight and went out the back door, the wind chilling her bare legs. The goats were gathered at the back side of the barn, probably eating the hay Jett had thrown down from above.

Passing through the gate, she called Jett's name, but the wind and the low murmuring of the goats smothered her voice. The penlight did little against the darkness, and she dreaded climbing the narrow wooden stairs into the loft. The hens clucked uneasily, disturbed in their nests.

"*Just like last time*," came the voice she'd heard in the pantry. Or it might have been the breeze whistling under the eaves of the tin roof.

Just like which last time? Katy thought.

"*The time Jett freaked out, and you found her in the barrel.*"

Maybe she was imagining a voice, but this voice was insistent, and the words tugged at her memory. The door was open, which probably meant Jett was inside. Gordon was a stickler for closing gates and doors, and hammered his point home at every chance. Jett wouldn't have left the door open despite her rebellious streak, because the bitterness of the punishment more than offset the pleasure of the crime.

Though the inside of the barn shielded the bulk of the wind, the open room was cold. She ran the penlight over the wall. The scarecrow hung on its nail, grinning in sleep. The back door was open as well, and the cluster of goats gave off a strong, musky odor. She hesitated, afraid of them, the moon shining on their curled horns.

"Get the fuck away from me, Fred," Jett yelled. She was among the goats, and must have risen to her knees because the top of her head was on level with those of the goats.

Katy ran among the goats, flailing the penlight as if it were a weapon. "Shoo, damn it," she said, pushing at the animals, careful of the flashing horns as the animals bucked and started. There were so many of them. It seemed as if the flock had swelled dramatically in just the last few days. She finally reached Jett and pulled her to her feet, and they backed away from the goats.

The animals fell quiet and still, all eyes on Katy and Jett as they retreated into the barn. The goats stared with interest (*hunger*, thought Katy) until Katy threw her weight against the barn door and it began its groaning path along its track. The goats hesitated, then moved forward as one, not in a rush but with purpose. Katy slammed the door home and took Jett's arm.

"Are you okay, honey? What happened?"

"I fell. I don't know. I saw something up there." Jett's gaping, tear-flooded eyes rolled toward the loft. "The scarecrow . . ."

"The scarecrow's hanging on the wall, honey. See?" Katy directed the light toward the spot near the stairs. The scarecrow was gone.

"Let's get out of here, before the goats come around front."

They linked arms and jogged out of the barn, not stopping to close the door. Let Gordon be pissed. He could come outside and deal with it himself. They were his damned goats, after all.

They reached the gate, and Katy fumbled with the latch. The goats had come around the barn but were not in pursuit. They stood in that mocking, silent way, working their hooves back and forth under the moonlight.

"Jeez, there's so many of them," Jett said.

"I shouldn't have let you come out here alone."

"Mom, I'm freaking out."

"I know, baby. We'll get you tucked in and everything will be all right. We'll get through this together."

"What about the scarecrow? He was walking around, he smiled at me, he—"

"There's no scarecrow, honey."

They headed to the porch, the scent of manure and brown oak leaves riding the wind. Katy looked back at the barn. The goats still watched, their dark noses lifted and ears twitching as if they were awaiting some unspoken command. Katy shivered and led Jett into the house. As soon as the door closed, she was overcome by the scent of lilacs and tomatoes and forgot all about the goats.

Alex surveyed the perimeter from the small glass windows along the front of his house. All clear for now, and Meredith was waiting the night shift at the Ruby Tuesday in Titusville. He finally had time to ponder his encounter of the day before, not distracted by her silly needs.

Goats as government conspiracy. It finally made sense to Alex. That's just how *they* would do it, come at him in the most unpredictable way possible. If only he had an Internet connection, he could go into some of the freedom organization chat rooms and learn from the fighters on the front lines. But he had no doubt the government was tapped into every Web server in the country, and that in big underground caverns near Washington, D.C., FBI agents sat before banks of computers, monitoring every e-mail.

If the government was behind the whole thing, then the man in the black suit must be some sort of genetic freak, the result of a secret experiment gone wrong. The fact that he was prowling near the Eakins compound meant only one thing: *they* were on to him. Four years of tax evasion wasn't that serious of a crime, not when Congress was stealing billions, but it was the principle of the thing. They didn't care about the money, they just didn't want word to get out that the government could be cheated and was therefore vulnerable. What better way to catch your enemy off guard than to come disguised as a backwoods preacher?

Except this preacher had been eaten alive. Even if he was an

FBI agent in disguise, such a stunt took some effort. Maybe *they* had used some sort of hologram. Classic brainwashing technique involved challenging the subject's notion of reality and eventually replacing reality with the desired set of beliefs. Alex nodded to himself, finished twisting a pinkie-sized joint, and lit up. He liked that answer better. Sure, he was paranoid, and like any freethinking man, he had good reason. But he wasn't crazy.

With the joint hanging from lips à la Bogart in *Casablanca*, he made his way to the back room, a space barely larger than a walk-in closet. He unlocked the two Case dead bolts and entered, searching for the candles he kept on an overhead shelf. Lighting one, he stood before his shrine: a wall covered with small arms firepower. His pride and joy was an AKR submachine gun, a favorite deadly toy of the Russian Special Forces that held 160 rounds. Alex had traded four pounds of seedless buds for the short-barreled gun, worth about eight grand on the street. The lethal and compact grace of the gun appealed to him as much as its country of origin. Not that the Russians could be trusted, either, but at least they were more sincere in their oppression.

Then there was the Swiss SIG 510 assault rifle. The good old Swiss claimed neutrality, but during every war of note, the country served as a clearinghouse for whatever loot happened to be pillaged by the victor. The Swiss made their weapons with all the love and precision they invested in their watches and chocolate. With bayonet, the rifle made a nasty but sleek package.

A row of well-polished handguns lay spread across a velvet-covered shelf. A Mauser C-96 was the centerpiece. No hidden arsenal was complete without a piece of German hardware. It was an older model, manufactured between the two World Wars, but it had a heft and sheen that justified its place in the collection, though he'd only been able to procure two ten-round clips for it. The Germans were arguably the most militaristic people in modern history, except perhaps for the Japanese, Montana freedom fighters, and Republican presidents.

He owned an Austrian-made Glock, a weapon currently in favor with police officers, though he preferred the proven accuracy of the Colt Python. Occasionally, Americans mustered up some pride in their craftsmanship, and the Colt had pedigree. The Beretta resulted from a sense of romanticism only, because he'd never bet his life on something Italian, unless it was manicotti or a young Sophia Loren. He owned a few other sidearms, a couple of M-1 practice grenades a staff sergeant had smuggled out of Ft. Bragg, and a Mossberg twenty-gauge shotgun. The collection also included the Pearson Freedom bow, which retailed at around six hundred dollars, unless you happened to be swapping grass for it. As for arrows, he went with Easton, mostly because he'd known a kid named Easton growing up in Chapel Hill. An array of knives completed the collection, though they were mostly for show. Alex wouldn't have invested in all that hardware if he was interested in hand-to-hand combat.

The other walls of the room held posters, antiestablishment stuff, an Abbie Hoffman portrait, psychedelic posters of nothing in particular, an art print of Che Guevara, the Cuban revolutionary who was as famous for his beret as for his celebrity death photos. Richard Nixon, the patron saint of all latter-day paranoiacs, glowered down with his sharp nose and sinister eyebrows.

As he had done in the well-lighted shed where his marijuana grew, Alex sat cross-legged before the wall that held his weapons. He sucked the joint down until it burned his lower lip; then he pinched it out and swallowed the roach. You couldn't leave evidence lying around, not when *they* might be closing in. He shut his eyes and enjoyed the silence, the Python cool in his lap. When the government agents came, he'd be ready.

Chapter Twenty-four

Mose Eldreth turned on the lights in the church, wanting to finish his carpentry work before tomorrow's service. He planned to stain the woodwork he'd installed, then coat it with polyurethane, but didn't want the congregation swooning from the fumes. If there was any swooning going on, he wanted it to be because of the sermon. He had a good one mapped out, based on the book of Revelation. Harmon Smith's return had served as inspiration.

Mose wasn't afraid to be in the church alone at night. The House of the Lord was the best sanctuary a man could hope for, even in uncertain times. *Especially* in uncertain times. Solom Free Will Baptist Church had ended up with a chunk of the Circuit Rider's legacy, in the form of one of the preacher's three graves. Mose didn't know what fate had befallen the Circuit Rider, but legend said preachers from three different congregations had conspired to slay old Harmon out in the woods. Sort of like Brutus and the gang teaming up on Julius Caesar. Like the Bible said, render unto Caesar what is Caesar's, even if it happens to be the business end of a back-stabbing knife.

Odus had tried to lure Mose into meeting with a handful of other people at the general store. Mose didn't see any sense in it.

Especially when he found out the Tester brothers would be there. David Tester's Primitive Baptist beliefs were sending a good two dozen people to hell, because they refused to get on their knees and do what it took to earn salvation. Sure, they'd get down there and wash each other's feet, then think themselves all humble and pure, but they believed it was up to the Lord to determine who was saved from eternal hellfire. By their reckoning, all folks were hopeless of their own accord. Damnedest thing. At least the congregation of the True Light Tabernacle, as slick as they were with their modern Good News Bible and electric organ, knew there was only one path to Glory, and that way was strait and the gate was narrow.

Mose flexed his back. After Odus had left, Mose had run another thirty feet of baseboard. He had a touch of rheumatism, but he wouldn't complain, not in the house of he who had suffered the agonies of the cross. Later, in his own bed, he could dwell on mortal discomforts. For now, he was in sacred service, and his hammer was a tool of the Lord.

As he set the last two nails on a corner piece, the hammer blows reverberated in the rafters. Mose went into the vestry to get the broom and dustpan. He couldn't have the congregation tracking sawdust everywhere, nor sneezing through the sermon. Mose was leaving the vestry when the church's front door banged open. A breeze skirled the sawdust, filling the air with the scent of pine and the night forest outside.

"Odus?" Maybe the man had forgotten a tool or had stopped by to see if Mose needed any more help. Or, more likely, to report on the meeting. Mose didn't want to know what those people thought. The Circuit Rider was beyond any of them. The Circuit Rider had a purpose, just like all of God's creations.

Something stirred outside, low sounds arising from the small cemetery. Mose leaned the broom against the lectern and picked up the hammer, comforted by its weight in his hand. He wasn't exactly afraid of Harmon Smith, but the Lord helped those who helped themselves.

The preacher walked down the aisle, as slow as a reluctant groom. He could use this fear in his sermon tomorrow, drum up some dread and paint an image of the everlasting lake of fire, where those who didn't accept the Lord as savior were doomed to be cast forever. Yes, fear was important, but bravery was a key part of the whole deal, too. The "valley of the shadow" and all that.

"Do not lead us into temptation, but deliver us from evil," he said. Beyond the open door, the night was clear, stars winking on the horizon, those higher up fixed like holes in a black curtain. The trees that crowded the cemetery stood against the wind, leaves scratching at bark. In the gaps of the forest, lesser patches of shadow moved among the trunks. A low fog had arisen, laying a moist gray wreath along the tops of the gravestones.

The mist had a peculiar quality and was different from the usual autumn fogs. Each fall, mountain folks counted the number of late fogs and used them to predict the number of snows due in the coming winter. But fog was supposed to be gray white, and this one had coils of black smut in it. The air stank of rotten eggs.

The fog appeared to be confined to the cemetery, as if laying down a cover so bad business could take place. It was thickest over the spot where pieces of Harmon Smith were buried, the Free Will congregation's share of its long-ago shame and triumph. Except Harmon's murder had been a triumph for the Lord, and worthy of rejoicing over. Why, then, was foul smoke seeping up from the crazy old preacher's grave?

Mose wasn't afraid. Harmon was back in Solom, as regular as a cicada, and he was making the rounds. Only God could say whether Harmon was looking for his horse or going around visiting his final resting places. And God wasn't telling, at least not yet. In Mose's sixty-five years on this good green earth, God hadn't shared a whole lot of the whys and wherefores. All God wanted was belief and faith, and sometimes it didn't seem to matter to him how he kept his people in line. Natural disasters, famine, the painful deaths of innocents, all could be argued as miracles instead of tragedies. The wayward ambling of Harmon Smith's soul was no less a mystery, but just as befitting. The devil walked the pages of the Bible through all the human generations, after all.

Mose felt a calling to visit Harmon's grave. Maybe this was one of God's tests of faith. Same as when he'd bypassed the chance to adulterate with Ginny Lynn Rominger a couple of decades back, or pushed away the bottle when it was offered in his teens. Same as when he took no more than twenty dollars from the collection come Sunday, though he was the one who tallied the bank account. Same as when he'd knocked over a road sign while speeding and had returned the next day and put it back good as new. He hoped he'd passed all his tests of faith, because he wanted to reach the Pearly Gates with a perfect score.

He waded into the fog, and though he told himself he wasn't afraid, his fist clenched around the hammer handle. The grass was spongy under his feet, the sweet green aroma battling with the cloying stench of the fog. He was midway through the cemetery, somewhere among the Harper and Blevins families, when the animals came out of the woods.

Goats.

White with black and tan spots, the goats marched like they had a destination. Their strange eyes sparkled in the celestial light, horns curved. Mose almost laughed. *That* was what had given him a fright? The herd must have busted out of a pen somewhere and smelled the thick grass, flowers, and shrubs of the churchyard.

He watched as the goats circled the cemetery, spreading out in formation. Mose was within ten steps of Harmon Smith's grave, but he'd momentarily forgotten the Circuit Rider in the wake of this new oddity. The goats were quiet, heads up, ears pricked and stiff as if hearing a command from an unseen source. When the circle was complete, cutting Mose off from the sanctuary of the church, a dark figure stepped out of the woods.

"Harmon," Mose said, loud enough so that God could hear, so He would know old Mose stood firm. "You got business, have you?"

The figure approached, tall and lanky, the silhouette of a hat revealed against the black background. He was as silent as the goats, and his footsteps made no sound. The air was still, and the fog grew thicker around Mose's waist. The preacher looked back at the rectangular light spilling from the church door. Would God forgive him if he showed just a touch of weakness, if he bolted for the safety of the church? That wouldn't be as bad as Judas's betrayal, or Peter's denying Jesus, or Pilate's washing his hands. There were a hundred worse failures in the Bible. And Mose was human, after all.

Except what kind of protection could a church offer? Harmon could walk through walls. The entire earth was God's church, and Mose was in as good à shape out here in the fog as he was in the biggest church ever built. Faith wasn't a place fixed in the real world, it was a golden patch in the heart of a good man.

The dark figure moved forward, steady, graceful. It was just behind the row of goats now.

Mose summoned his courage to speak again. "I say, Harmon, wonderful night we're having. Fog's a little chilly, but the sky's as clear as creek water."

The figure didn't answer. It moved between two goats and entered the cemetery.

Something was different about the shape of the hat. Harmon's was rounded on top, the brim wide and stiff. This one was flattened and frayed around the edges. The clothes weren't solid black, either. Harmon had worn a coarse, white linen shirt, but this creature sported a darker fabric. Did restless spirits have any need to change clothes?

Something curved from the thing's right hand, pale and wicked as a goat's horn.

Mose eased back a couple of steps, bumping against a grave marker. It tumbled over, crushing a bouquet of plastic flowers.

"All right, Harmon, you made your point," Mose said. "I'm not as brave as I'd like to be."

The figure moved past the goats, and the fog seemed to swirl around it, as if caressing its skin. Mose could make out more features now: Harmon's face was covered with a cloth of some kind, and had bone-colored buttons over his eyes. Straw protruded from the sleeves and collar of the shirt, and the hat was a beat-up planter's style, woven with reeds.

And in the thing's gloved hand was a reaping sickle.

The cloth mask moved in the area where the lips would be, though a dark stitch was the only mouth. "No one can serve two masters," the thing said, in a voice as dry and old as dust.

Mose forgot all his brave talk and tests of faith. He spun, look-ing for a path through the gravestones, but the fog had grown thicker and obscured the trees. The goats no longer circumscribed the cemetery. He turned back to face the thing, and the hat and clothes finally triggered an image in his mind.

Scarecrow.

A scarecrow in a cemetery.

One that talked and carried a sharp thing.

A curl of bone poked up from the fog to Mose's left, then an-other flashed to his right. The goats were coming beneath the fog, as silent as sharks closing in on their prey.

The scarecrow was close enough that Mose could count the holes in its ivory button eyes. The choking aroma of chaff crowded the sulfurous stench of the mist.

"Why?" Mose asked, and the question was as much for God as for the scarecrow.

Neither answered, and the sickle rose and fell.

Jett had the blankets pulled up to her chin, but still she shivered. Katy put a hand to her forehead, a typical Mom thing, but Jett didn't have a fever. Unless you counted bogeyman fever. She had that big time.

The man in the black hat was bad enough by himself. Now he had the scarecrow creature on his side. She closed her eyes and saw the cheesecloth face, the stitched grin, the button eyes, the wicked curve of the sickle. Worse was awakening among the goats, who had milled about her sprawled body, nudged her with their horns, and pressed wet noses against her flesh.

"Sure we shouldn't take her to the emergency room?" Mom asked Gordon, who stood in the doorway as if he were late for an appointment.

"No bones broken," Gordon said, speaking with the authority of a former Boy Scout. "And both her pupils are the same size, so she's not concussed."

"I feel okay," Jett said, though she was tempted to feign some sort of internal injury so she could get out of the Smith house and into the relative sanity of a hospital. But that would mean Katy would eventually wind up here alone with Gordon. And with the man in the black hat, the goats, and the scarecrow creature. And with whatever else had been bothering Katy lately. Jett needed to stay and watch over her.

"Well, we'd better keep you out of school tomorrow, just in case," Katy said.

"You should have been more careful," Gordon said.

"The barn was dark," Jett said.

"I was hoping you'd be able to pull your weight around here. You're a Smith now."

"Gordon, she's just had a bad fall," Katy said, defending her daughter for the first time in weeks. "No need to be mean."

"I wouldn't be surprised if she was out there doing drugs. Maybe that's why she lost her balance."

Katy's voice rose in pitch. "That's your answer for everything, huh?"

"Well, you knew how I was when you married me."

"No, I didn't. Not at all."

Gordon glowered, shook his head, and faded back into the hall. Katy stroked Jett's cheek. "I'm sorry, baby. Things aren't going too well right now."

"Something's happening, Mom."

"I'll have a talk with Gordon—"

"No, I mean something weird is happening here in Solom. With you. With *us*."

Jett sat up, letting the covers slide from her shoulders. She was dressed in a nightgown and a black tube top. She didn't really need a bra yet, but liked the black accessory, especially at school. But now, with the world gone doomsday freaky, the whole Goth thing seemed a bit silly. Jett fought a hand out from under the blankets and gripped Mom's wrist.

Mom scooted to the edge of the bed and faced the window. The world outside was silvered by the moon, the light rimming the dark and silent walls of mountains. "I'm being haunted," Mom said.

"Like, by a ghost?"

Mom nodded. "I think so. Sometimes I think the ghost is me."

"Don't tell me you're going nuts, too? No wonder Gordon's pissed off at you."

"And I saw a man at the top of the ridge yesterday, standing by the fence near the Eakins property. He was just standing there, looking over the valley. The goats had gathered around him."

"Was he wearing a black suit? And a hat that was kind of rounded, with a wide brim?"

"Have you seen him?"

"Twice, at school. And today I saw him outside the house, just before you got home. I was so scared, I hid in the attic, only something was up there. Some kind of creepy scarecrow. And he was in the barn, too. He had a sickle, and he chased me, and that's why I fell—"

"You sure it wasn't Odus? Maybe he hired somebody new."

"But this guy isn't new at *all*. He's like two hundred years old. His face looks like somebody melted candle wax over a skull."

"Hmm. Maybe you hit your head harder than you thought."

"I swear, Mom. I wasn't doing drugs." *At least, not much.*

"I believe you, honey. But none of this makes sense."

"Like, you think *ghosts* are real but my weird trips are all in my head?"

"I can't think here. I should go to the kitchen."

"*Fuck* the kitchen, Mom. What's happening to you?"

The expletive caused Katy to blink. "Don't cuss, Jett. It's not ladylike. You're a Smith now, and we need to behave like Smiths."

"But I'm not a Smith. Neither are you."

"That's not what she says."

"She *who*?"

"The woman in the pantry."

"Jesus, Mom, are you on pills or something?"

"She's nice. She wants me to be happy and take care of Gordon, just like she did."

"Hell-*o*. You're scaring me as much as the scarecrow did."

"The scarecrow is a Smith. He's been in the family for generations."

Jett waved her hand in front of Katy's eyes, but Katy was nearly catatonic, staring at her reflection in the window. "Mom. You're not hearing me. Solom is going goat-shit crazy."

"The best thing is to get some sleep. I'll talk to Gordon about it. He'll know what to do."

Sure, Gordon, always knows what's best. That's why we're one big fucking happy family, getting through it together, fighting the good fight.

"I love you, sweetie." Mom hugged her, and the embrace reminded Jett of how things used to be, back in Charlotte before marijuana and the divorce and the first stirrings of puberty. Jett held on as if the universe were crumbling away beneath the floor, and the bed were the last tiny island of sanity and hope. Warm tears ran down her cheeks. Everything was going to be okay, as long as they stuck together.

Unless the scarecrow dragged his scratchy sack of straw out of the barn and came calling on the house. The September wind picked up, whistling around the window frame, and bare branches clicked against the side of the house. Or it could have been the point of the sickle, *tap-tap-tapping*, probing for an opening.

"Will you sleep in here, Mommy?" Jett hadn't said "Mommy" in years.

"A wife's place is by her husband," Katy said, staring out the doorway into the hall.

"Mom?"

Katy stood and walked across the room like a zombie in an old black-and-white movie. She paused at the door, blew a kiss, and turned off the light. "Pleasant dreams, Jessica."

"*Mom!*"

The door closed, throwing the room into darkness. Jett, panicked, fumbled for the bedside lamp, and flipped the switch. She huddled in its glow as if it were the world's first campfire keeping back all the beasts of the night. Every rattle of a leaf outside became the footfall of a straw man, every creak of the wind-beaten house was a straining bone of the man in the black hat, each flap of loose shingles was the fluttering wings of some obscene and bloated bat.

Mom had gone over. Jett couldn't rely on her. So much for getting the fuck through it together. She waited a few minutes until she was sure Katy had gone into her own bedroom. The she tiptoed to the door and cracked it enough to check the hall. It was dark but empty, as far as she could tell. Jett tiptoed to the staircase. She was passing by the linen closet when she remembered the access hole and the scarecrow's box in the attic. Maybe it slept away the day there, like a vampire in its coffin. She quickened her pace, socks slipping on the wooden floor. She descended the stairs so quickly she couldn't recall touching any of the treads.

In the den, the banked fire threw a throbbing orange glow across the room. The phone was by the sofa, and she plopped down and dialed. The trophy heads on the wall glared down at her with glass eyes that seemed animated in the firelight. On the third ring, Dad answered.

"Hello?" His voice was cracked with sleep. He was an early-to-bed type, especially when a woman was around.

"Dad?"

His voice cleared. "Jett? What time is it?"

"Nearly midnight."

"What's wrong?"

"It's Mom. She's losing it and everything's going to hell."

"Where is she?"

"Upstairs."

"That doesn't sound so bad."

"She just told me she was a ghost."

"Shit."

"We need you."

"Is it bad?"

"Badder than bad. But I can't talk now. Gordon might catch me out of bed. But please come."

He sounded fully awake now. "Okay. I'll get there first thing in the morning, if you think you'll be okay until then."

"Maybe," Jett said, listening for cold fingers trying the front door handle.

"Solom. I guess it's about time I paid a visit, anyway."

"It's a real happening place, Dad. Maybe too much."

"Don't worry. Everything's going to be all right."

"So I keep hearing."

They talked for a minute more, then said their good-byes. After Jett hung up, she knelt before the fire and stared into the pulsing embers, waiting for the soft touch of boots on the front porch or the whisper of straw-filled sleeves in the attic.

Chapter Twenty-five

The sun came up on a brisk, clear Sunday. Frost laid a sparkling skin across the ground, but quickly melted where touched by the autumn light. Odus had slept uneasily, visions of the Circuit Rider galloping across his eyes whenever he happened to drift. He tried to remember what Granny Hampton had said about the Circuit Rider, if the old-timers had some means of warding him off. Didn't seem likely, because even after all these years, Solom was still a stopping point for Harmon Smith. The other mountain communities on Harmon's original rounds had probably all seen their share of mishap and death. Odus would bet that anybody following the histories of Balsam, Parson's Ford, Windshake, Rocky Knob, and Crowder Valley would see a trail marked by bloody hoofprints, at least every seventeen years or so. Seventeen years seemed to be the gap between Harmon's visits, for whatever reason. Odus didn't have a head for numbers, and he couldn't parse out any reason why seventeen would be special. But Rebecca Smith's death was generally attributed to the Circuit Rider, and that had only been five years ago. The Circuit Rider had a lot of territory to cover, stretching into East Tennessee and Virginia, and even a man on a hell-driven horse could only cover so many miles in a day.

Odus dressed in a pair of overalls that were dirty and stiff but had aired out for a couple of days. He scrambled a couple of eggs and rummaged in the counter. Like any common drunk, he knew exactly how much liquor was in the house and that on a Sunday, a bottle would be hard to come by unless he felt like visiting a bootlegger and paying a king's ransom. Odus had tucked back a pint of Old Crow, and the bourbon lay golden and gleaming in the glass, greasy and somehow thicker than water. He'd been tempted to polish it off last night, especially after Harmon had walked into the general store pretty as a show pony, as if knowing they were talking about him and daring them to make a play. But liquor tasted better on a Sunday and mock courage might serve where plain old backbone failed.

Because Odus was going to hunt down the Circuit Rider.

After Harmon had mounted Old Saint and vanished into the dark, off toward whatever errands called such a creature, Odus and the others had gone onto the general store's porch. The others were shaken, excepting old Sarah, who had been around for a few of Harmon's past visits, though she claimed this was the first time she'd ever seen him up close. Sure, David Tester had talked big, quoting some Bible passages from books that Odus had never heard before, with names like Nehemiah and Malachi, but he was as scared as the rest.

David had quoted Malachi as having set down these words in the old days, back when pretty near everybody with a beard, a high fever, and a clay tablet could be a prophet: "Surely the day is coming, it will burn like a furnace. All the arrogant and every evildoer will be stubble."

Then David went on to say that the dead horseback preacher had been quoting from the book of Matthew, when Christ delivered his Sermon on the Mount.

Odus didn't feel much like an evildoer. Sure, he cheated the government and big corporations and rich Floridian tourists, but he never cheated a human being. His reputation as a handyman was built on his word. He delivered what he promised, and he was never a day late about it, either. He treated people fair and expected the same. That was more than Odus could rightly say of the Lord, at least from what he'd seen. So he couldn't see why the Lord would want to set something like the Circuit Rider loose on Solom, especially since most of them were decent, churchgoing folks.

But it didn't matter whether Harmon had ridden up through the gates of hell or whether he'd clopped down a set of golden stairs. Odus could track the Circuit Rider down, because, ghostly stallion or not, the animal had left hoofprints in the muddy parking lot. With a flashlight, Odus had followed the tracks until they disappeared on the asphalt of Railroad Grade Road, though the prints faded and vanished within minutes of the animal's passing. Chances were that Harmon was hiding out up in the woods, probably on his original land at the foot of Lost Ridge where the Smith house sat. Even a dead man probably took comfort in familiar surroundings.

Odus hadn't mentioned his plan to the others because he didn't see that they could offer any help. Ray had a country lick of sense, but he was too steamed at his brother to work as a group. Sarah had too many years on her, Sue Norwood was too young, Lillian was an outsider, and David couldn't shake free of his Bible enough to tackle such a thing.

Odus hunted in the fall and usually got himself two or three bucks each season. The venison could be frozen or canned, and he traded the meat for vegetables and fruit. It was another way to keep from holding down a regular job. Now the tracking skills would come in handy, though a Winchester .30-30 wouldn't do the same job on Harmon Smith that it did on a white-tailed deer. Odus figured he'd find the right weapon when the time came. He threw a can of Vienna sausages, a couple of apples, a Thermos of coffee, and the bottle of Old Crow in his leather hunting pouch, hauled it and his fishing rod to the truck, and headed for the river road.

Mark Draper pulled up to the Smith house just before 9:00 a.m. Jett had e-mailed him the directions a few weeks back so he could pick her up for the Thanksgiving weekend. He'd been to the mountains before, but never this deep into them, where Tennessee and Virginia met North Carolina in a craggy collision. Mark had asked Katy as few questions as possible about Gordon. While he was curious, as all ex-lovers are, he didn't want to give her the satisfaction of that curiosity.

Gordon Smith seemed to be doing all right for himself, judging from the restoration work on the old farmhouse. The new tractor by the woodshed probably cost twice as much as Mark's Honda Accord, and Jett had told him the Smith property contained over two hundred acres. Goats milled around the barn, and a row of chicken roosts was lined across the barn's front wall. The rich tang of manure filled the air, but the air contained a freshness and greenness despite the season.

Mark got out and wiped the last sleepiness from his eyes. Three cups of coffee hadn't changed the fact that he'd left Charlotte before sunup. Now he had to take a whiz, but he ordered his bladder to calm down. He didn't want his first sentence to Katy's new husband to be, "Could I use your bathroom?"

He was approaching the porch when the door opened and Jett's head poked out. "Daddy!" she squealed, and despite the grin that spread across his face, a dagger of memory pierced his heart. She'd sounded the same way when he picked her up after her first day of kindergarten. Now she was living under another's man's roof, his ex-wife was sharing that man's bed, and he was years older and wearier.

They ran to each other and Jett jumped into his arms, nearly knocking him over. "My, you're getting big, honey," he said. "This fresh air must be doing wonders for your appetite."

"Daddy," she repeated.

"Let's have a look at you." Mark held her hand as she twirled like a ballerina. She was in flannel pajamas and wore gray bunny slippers. Her hair was dyed a shade darker than she'd worn it in Charlotte and held a hint of purple. She had grown at least an inch, maybe two, since he'd last seen her.

"Thanks for coming."

"I told you I'd be here whenever you needed me."

"And I need you. We need you."

Mark gave her another hug. "What did your mother say about my coming?"

Jett looked at the ground. "I didn't tell her."

Katy appeared in the open doorway, hand at her throat, clasping the front of her nightgown together. She was as beautiful as Mark remembered, red hair shining in the sun like lustrous copper, freckles dappling her cheeks, her pert lips parted in an unspoken question.

"Hi, Katy," Mark said, feeling stupid. He waved.

She blinked twice and rolled her green eyes. "What in the world are you doing here?"

"I came to see my daughter."

"You can't just show up out of the blue. We have a custody agreement."

"I asked him to come, Mom," Jett said. "To help us."

Katy looked at the two of them as if they were co-conspirators in some bizarre practical joke. "We don't need any help."

"You don't think so, but you're spaced out, Mom."

"I'm perfectly fine," she said, but looked at the barn as if she'd misplaced something and couldn't remember where she'd last seen it.

"What kind of trouble are you in?" Mark asked Katy.

"I don't know. Something about the barn. And recipes."

"Can I come in?"

"I'll have to ask Gordon."

"Where is he?"

"Taking a shower."

"Okay, I'll just wait here with the world's bestest girl." He put his arm around Jett as Katy went back inside. "So what's all this about the barn?"

"Well, it's kind of hard to explain."

"Look, we've always been honest with each other, even when we mess up. If it wasn't for my drug use, you might not—"

"This isn't about drugs, Daddy. It's about the goddamned man in the black hat and the scarecrow boy and the goats that tried to eat me, and maybe about Mom losing her mind. She thinks the house is haunted."

Mark wiped his mustache, unable to comprehend what his daughter was saying. Had she dragged him up here for some dramatic story? He was glad to see her, but if she started lying to get attention, he predicted trouble ahead for both him and Katy. So far, Jett hadn't punished either of them for the divorce, but she no doubt harbored a seething anger.

He was about to question her when Gordon came onto the porch. Mark nodded in greeting, straightening his spine and lifting his head, because Gordon had at least three inches on him. Jett led Mark up the porch and made introductions. Mark gripped Gordon's hand, wondering whether to go for the macho thing and try to squeeze the hardest. Instead, they both pressed flesh as if afraid of catching germs.

"Come in," Gordon said, turning and going back inside. "Make yourself at home."

Jett gave him a sideways glance as if to say, "See what I have to live with?"

They sat in the study. Katy fidgeted, hustling around the room and arranging magazines, Gordon's collection of religious relics on the mantel, and the plastic cases of DVDs that were stacked in front of the television. Mark noticed folded blankets stacked beside the sofa and wondered who had been sleeping downstairs. He was alarmed to find pleasure at the thought of Katy's abandoning her marital bed. Whatever her sleeping habits, she certainly was a lot fussier about housekeeping than she'd been when they shared the same roof.

"Can I get you something to drink—" Mark could tell by her exhalation that she almost said "honey," one of those lingering endearments that were difficult to shake off despite a legal document terminating such pleasantries. Mark himself knew the price of a relaxed guard, having lost a recent girlfriend by accidentally calling her "Katy" in a moment of passion. Gordon didn't seem to notice, but Jett sat forward on the sofa, attuned to the air of expectation that filled the room.

"I had coffee on the way up," Mark said, and that reminded him of the pressure in his bladder.

"So, to what do we owe this surprise visit?" Gordon asked.

"I'm sorry. I thought Jett had cleared it with you guys. I would never intrude otherwise."

"You didn't think to call me?" Katy asked, standing by the cold fireplace holding a throw pillow against her stomach. He admired her long fingers, the nails painted cherry, the freckles scattered across the backs of her hands like star maps he'd once memorized.

"I—"

"It's some personal stuff," Jett cut in. "I didn't want you to make excuses and keep him away."

"Jessica, we all appreciate your need for a broad support network," Gordon said. "But in my house, I need to know what's going on. We'll let it slip this one time, but from now on, everything gets cleared through me, okay?"

Gordon flashed Mark a wink that suggested "Oh, what we fathers have to go through, right?" A freshet of anger sluiced through Mark's veins. *Pompous ass. Wearing a turtleneck sweater on a Sunday morning, looking like Captain Nemo with that same sanctimonious burden of saving the world from itself.*

"How about breakfast?" Katy said. "I was making some scratch biscuits."

Scratch biscuits. The old Katy couldn't even handle Bisquik, and microwaving yeast rolls had been about the peak of her culinary skills. Country life must have inspired her. Or beaten her down. He found himself scrutinizing her as he listened to Gordon. Had she lost weight? She'd done something different with her hair, the trendy, cheek-sweeping cuts she'd preferred giving way to a longer, more free-flowing style that feathered across her collarbones. Damn. She was still beautiful, but then, that had never been one of her shortcomings.

"Actually, I was hoping to take Jett out for breakfast, if that's okay. Where's the closest McDonald's?"

Gordon gave one of those bluff, hearty laughs that were simultaneously cheerful and irritating. "Try Titusville. That's our college town. Population fourteen thousand when the semester is in session. Three thousand during Christmas break. But it's a twenty-minute drive, probably longer on a Sunday when the little old ladies drive their Olds Cutlasses to church."

"Let me fix you something here," Katy said. "We have fresh eggs and bacon, and I have a new waffle iron, too."

Mark shot her a glance. Gordon didn't have enough parental experience to pick up on the subtleties, but Katy should know the point of the suggestion was for Mark and Jett to spend time alone.

"How about the general store?" Jett said. "We can get something from their deli. You and me, Dad, just like when you used to drop me off at school."

Mark searched Katy's face for any hint of a sting, but she seemed lost in menu planning. "That sounds great, pumpkin. A real-life general store, huh?"

"Yeah, it's like a hundred years old and it's full of weird old stuff you never need."

"Sounds great. Is it open this early?"

"Sure," Jett said. "The woman who owns it lives next door. Except it's more like she lives at the store and just sleeps at home."

"Sounds like the ticket to me." Mark stood, half expecting Katy to invite herself along. He wasn't sure whether he would mind or not. Making Turtleneck Boy jealous would almost be worth the trouble, but Mark didn't want to reopen old wounds. Or risk fanning old embers, either.

He was being a selfish ass, as usual. This was about Jett, not any of the three adults.

"Is that okay with you guys?" Mark asked.

Gordon and Katy looked at each other, Katy obviously awaiting her husband's response. Gordon nodded at her, then Katy nodded at Mark. Jett grabbed his arm and squeezed in joy.

"Do I need to have her back at any particular time?" Mark asked. "Like for church?"

"I attend services, but Katy and Jett don't," Gordon said. "My spiritual interest is purely academic, though."

I'll bet it is, Mr. Penny Loafers. If God walked in the front door, you'd invite Him into the study for a sherry and a chat about ways to improve the cosmos.

"Great, then," he said. "I'll have her back in time for lunch."

"I'll make a casserole," Katy said. "Table for four?"

Jett surreptitiously shook her head. Mark was beginning to see why his daughter was freaked out. The woman who had been his wife for ten years and girlfriend for a couple of years before that had become a completely new woman in the four months she'd been in Solom. Perhaps this was the real Katy, and the one he'd known had been inhibited and repressed. Though that made no sense, because Katy had always been independent and, if anything, a bit too strong-headed. Her head now seemed to be filled with little more than the back pages of *Good Housekeeping*.

"I don't think I can stay for lunch," Mark said. "I've got some clients to check on this evening. Self-employed people work seven days a week, remember?"

Katy smiled, but it wasn't the sardonic grin she always flashed when she was pissed about his workaholic ways. "That's nice. Gordon is a hard worker, too."

"It's not work when you enjoy it, isn't that right, Mark?" Gordon said. "Religion fascinates me, and faith is even more mystifying. As Mark Twain said, 'Heaven goes by favor. If it went by merit, you would stay out and your dog would go in.' "

"Well, may we all be dogs in the next life," Mark said, wishing he'd smoked a joint before meeting Jett's new stepdad.

Katy was determined to pull off a nice soufflé, figuring Jett would talk Mark into staying for lunch after all. Gordon was attending one of the churches, probably the True Light Tabernacle, and she figured he'd be hungry afterward. Part of her was also hoping to impress Mark, give him yet another reason to regret her loss. Seeing her ex-husband had shocked her in ways she never would have expected, and she wondered if Jett had planned the rendezvous so Katy wouldn't have time to psychologically prepare for his arrival. Katy had done a good job of hiding her feelings. The physical attraction was still there, but for a grown woman, attraction was tied to love or at least like.

She opened a drawer to find an opener for the can of evaporated milk. The key lay in the drawer, among measuring spoons, whisks, peelers, and spatulas. Someone had moved it. She'd left it in the *other* drawer, the miscellaneous drawer that was rarely opened.

She couldn't resist picking up the key. A floral smell drifted from the hallway, and barely audible footsteps trailed up the stairs. Katy frowned at the eggs she'd cracked into a metal bowl. Well, if she hurried, the eggs wouldn't go bad.

Katy ascended the stairs, following the faint aromatic thread of lilacs. It led to the linen closet. Someone had left the door open, and the attic access was ajar. Katy perched on her tiptoes and pulled the string, and the access door yawned wide, the ladder unfolding as the door dropped. Key clutched in her fist, Katy climbed into the darkness above.

Her eyes adjusted to the gloom, the morning sun piercing the ventilation shaft on the east gable and throwing yellow stripes across the attic. Dust floated in the sunlight, and a stray wasp cut a slow arc in the air. Katy stooped under the low rafters and navigated the clutter until she came to the dresser with the dusty mirror. The silver-handled hairbrush was still on the dresser, with an old stool pushed in front of the mirror as if someone had been checking her reflection.

"Rebecca?" Katy's voice was muffled by the insulation, furniture, and boxes of old clothing that lay scattered and stacked like a museum to unwanted things.

A rustle arose from inside one of the boxes.

"I don't want to take your place," Katy said.

"*He wants you.*"

Katy wasn't sure whether she'd actually heard the words or if the breeze had whispered through the ventilation screen.

The access door slammed shut with a rusty scream of springs and hinges, making the attic even darker.

Katy backed away from the sudden noise. She bumped into the long wooden box that contained the strange outfit she'd discovered on her earlier visit. She forced herself not to think of the box as a coffin. The clothes inside had probably been the relics of a previous Smith generation, left to molder as moth bait. Except, why had the clothes *moved*?

The surface of the mirror grew bright with collected light. Katy glanced from the mirror to the cramped attic. The reflection was somehow different from the reality that pushed itself against the silvered glass. She fell to her knees, looking from the mirror to the dimly lit attic, trying to comprehend the juxtaposition of elements. There lay the golden strips of sunlight, the oblique darkness of the old bureau, the array of boxes, and the slanted brown rafters. What was missing?

She tore her gaze away from the mirror. An image of Jett

popped into her head: Jett under the blankets in her bedroom, confused, eyes wide in panic. Her daughter had been trying to tell her something.

Scarecrow creature. Man in the black hat. Goats.

Why had Jett called Mark?

Katy should have been able to protect both of them. That was why she'd gotten divorced, why she'd married Gordon. Why she'd given up a banking career. None of it meant anything without Jett.

Sacrifice. It meant the same thing as "motherhood." Fathers never understood. They shot their sperm and went about their business.

But what had Katy been doing these past few weeks?

She looked down at her clothes. This wasn't her. The clothes didn't fit. They itched.

She shook the sleeve of her dress and bits of straw fell out.

The key was warm in her hand, almost electric.

The light shifted with the rising of the sun, and a shaft of yellow fell across the dark slot in the middle of the bureau. A keyhole glared in the brass workings beneath the double handles.

"*Open me*," Rebecca said, the words hollow and muffled, as if spoken from the depths of a coffin.

"You're dead."

"*But you're not*." One of the hens cackled in the barnyard outside, a frantic and rattling punctuation to the eerie stillness of the attic. "Not yet, anyway."

Katy approached the bureau, avoiding the gravity of the mirror. The key lifted her hand as if magnetized and she followed it between the dusty cardboard boxes and linen-draped humps of furniture. She pushed the key into the bureau lock, or else the key pulled her hand, she couldn't be sure. Then the lock was turning and the doors groaned open like a death angel spreading its wings.

Chapter Twenty-six

"I'll take Jessica now," Gordon said.

Mark looked up from the table. Jett had plowed her way through a glass of chocolate milk, half a Spanish omelet, two strips of bacon, a piece of white-bread toast slathered with margarine, and still had a cream-cheese cinnamon bun at her elbow. Mark was drinking coffee, the house brand, and wished the woodstove had been stoked recently. He was not used to the mountain chill, and the general store had obvious shortcomings in weatherproofing. The twin aromas of fried liver mush and onions fought for dominance in the air. However, the place was not without charm, if you didn't count the six-foot-four guy standing over him who set off every bullshit alarm in Mark's body.

"I thought I was supposed to take her back to your house," Mark said.

"Plans have changed," Gordon said. His smile was midway between smug and confrontational and he was outfitted in his Sunday best, collar stiff and uncomfortable, the kind of clothes built for sitting upright in church or lying prone in a coffin. Gordon's face was flushed, as if he'd jogged a half mile before walking in the door.

Jett looked at Mark with those wide, pleading eyes. He'd let her down plenty already. He'd fucked up with the drugs, he didn't take the steps that could have saved his marriage and his family, he hadn't grabbed on to the things that were most important in his life. And now they were drifting out of his reach, like fairy dust or pot smoke, insubstantial, unreal, pieces of a lost and long-ago dream.

He could sit here and drink coffee or he could tell Gordon Smith to go the fuck down the deepest hole in hell.

"We're still finishing our breakfast," Mark said. "Adolescents need their nutrition. Haven't you read the parenting manuals?"

"I know what's best for her," Gordon said, his gaze unwavering. "And for Katy. You had your chance, after all."

Mark's grip tightened around his coffee mug. He didn't know whether to dash the liquid onto Gordon's three-hundred-dollar jacket or to shatter the ceramic and bring a shard up to slice his own jugular.

"It's okay, Dad," Jett said. "Call me when you get back to Charlotte." She reached across the table and put her small fingers on his forearm. Her nails were painted dark violet to match her eye shadow. His girl had style, at least. And a flair for the dramatic.

"I don't feel comfortable leaving things as they are," he said to her, hoping his expression revealed he was worried and didn't want Gordon to know.

"We'll get by, Daddy," she said. "You know what Mom always says."

The words were like rabbit punches to the kidney. That was a Katyism, said when bills were stacking up or some medical problem arose. When things seemed darkest, when love seemed ephemeral, when only fools believed "forever" was more than just a weapon in a poet's arsenal. "We'll get through this together" had been one of those lines that still rang even after the "together" part was over.

Coming from Jett, the words were almost a mockery, an echo that whispered of failure. Because they weren't getting by. Jett had told him the weirdest damned stories, and after he'd gotten past his initial instinct to assume she'd graduated to hard drugs, just like her old man, he had almost started to believe her. Tongues could lie, but eyes had a difficult time. Especially the eyes of the young.

"When can I see you again?" Mark asked her.

"We'll talk about that," Gordon said. "The three of us. We'll let you know."

Gordon reached down and took Jett's wrist. She wore the expression of a prisoner being hauled away after court sentencing.

"It's okay, pumpkin," Mark said. "I'm glad I got to see you."

They stood and hugged, Jett giving him an extra squeeze. He stroked the top of her head and stooped to kiss her cheek. She was on the doorstep of womanhood, and he'd miss her crossing the threshold. Gordon would be ushering her through that passage, because Gordon was stable and wealthy and reliable. The kind of man every woman needed as a husband and every daughter needed as a father.

Except the corners of Gordon's mouth flirted with a smirk. Which Gordon was the real one?

"Call me," Mark said as the pair walked down the aisles of the store, between rows of bark birdhouses, snow shovels, bushels of apples, pumpkins, dried Indian corn, and gourds.

After they left, Mark sipped his coffee. It had gone cold and bitter, a fitting juice for his heart. His daughter had told him Katy was possessed, a man in a black hat was stalking her, a scarecrow had attacked her, and goats were trying to eat her. It sounded like a direct-to-video movie, and yet her face had paled and hands trembled as she told her tale. Despite her talent for drama, she had spoken with quiet conviction, as if fully expecting not to be believed. She'd finished speaking, crunched some bacon, a couple of dark red crumbs on her lower lip as she'd asked, "What now, Daddy?"

It was a question Mark pondered as he finished his coffee and the tables around him filled with lunch customers.

The key turned in the lock with a sharp groan of relief. The bureau gave forth a smell of lilacs so strong that Katy nearly sneezed. Beneath the floral sweetness lay the stink of something warm and wet, like damp and rotted hay. The bureau was empty except for a rumpled pile of clothes on the middle shelf. Katy looked behind her, half expecting Rebecca to finally seep out of the shadows. But Rebecca hadn't harmed her yet, so why should she be frightened? After all, Rebecca had been part of this house long before Katy's arrival.

Katy was tempted to ask Rebecca what was so important about the clothes that they needed to be locked away. Maybe Rebecca had her own motives. Jealousy might stain the soul even unto death, though Katy couldn't imagine the grave being much colder than Gordon's bed.

She pulled the tangle of clothes from the shelf. A plain flannel shirt, pocked with tears, loose threads, and moth holes. Except the sleeves and cuffs were moist, painted a color that was darker than the shadowy attic. A pair of faded jeans was beneath the shirt, and under the hump of clothing was a battered planter's hat. As she pulled the hat from the shelf, something heavy thumped to the floor, barely missing her toes. She bent and picked it up.

A sickle, the same as the one that hung on the wall of the barn. Except this one was clean and had a honed edge, while the one in the barn was rusty from lack of use. Katy held the curved piece of steel before her. Could this be the same one from the barn, only with the blade polished and sharpened? When was the last time she had been in the barn?

Short pieces of straw were scattered among the clothing. At first Katy thought the hat was unraveling, but the straw was tucked into the folds of the shirt, adding another scent to the strange mix. She laid the sickle on the shelf and lifted the shirt toward the shafts of light leaking from the nearest vent. The wet sleeves slapped at her arms as she carried the shirt to the mirror. The mirror reflected the faint light and allowed her to recognize the pattern. It was the same shirt worn by the scarecrow in the barn.

And the sleeves were dark red with drying blood.

Katy tossed the shirt to the floorboards in disgust. Maybe someone had killed an animal in the shirt, then stowed it away in the attic. Then why was the blood not completely dried? Neither

Gordon nor Odus had killed any farm animals since Katy and Jett had moved in. Certainly not in the last day or two.

"Blood in the attic?" Katy asked, half to herself and half to Rebecca, though she still didn't quite trust the opinion of a ghost.

Behind the dresser, the lid on the long wooden box creaked open, then fell closed with a soft *thwump*.

Every country attic had rats or squirrels or possums. She had disturbed some nesting animal, that was all.

Katy remembered the clothes in the box, coarse fabric like those that had adorned the scarecrow. Except they had been dry, and not under lock and key.

Tiny scurrying under the dresser. The quick claws of some rodent. Clicking on wood.

Katy dropped the shirt and gripped the wooden handle of the sickle. It fit her palm as if personally carved for her.

She backed toward the attic door. The clicking multiplied as more small, sharp toes scrabbled among the boxes, furniture, lamp shades, and the huddled hulk of an old wheelchair. Katy reached the door with its folded ladder and pushed downward. The door had no latch, and should have swung free. But it stuck tight as if someone were on the other side, bracing it closed.

She placed her foot on the door, slowly sweeping the sickle in front of her, reaping air as if to ward off the unseen creatures that flirted with the shadows. That's when she looked back at the dresser. On the stool, perched before the mirror, was a woman in the same dress that Katy was wearing. A pale, delicate, freckled hand swept the silver-handled hairbrush in curling motions as if smoothing tangles. Except there was no hair.

The woman had no head.

The body turned on the stool, the hairbrush descending to rest in her lap, a ragged, transparent stump of flesh protruding above the lace collar. "Am I not pretty enough for him?" Rebecca asked.

How can you speak when you have no head? How can you speak anyway when you're dead?

Katy climbed onto the narrow access door, then began jumping, staying hunched so she wouldn't bump her head on the joists. She couldn't look away from that headless figure, the woman whose place Katy had taken in the Smith house, even though the scurrying was on all sides and shapes wriggled in the eaves.

On the fourth jump, the door gave way and she plummeted into space, the sickle falling from her hand as she bounced off the shelves in the linen closet and tumbled into the upstairs hall.

As the world went gray, the staccato scurrying continued above her, and beyond that, as soft as lamb's breath, came the whispering stroke of a hairbrush through ethereal tresses.

Odus figured the Circuit Rider would be either at one of his three Lost Ridge grave sites or else up on the Snakeberry Trail where he'd been killed. The Circuit Rider had somehow found his faithful horse, and was mobile again.

Odus figured he'd need a horse himself if he was going to roam the back-mountain trails. A motorcycle would probably work better, but the engine noise would kill any element of surprise. Plus he didn't think he could hot-wire a Harley without rousing half the police in the county. Besides, it seemed only proper to track the Circuit Rider by horseback. Since Odus was going into this showdown without any weapons, he figured he ought to make up the rules as he went along, on the theory that like could slay like.

Odus parked his truck on a gravel lot by the river at the McHenry farm. He was near the bridge that led to Rush Branch Road, a steep strip of crumbled asphalt that gave way to mud as it wound around the mountain. The Smith property lay on the other side, in the valley at the base of the mountain. The Primitive Baptist Church stood near the peak, just where the pavement ended. Some three-story houses were perched on the steep slopes here and there, up where the late wind shook the walls, but they were mostly summer homes for Yankees and were empty this time of year. It would be easy to ignore their fences and NO TRESPASSING signs. The Circuit Rider certainly wouldn't observe human laws, and Odus had to adopt that same mind-set.

He found a horse on a riverside pasture, a stretch of flat bottomland that would have been developed for condos already if not for the spring floods that sometimes washed over it. The horse was a pinto mare of mixed colors, probably two or three years old. It shied away as Odus approached, which was just fine because Odus needed to lure the horse out of sight of the river road. The horse was pastured with cows, a mistake on Old Man McHenry's part, because horses didn't know how to behave after spending time with cud-chomping sacks of sirloin. Odus had helped McHenry put up some hay last fall and knew his way around the barn. The house was up the road a quarter mile, so Odus was concealed while he rummaged. The horse followed him to the barn because it smelled the apple in Odus's pocket and, despite the bad bovine influence, an apple to a horse was like a sweet lie to a woman. They both got you what you wanted.

In the barn, Odus rounded up a halter and reins. He didn't like sliding the steel bit in the horse's mouth. Folks said horses didn't mind, but it looked uncomfortable anyway. He gave the pinto the apple to work on while he cinched the saddle. Odus had done some riding here and there in his work as a hired hand, occasionally putting in some saddle time to exercise horses for lazy people. He was no Gene Autry, but he knew enough to keep from getting bucked.

The church crowd would be filling the roads any minute now, and he'd have to either use the bridge or find a shallow spot to cross Blackburn River. He liked the idea of fording the river. That's probably how the Circuit Rider did it. With any luck, or some kind of higher power pitching in a little help, Odus would be able to track Harmon before nightfall. Because night was a time when things like dead preachers grew more powerful. Odus didn't need a scientist to tell him that. Dark things loved the dark, and the dark loved them right back.

Odus swung into the saddle and gave the pinto a twitch on her flank. "You got a name?" he asked her.

The horse whinnied, spraying a few specks of apple.

"I'll take that as a 'yep,' " Odus said. "You speak human better than I speak horse, so I'll just have to make something up. Harmon has Old Saint, so let's call you 'Sister Mary.' What do you think of that?"

Sister Mary's snort might have signaled disgust, or it could have been a request for another apple. Either way, she headed out of the barn when he gave the reins a shake. He guided Sister Mary past the cows, who stared as if they'd bought tickets, and toward the river. Just before Sister Mary put a tentative hoof in the cold water, Odus glanced up the ridge at the next pasture. McHenry's goats were lined along the fence, as menacing as the Apache warriors in a wagon train western.

"Don't pay them no mind," Odus said. "We got business elsewhere."

He gently bounced his knees against Sister Mary's ribs and they entered the current.

Crisis of faith. That was the only explanation. Mose Eldreth hadn't shown up for services, leaving his congregation high and dry in its time of need. David should have felt disappointment or perhaps pity, for he understood as well as anyone the flesh was weak. But the emotion that struggled for dominance in the mix was triumph, as if God had whittled away one more competitor for precious space in heaven.

Primitive Baptists shouldn't gloat, he knew. Only the Lord knew the whole truth about Mose, and it was always possible that God had sent Mose away on some sort of quest or mission. In which case, David's triumph was actually failure, because it meant Mose was at least one step ahead on those golden stairs. But none of that mattered now.

Clayton Boles, a semiregular at Solom Free Will Baptist, had shown up at David's church fifteen minutes after service started, sliding into one of the back pews. His entrance was obvious: only a dozen faithful had shown up that morning, none of them under the age of fifty. David had even paused in his sermon, a rambling discourse on the enemy within and a human's inability to personally remove the burden of sin. Clayton nodded and blinked and David had offered a public welcome. The Primitives didn't mind an occasional guest; Gordon Smith popped in every three months or so, and relatives sometimes sat in, especially during foot-washing ceremonies. But if Clayton thought he was going to join the fold, he'd have to rid himself of a lot of self-serving ideas of getting saved. Clayton would have to get humble, an idea that far too many Christians of every stripe resisted.

After the sermon, while the members of the congregation were shaking hands, David took Clayton to the side and found out about Mose's dereliction of duty. Word of the Circuit Rider had gotten around, at least among the locals, and Clayton confessed that he figured any port in a storm, because evil wouldn't befall him while he was in a church, no matter what kind of sign was posted out front.

"Damnedest thing, though, Preacher," Clayton had said. "The grass in the graveyard was tore to hell and gone, like somebody stampeded a herd of cattle through. And there was a scorched patch around Harmon Smith's grave."

Around one *of his graves*, David almost added. Instead, he quoted from Matthew: "Do not worry about tomorrow, for tomorrow will worry about its own things. Sufficient for the day is its own trouble."

David waited until the congregation left, then changed clothes in the little room that was more of a broom closet than a vestry. By the time he emerged, the sun was nearly straight up in the sky. As surely as the dawn was a symbol of rising and renewal, dusk was a time of despair and destruction. Whatever Harmon Smith had planned for this go-round of the circuit, it would happen tonight. That gave David less than seven hours to come up with a way to preserve his church and his community. Even though God had already predestined the outcome, David felt a need to act.

He went to his pickup truck and took a shovel from the bed. The oaken handle was strong and sure in his hands, a sacred staff if there ever was one. He navigated the scattered markers that surrounded Rush Branch Primitive Baptist Church and proceeded to the worn and nameless slab of limestone that was cracked down the middle as if lightning had been buried there.

The holes that had pocked Harmon Smith's grave were larger, the dirt fresh, as though some creature had burrowed its way in. Or maybe *out*.

Only one way to know for sure. David drove the shovel blade

into the moist soil with a sound like a hatchet into meat. He drove the metal deeper with his boot and turned. He was a grounds-keeper, and this was his turf. Here, at least, he had a chance. If he could beat the sinking sun, that was.

Chapter Twenty-seven

"What's wrong, Mom?" Jett asked

"I fell." Katy stood at the sink, rinsing her hands. She had a cut on her chin and one eye was bruised and puffy.

"Good Lord, Katy, how could you get hurt cleaning house?" Gordon said.

"I was in the attic."

Gordon glared at her, almost owlish with his beard and glasses, with sinister, prey-hunting eyes. "I didn't give you permission. We have valuable antiques and family heirlooms up there."

"I'm part of the family now."

"You're not a Smith yet. You're a Logan."

"Where's Mark?" Katy asked Jett. Her head throbbed. The image of the headless Rebecca at the mirror still haunted her, as if the image had seared itself against the plate of her forehead.

"Gone back to minding his own business," Gordon said. "We don't need any outsiders. We can solve our problems by ourselves."

"I saw the clothes. And the sickle."

"What are you talking about?"

"From the scarecrow in the barn."

"The scarecrow is out there hanging on the wall. Where it always is."

"No, it's not," Jett said. "I told Dad about it. You guys don't believe me, but he does."

"That's enough of this foolishness," Gordon said. He grabbed Jett's wrist and pulled her toward the front door. "Come on, you two. I'll show you the scarecrow is just a sack of rags and straw, not some evil creature."

"Let her go, Gordon," Katy said.

Jett tried to struggle free, but Gordon was too strong and heavy. He tugged her outside, Katy right behind them. The fence gate was open. Katy wondered where the goats were. The barn door was open, too, afternoon sunlight boring through the gap and painting the dirt floor in patches of amber. The rich smell of manure and hay filled the air. The chickens clucked uneasily in their nests.

Jett gave up resisting and allowed herself to be guided into the barn. Katy wondered what she had told Mark. She couldn't believe Mark would just drive away after hearing such strange tales. But he'd always believed what he wanted to believe, despite pleas or evidence.

"The scarecrow's right there," Gordon said, pointing to the spot on the wall above the loft stairs. The figure wasn't dressed in the bib overalls and flannel shirt that Katy had seen in the attic, inside the locked bureau. This figure wore a dark suit of a heavy material like wool. Straw spilled from the sleeves and ankles of the suit, and the yellowed collar of the white shirt stuck up around the collar. The scarecrow had no head.

"That's not the one," Katy said.

"Yes, it is," Jett said, excited. "That's the man I saw. The one in the black hat."

"I don't see a hat," Gordon said. "Odus must have taken the other scarecrow for some reason. Those clothes look old-fashioned, maybe even antique."

"What's going on, Gordon?" Katy asked.

"The scarecrow hungers," Gordon said.

"Where are the goats?" Jett asked.

Gordon looked around as if noticing their absence for the first time. "He's taken them."

"Who?" Katy touched the welt over her eye. The upper and lower eyelids were swelling together and she could barely see. The side of her face felt as if a pint of hot water had been pumped under her skin.

Katy squinted at the shape on the wall. Hadn't the original scarecrow been shorter? No. That was the kind of thing that crazy people thought. Crazy people who believed they were being haunted by their husband's dead ex-wife.

The sickle was absent from its wooden peg.

"It moved," Jett said, grabbing Katy's arm. Katy looked at the gangly, splayed form. A few pieces of straw fell from its cuffs as if an animal were moving inside it. Katy recalled the toenails skittering on the attic floor.

"It's the wind," Gordon said. "Odus left the barn door open."

"Let's get out of here," Jett said.

"Go on back to the house," Gordon said. "I'll close up the barn."

Katy nodded and put an arm around Jett's shoulder. The two of them went into the barnyard. Katy stopped by the chicken roost. "What did your dad say when you told him about this place?"

Jett shrugged and stared at the ground. "Nothing much. He thought I was weird. But he didn't laugh at me." She looked up, her blue eyes vibrant and imploring. "I wish—"

Katy reached out and hugged her daughter, pulling her close. The girl was getting tall. The hair on the top of her head brushed Katy's wounded chin. "Shh. Wishing for lost things isn't a good idea. We have to work with what we've got."

"Yeah, yeah, yeah. 'We'll get through it together,' right?"

"Exactly." Katy brushed away Jett's bangs and planted a kiss on her forehead.

"I just wish Daddy were here."

Katy had no response for that. She had failed her daughter and her marriage. Maybe if she had tried harder, been less self-absorbed . . .

No. Gordon was her husband now and she was determined to make it work this time. All it took was sacrifice.

"Let's go in the house," Katy said. "I'll make us some cinnamon rolls. I found a great recipe."

"What about the scarecrow and the man in the black hat?"

"Gordon will take care of it."

"Do you love him?"

Katy pulled away from the hug. "What kind of question is that?"

"I don't know. I saw the way you were looking at Dad, and you've never looked at Gordon like that."

"Gordon is a good man and he'll make a good father if you give him a chance."

"I don't want another father. I want mine."

"I'm sorry, honey. We've turned that page. This is our new life."

Jett pushed away. The hens squawked at the disturbance, flapping their wings, tossing soft feathers in the air. Inside the barn came the slam of a large wooden door.

"I don't want a new life. Especially if it's this one." Jett went through the gate and into the house.

Sister Mary proved to be a rugged animal, despite a lifetime spent in the companionship of cows. Odus had guided her up the mountains and traversed the roughest trails he could find, twisted paths that were scarcely wide enough for deer. He half expected the horse would put her nose to the ground like a bloodhound and instinctively know they were on the scent of something bad. Odus figured that two hours had passed, and maybe Old Man McHenry had already noticed somebody had stolen his pinto mare.

At one point, the forest gave way to a granite shelf, with rocks settled into the Appalachian soil like droppings from some ancient giant bird. Odus tied Sister Mary to a stunted balsam and gave her some of the bread from his sandwich. As she smacked her lips around it, Odus eased to the edge and looked down in the valley below. Solom was sprawled like a faded patchwork quilt of yellow meadows, brown forests, and the small gray squares of houses and barns. The river wound like a loose length of spilled yarn through the bottomland, the water white where it tumbled over rocks. The two-lane road followed the river, except for an intersection near the general store where the covered bridge, post office, and Sue Norwood's shop cluttered up the geometry.

This stony point looked like the kind of place where the Circuit Rider would step out and survey the community. Maybe this had been part of his original route, back when he was a Methodist preacher sent down from Virginia. If so, he might have passed his eyes over the green valley and decided it was just the kind of place to set up shop. A Holy Land, of a sort, one maybe just a little bit remote from the eyes of God, where a fellow could practice the kind of rituals he wanted.

Sister Mary let loose with a wet snort.

"All right, don't get your neck hairs in a tangle," Odus said. He went back to the horse, unhitched her, and mounted. His rump was a little sore from the jostling ride, but it wasn't sore enough to complain. He pulled the Old Crow from the knapsack and gargled on a two-finger slug. He was slipping the bottle back into the pack when a twig snapped in the thicket behind him.

"Who's there?" Odus said, and despite all his high-spirited notions about not needing a weapon, he wouldn't have minded a rifle right about then. Not that there were any wild animals left in the mountains big enough to threaten a man or a horse. The occasional bobcat was about as predatory as it got these days.

Whatever was thrashing around in the brush didn't answer. Not that Odus expected a reply. He eased Sister Mary down the path a little, wanting to put some distance between them and the cliff edge. Sister Mary seemed to notice her passenger's unease, because her ears pricked up. Odus gave her a pat on the side of the neck to calm her.

He was twenty feet down the path when the goat emerged from the stand of laurels. Odus almost laughed in relief. Except the goat's head was tilted sideways, the way a man might look at a car he was thinking of buying. Or maybe which steak from the butcher's counter he craved for that night's supper. Sister Mary drew up short without Odus having to pull back on the reins.

"Get on," Odus said to the goat. The goat was nearly a quarter the size of the horse, fat and white, a string of dirty fur trailing from its belly to the ground. Its eyes were rheumy, the corners full of yellow pus. It stank of piss and the musk of its rutting scent. The horns spread wide, with just the slightest bend to them. Its lower jaw dropped, the worn and stained teeth showing in a corrupt grin. Odus recognized the animal now, from Gordon Smith's flock.

What was it doing loose up here? Gordon had walked the Smith fence lines in early August, just before the second cutting of the hay. The wire was in good shape, and locust posts took decades to rot. Goats had a reputation for breaking boundaries and getting into where they weren't wanted, but it didn't make sense for the goat to climb up into the laurel thicket. Laurel leaves were poisonous, and not much else was green this time of year except balsam and jack pine.

The goat didn't look like it cared for green. The strange, glittering pupils fixed on Odus as if the two were gunfighters squaring off in the Old West.

The goat lowered its head, the scruff of beard pressed against the shaggy chest, showing the serrated grooves of the two brown horns. The animal pawed at the ground with one hoof, like a Spanish bull preparing to charge a red cape. A goat was far more dangerous than most people thought, because its neck was strong and horns hard and sharp. If the horns tore into the horse's abdominal cavity, the goat would likely pull away with intestines entwined like spaghetti around a twirled fork. The laurels on each side were too thick and tangled to allow escape.

Odus peeked over his shoulder to see if a path led down the side of the cliff, and that's when the goat charged. It came in low, at Sister Mary's knees. The horse shrieked and bucked, flailing its front legs in the air. Odus clung to the reins and hunched over the horse's neck, one boot flying out of its stirrup. For a moment he was weightless, and then he crashed back down into the saddle, slamming his testicles against the hard leather. Sister Mary reared again, this time catching the goat in the forehead with one steel-shod hoof. The goat let out a gurgling bleat and drew back, a gash opening just above its eerie eyes, blood flowing down the snout. The goat retreated a few unsteady steps and wobbled a moment as Sister Mary hopped forward, not giving Odus a chance to regain control.

The goat fell to its knees, lapping at its blood with a grayish pink tongue. Sister Mary took a long couple of strides and leaped over the goat, once again lifting Odus out of the saddle, with gravity doing its work and plunging him right back down.

Sister Mary galloped along the path, branches slapping at

Odus's hands and face. He glanced back and saw the goat was still lapping at its own leaking fluids. They had gone perhaps a hundred yards when Odus pressed his knees against the mare's flanks and urged her to slow down. At last she came to a stop, panting from the effort. Odus reached into the knapsack and treated himself to a shot of bourbon, his hands shaking. Somehow the encounter with the goat was creepier than the Circuit Rider's uninvited stop at the general store the night before.

One thing was for sure, the Circuit Rider appeared to have a few friends on his side. All Odus had was a pinto horse, a half pint of eighty-proof, and a stubborn streak. He guided Sister Mary higher into the forest, where the tributary springs that fed Rush Branch squeezed from cracks in the gray, worn granite. In the world's oldest mountains, where the headwaters of one of the oldest rivers leaked like the tears of a tired widow, Odus figured this was as good a place as any to serve as a cradle of evil.

And Odus planned on rocking that cradle.

Mark Draper checked into the cabin at four in the afternoon. He'd driven around Solom to get a feel for his daughter's new home. She hadn't exaggerated when she'd called it a "one-horse shit bag of a town," and though he'd chastened her on the use of the expletive, he'd had to grin around the straw of his 7-Up. He hadn't grinned as much as he'd wanted, because Jett's story was way too disturbing. As fantasy, it suggested dementia. As truth, it suggested the need for escape.

He couldn't just drive down to Charlotte and hope everything would work out for the best. Mark wasn't an optimist by nature, and that was probably wise, given his penchant for fucking up his life.

He wouldn't fuck this up, wouldn't let Jett down. He paid for the room with a credit card, shocked at the $150 fee for one night. Reading his expression, the Happy Hollow clerk explained that it was the fall tourist season, and with the leaf-lookers who would soon be swarming the highways, he was lucky to find a room at all. Mark thought of driving back to Titusville where a Holiday Inn,

Comfort Suites, and other chain hotels feasted on the college. But he felt a need to be near Jett. And Katy, too, as much as he tried not to let his mind wander down that road.

He hadn't packed any clothes, but he always carried a shaving kit in his trunk. He sometimes traveled in his job, and more than once had been caught out of town and having to make a trip to the drugstore for shampoo and toothpaste. The cabin was dark and cramped, the sort of place that was just uncomfortable enough to let flatlanders feel they were "roughing it." However, an eighteen-inch television stood on the kitchenette counter, and the bed's mattress was thick and soft.

Mark pulled out his cell phone and sat on the bed. Should he call Jett and tell her he was hanging around? Probably. Katy or Gordon might answer the phone, but he could bluff them, pretend he was calling on his way down the mountain. He thumbed the button. No bars. The valley must be dead. He hadn't noticed any towers on the ridgetops. Perhaps the telecommunications and cell phone companies had yet to mark this end of nowhere.

The cabin didn't have a phone. He'd have to walk down to the check-in desk and borrow one. He'd also noticed a pay phone down at the general store, the old-fashioned kind that still took coins. The store was only about three hundred yards down the road, a nice hike that would let him get a feel for the little community.

First things first. He pulled the slender glass vial from his shaving kit and shook it. A fine, white powder lay in the bottom. Fine Peruvian flake, at least 30 percent pure. The kind that would blow most street crud away, devoid of the milk sugar and strychnine that polluted most cocaine. Mark had his connections. After all, he'd spent a great deal of energy making them, at the same time he was losing touch with his wife and daughter.

Fuck it.

He took the lid off the vial and carefully dumped a little mound on the coffee table. Two hundred bucks' worth. He flipped open his wallet and took out a credit card. Using the card, he pushed the coke into two neat lines. Next, he rolled up a five-dollar bill into a tight straw. The big shots used hundreds, but Mark's habit kept him broke. He bent over and snorted the right line into one nostril, tilted his head back, and sniffed. The coke draped a frozen sheet over the base of his skull and his heartbeat accelerated. He bent and tooted the left line into his other nostril, his nose and cheeks going numb. He wiped up the stray dust with one pinky and rubbed the dregs of the coke around his lips, then sucked his pinky clean.

Yeah. Walkin' time. Let's see what the fuck Solom's got to offer a man who's as high as a god and as lowdown as the devil.

He was at the door before he'd even thought about standing, his thoughts racing, trying to stack the images of Jett's story: goats, ghosts, some guy in a black hat, a scarecrow. Now that he was jumped up, the whole thing seemed ridiculous, yet appealing in a strange way. Like some kind of cryptic mystery. He didn't believe in the supernatural. Even though he'd read Stephen King like everybody else on the planet, he couldn't quite get his head around Katy's haunting. More likely his ex-wife was being dramatic in an effort to win sympathy from Gordon. That was just like her, making a play for attention. Maybe to divert Gordon away from Jett's problems, or to pull that selfish "me first" business that had put paid to their marriage.

Mark walked fast, down the hard-packed road and past the Happy Hollow office. A number of other cabins were tucked away in the woods, all offering the occupants privacy without ever letting them lose sight of the Pepsi machine in front of the office. Mark came to the entrance at the highway, then decided to cut across the road instead of making straight for the general store. The river beckoned, a jeweled, frothy dragon, chuckling as it slithered around rocks. The air was wet with the smell of mud and decaying vegetation, and goldenrod shimmered along the banks. The back of Mark's throat tingled, and his feet seemed to be hovering two inches above the ground with each step.

A little trail among waist-high weeds marked what was probably someone's favorite fishing hole. Mark looked up the road and saw a couple of pickup trucks parked in front of the general store's deck. A man in a denim jacket was using the pay phone. Mark headed down the trail, beggar's lice sticking to his trousers, a stray blackberry vine grabbing his sleeve. He scarcely felt the briars that stitched his forearm.

At the river's edge, the mud gave way to smooth pebbles. The water was clear as glass, though its motion distorted the colorful stones along the bottom. A fish raced by, sparkling in the diffracted sunlight before disappearing in a deep, shadowed pool beneath the branches of a drooping sycamore. Nature was a trip. He'd have to get out more.

He was about to walk back to the road and see if the phone was free when something splashed upstream. An old concrete dam spanned the river fifty yards away, though it was more holes than anything. A decrepit mill sagged at one end of the dam, a wooden waterwheel dipping into a gray concrete channel. Most of the wheel's paddles were missing, so it didn't turn steadily. Instead, it juddered and spun a few feet at a time, wobbling like a giant tire with loose lug nuts.

"Help!" someone shouted.

The sound had come from the same general direction as the splash. The white noise of the rushing water confused Mark, or maybe it was the Peruvian flake banging pipes in his brain. He started up the bank toward the sound. That was when he saw the boy attached to the paddle wheel. It looked like his clothes had snagged and he was pushed under the water. Mark waded into the river and fought against the current.

The wheel turned, lifting the boy, who looked to be no more than ten. He was dressed in ragged overalls and a flannel underwear shirt, and as the wheel brought the boy higher into the sky, water poured from his bare feet. The boy was silent, but had seen Mark and raised a weak, desperate hand toward him. Mark plowed through the knee-deep water. The coke had kicked in enough that the river seemed no more powerful than the spit of a garden hose, but time had stretched out so that Mark didn't seem to be making any progress. The wheel took another hesitant roll and the boy was now at the top, his back arched against the metal framework.

As Mark watched, realizing he should have run up the road and then down to the dam, the wheel moved again, and the boy descended headfirst toward the water. His dark hair hung like a dirty mop as he struggled to free himself. He grabbed one of his overall buckles as if to unfasten it, but his fingers weren't strong enough to fight his weight against the strap. Mark was twenty yards from the boy now, sticking to the shallows near the overgrown banks, kicking water into his face as he ran, knees high like an old-fashioned

fullback's. The boy's head went under, and the wheel seemed to
hesitate, as if chocked by the boy's head pressed against the bottom
of the channel. The wire-and-wood frame shook as the boy's legs
flailed in the air. Then the wheel turned again, dragging the boy
fully under and pinning him on his belly.

The water was deep near the base of the dam, the edges rimmed
with stonework. Mark had to swim the last ten yards, though the
current was much weaker where the force of the water spent itself
straight downward. He reached the dam and grabbed a chunk of
shattered concrete, pulling himself out of the water. He couldn't
tell if it was an effect of the cocaine or the angle of the sun off the
water, but the drops that poured around him each seemed to contain a tiny rainbow.

The wheel still juddered in place, hung up because of the boy
lodged at its lowest point. Mark pulled himself over to the channel,
scrabbling for purchase on the slick and jagged concrete. He
reached the wheel, wondering if the boy had already drowned,
wondering how he could fight thousands of gallons of water, wondering if he'd failed somebody again. Just as he reached the wheel,
it issued a moist, rusty groan and turned. Mark braced himself, expecting to see the boy's slack face, eyes shocked wide in death.

Instead, the wheel was bare, save for a few wooden blades dangling from the metal frame.

Mark looked into the river below. The boy couldn't have
plunged past without Mark's seeing. He eased along the top of the
dam and examined the upstream edge of the wheel. No body.

Shit. Cocaine didn't give you hallucinations. Not unless you
were in the screaming pink pain of serious withdrawal.

Mark scanned the road that ran parallel to the river. Through the
trees, the general store stood with its green metal roof, white siding
boards, and black shutters. Farther upstream was the wooden covered bridge marking the highway that led to Titusville. An old
house, its windows broken, huddled at a high bank of the river,
boards warped where past floods had touched it. Solom seemed
abandoned, as if everyone had driven away for the season and
locked up their buildings.

Mark pushed his hair out of his eyes. The water upstream
looked too deep to wade, and he was too weary to try it with his

sodden clothes. He'd have to navigate the top of the dam, walk to the other side of the river, and push through the weeds to the covered bridge. The wheel clicked forward a few feet, like a roulette given a halfhearted nudge.

That's when Mark looked at the window of the mill house. In the shadows stood a man in a hat, which might have been black like the one Jett had described. Mark couldn't discern any features, but he was struck with the notion of being watched. The man was motionless for a moment before slipping into the deeper darkness of the ruins.

Chapter Twenty-eight

Sarah usually closed at six in the evening on Sundays, figuring the second shift at the Free Will Baptist Church would bring in a few customers on the way, those who needed a cup of coffee, Moon Pie, or giant Dr Pepper to fuel them through the service. She couldn't understand why some Baptists felt the need to go to church three or four nights a week. She always thought it would be simpler just to do a little less sinning than more begging for forgiveness. But a dollar was a dollar, no matter the stains on the soul who spent it.

She'd had only two customers in the past hour, loud Yankee fly fishermen who prowled the aisles and hadn't bought so much as a pack of Wrigley's, though they'd held up a number of the more esoteric items and laughed in that slick, mean way they taught up in New York. Too many tourists, and Yankees in particular, had a way of waltzing through her store as if it were a museum, as if none of the merchandise had price tags. As if the whole shebang were there for amusement and not to help feed and clothe a poor old hunched-over Appalachian Jew.

So shutting down early had crossed her mind, because a feeling was creeping up from the soles of her feet that tonight was going to be a doozy. It was almost like the earth itself was sending up bad vibes, that the billion-year-old rocks and mud of the world's oldest mountains sensed something unclean was walking over them. If tonight was going to be a doozy, and the Circuit Rider had found his horse, then going home and worming deep under the quilts sounded like a good idea. Dollar or no dollar.

Sarah was closing out the cash register, figuring to turn over the sign on the door (from COME ON IN—WE'RE BROKE! to MISSED YOU—AND YOUR MONEY, TOO!) even though it was only four o'-clock. Word had gotten around about her fainting spell, so any regular who dropped by would understand. As for the tourists, like those who rented out the cabins on the hill, let them haul their big white rumps into Titusville and mingle with the Tennessee welfare moms in the Wal-Mart.

She was counting the twenties—not enough of them to suit her—when the screen door spanged open and a man thrust himself through. He was soaking wet, one shirttail hanging out, the knees of his trousers scuffed. He was missing one shoe, and the toe of his sock make a spongy slap with each step. The man's eyes showed white all around the iris, as if a doctor had just given him a surprise proctology checkup.

Sarah recognized him from earlier in the day, when he'd stopped in for lunch with a young girl. She'd seen the girl around before; you could hardly miss her, the way she waltzed around tarted up in lipstick and black eyeliner. The girl's redheaded mother came in from time to time, buying eggs, baking powder, and flour, and occasionally asking kitchen advice. The redhead had married Gordon Smith, a fact that had been the talk of the community back in June. This man, though, didn't seem to fit that family picture.

He was probably playing fisherman and had walked himself out of his hip waders after a sip too many. Or maybe he'd rented a canoe from Sue Norwood and taken a spill down by the island park along the first stretch of white water. He didn't look hurt, but his face was blanched the color of the provolone cheese she kept in the dairy case. Might be one of those drugged-out meth junkies she'd read about, who seemed to be everywhere these days, cooking up the stuff in their car trunks. She didn't know what meth was, exactly, or what it did to people, but she wouldn't be surprised if it led you to fall in the river.

"You okay, mister?" She slipped the twenties under the cash register in case he took a notion to rob her. The shotgun beneath the counter was loaded and handy, if need be. She'd made certain of that after the Circuit Rider's recent visit to her store. Not that buckshot would do any good against something two hundred years dead, but it was the *comfort* of the thing that mattered.

"I don't have any change," he said. He didn't talk Yankee, but he sure wasn't local.

"Well, normally we take credit cards, but I'm just about to close."

"No, I mean—I need to use your phone."

Their eyes settled on the store's rotary-dial phone, a battered black relic that looked like something from a 1950s government office. Sarah liked the sound of a good, solid ring, not the little kitty puttering of those modern phones. A woman of years could hardly hear such a contraption. Most people carried their phones in their pockets these days, as if it were a virtue never to spend a minute totally alone. The pay phone out front barely earned its keep these days, and the BellSouth man had threatened to take it away until she convinced him it was a proper companion to an old country store.

"That's not a public phone," Sarah said, annoyed that a drenched-to-the-gills outsider had the nerve to barge in and take over the place. As if it were a museum built for his amusement and convenience. Sure, he'd tipped well after his earlier meal, but that was hours ago.

The man put his palms flat on the counter and leaned forward, water dripping from his chin to dot the scarred maple. He panted, his breath ruffling the cellophane in the jar of cow-tail candy perched by the register. He didn't smell of liquor, so that ruled out the "drunk fisherman" theory.

"I have to report a drowning," he said.

"Oh, goodness, why didn't you say so? Whereabouts?" Sarah grabbed the phone and put her finger in the last hole on the dial, ready to spin out 911.

He waved behind him, toward the old dam. "In the mill. A boy got caught in the waterwheel."

Sarah was halfway through the spin when she lifted her finger away. "About ten? Wearing scrub overalls and a long john shirt?"

The man's eyes grew even wider, near the size of pickled eggs. "Did you see him, too?"

"I seen him," she said. "Not lately, though."

He reached to grab the phone from her, but she slapped his hand away. "Hurry," he said. "There might still be a chance—"

"That was little Johnny Hampton you saw," she said. "No need to hurry on his account. He's dead."

"I didn't see his body. He just went under. He might be some-where downstream."

"He ain't downstream."

"Please, ma'am." His hands were shaking, and he sniffed a rope of snot back into his head. Sarah was sticking with the "meth junkie" idea, but meth wasn't what had triggered the man's horri-ble ghostly vision.

"He went around and around the wheel, didn't he?" Sarah said, calm now, no longer afraid of him. Instead, she felt pity. Solom's dead were meant for the eyes of Solom's people, not those of out-siders. The Circuit Rider must be whooping up some god-awful bad juju if just any-old-body was able to see his victims.

The man pushed the wet hair from his eyes, stepped back, and looked out the store windows, as if checking to see if the dam was visible from the counter. He shuddered, and whether it was from the cold or the shock, Sarah couldn't say. She doubted if the man could, either.

"I didn't see it *this* time," Sarah said. "I saw it nearly twenty years ago."

The man faced her again, one eyelid twitching. "The boy?"

"I wasn't the first, and you ain't the second," Sarah said. "Johnny makes an appearance every now and then. Along with the rest of them."

"The rest of who?"

Sarah had lost him. She should have known better. Solom kept its secrets, and outsiders never understood. "Where's the girl? The one you ate lunch with?"

"My daughter? She's back home." The man choked on that word *home* as if it were a sour green gooseberry.

"Keep her there. Now, be on about your business."

The man lunged forward and grabbed the front of her cardigan sweater. A speck of spit landed on her cheek as he spoke. "If there's some kind of danger, you need to tell me."

"Hey, mister, ain't no call for that." Sarah dug her fingernails into the man's wrists and squeezed until he looked down. He let go of her and studied his palms as if stigmata had appeared there.

"Sorry," he said. "I—damn . . ."

"Things are walking," Sarah said, pity filling her. If the redhead was his ex-wife and the little tart was his daughter, that meant they were now part of Solom, since they'd married into the Smith clan. They'd be bound up in whatever business the Circuit Rider had in store this time.

"Harmon's things," she continued. "The ones he's taken away. They come back when he comes back. It's best for you to make sure your daughter stays in tonight, and get yourself as far away from this valley as you can. This ain't your business."

"If my daughter's involved, I'm not going anywhere," he said.

"Suit yourself. But I can't help you."

"She was telling me about a man in a black hat."

"Harmon Smith." Dark blotches formed across Sarah's vision, drifting like jagged thunderclouds. She wouldn't black out again. She had nothing to fear. Harmon didn't want her, not this time, or he would have taken her the day he walked into the store.

"I think I saw him down at the dam. Where is he?"

Sarah braced herself against the counter, fighting off the dizziness. "Everywhere. In the trees, in the river, in the barns. The best thing we can do is lay low until he rides off for the next stop."

The man shook his head. The river chill had sunk in, and his lips quivered. Steps clattered across the wooden porch. The door opened and Sue Norwood entered the store, a rock climber's pickax in her hand.

"Are you okay?" Sue asked Sarah, lifting the pickax as if she knew how to use it.

The man raised his hands, palms showing in a submissive gesture. "Hey, I was just leaving."

Sue looked at Sarah, who nodded. Sarah was bone tired, seventy years of standing up to gravity and worry and fright finally coming down square on her shoulders. Who cared if Harmon swooped in and reaped her? One less Jewish shopkeeper in the world wouldn't make a damn bit of difference in the big scheme of things.

The man eased around Sue, the toe of his sock slapping like a wet fish against the floor. After he was gone, Sarah sagged into the little rocker she kept behind the counter.

"This is my town, too, even if I've only lived here for a few years," Sue said. "I'm going after the Circuit Rider."

"You and everybody else," Sarah said. Though she had a feeling they wouldn't have to do much seeking. Harmon Smith had found his horse, and that meant he'd be making the rounds in due time.

David Tester's hands were callused from years of landscaping, but a blister arose on the pad of his left hand before he reached Harmon Smith's coffin. As the shovel bit deeper, the soil became darker and gave off a rank, swampy smell. If Harmon had been buried for over two centuries, then the coffin was likely rotted away. The grave might contain nothing but a few bones, given the lack of preservation techniques employed during Smith's era. But that was wrong, too, thinking of Smith as belonging to one era, when every generation in Solom earned a visit from the Circuit Rider.

The shovel blade finally met a soft resistance, and David looked up at the sky. He hadn't cut a sharp rectangle into the ground the way grave diggers shaped them to receive a coffin. David's hole was sloped and uneven, showing the roots and gravel that had slowed his path through the clay. The wood was soggy, but preserved somewhat by the clay, and David had to chew through it with the shovel blade. He wouldn't have to clear the entire lid of the coffin to find what he sought. He rammed the shovel down time and again, the sound of the blows baffled by the walls of dirt. The wood gave way, and David twisted the blade to widen the opening.

A foul odor arose from the voided coffin, like rotten eggs scrambled in formaldehyde and served up with slices of spoiled pork. David pulled a bandana from his back pocket and wrapped it around his mouth and nose, tying it behind his neck. He was reaching for the shovel when the sodden wooden planks gave way beneath him. He plunged knee-deep into the gap, the stench rising around him in putrid waves. His boots splashed in unseen muck. He clawed at the clay banks, trying to pull himself up, but his movements triggered a tumble of loose soil from the rim of the hole. Clods rained down and bounced off his shoulders.

"You looking for something?"

The voice came from above and below at the same time, as if piped in by some insane and remote sound system. David recognized it from the night before. He looked up, and the Circuit Rider was framed against the blue afternoon sky, sitting astride his legendary horse. His back was to the sun, like the lone hero of a western, throwing most of his face into shadow.

David sank another six inches, the jagged wood scraping against his thighs. He grabbed the shovel and spanned the broken top of the coffin with the handle, hoping to halt his descent. He didn't want to die this way, another one of Harmon's victims. Even if it was predestined by God, David fought the urge to surrender. He could imagine his congregation whispering about his failure, he pictured the men casting votes for the next elder, he could see the church abandoned and forlorn, good for nothing but the winter nests of rodents.

"I was looking for *you*," David said, his voice muffled by the cloth over his mouth. He braced against the shovel handle even though he was now waist-deep in the cool morass. The stench had grown even stronger, despite the protective bandana.

"You got your holdup mask on," Harmon Smith said. "You fixing to rob a bank? Or just a grave?"

"I needed to see how many pieces of you were buried in my churchyard."

"To see if you got your fair share?"

"You've got three graves."

"And I don't have use for any of them," Harmon said. He twitched the reins and Old Saint took a step forward, knocking a bucket's worth of dirt around David's waist.

David could feel things moving around his legs, loathsome and slithering creatures. He tried to tell himself that an underground spring must run beneath the graveyard, carrying water from the creek, and the creatures were salamanders preparing for a long winter's sleep. But they were too big to be salamanders. And salamanders didn't have teeth . . .

Predestination. David looked past the gaunt face and potato-beetle eyes of the Circuit Rider to the faint rags of clouds above. Somewhere up there, God sat on His almighty throne and watched it all play out, even though He already knew the ending.

Must be kind of boring, even when the entertainment was as rich as watching a preacher die in a deep hole only to have his soul tied with Harmon Smith's return to the area. How many times would David have to play out this little scene again? How many times would he have to die and be reborn, a puppet in Harmon's little stage show? Jesus Christ might come again, but Harmon Smith would come back not only once, but over and over and over.

"I tried to follow Your ways," David said, slipping another few inches into the mire. He could no longer move his feet.

"Well, that's mighty obliging of you, Elder Tester. A shame your ancestors didn't walk that path."

"I wasn't talking to you, you sorry bastard."

The Circuit Rider laughed, a rattling ululation that silenced the birds in the trees surrounding the graveyard. Even Old Saint blew a moist snicker. He lifted a bony hand, one that was like parchment wrapped around a bundle of broken sticks. His index finger aimed at David as if preparing to shoot fire or a lightning bolt or a magic spell.

"No respect for a fellow man of the cloth," Harmon said. "That's what caused such grief for the people of Solom. If they hadn't given in to jealousy and coveting, all of us would have lived in peace. But they had to go and kill me. And I couldn't allow that to be the end of it. Neither could he who gives life."

David tucked his forearms over the shovel handle and lifted. He thought he was gaining ground, though it felt like one of his boots was sliding off. Something bumped against his knee and sent a sharp flare of pain up his leg.

"All the people who hurt you are long gone," David said between tight lips. "Didn't the Methodists teach you to forgive?"

"Oh, I gave up the Methodist ways. That's why people got so riled. I went back to the older religions. If you want God to grant increase and to bless the orchards of your life, then you offer Him blood. Fair enough trade. Life for life."

The dark morass sucked at David's lower body, a moist, hungry thing. He wondered if this was really the way God wanted his life to end. What if he let go of the shovel and slid on down into the suffocating mud?

"Did you find what you were looking for?" Harmon asked, adjusting the brim of his hat. Old Saint kicked at the loose dirt, triggering another small avalanche onto David's shoulders.

"I wanted to see if your grave was a doorway to hell. Or if the Primitive Baptists had earned their piece of your corpse."

The Circuit Rider tipped his hat. "Well, I'll leave you to your business, then. For where your treasure is, there your heart will be also."

He whipped the reins against Old Saint's neck, and the horse reared and whinnied, the front legs coming down with so much force that David feared the bank would give way and the horse and rider would fall on top of him. The horse wheeled and the hoof-beats thundered off across the graveyard. David slipped another couple of inches into the mud and was losing his battle to brace himself with the shovel handle. How could God allow a true believer to die in someone else's grave?

Something slithered into his remaining boot, then up his pants leg, scraping rough scales against his bare skin. David tried to kick, but the mud held his leg firm. In his struggles, he lost his balance on the shovel handle and slid into the mud until it was past his waist. The pressure on his abdomen made breathing difficult. He thought of offering a final prayer, but if God had already decided, as the Primitive Baptists believed, then it would be a waste of air.

He was just about to let himself slip down into Harmon Smith's tainted coffin when a snake fell across the back of his neck. He slapped at it, frantic, and found it was coarse and fibrous. It wasn't a snake.

It was a rope.

"He would let you die that way, but I won't," the Circuit Rider said. "After all, the Good Book says to bless those who curse you and do good to those who hate you."

David grabbed the rope. The Circuit Rider had tied his end to the saddle horn and nudged Old Saint so the horse backed away, chest and flanks flexing as it fought for purchase in the graveyard grass. The walls of the hole gave way in large chunks, but David wrapped the rope around his wrists and shielded his face from the barrage of dirt. He thought his arms would be ripped off at the shoulder blades, but his body slowly pulled free of the mud and the two feet of loose dirt that had piled around him. He slid on his belly up the slope of clay and then lay gasping and shivering on the grass.

The rope fell beside his face in a rattlesnake's coil.

"A good tree cannot grow bad fruit," Harmon Smith said. "And a man cannot serve two masters."

Once more, the horse's drumming hooves faded into the distance, leaving David weak and cold, and beyond the numbness, maybe a little angry. Whether at himself, or Harmon Smith, or God, he couldn't be certain.

Chapter Twenty-nine

Katy waited until Gordon excused himself from dinner. He'd eaten only half of his sautéed chicken breast and had barely touched his wax beans and sweet potato pie. Katy finished her own plate and began collecting dishes. Jett, who had remained sullen and silent throughout the meal, shoved her glass of milk away and crossed her arms.

"What did you tell your dad?" Katy asked.

"That's between him and me."

"Honey, remember the deal. We'll get through this together, okay?"

"Okay, I'll share if you share. What's the deal with this ghost you keep talking about?"

Katy dropped a piece of silverware as she stacked dirty dishes with shaking hands. "Nothing. I think I was just suffering delusions."

"And a 'delusion' just happened to give you a black eye while we were gone?"

"I was up in the attic looking for something—"

"Something in a long wooden box, right?"

"No. I found a key. And I thought it might fit one of the bureaus up there."

"Well, I'll tell you what *I* found in the box. A scarecrow. Just like the one that used to hang in the barn. Not the one that's hanging out there now. Somebody switched them."

"Why would they do that?"

"Maybe they needed to borrow the clothes."

"You didn't tell your dad any of this, did you?"

"I told him everything. The parts I know, at least."

"You didn't tell him I thought I was being haunted—"

"He loved that part. I thought he was going to laugh right into his coffee. Good old Dad. He can't handle any alternate reality unless it's caused by drugs."

"You shouldn't talk that way. Mark loves you."

"Yeah, but he loves drugs more. I could see it in his eyes. He's still just a sniff monkey, despite all the big talk about being strong for the good of the family. But you've heard that line plenty of times, huh?"

Katy left the room, dishes piled against her waist and smearing butter on her blouse. She didn't want Jett to see her tears.

They should get out of the house. Jump in the Subaru and drive down to Florida, stay with Katy's mom for a while, dig in the flower garden, and get sane. She needed time to sort things out. Rushing into a bad marriage was one thing, but dragging Jett along made it worse. And now she was hallucinating, or maybe cracking up.

Yet the smell of lilacs was real. It was strong in the kitchen, heady and thick, as if Rebecca had walked through the room only moments earlier. But Rebecca was dead. She'd had her head sheared off in a car crash. Rebecca wasn't keeping house any longer, nor was she brushing her invisible hair. No scarecrow lived in the attic. The man in the black hat was probably Odus, dropping in at odd hours to catch up on chores. Jett had merely seen a shadow, a trick of the moonlight, and her youthful imagination did the rest.

They couldn't *both* be going crazy.

But the goats were real. They were cunning and sinister and dangerous. Gordon talked of them as if they were family, and he showed them more affection than he showed his own wife and stepdaughter. He tended and nurtured his flock, but offered no warmth to the humans living in his house.

"Mom," Jett said from the doorway.

Katy was at the sink, elbow-deep in suds. The clock on the wall read a quarter till six. She'd been standing there fifteen minutes. Only two plates stood in the dish rack, and she could see her blurred reflection in the nearest one. For a flicker of an instant, she appeared dark-haired, smiling, eyes as mysterious as those in the locket she'd found in the attic. Rebecca's face had superimposed itself over hers, and a ragged rim of flesh encircled her neck.

She reached up to touch the wound, but found only the lump in her throat.

"You're blanking out again."

"No, I'm not. Everything's fine. We'll get through this—" Katy couldn't bring herself to finish. It was all hollow, the whole new life she'd tried to build was just a stack of cards waiting for a breeze. She despised cooking, and God had invented the dishwasher for a reason. These clothes were too cheerful and bold, too goddamned *chirpy*.

She was trying to be someone else. Someone whose head had never been found.

"Jett, I think we need to leave."

"You mean go back to *Dad's*?"

"No. That wouldn't be right. But I can't stay in this house another minute."

"What about Gordon?"

"I'll call him later."

Jett grinned, the first real joy she'd shown since moving to Solom. "Wow, Mom. I'm impressed. You've really got some fucking balls."

"So to speak."

"Oh, sorry. I wasn't supposed to cuss."

Katy turned off the water. She didn't even set the dirty dishes in the sink to soak. Let Gordon wash his own damn dishes. It was his house, after all. His and his dead wife's.

"Go upstairs and throw some things in your knapsack," she said, the weariness lifting from her body. "Clothes, toothbrush, pajamas.

Just enough stuff for a few days. We'll come back and get the rest after I've had a chance to talk with Gordon."

Jett raced across the room and lifted her arm, open-palmed. Katy did the same and Jett leaped and slapped a high five. "You rock, Mom. I love you."

"A hug and a kiss aren't cool enough?"

Jett hugged her and gave her a quick kiss on the cheek. "Ooh, gross, Mom. Where did you get that stinky perfume?"

"I'm not wearing perfume."

"Smells like flowers."

"Must be the cinnamon I put on the sweet potatoes."

"Whatever. Let's blow this nutty little peanut shack."

Katy followed Jett up the stairs, wondering if she was making another mistake. She had probably stayed in her relationship with Mark several years too long, but what if she was skipping out before she'd given Gordon a chance? No doubt Gordon could explain everything and ease their fears, show them that ghosts weren't real and scarecrows were nothing but straw and cloth.

No, he'd had plenty of chances. Katy couldn't love him or even trust him, despite his pledge to protect her and take care of Jett. All she had to do was imagine his face during that morning they'd had intercourse, when he'd opened his eyes and seemed shocked to find her on top of him. As if he was expecting someone else.

Besides, as Jett would say, Solom was one seriously fucked-up piece of real estate.

Alex fired up a bowl of sweet, homegrown weed and puffed it until his lungs were scorched. Despite the pleasant buzz from the smoke, Alex couldn't relax. Something heavy was coming down in Solom. He had a feeling it wasn't the secret agents he'd always feared, or the Internal Revenue Service coming to seize his land as punishment for his income tax evasion. No, this had all the vibes of a world-class cluster fuck.

Alex had convinced Meredith to stay in her apartment near the college. Despite her physical gifts and generosity, Alex liked his space. He needed to get his head together, which seemed to be a full-time job these days. He put the pipe away and went outside to check on the garden. The garden did what drugs and sex couldn't do: it filled him with a sense of purpose and accomplishment. Growing good crops, especially mythical mother-lode mind-fuck marijuana, was about as close to God as a human being could get. Crops made the world a better place, especially dope, which was the equivalent of Eden's apple when it came to granting wisdom. As a fringe benefit, self-reliance also stuck it to the Man, because the government couldn't tax such products.

Alex peeked through the curtains to make sure nobody was watching from outside. Dope possessed the strange power to make him feel bulletproof and paranoid at the same time. Behind the safety of locked doors, he was master of his fate. When he stepped under the big sky, all manner of rules and laws took effect, whether they were natural or contrived by the two major political parties to ensure that nothing changed, that all the stars stayed fixed in the heavens and all the crooks in Congress defended their incumbency.

Looked safe outside. No cops, no Weird Dude Walking. The sun was about half an hour from hitting the tops of the trees on the western mountains. In September, dusk arrived quickly and the shadows stretched longer and longer until they tangled in dark armies. It was nearly six o'clock, which meant the bell in the steeple of the Free Will Baptist Church would soon sound its Sunday call. Birds twittered in the surrounding trees, as sacred a music as any that had ever droned from a church organ. If the birds were talking, that meant everything was normal, despite the eerie flutter in the pit of his stomach.

Alex went out onto the deck, binoculars in hand. Through a cut where the road wound among the trees, the Smith farm was visible. Focusing the lenses, he saw the new Smith woman, the redhead, walking toward the barn. Alex didn't like spying, because it was too close to what the CIA practiced against its own citizens. But survival instinct told him there was a big difference between being nosy and being informed. As he watched, the redhead veered toward the fence, then pulled back as a clutch of goats came trotting toward her from the rear of the barn. Probably the same damn goats that had eaten Weird Dude Walking.

Alex shortened the lenses so he could scan his fence line. The spot he'd repaired near the garden was still intact. He'd fantasized about planting some sort of booby trap, maybe a razor-studded spring that could be triggered by a trip wire. But the fence was technically on Smith property, and that would be crossing the line. Neighbors deserved a little extra tolerance, even if their livestock fed on old preachers as if they were a Jesus biscuit in a Catholic chow line.

Alex put down the binoculars. All was right with the world, at least his portion of it.

Then he saw the shed.

The doors were open, one of them hanging askew on a single hinge. The grow bulbs threw their blue-tinted light against the greater might of the orange sun. Something had forcibly broken in, or maybe *out*. Except there was nothing in the shed but . . .

Thirty-seven beautiful creatures. His babies. His family.

Alex hurtled down the deck steps three at a time, the binoculars swinging from the strap and banging against his chest. One of his paranoid fantasies was that someone would learn about his hobby and try to rip him off, a fellow stoner who didn't groove on the righteousness of karma. That's why he was careful in choosing his customers. And the government was to blame for criminalizing a harmless flower and linking it to violence and theft, when it was put on earth to be shared in peace.

He ran the fifty feet to the shed and looked in, barely able to breathe. Most of the pot plants had been ripped up by the roots, though a few bare and broken stalks poked toward the ceiling like skeletal green fingers. Stray leaves lay scattered along the floor, and one light fixture had been torn from the wall. The black plastic sheeting beneath the buckets was ripped and gouged. And on the cinder blocks that served as a step was a mucusy gray-white smear that could only be one thing.

Goat shit.

The fuckers had trespassed onto *his* land, broken into *his* shed, chomped down on the fruit of *his* labors. He didn't know how they'd circumvented the fence, but the ground was scarred by cloven-hoofed footprints. Alex, his heart pushing broken glass through his chest, followed the tracks behind the shed to the fence. There, the wire had been trampled as if pressed down by a great weight, dragging down several locust posts. The wire was pocked with tufts of goat hair, and the musky stench of a rutting billy tainted the air.

On the Smith side of the fence, leaves had been scuffed and scooted around. Clearly evident against the dark humus was the imprint of a horseshoe. As if some rider had urged his horse to stomp down the fence and allow the goats access. Maybe the horse had even kicked in the shed door for them. Alex was sure that, if he checked beside the padlock, he'd find the arc of a horseshoe embedded in the wood.

Alex wondered if Weird Dude Walking was no longer walking. Maybe he'd mounted up in order to make better time. On whatever road he was headed down.

Didn't matter.

The Dude had fucked with private property. And so had those creepy-eyed, stink-making, beard-pissing goats.

The Bible said to forgive trespasses, but Alex didn't hold to the Bible. In Alex's belief system, trespasses meant one of two things: either you build a bigger fence or you go after those who didn't respect boundaries.

Alex went back to the house, to the walk-in closet that held his arsenal. There was hell to pay and Alex planned on delivering the invoice.

He only takes one.

That had been the way of Solom for as far back as the legends reached. All a body had to do was keep his head down, stay inside, and wait for somebody else to get claimed. That philosophy had served Arvel well for sixty-eight years and counting. As a boy, when he'd first seen the Circuit Rider on the little goat path that led to his Rush Branch fishing hole, he had managed to escape for some reason. He'd tried to tell his dad, a no-nonsense, up-with-the-sun Free Will Baptist, about the encounter, but Dad cut him off at the first mention. The Circuit Rider wasn't real, and that was that, and no amount of blabbing and blubbering would change that. Except Dad's wrinkled-raisin face had grown as pale as a potato root, leaving Arvel to figure that Dad must have had his own little run-in with the dead preacher.

Arvel had kept himself scarce for the next two days, feigning a bellyache so he wouldn't have to go to school or do chores. That wasn't much of a stretch, because he was so nervous he puked every time a spoonful of food hit his gut. From the bedroom he shared with his brother Zeke, he could see the Smith barn, and under the moonlight shadows sometimes moved in the hayloft. He'd clamp his eyes tight, but one of them would end up creeping open like the lid of a vampire's coffin. He didn't sleep much those two days.

Then, his brother didn't come home from school. The county schools had buses, but the Wards and other kids in their area had to walk a mile down to the river to catch one. The bus stop was a favorite spot for shenanigans, with a dozen kids of different ages killing time with jokes, pocketknife stretch, and the occasional round of post office or show-me-yours-and-I'll-show-you-mine. Zeke had taken up cigarettes, another favorite pastime at the bus stop, but none of the other kids dared smoke. Of course, that made Zeke the idol of the dirt-road neighborhood, but he also knew he would get his rear end worn to a pile of rags if the folks caught him. The kids said he showed them the pack of cigarettes that morning, unfiltered Viceroys in a shiny pack he must have swiped from the general store.

As big a show-off as he was, Zeke thought he'd best slip off into the woods to do his puffing. Arvel guessed his brother was just as afraid of coughing and hacking in front of the others as he was of being spied by an adult. Whatever the reason, Zeke went into a laurel scrub and lit up. The kids watched for the trail of smoke to be sure that Zeke wasn't joshing them, then turned their attention back to their games. It was only when the bus rolled up and one of the kids hollered Zeke's name that they realized he'd been gone way too long to just smoke a cigarette.

Arvel's best friend, J.C. Littlejohn, had gone into the laurel to find Zeke. The bus driver honked and the other kids shouted names, according to J.C., but Zeke didn't come out of hiding. J.C. found him sprawled on the ground, belly down, the moist butt of the Viceroy inches from his lips, the ember on the lit end burning a hole in a dead leaf. Zeke's Kedd sneaker had lodged in a protruding root and he'd tripped. Freak accident, the county coroner said. His forehead hit a tree trunk and snapped his neck back, killing him instantly.

And Arvel's first thought upon hearing the news: *I'm glad the Circuit Rider took him instead of me.*

He was having a similar thought now. Betsy had come home from the hospital and was going to be just fine. That was the trouble. Arvel had been hoping that Betsy would be the one the Circuit Rider took this time. Not that he wished ill of Betsy, but after all these years, he was still so sweat-shaky scared of the Circuit Rider he'd rather die a thousand different ways than end up done in by the Circuit Rider. Because them that the Circuit Rider claimed had a way of showing back up.

Arvel had seen his brother a decade after his death, when Arvel was newly married and had taken over running the farm after Daddy's final stroke. Arvel made a habit of keeping watch on the Smith barn, and his adolescence was haunted not by his brother's fluke accident, but by the shifting wedges of darkness that seemed to cavort just beyond the sunlit windows. On a cold March morning, when Arvel was on his way to slop the two hogs, Zeke was standing by the collard patch, barely visible, wreathed in the fog as if he were woven into it. His head lolled to one side like an onion hanging by a piece of twine.

"Soon as he finds his horse, you can come join me," Zeke said, the words seeping out of the mist as if growing up from the dirt. "Gets lonely over here waiting."

Arvel dropped the slop bucket, splashing sour milk, table scraps, eggshells, and apple peels on his jeans. He ran back into the house, where Dad saw the smelly clothing and whooped him for spilling the slop. Dad sent him back out to retrieve the bucket, and Arvel had no choice, you didn't cross Dad on pain of death or worse. Zeke was gone when he reached the spot by the collards. Arvel didn't look too hard for his dead brother. Instead, he found an excuse to hang around the house or work in the barn for the next several days, only venturing to the garden in broad daylight.

And even through the fear of that encounter, another thought had pierced through like sunshine through a church's plate-glass window: *I'm glad it was him and not me.*

Which is the same way he felt when he'd come into the kitchen and seen Betsy sprawled on her back by the stove. The gouge in her side was the mystery. The Circuit Rider wasn't known to mutilate his victims. Sure, they didn't die pretty, but almost always whole. Some said that Rebecca Smith had been taken by the Circuit Rider, but Arvel figured that was just a plain old car wreck on a twisty mountain road. Harmon Smith hadn't been seen in the days leading up to her accident, and it hadn't really fit the pattern of the preacher's rounds.

But he was back now, that was for sure. The first night that Betsy was confined in a Titusville hospital room, Arvel had lain awake until 3:00 a.m., listening for the sound of hoofbeats outside, his heart jumping every time Digger let out a bark. Once he'd gone to the window to check on the Smith barn, but the windows were dark and the moon was buried behind the clouds. Last night, he'd curled up on a couch in the hospital waiting room, a magazine in his lap as if he were expecting a diagnosis, and had napped just enough to have a nightmare of the Circuit Rider chasing him down the goat path from the fishing hole.

He poured a cup of tea for Betsy and checked the lock on the back door. He didn't know if locks would keep the dead preacher out. For all he knew, the door had been locked when Betsy had her little accident. She had no memory of falling or hitting her head, only a headache she compared to the one she'd had the morning after Arvel got her drunk on moonshine and became engaged to her the old-fashioned way.

Betsy was local, half Rominger and half Tester, and she knew about the Circuit Rider, like everyone else who grew up in these parts. She didn't talk about it, and didn't seem to connect her accident with the preacher's return. So there was still a chance that Betsy was the intended victim. The preacher could certainly do worse: Betsy was a decent cook and didn't run her mouth too much, she was beholden to men and honored the local traditions. She could can a mean batch of relish or sauerkraut, wasn't above butchering a chicken, and put up with Arvel's fumblings about once a month when he needed satisfaction. Arvel didn't know exactly what the preacher did with them after he got them, but he didn't want to find out. All he knew was if he survived this time, he probably wouldn't live long enough for another turn of the Circuit Rider's wheel. And that was plenty fine with Arvel.

This was Sunday, the very day Harmon Smith had been killed all those years ago. If ever there was a day for the preacher to carry a grudge, this would be it. And no doubt Zeke would be out tonight, maybe hanging around the garden carrying a hoe or flitting through the apple orchard like a shredded kite.

He added a spoonful of sugar to the tea and carried it up the stairs, glad that he wouldn't be alone tonight.

Chapter Thirty

Jett tucked a stone-washed denim jacket, a pair of black stockings, and a sweat suit into her backpack. She looked around the room. She'd never really settled into this place. Maybe it was Gordon's dreariness hanging over the entire house, or the faceless generations of Smiths who had lived in this room before her. A Brandon Lee poster and a diaphanous black scarf over the lamp shade didn't make a place any more inviting to a Gothling.

Mom had said to hurry, so Jett flipped through the CD stack. She passed over the Bella Morte, Marilyn Manson, Nine Inch Nails, the music that had once seemed to match her mood. Now it all seemed so childish. Nihilism was great when it was part of a stage character, like makeup and black-leather props and facial piercings. But when you had stared nothingness in the face, and it stared right back and grinned, then the romanticism was lost. Jett nudged the CDs aside and plucked up some of her mother's favorites. Robyn Hitchcock's *Queen Elvis*, Tommy Keene's *Songs from the Film*, the Replacements' *All Shook Down*, XTC's *The Big Express*. Seemed like music to escape by, stuff that let you be yourself with no questions asked. Songs that made you feel stoned without drugs.

She crammed a couple of changes of day clothes in the bag. She didn't know if she'd ever see this room again, or the rest of her stuff. It depended on how well Gordon handled Mom's leaving. He might go postal and come after them with both guns blazing, or he might just as easily sit by the fire with a glass of wine, intellectualizing the reality of abandonment. That was the problem with Gordon. He didn't seem human, so you couldn't expect a human reaction.

After packing, Jett slid open her desk drawer and reached to the underside of the desk where she'd taped her bag of pot. She was a veteran of room searches, and though Mom had sworn to trust her, Gordon had no doubt rummaged a few times. She pulled the Baggie free and checked its contents. Enough to get her through the week. And then what?

Reality.

A reality far from a creepy stranger in a black hat, a gooned-out living scarecrow, a goat that sniffed your skin as if you were an apple pie, a ghost that haunted your mom.

Fuck it. Those would all be memories one day, and the more time that passed, the less she'd be able to see them. In a year, she probably would be able to tell herself it was all just a stoned nightmare. She tossed the pot back in the drawer. Let Gordon find it. Maybe he'd cram some into his pipe and see what all the fuss was about. Might loosen him up a little.

Textbooks lay scattered across the desk. No need to worry about that geography test next week. The sun was touching the mountains, and the first long shadows reached between the curtains. She wanted to be out of Solom before dark, and would bet her leather bracelet that Mom felt the same way.

Jett snatched Captain Boo off the bed, flung the backpack over her shoulder, and ran down to meet Mom at the car.

"There's just one thing about this," Sarah said.

"Whatever," Sue said, still clutching the climber's pickax. "I'm already nuts to believe any of this, so just lay it all out."

"The Circuit Rider only takes one. He had his shot at me, and I didn't cut the mustard with him for whatever reason. Not that I'm complaining, but I don't know if I want to double my odds. And it may be that he's ready to take on outsiders like you. After all, a soul's a soul, no matter where it comes from."

"I'll take my chances. I worked too hard to get established here. I'm not going to run off without a fight."

"That's a lot of gumption for a little thing like you. But that pickax might not do any good against a dead guy."

Sue swung the pickax handle against her other palm and caught it with a smack. "It feels right, somehow. Like you're supposed to use something that's part of who you are."

"In that case," Sarah said. She rummaged under the counter and brought out the twenty-gauge shotgun. She broke down the barrel and checked the shell. The gun hadn't been fired in five years but the powder had been kept dry. She reached up on the shelves behind her where she displayed ammunition for sale. Pulling down a box of bird-shot shells, she opened it and slipped three of them in her pants pocket.

"If I need more than three shots, the last one is for me," she said, pointing her thumb to her chin to show she'd blow her own head off before she let the Circuit Rider gallop her soul off to hell. Except part of her wondered if, by committing such an act, she would be volunteering to play the part of victim.

They stood looking at each other for a moment, sheepish expressions on their faces. "What now?" Sue asked.

"You got your Jeep?"

"It's by the shop."

"Let's take a ride, then."

"Where?"

"If you want to catch a mouse, you have to think like a mouse. If you want to catch a contrary preacher that's two hundred years dead and won't accept it, then you have to think like one of those, too. And if I was the Circuit Rider, I'd head for high ground."

"High ground? You mean Lost Ridge?"

"Can't think of any better place for a soul to get lost, can you?"

"Closer to heaven."

"Turn over the sign on the door and I'll close out the register. If there's a chance I'm dying tonight, I don't want some Yankee lawyer claiming the petty cash as part of my estate."

"You're a woman after my own heart," Sue said.

"Except I ain't got one."

Ray was changing the plugs on his Massey Ferguson when he saw a goat moving across his meadow, hobbling as if it had blown a knee joint or gotten a thorn up in between its cloven hoofs. The animal moved between the giant rolls of hay that were still green and moist. Ray recalled the headless goats he'd found in the field. He'd buried the goats behind his blackberry patch, using his tractor to gouge a hole in the ground. The heads had never turned up.

Ray figured the Circuit Rider would be afoot tonight. After Harmon Smith's appearance at the general store last night, Ray thought the preacher was toying with them, letting them know he could take one of them at any time. Ray wasn't particularly afraid of dying. He'd given up on religion, and the Primitives didn't really believe you could do anything about the fate of your soul, anyway. His younger brother David hadn't reached out to try to bring Ray back into the church. David had always been the smooth talker of the family, the one who'd learned to read before grade school. Ray had studied shop and auto mechanics before dropping out in the eleventh grade, while David had gotten a degree at the community college. Never mind that David was practically nothing but a glorified lawn mower man these days, while Ray worked for himself running a backhoe. David was the one the church members had selected to be elder.

The church had a hand in Harmon Smith's death. It wasn't something the Rush Branch Primitive Baptists were either proud of or ashamed of, it just *was*. Like that lame goat that made its way between the rolls of hay, making a drunken beeline for the fence. Ray put down his ratchet and wiped his hands on a rag. As he watched, the goat eased against the wire, its left foreleg twisted as if the bone had snapped. Goats were known for breaking out of any kind of pen, and this one must have pulled a Houdini act once already. But there was no way it would make it over four feet of hog wire topped with two strands of barbed wire.

Yet the goat reared up, put its broken limb on top of the hog

wire, and dragged itself up. Then its other leg hooked on a strand
of wire, and the rear hooves fought for purchase. The damned goat
(a billy, judging by the sac that swung between its rear legs) was
climbing the fence like a brain-damaged monkey. It put its chin
over the top strand of wire, puncturing its flesh and sending a dribble of blood down the dirty white fur of its neck. Then it reposi-
tioned its legs and shoved forward until its chest, and then belly,
were suspended on the top wire. The barbs must have been shred-
ding its stomach, but the goat didn't mutter a grunt of complaint.
Instead, it worked like it had a mission, wriggling until the bulk of
its weight caused it to flop onto the other side of the fence. It stood
on shaky legs and stared at Ray, eyes red and mucusy. Could goats
get rabies?

Ray looked in his toolbox. He pulled a rusty plumber's wrench
from the depths. It was two feet long and weighed at least eight
pounds. Ray swung it before him, testing its heft.

The goat didn't charge. Instead, it planted its broken leg and
took an awkward step, then another, blood seeping from its scored
belly. It was heading past the potato patch and up into the woods.
Toward the rocky slopes of Lost Ridge.

Ray waited until it was past the spot where he had buried the
goat corpses, then followed, keeping a distance of about forty feet.
He could track the thing easily from the red splashes that pocked the
ground to the cloven hooves in the mud and the dragging little rut
made by the crippled leg. It was headed for the top of Lost Ridge
and the twists of Snakeberry Trail, where the Circuit Rider had
once paid the final price for his sins.

The Bible said if you wished hard enough, you could move
mountains. But this mountain belonged here, huddled over Solom
like God's black watchdog. The Circuit Rider belonged to the
mountain as surely as did the rocks and springs and laurels. Up
there, Ray could spit in Harmon Smith's eye and show God that he,
and not David, should be the chosen one.

The job would serve even better with a witness to his faith.
Brother Davey would probably be holed up in the church, on his
knees in fear, begging for the Lord to deliver him from an evil that
God had sent for just that purpose: to test the weak.

Ray didn't realize he carried the plumber's wrench with him as he walked to his truck, or that dusk was reaching its fingers across the valley.

Odus reached the ridgeline and dismounted, letting Sister Mary nibble some dried-up rabbit tobacco as he scanned the granite boulders and stunted cedars that had been swept by the wind for ages. The path had narrowed and grown rougher, used mostly by foxes, the occasional black bear, and deer. Yet this would have been the way Harmon Smith would have crossed, to head down the other side to Virginia or eastern Tennessee. The valley cut through gaps at each end of Lost Ridge that would have resulted in less of a climb, but they were each nearly ten miles out of the way. A car had no trouble with the extra distance, and the state highway department had stuck as close to the lower elevations as possible. But Harmon Smith had ridden in the days before highways, and still marched to the echo of that long-dead era.

Odus had expected some sign, a hoofprint or a broken tree branch or maybe even Old Saint's spoor, whatever that might look like. But all he'd found were crackling leaves, hardwoods damaged by acid rain and insects, and the cold September air at forty-five hundred feet of altitude. He'd spooked a few ravens, and a red hawk had cut an arc in the indigo sky before diving for some unlucky rodent, but the forest had been quiet. He went for the whiskey bottle again, letting the Old Crow warm his tongue.

"Looks like I took us on a wild-goose chase," he said to the horse. Sister Mary flicked her mane out of her eyes as if nodding in agreement.

A clatter arose, like the sound of wood against stone. Or the clop of a horse's hoof.

"You've come a long way," came a voice from the thinning trees. "Seek and you shall find, knock and the door shall be opened."

"I *do* want something," Odus said, in the general direction of the voice. He could never forget the cold, deep tones of the Circuit Rider. Outside, the voice seemed to boom even more than it had done inside the general store. "I want this to be over. I want *you* to be over."

"Come to me, all that are weary and carrying heavy burdens, and I will give you rest."

"The folks that are alive today didn't have anything to do with what happened to you. Why don't you just go on and leave us in peace?"

"I desire mercy, not sacrifice."

An unseen horse whinnied. The laurel branches quivered, parted, and the horse stepped out, black with a pure white chest the way the legends described him. He stood a good head taller than Sister Mary, whose ears twitched at the sight of the animal. The Circuit Rider was astride his horse, sitting tall in the saddle, head tilted down. Even looking up at him from below, Odus had a hard time distinguishing his features. The dying sunlight was at the Circuit Rider's back, the sky cast purple with shredded sheets of pink. The shadows of the trees seemed to grow up from the ground and enshroud the mounted figure.

Odus wondered if this was the showdown he'd been seeking. Maybe he was supposed to jump on Sister Mary, ride hell-bent for leather toward the dead preacher, and tangle with him head-on. If he'd brought a firearm, he probably would have faced him down like a tin-star hero. Odus had counted on making up the rules as he went along, forgetting that the Circuit Rider existed under its own set of rules. Odus wasn't that good at reading, but he doubted if there was an instruction manual on taking down a mythical creature. Even if that creature showed a jagged arc of grinning teeth beneath the wide brim of its hat.

"We're not the ones who killed you," Odus said.

"You belong to Solom. That's reason enough."

"It ain't the *place* that sinned. It was just a few preachers who did you in, the way I hear it. And they're dead. They faced their judgment long ago, before him that has power over all of us."

The Circuit Rider's head lifted, and Odus recognized that strong, jowly Smith chin. The hidden eyes suddenly flared like a campfire's embers urged by the wind. "You think I like making these rounds? You think I have a choice? Did you ever consider maybe something's got power over *me*? For the Bible says, 'If you are forced to go one mile, go also the second.' "

Odus gripped the dangling reins and held Sister Mary's head

tight. The pinto tried to back away, but the terrain was too rough and dangerous. A stench drifted off the Circuit Rider, the smell of a dead skunk in the road, but a whisk of wind carried it off, leaving only the strong, green smell of pine and the earthy aroma of fallen and decaying leaves.

"I've come to stop you," Odus said.

"I wish you could," the Circuit Rider said, relaxing his pale hands and patting his horse on the neck. "Narrow is the gate and hard is the road that leads to life, and there are few who find it."

"Why don't you just step down off that saddle and let it go?"

"Told you, I got a mission. I didn't ask for it. It was given to me."

"I don't believe in the devil."

"Neither do I, Mr. Odus Hampton." The Circuit Rider leaned to one side and spat, as if ridding himself of two hundred years of bitter trail dust. "I knew your daddy. Good man. I could have taken him in the summer of seventy-seven, when he was up on a ladder cleaning out gutters on the Smith house."

"He worked for Gordon's daddy."

"And you work for Gordon. Some things don't change in Solom."

"I reckon one thing's going to have to change."

"Not tonight. Not here and now, between you and me."

"I'm afraid so, mister." Odus's throat was dry, but he wouldn't let his voice weaken or crack.

"Who do you think brought you here? Don't tell me you woke up this morning and it just popped into your head to steal a horse and ride to the top of Lost Ridge."

"I did some studying on it first."

"That's the trouble with you folks. You think you're the boss of your arms and legs and mind, you think your soul is separate and free from your flesh. And I'm here to tell you otherwise."

"You're sounding a lot like Elder David and them Primitives."

"Elder David is a good man, but not good enough. His faith is weak."

The chill that had crept over Odus's skin had only a little to do with the day's fading warmth. As the sky grew darker, the shadows around Harmon Smith lessened, as if the man were absorbing the blackness. More of his face was visible, and the meat over his jaws looked to be the texture of crumbling wax. Old Saint had stood stock-still during their conversation, while Sister Mary pawed the ground, shuffled, and snorted in dismay. Odus noted that maybe being dead had its advantages when it came to the equestrian arts. No saddle sores.

"Well, I found you, so that means there's a reason, doesn't it?" Odus ached for a shot of whiskey, but then wondered if the ache was due to his own need or was caused by the whim of some bearded guy behind the clouds. He had little use for religion, but, like most hopeless sinners, he wrapped his hands around it when it was the only rope available for climbing out of a dark pit.

"You're not special, you're just early," the Circuit Rider said.

Confused, Odus figured he'd best keep the creature talking while he came up with a plan. "Did you kill them two tourists on the Switchback Trail? You're only supposed to kill one and then be on your way. That's how it's always been, as far back as they remember to tell it."

"It's not about what you want or what I want. If it was up to me, Old Saint would just haul me off into the mist of a mountain morning and that would be that."

"You're evil, though. How can a man of the cloth go around killing like that?" Odus was casting about for a fallen tree branch or a loose jag of granite. He felt foolish now for not bringing a gun. He still wasn't sure what sort of weapon would work, if any. His was a mission of faith, despite the Circuit Rider's mocking.

The Circuit Rider ran a gaunt, crooked finger through a hole in his jacket. "Cloth is like flesh, it goes to worms. The spirit is the thing that doesn't die."

The Circuit Rider lifted his head and glanced above them through a gap in the canopy, his mouth curling up at one corner. A beech leaf spiraled down from the twisted branches and fluttered across his face. The woods were hushed in that moment as the birds and wildlife changed shifts, the daytime animals settling into holes, nests, and protective crooks of tree limbs while the nocturnal creatures roused from their slumber.

The silence was disturbed by a faint buzzing from below, as if a giant nest of hornets had been stirred with a stick. Harmon Smith's cracked lips bent like a snake with a broken spine in something that might have been a smile if seen on a human face.

"I suppose the others got the same idea you did," he said. "Funny how you give them a choice and they make the wrong one every single time. Few find the true way."

The buzz grew louder, changed into a roar. It was a vehicle engine. Somebody was climbing the rough logging roads that crisscrossed the mountain. And those roads led to the top, where Odus stared down his adversary. His brow furrowed in doubt. He was supposed to do this alone, wasn't he?

At that moment, Sister Mary reared, flailing her forelegs in front of her, stripping the leather reins through Odus's palm, cutting into his flesh. She broke and galloped into the trees, neck stooped low and ears pinned close to her head.

The Circuit Rider stroked Old Saint's mane, and the revenant horse chuckled softly in response. "I guess your friend there just exercised her free will, huh?"

Odus took two steps backward, toward the rocky ledge that led to one of the logging roads. It was a thirty-foot drop. He could try to climb down, but he pictured his fingers gripping the granite ledge and Old Saint bringing a heavy, scarred hoof down on them. He could follow Sister Mary and blaze a trail through the tangles, or he could stand his ground and see what God had in store for him.

None of the options settled the squirming in his chest and gut. The courage that had surged through him since this morning now seemed foolish and silly. He had no special gifts or weapons to bring to bear against a supernatural creature. He'd fallen back onto a sort of crippled faith, believing God would provide in Odus's hour of need. But Odus didn't consider that he'd never been a deeply religious man, and that faith couldn't be turned off and on like tap water.

"You fear me, but only because you don't understand me," the Circuit Rider said, over the increasing roar of the engine. "If the shepherd has one hundred sheep, and one of them goes astray, does he not leave the other ninety-nine on the mountains and go in search of the one that went astray?"

The Circuit Rider wheeled his mount and trotted back through the laurel thicket. The branches shook from his passage as if horse and rider were as solid and real as any living creature. But the smell of decay lingered, a smell that hinted of grave dirt and spent fires and blood dried black.

Chapter Thirty-one

Jett opened the door to her room to find Gordon standing there.

"Where do you think you're going, Jessica?" he said, hands on his hips, blocking the hallway.

"Um, out for a drive with Mom."

Gordon grinned, and it looked like the expression of a cartoon possum, eyes narrow behind his thick lenses. "Mrs. Smith isn't driving anywhere. She told me so."

"Where is she?"

"In the attic."

Jett leaned to the side and looked past Gordon. The linen closet door was shut tight. The closet was too small for the attic ladder to unfold without the door open. Either Gordon was lying or else he'd shut the access door with Mom up there. But why would Mom go up there, especially after the ghost had scared her silly?

Jett decided Gordon was lying, and figured that deserved a lie in return. "I was smoking pot that time in the barn," she said. "When I saw—I mean, *thought* I saw—the scarecrow the first time. I guess I just freaked out."

Gordon's eyes narrowed. "You know the rules. No drugs in this house."

"Well, technically the drugs weren't in the house."

"I'll have no sass from you, young lady. You're a member of this family now and I'm your stepfather."

Jett's cheeks flared red in defiance. "You'll never be my dad, no matter how hard you try."

Gordon reached out as if to grab her arm, but she ducked past, slinging the backpack around. She tried to crawl between his legs but he brought his knees together, clamping her like an oversize vise grip. Her sides ached from the pressure, but she wiggled while he reached down to her. Gordon was shouting, his voice scarcely recognizable. Some of his words sounded like Latin, intoned like the traditional liturgy of a Catholic priest. Like something out of *The Exorcist* or some Goth band's hokey attempt at demonic incantations.

Gordon had one of her boots, but they were recently polished and he lost his grip. She kicked free and crawled on her hands and knees down the hall, her mind blank except for the unbidden thought, *How could Mom have been dumb enough to fall for this idiot?*

Then she regained her footing and sprang forward, launching herself down the stairs three steps at a time, clutching Captain Boo. She toyed with the idea of sliding down the railing, but there was a large wooden sculpture on the bottom newel post, and Jett pictured herself breaking a leg, lying there flopping and moaning on the landing while Gordon loomed over her.

What would he do to her? Even if he knew they were running out on him, which wasn't likely, considering what a wet mop Mom had been lately, surely he wouldn't do anything worse than scream and yell. Yet he had tried to physically restrain her upstairs, and she'd heard some guys went into possessive rages when a woman ditched them. His heavy shoes punished the stairs behind her.

When she reached the first floor, she dared a backward glance and suffered an acid flashback.

At least, she *hoped* that's what it was, because a woman was floating—*floating!*—behind Gordon.

She was thin as threads, almost invisible, and she was pulled forward as if riding in Gordon's back draft. Her lack of flesh was almost as startling as the fact that she had no head.

Jett hadn't seen anything that bizarre on her actual acid trip, and couldn't imagine how a flashback could be so intense and disturbing. But accepting it as a drug-induced hallucination made it somehow easier to assimilate.

Of course *there's a ghost in this house. Why wouldn't there be, when creepy scarecrows live in the attic and the barn, when goddamned goats scarf your dope and try to eat your ass, when a man in a black hat peeps in your windows?*

Jett was nearly out of breath when she reached the door, but she had twenty feet on Gordon (and thirty feet on the headless ghost). She threw open the door and was racing across the porch when she saw them.

Goats, dozens of them, a veritable army of horned stink factories, staring at her with their weird, glittering eyes. They blocked Jett's path to the driveway and surrounded the car. Mom sat in the driver's seat, clawing her cheeks in anxiety. One of the goats lowered its head and gave the driver's side door a solid thwack with its horns and forehead.

"Going somewhere?" Gordon said behind her, and she could hear the smile in his voice.

Alex had a passing knowledge of tracking and hunting, and though he was mostly a vegetarian, he figured being able to round up meat for the dinner table might be a handy survival skill when the Republicans and Democrats finally toppled the Statue of Liberty. So he'd learned the basics and had even killed some small game with his bow and arrows. Of course, he was a crack marksman. That was required of any member of the antigovernment militia, even if you were only an army of one.

So Alex had no trouble following the goats' hoofprints through the woods. Even his sister, a Boston lawyer, could have followed this trail—the fuzzy beasts had practically trampled a superhighway through the underbrush. The carpet of leaves on the forest floor was scuffed, branches hung broken and nibbled, and of course there was the occasional pile of plum-sized goat turds. In his haste, Alex hadn't paid close attention to the ammunition he'd loaded into his shoulder bag, but he figured he had at least six rounds for each of the goats. Plenty enough lead to teach the Satan-faced little fucks not to mess with *his* property.

The trail followed the ridge. Wherever they were going, they were making a beeline for high ground. Alex understood the chemical processes by which marijuana played with the synapses. Marijuana required heat before the cannaboids were activated, so you had to smoke it or cook it in brownies or oil for the pot to do its stuff. But maybe goat neurology was different. Maybe goats could get stoned just from the raw green leaves. That seemed to be the only reason they would break into his shed and gobble up good bud that would net twenty grand on the street.

Unless they were smart enough to know what the pot meant to him.

Maybe they were part of some secret government experiment, too. He'd read about how the spooks trained dolphins to carry explosives toward enemy ships and trained chimpanzees to infiltrate bunkers. No doubt the same government that publicly frowned on genetic research was going gangbusters in their underground labs, splicing all kinds of stuff together, putting microchips in the heads of animals, developing entire battalions of remote-controlled killers.

Alex stopped and adjusted the strap of the submachine gun, the Pearson Freedom bow tucked under his armpit. Maybe the goats were fucking with him on purpose. Maybe they were trying to . . . well, to get his goat. The FBI had found out about his stash and his weapons and his tax evasion, and instead of coming up and knocking on the front door with a warrant, they'd concocted the most screwed-up, expensive, and outlandish revenge possible. Yeah, that was what the U.S. of A. was all about.

Well, revenge worked two ways. Alex patted the Colt Python at his side. The ripped-up ground was moist, the goat shit fresher as he climbed the slope of Lost Ridge. He was gaining on them, even with darkness settling in. And if the universe was as just and fair as Alex always believed it was, especially while brain-basted on a thumb-sized joint of God-green smoke, then he'd have his revenge before the sun surrendered to the night.

An engine roared in the distance. Motorcyclists or kids on all-terrain vehicles sometimes prowled the old logging roads, disturbing the peace, trespassing, and generally raising hell. If he came across one, Alex just might put a slug in a rear tire. From the camouflage of the forest, he wouldn't be seen, and he'd bet his pair of Herman Survivors that the driver in question would fishtail his ass back to civilization, riding the rim or not.

Alex was in a good mood, despite the loss of a season's worth of crops. The evening's events felt natural, as if they had already happened, as if this were a stage play and the parts had been written ahead of time: Alex, the dark storm of vengeance, and the goats in their supporting role of government vermin. He might even encounter Weird Dude Walking, who seemed to be a part of all this craziness. Maybe Weird Dude was some sort of upper-level federal agent, in the National Security Agency, even. Alex realized maybe that particular line of paranoid delusion was probably a bit too extravagant, but it pleased him nonetheless.

He shifted into a double-time jog, eager to catch up with whatever was awaiting him at the top of the ridge.

"Shit, shit, shit." Katy beat the steering wheel as the goat rammed its head against the door a second time. Another goat, this one a hoary old-timer, with gray and white streaked among the brown patches on its face, reared up and settled its front hoofs on the bumper and glared at Katy over the hood.

She'd tucked her suitcase in the trunk and had just closed the front door when the goats appeared. She had looked over the driveway and the gravel road, checking things out before fleeing, and the coast had been clear. Admittedly, she'd been looking for Gordon and not goats. She figured he was still out making whatever weird farm rounds he kept on Sunday evenings.

The goats had appeared out of nowhere. First came Abraham, the only one she could distinguish because of the right horn that corkscrewed crazily behind his ear. Abraham had waltzed down like a show pony, in high spirits, even kicking up and clicking his back hooves. Katy had grinned at that one, even though Abraham had broken out of the fence. That was Gordon's problem. Katy mourned briefly for the perennials she'd planted along the front porch, the forsythia, hosta, and snowball bushes that the goat would no doubt munch, but this wasn't her house anymore. If it had ever been.

She'd checked her watch and noted it was a quarter after seven. She debated running into the house and getting Jett. She'd also forgotten to call her mother and announce their unexpected arrival. When she looked up from her watch, three goats came around the house like a gang of gunfighters in a spaghetti western. That was when the first alarm had gone off inside her head, an insistent, irritating beeping.

She was about to open the door when the rearview mirror revealed a half dozen more, popping up as if they had formed from smoke. She didn't like the look of their eyes. And while she hadn't quite believed they were dangerous before—despite her own creepy encounters; after all, a goat was an herbivore, not a carnivore, right?—she accepted it now, because the goats moved with a common intent, as if they shared the same mind and the same hunger.

When Jett opened the front door, Katy wanted to scream at her to go back inside the house. Then she saw Gordon behind Jett, and the ghost—*Rebecca*—behind him, and figured goats were the lesser of three evils. Jett paused at the edge of the porch, clearly sizing up her chances of making it to the car. By now dozens of goats filled the yard, their restless legs kicking in the dusk, their hooves pawing the ground, ears twitching.

Katy decided she needed to improve the odds a little. As the butt-head slammed her car door for the third time, she turned over the ignition key. The Subaru engine roared to life, and she threw the gearshift into drive and hit the gas. The goat perched on the bumper (for some reason, the name "Methuselah" came to mind) lost its balance and bounced off the grille with a meaty thump. Gravel spat from beneath the wheels like Uzi slugs, and startled goats emitted bleats of surprise and pain. The fishtailing rear of the Subaru slewed into a small group of the creatures, scattering them like soft bowling pins. Katy heard limbs snap, and a stray horn clacked against a side window and caused the glass to spiderweb.

Some of the goats danced out of the way, their long, angular faces almost comical with those obscene eyes set deep beneath heavy brows. Katy navigated an arc, parking the passenger's-side door at the foot of the porch steps. She leaned over and flung the door open as Jett hopped toward the car. Gordon looked shattered, as if he wanted to cry but couldn't find any water in his dried-up heart. Katy would almost have felt sorry for him, but she was pretty sure he was distraught over the dead and injured goats and not over losing his wife.

"Shit, Mom, you rock," Jett said as she climbed into the front seat. Katy was already pulling away before the door closed.

The goats had by now figured out a monstrous steel predator was in their midst, and they had parted like the waves of the Red Sea.

"Moses," Katy said. "Did he have a goat named Moses?"

"That one," Jett said, pointing to the left. "The one with the black hairs in its beard."

Katy veered out of the way and clipped Moses head-on. The goat bounced up on the hood and pressed against the windshield. For one horrifying second, Moses glared through the glass at Katy, as if admonishing her for breaking some unwritten commandment. Then he rolled to the side and was flung from the car, which was by now halfway down the drive to the Ward house. When Katy checked the mirror, Moses was flopping and flailing on the hard-packed road.

"Sweet!" Jett yelled, as if this were a sequel to *Thelma and Louise*, only this time cowritten by Federico Fellini and George Romero.

"Fasten your seat belt," Katy said, her hands no longer trembling. She hadn't had time to be frightened—well, not such a much of it—but now the reverse endorphins were kicking in and the blood drained from her face, her bruised eye throbbing.

"I saw your ghost," Jett said after obeying the parental command. She put her backpack in the floor between her legs, opened it, and rummaged while Katy aimed for the paved highway.

"It's not *my* ghost," Katy said. "I'm still very much alive, thank you."

Jett pulled a CD from her backpack, opened the case, and slid it into the player. She punched a button and Paul Westerberg's "Knockin on Mine" blared from the speakers like a bad attitude in A major.

Neither of them noticed the ghost sitting in the backseat, its head in its lap.

Sue parked the Jeep beneath a stand of balsam, gnarled trees whose bones had been bleached white by acid rain and foreign pests. A number of native tree species were in decline because of exotic diseases that had been brought to the country from Asia, usually piggybacking on landscaping plants. Human vanity had led to this imbalance of nature, as it did to most imbalances. The regional tourist economy, and Sue's personal economy, was threatened by the damage to scenic beauty.

Perhaps Harmon Smith, the Circuit Rider, was another such blight, invading a realm where he didn't belong. The Circuit Rider was just as much a threat, because he couldn't be caged and put on display at five bucks a head. Instead, he literally killed her customers, if indeed he had done away with the Everharts while they were cycling. Plus, somebody had to pay for the damage to the bicycles. Though the Circuit Rider couldn't pay in a pound of flesh, Sue hoped to extract some sort of substance.

"Ready to rock and roll?" she said, looking over at Sarah. Maybe ancient wisdom had something on the brashness of youth, because Sarah gripped the safety bar on the dash in front of her and stared straight ahead at the woods.

"I don't know why you brung me along," the storekeeper said. "If I was meant to take care of Harmon Smith, I expect I'd have done it many moons ago."

Sue brandished the pickax, letting it catch the last rays of sunlight. "Maybe you didn't have the right tool."

"And what in tarnation am I supposed to do with that? Hammer it into his heart like he's some kind of ass-backwards vampire?"

"I think we'll know when the time comes. I'm just flying by the seat of my pants here."

"You act like you've done this kind of thing before."

Sue flicked the headlights, strobing the silent trees. "No, I just don't want to be waiting for the next time Harmon Smith decides to come around. Solom is my home now."

"You younguns are so full of piss and vinegar. It's a wonder any of you ever live to be old."

"Well, Miss Jeffers, I don't mean to be disrespectful, but if the people of Solom had faced this problem right at the start, maybe it would all be over by now."

Sarah's voice broke, nearly becoming an old woman's whine. "We couldn't figure out what he wanted. We figured he'd just come to claim somebody and that was that, and each time he went away, the ones who weren't picked just counted their blessings and went about their business. That might be the worst of it all. Because, until he comes back again and you start seeing the people he killed, you somehow manage to *forget*."

Sue wrestled a flashlight from beneath her seat and flung open her door. "Well, nobody's forgetting this time."

"I hope it ain't you," Sarah said. "But I hope it ain't me, either, and if it does turn out to be one of us, I'd rather he carry you over. Nothing personal, mind you."

Sue almost smiled, despite the knot in her stomach. Her bravery was mostly false, but Sarah was clearly shaken, and Sue felt a need to be strong for both of them. She believed Harmon Smith would be impressed by a lack of fear. She went to Sarah's door and helped her out, then played the flashlight around beneath the dark canopy of the forest.

"Where to now?" Sue asked.

"Right here," came a voice from the trees.

When Mark Draper arrived at the Smith house, both vehicles were gone from the driveway. He knocked on the front door with no answer, then walked around the house. He didn't know how Gordon Smith would react to trespassing, but a tingling at the base of Mark's skull told him something was wrong. After hearing Jett's stories and seeing the dead boy in the waterwheel, he was willing to believe his paranoia was real and not a side effect of the cocaine.

Mark was about to drive back to the general store to call the sheriff's department when he saw the barn. The doors were swung wide, and the gate was open. Twin tire tracks led into the old wooden structure, and the tracks looked fresh. That was where Jett had been attacked by the scarecrow and the goats, and he figured he'd at least take a peek. He owed her that much. He hadn't believed her this morning. Now he realized, maybe for the first time in his life, that he expected her to lie. Because she'd learned it from him. Along with other bad habits. His failure cast a bigger ripple than a mere broken marriage and a troubled childhood, because Jett would be carrying that bad karma with her even when Mark was worm food.

As he approached the gate, he noticed splotches of blood on the gravel driveway. The blood led into the barn.

"Shit," Mark said, breaking into a jog even though his knees were trembling. Dusk seemed to settle more heavily with each step, and the dark heart of the barn beckoned him like a carnival funhouse. Chickens emitted clucks from a row of cages along the front of the barn, and in the otherwise brooding silence, the clamor added to his uneasiness. What if the blood were Jett's? And what if something had happened to her just because he didn't believe her?

The wet drops reflected in the scant light that leaked through the doors and windows. Mark followed them to a set of narrow wooden stairs, where the drops were larger and stood out like black paint against the gray, bleached boards. Mark hesitated only a second, making sure none of the goats that Jett had talked about were around.

Man-eating goats.

That was about as loopy an idea as, say, a dead boy crying for help. He shivered and ascended the stairs, stepping as carefully as he could, though even missing a shoe his footfalls sounded like the beating of a kettledrum. Or maybe the noise was his pulse pounding through his temples. He leaned against the wall for balance, not trusting the skinny, cockeyed railing. His hand brushed cloth and a dusty snuff of dried straw and chicken manure assailed his nostrils.

He fought off a sneeze, eased up another few steps, and his hand struck cold metal. He ran his hand along the smooth length and came to wood, then back up into a sharp edge. Some type of cutting tool. Mark lifted it free of its support and checked its weight. It was a long scythe, the kind the Grim Reaper carried in cartoons. The curve of the blade made it awkward to handle in the confined space, but gave Mark a sense of security.

At the top of the stairs, the blood had pooled on a short landing, as if whatever—or whoever—was injured had struggled to open the door that must lead to the hayloft. The blood gave off a bright, warm smell that reminded Mark of seawater. He tried the latch, and his hand came away slick and moist. He wiped his hand on his slacks and eased the latch up. The door swung open with a slow groan of hinges.

The hayloft access was open on the far side of the barn, and the first glimmers of moonlight cast the pastures and surrounding hills in silver, as if the scene had been electroplated. The air was rich with chaff and the sweet smell of an early dew. Mark was tempted to call out for Jett, but what if someone was holding her prisoner? The scarecrow thing, or whatever?

Mark hefted the scythe and held the blade in front of him, taking careful steps forward. Something could be hiding in the hay bales to either side of him, and he couldn't swivel the scythe fast enough if he was jumped. Light from the gaps in the boards threw lustrous stripes across the floor, giving the illusion of prison bars. Mark was in the middle of the hayloft when he glanced out the window and saw Gordon's Chevy Tahoe parked up on the hill. The truck appeared to have been driven through a section of fence, because barbed wire curled around it and a broken fence post lay across the hood. The truck's driver's-side door was open, and the cab appeared empty. Mark was edging toward the window for a closer look when he heard a whisper of movement behind him, the soft rattling of corn husks or the stirring of a rodent. He spun, the scythe causing him to lose his balance.

Silhouetted against the silver spill of moonlight was a man in a hat.

The one Jett had told him about.

Mark squinted, trying to pool enough light in his pupils to make out the face. It appeared to be covered by a rough, grainy cloth. The rest of the clothing was ragged, with frayed strips fluttering in the breeze that carried the smell of autumnal decay from the valley outside.

"Where's Jett?" Mark said, his voice thick from dust.

The man didn't move.

The man in the black hat, Jett had said. But as his eyes adjusted, Mark saw that the hat wasn't black. It was a straw planter's hat, dented and torn, with stray sprigs of reeds sticking out at odd angles.

Mark took two steps forward, then went weightless, and he pushed the scythe across his chest as he realized he was falling. A square was cut in the floor, wide enough to drop through a bale of hay (*or a man,* he thought), and his rib cage banged, and then his chin, as he kicked to keep himself upright. The floor couldn't be more than twenty feet below, but it was hard ground, packed by the hooves of generations of animals.

And as Mark struggled to keep a grip on the scythe, fighting to keep his elbows on the long wooden handle, he was suddenly sure that goats—*carnivorous goats*—were milling down below him, as silent as sharks cruising a chum-stained sea.

He pushed his legs out, swinging like a drunken gymnast in a surreal Olympics, then lifted himself until his belly was across the scythe handle. He reached one hand and found the hayloft floor, his index finger ripped by a protruding nail head. Blood trickled down his finger to the pad of his hand, where it fell to the barn floor below. The unseen movement beneath him increased in intensity, and hooves padded softly in the dirt. But that didn't matter, because he had his balance and then his other hand was gripping a floorboard and he pulled himself forward, forward, and he had a knee on the scythe handle and he was going to make it—

He looked up to see the scarecrow standing over him, a crescent moon of metal arced above its straw hat. Mark couldn't be sure, but the stitched face seemed to be grinning. Then the sickle swept down, slicing into Mark's left wrist all the way to the bone. The whole arm went numb, but he kept a grip with his right hand, even though his blood pressure plummeted and his skin grew cold as he went into shock. As the sickle reaped its sick harvest a second time, Mark let go, and as he fell to his death, he concentrated on Jett's face but all he saw was the long, endless tunnel of a final failure.

Chapter Thirty-two

Katy pushed the Subaru a little fast for the winding road that followed the river, but she was in a hurry to get as far away from Solom as possible. She switched on the headlights as they passed the general store, noting that the store's porch light wasn't on. Usually, its deep yellow glow flooded the valley, drawing insects from the riverbanks and reflecting off the plate-glass window of the post office. All the buildings were dark, even the True Light Tabernacle, the squat brick building with the teepeelike steeple.

"Looks like Solom shut down for the night," Katy said over the sweet, aching strains of Westerberg's "Runaway Wind."

"What?" Jett cupped a hand to her ear, and Katy turned down the volume a little.

"Solom," she said. "Something weird's going on."

"Hey, not our problem, Mom."

"Got your cell phone?"

"Yeah, but it's about as useful as frog's wings in this valley. Where's an ugly cell tower when you need one?"

"I thought we might call your dad."

Jett's grin flashed in the green glow of the dashboard lights. "Are we going there?"

"No, I just thought we ought to tell him. He should be back in Charlotte by now."

"Damn, Mom. This is an emergency. Forget about your pride for a sec, okay?"

Katy eased up on the gas pedal. "There's a lot you don't know, honey, and a lot that you don't need to worry about."

"Come on, I saw the way you guys were looking at each other this morning. There's still a spark, just like Paul says in this song." She reached over and cranked the volume as Westerberg plowed through a chorus fraught with romantic desperation, and then she turned it down again. "I never saw any spark between you and Gordon. Not even hatred. Just a pair of flat-out fucking zombies."

"No cussing, honey," Katy said automatically, but was thinking: *out of the mouths of babes.* Jett had seen what Katy refused to see. But Katy had larger issues to consider than sparks, happiness, or love. She had to make good, she had to provide Jett stability, she had to make up for a failed marriage by making the second one work. She had to have a happy family whether she wanted one or not.

Except that perfect plan hadn't exactly worked out, had it? She'd ended up playing second fiddle to a woman who couldn't even hold an instrument.

She glanced into the rearview mirror, wanting to see the outline of Solom vanishing into the past, one more wrong turn on the road to wherever she was meant to wind up. The full moon had risen and segued with the setting sun so that full darkness had never touched the sky. It had gone from deep purple to milky silver, though the hills lay beneath it like black sleeping beasts. A few wisps of ragged clouds spread themselves across the dust of the Milky Way. Katy had never noticed how few streetlights there were in Solom, and how the stars stood out by contrast, even while fighting the dominant glow of the full moon.

"Up ahead is where Gordon's wife wrecked," Jett said, pointing to a steep cut of bank that led down to the river. Hard trees danced just beyond the headlight beams. "The kids at school said the car flew off the road and flipped. She wasn't wearing her seat belt and—"

"Her head was cut off."

"I saw her, Mom. You weren't lying."

"I never lie to you."

"Bullshit. You lied about lots of things."

"Only to myself." Katy found her foot going from the accelerator to the brake.

"Mom? What are you doing?"

"She needs to stop," came the voice from the backseat. Even with Westerberg singing over a tortured blues guitar lick, the voice carried and filled the interior of the car, as if it was coming from the speakers.

Katy swerved the steering wheel, bouncing to the narrow shoulder as the tires grabbed for traction. Jett jerked forward, straining against the seat belt. "What the fuck?" she said, her voice reverting to a prepubescent screech.

Rebecca, or what there was of her, leaned over the front seat. The milk-white threads of her ghostly flesh caught the sick glow of the dash lights. Her head was on, her face nearly blank, though her black lips held the hint of a smile in the mirror. Even ethereal and dead, with a gruesome wound around her neck and the shadows of her bruises on her face, Katy noted that she was beautiful. The first wife whom Katy could never replace.

Jett wriggled from her seat belt and flung the passenger door open. "Get the hell out, Mom!"

Katy's fingers hesitated on the seat belt latch. Westerberg was singing about the dice behind somebody's shades. The soft, eternal whisper of the river blended with the music, and the night air carried the smell of mud that had spent eons working its way down from the high granite peaks. Rebecca had died here, and hadn't been allowed to haunt this place. She had been banned from moving to some greater reward or perhaps a greater punishment than any cruelty this world could administer.

Weren't ghosts supposed to haunt their place of dying? But Rebecca had been bound to the Smith house, perhaps the place of greatest happiness or sorrow in her life. Not here, by a cold and remorseless river.

Katy could hop in a car and run away, but Rebecca was destined to stay with Gordon.

Their gazes locked in the mirror, and Rebecca gave a slight nod as if she understood Katy's thoughts.

"They found me here," Rebecca said.

Jett pounded on the hood with her fist. "Mom, get the fuck *out.*"

Katy released her seat belt, but didn't get out. Instead, she killed the engine, taking the headlights with it. In the vacuum of silence, the night sounds filled the car, surrounded her: a breeze rustling the dried weeds along the river, bullfrogs croaking in a symphony, a short spill of water churning against the rocks, the engine ticking as it cooled.

"But you didn't die here," Katy said, the deeper, less calm part of her mind screaming: *you're talking to a* ghost!

"No."

Jett ran to Katy's side of the car, pulled open the door, and pulled Katy's arm. "Get out, Mom. Get away."

"It's okay. She's not going to hurt us." Something made Katy add, "She *can't* hurt us. She's dead."

Jett kicked the side of the car in frustration. "I don't think she's nearly dead enough."

"Look at her. She's trying to tell us something."

Rebecca's smile widened in the mirror, and though it was still a creepy, elusive, unnatural thing, Katy turned to face her. She expected a corpse smell, a graveyard wind of what passed for breath among the dead, but there was none. Ragged flesh circled Rebecca's neck. However she had lost her head, it had not been by a clean stroke. Something, perhaps a piece of dull, jagged metal, had worked and rasped and gnawed at the meat. Rebecca was wearing the dress from the closet, the one with the autumnal print, though the dress was as translucent as the woman wearing it. The bustline would have been flattering if not for the wound.

"I died at the Smith house," Rebecca said, her dark eyes far away, as if staring into the cold waters of the river Styx.

"But what about the car wreck?" Katy said.

"Gordon brought me here."

"Did the Circuit Rider kill you?"

"No. I'm a sacrifice."

"A what?"

"Sacrifice."

"Who killed you?"

"I'm a sacrifice."

"That's just great," Jett said, still standing by the open door. "Out of all the dead people in the world, we get the only one with a defective voice chip."

"Shh," Katy said. Distant headlights flickered in the valley behind them, then disappeared as the vehicle rounded a curve. A dog barked from a distant hillside, the sound lost and lonely under the full moon.

"Who killed you?" Katy repeated. She felt a strange affinity for the woman, now that she had accepted that dead people were just like the living, only less afraid. She and Rebecca had shared the same kitchen and the same husband. Now they were sitting in a car together, talking about Rebecca's death as if they were discussing cosmetics.

"I'm a sacrifice," Rebecca said. "For his goats."

"Goats? *Gordon* killed you?"

The morose eyes blinked, momentarily shielding Katy from their dark sorrow and pain.

"I knew that fucker had a screw loose," Jett said.

"Try the phone," Katy said, handing her the cell unit.

"Who do you want me to call? Ghostbusters? The FBI? Scully and Mulder?"

"Nine-one-one for a start."

"And what am I supposed to tell them, assuming we've found the one little patch in the valley where there's a signal?"

"Tell them we have to report a murder."

"And you're going to take *her* word for it?"

"Shh. Go on, so I can talk to Rebecca."

"Great. You're as nutty as the rest of them."

"I love you, too, dear." Katy turned her attention back to the dead woman in the backseat. "Well, what do we do now? Are you coming with us, or are you like the 'vanishing hitchhiker' in that urban legend and are going to disappear the moment we get where we're going?"

Rebecca's answer, rising from the pipes of an ethereal hollow inside, was neither of the two options Katy had offered.

* * *

Odus thrashed through the laurels, calling for Sister Mary. He was mostly sober now, the braving effects of the Old Crow dissipated and leaving in its place a painful veil of fog. Some shining knight he'd made, some hero. His image of a tin-star stud riding into a dirty town with six-guns blazing had been reduced to a hungover cowpoke who'd lost his ride.

The September darkness had not settled over the sky so much as it seeped up from the cool, ancient mountains. The black stuff of night had crawled around the rude and rounded chunks of granite, out from between the roots of old-growth ash and beech and hickory, up from the hidden holes in the world. Now it knitted its single, all-consuming color in a smothering straitjacket, there at every turn, ready to match every breath, flowing into Odus's lungs and claiming its rightful space. Odus had never felt so much like an invader on this planet as he did now. In fact, he'd never given it any thought at all.

He'd hunted these peaks, had sought squirrels and wild turkey and the occasional black bear, but he'd always come here as a conqueror. Now, entangled in its inky depths, his bearings lost, he recognized the futility of laying claim to something as old as the Appalachians. No human owned these mountains. If anything held deed to these stony and storied lands, it was creatures like the Circuit Rider, those not bound by time and space and the sad, small worries of the mortal.

Unseen branches tore Odus's hands, and waxy leaves slapped his face. He rested for a moment, squinting through the canopy to the scattered stars and the comforting cast of moonlight above.

"God, if you're up there, now would be a great time to lend a little hand here," Odus said, the prayer sounding stupid even as it left his lips. Why should God listen to a man who hadn't stepped foot in a church in two decades, who hadn't cracked a Bible since Sunday school in Free Will Baptist Church, who hadn't felt a single spiritual twitch since the day Preacher Blackburn had dipped his head into the chilling waters of Rush Branch and pronounced him washed free of sin?

However, his prayer may have been answered, or at least coincided with an earthly event, which amounted to the same thing when you dropped the fancy cloth and got down to brass tacks.

Needles of light broke through the branches ahead. This light was filtered by the leaves but was a solid force, pushing at the suffocating darkness and promising hope. Odus worked toward it, his footing more sure now as he could make out the black lines of trees and didn't have to feel his way through the vegetative maze. He heard voices as the light grew stronger and recognized one of them: Sarah from the general store. What business did a seventy-year-old woman have on top of Lost Ridge at this time of night? Of course, Odus could ask himself the same question, and maybe the same answer would serve for both of them.

"Hello," he shouted through the trees.

"Who's there?" Sarah said, her voice snapping like a soggy twig.

"Odus."

"Well, come on out of there and count your blessings that I didn't let loose with some buckshot first. It ain't wise to go sneaking up on a lady in the dark."

"I wasn't sneaking, I was walking," he said.

"Is this your horse, then?" came another voice, and Odus placed it as belonging to Sue Norwood, the young woman who'd been at the meeting at the general store last night.

Guided by their voices and the intensifying glare of car headlights, Odus threaded through the edge of the laurel thicket and stood in a little clearing at the end of a logging road. He stepped into the comforting cone of light and shielded his eyes. Sister Mary stood by the Jeep, snorting, head twitching up and down, and Odus couldn't shake the feeling that Sister Mary was laughing at him.

"Well, she's not rightly mine," Odus said. "I kind of appropriated her for a holy mission."

"See?" Sarah said to Sue, who was holding Sister Mary's reins. "I'm not the only one who's been touched in the head. The whole blamed place goes crazy whenever Harmon Smith rides into town."

"It seemed like the thing to do at the time," Odus said. "I mean, when you hear a calling, do you stop and ask questions, or do you just follow that voice?"

"You follow it," Sue said, and Odus could see the pickax in her hand, brandished like a Crusader's sword.

"That little pig-sticker won't do a thing against the Circuit Rider," Odus said, then noted the shotgun cradled across Sarah's arm. "I reckon a twenty-gauge won't, either."

"Oh yeah?" Sarah asked. "And what exactly do you have in your bag of tricks there that's supposed to kill a dead preacher? A Mason jar of holy water? A slingshot and a silver dime? An empty liquor bottle?"

Odus's face flushed. He'd tossed the Old Crow bottle into the hollow of a rotted-out stump, but first he'd briefly considered its potential as a spiritual battle-ax. Now the idea seemed as silly as Sue's and Sarah's weapons of choice.

"Okay, own up to it, we're poking in the dark with a limp stick," he said. "What now?"

"Wait, I reckon," Sarah said. "Harmon crashed our party last night, but I think tonight he's playing host."

"The air feels strange," Sue said. "Like it's carrying a mild electrical charge."

Odus had been so wired with tension his senses had been honed and focused down to the tight ache in his gut. Having found company, and his horse, he was able to relax enough to draw in the moist night air. The inhalation carried the fragrance of balsam and wet leaves, rich loam and moss, the safe, healing aromas of the high forest. But beneath that, like a corpse's smell oozing from beneath the undertaker's applied mask of perfume, was a corruption of sulfur and ozone, of decay and a pervasive stink of something that didn't belong in this world. The smell almost had a physical presence, as if it was lightly stroking his skin, coaxing him into vile acts and thoughts.

"I expect the others will be joining us," Sarah said.

"He's leading us here?" Sue said.

"Jesus had his Sermon on the Mount," Odus said. "Maybe Harmon's ready for his turn."

"You don't think . . . he's the *devil*, do you?" Sue said this with the tone of one who'd relegated such ideas to the realm of B-grade horror movies and backwoods tent revivals.

"Or a dybbuk in Jewish lore," Sarah said. "Not that I'd know anything about that."

"Maybe that's a question for Gordon Smith," Odus said. "He's the one with all the smarts on that stuff. Come to think of it, I wonder why he's never talked about it much."

"Ashamed, maybe," Sarah said. "It's the same bloodline. And we all got some kin that we don't talk about much."

Sister Mary stepped forward, onto the stage defined by the headlights, and Sue dropped the reins so the horse could reach Odus. Sister Mary brushed Odus's satchel with her nose, and he unzipped it and brought out an apple. As she munched it with a curious, sideways twist of her jaws, Odus was reminded of the goats and their increasing numbers, how they were being born outside their natural gestation period.

"Flock," he said, dimly recalling material from Sunday school, when the class leader sold the kids on religion with coloring books and posters. Jesus was often pictured with a flock of some kind, whether it was sheep, children in robes, or grown-ups whose skin colors were varied enough and in the right proportions to make you think that, sure, black folks could get to heaven, too, only there probably wouldn't be too many of them, and God would surely give them a place off to themselves. The common theme was that gathering of creatures around Jesus, as if the Son of God would get lonely if he didn't have living things milling around him, waiting for a wise word or a bit of free food.

"Flock what?" Sarah said.

"The goats made me think of it," Odus said. "They've been breeding like rabbits in the past year, especially on Gordon's farm. I could hardly walk through the field without hearing them rutting in the weeds. Made me think that Gordon was on some kind of power kick, like he needed to be the king of the heap. Like he needed a flock so he could feel good about himself. I figured that was why he married a woman who had a kid, too."

"What's that got to do with the Circuit Rider?" Sue said.

"He wants a flock, too. And we're it."

Sarah looked around, as if afraid of what might lurk beyond the false security of the headlights, the shotgun tilted to the ground. "What in the world does he need with *us*? He should have killed somebody and been gone already."

"Maybe he needs something different this time," Odus said. "Notice we both said *need*. Like we have to serve some purpose."

"And maybe that's why we feel like we're on some sort of mission," Sue cut in, her voice excited, reminding Odus of just how young she was, and how new to Solom and its strange ways. But she seemed to be a fast learner, or else was as loopy as the rest of them. Odus had sometimes wondered if there was some mineral missing from the local water sources, or if some element was too rich in the underground springs, and that it had slowly poisoned the minds of everyone who stayed here too long. After generations, no doubt the madness was inherited. But if cheap bourbon had never clouded his mind for less than a day at a time, then why should plain water have that power?

"Others will be coming along shortly," Odus said, realizing how pitiful and small his lone effort had seemed, riding into the mountains like the long arm of justice.

"Well, we ain't serving nothing by just standing here," Sarah said. "I guess we ought to go hear our sermon."

"Where do we look first?" Sue asked.

Odus stroked the lean, sinewy neck of Sister Mary, who nuzzled against the flannel of his shirt. "I think our animal friend here knows the way."

Animals.

Alex Eakins sensed their presence as he threaded his way up the narrow mountain trail. This path had been marked by buffalo and elk, which had walked these ridges in great numbers before European hunters had permanently removed them from the landscape. Bears, bobcats, deer, foxes, raccoons, opossums, and other creatures had used the route in their stead. Mountain lions had once lurked in the branches above, waiting for easy game. Alex could feel the power of all those thousands of feet, hooves, and paws that had passed here before. But mostly, he could smell the raw musky funk of goat shit.

As daylight had failed, he'd relied on the flashlight to follow the goats' trail. When night had finally pulled its dark sheet over the sky, his other, more primitive senses had emerged at their keenest. The air was chilly, ripe, and moist, full of the fecundity of fall's decay. The forest had a taste that lingered with each breath, the acidic tang of oak, the bitter bite of wild cherry and birch, the muddy richness of a hundred seeping springs. His power at detecting scent had also heightened, until he found he could smell not only the goats' spoor, but their fur and their ripe rutting aromas as well. Several times he thought he'd heard dozens of them moving through the unseen trees ahead, and wondered what he would do if he stepped into a clearing and found them all staring at him.

Alex patted the bow. He'd handle it, by the grace of God and the pissed-off fury of a man who had suffered trespassing.

His footing had grown more treacherous, the soles of his boots slick with the offal of those he pursued. The soil, though packed down by the centuries of use, had been scarred and tilled by the goat hooves. They were mountain creatures by nature, browsing the high forests when left in the wild, where their sure footing gave them an advantage over predators. But Alex felt his weapons and determination made him equal to the task.

The degree of the slope leveled out a little, allowing him to catch his breath. Near the peak, the trees thinned and moonlight spilled over the gleaming protrusions of granite. The gray boulders were scarred by moss, worn smooth by the slow work of a hundred thousand rains. The path narrowed as it wound between the rocks, and the hoot of an owl made the mountaintop seem like the last outpost on an alien boundary. Alex didn't contemplate the danger of breaking a leg or falling from a ledge. His path was sure and righteous. Revenge always delivered its own justification.

Below, through a gap in the trees, he could see the few twinkling lights of Solom. The bulb on the porch of the general store cast its pumpkin-colored glow, the center of a constellation of houses. The river road was like a dark black snake winding through the valley, and icy moonlight glinted off metal barn roofs. The trees thinned and Alex came to a clearing. He paused and listened, the wind playing through the dead and dying leaves. A soft murmur arose, like the babbling of a brook. After a moment, he recognized the sound as that of lowering goats, their bleats muted but uneasy. The bastards were just ahead, probably milling around in stoned-out glory, chewing bark and rocks in their advanced stage of marijuana munchies.

Alex slipped an arrow into the Pearson bow and made a stealthy approach. The ridge seemed brighter here, as if a last finger of daylight held a tentative grip. Alex eased his way through a stand of laurels and saw what was in the clearing.

Weird Dude Walking stood in the center, on a large slab of stone. The goats knelt around him, their heads tilted up as if awaiting words of capricious wisdom. Car headlights glared from behind the opposite stand of trees, moths swirling in the twin beams. Three people stood in silhouette among the trees.

Alex drew back the bowstring, intending to send an arrow through the dude's heart.

Weird Dude Walking turned to where Alex was hidden in the vegetation. "Welcome, friend," he said, his voice like smoke.

Chapter Thirty-three

A chauffeur for the dead.

Katy guided the Subaru off the highway onto the old logging road, sure that the last bit of sanity had slipped from her, leaving the nerves of her brain raw and exposed.

Why else would she be taking directions from a ghost? Her instinct had been to stay on the highway and make time to Florida, maybe stopping at a Holiday Inn halfway between. Anything that would have put distance between Jett and Solom. But Rebecca's lost voice had connected with her on some primal, feminine level. They were two women who had traveled the same path, though Rebecca's had ended too early and violently.

"Well, Mom, this is just great," Jett said. "You brought me here to get me off drugs and then you drop me right into the biggest bad-acid trip in the universe."

Jett had been reluctant to get back in the car after Rebecca had shared her story. But Katy's determination had convinced Jett they had a duty to obey. It was a little like a stray kitten that comes yowling in hunger around your doorstep. Never mind that this particular feline could remove its head and was built of see-through supernatural stuffing.

"Just hang on, honey," Katy said. She glanced in the rearview. Rebecca was gone but her words came as if she were leaning over the seat: *up the mountain.*

Up, an ascension, as if the journey had a spiritual as well as physical element. But didn't all journeys? If you thought of life as a road that must be traveled, then you had all kinds of exit ramps, signal lights, pit stops, and, eventually, a vehicle breakdown. Each fork was an opportunity, as the poet Robert Frost had pointed out, but no one had ever figured out if each road taken was a choice or an obligation. If you took the road less traveled, was it because you wanted to, or because you were compelled?

Katy decided this road was definitely the one less traveled, because the Subaru bottomed out in the ruts, the arcs of the headlights bouncing ahead like light sabers cutting a path through the wilderness. The car was all-wheel drive, which gave it enough traction to navigate the roughest parts of the old road, but it groaned in protest as it leaped and jittered like a two-ton electrified frog.

"Mom, what are we supposed to do when we get there?"

"I don't think we're supposed to know," Katy said.

"You just have to get there," Rebecca said, suddenly whole again, or the closest she could come to that state.

Jett jerked away, sitting forward in her seat, fighting the tension of the seat belt. "Hey! Don't do that. You're freaking me out enough already without popping out of thin air."

"I'm a ghost," Rebecca said. "What else do you expect me to do?"

"I see years of therapy ahead," Jett said.

"Just imagine the stories you'll have to tell your grandkids," Katy said, wrestling the steering wheel as the car lurched over a fallen sapling.

"If I live that long. Let's not take that for granted yet. We're on a place called 'Lost Ridge' with a headless woman in the backseat."

"They're waiting," Rebecca said.

"They?" Katy asked.

"The ones who are supposed to be there."

"What's with the riddles?" Jett said. "If you know what's going to happen, why don't you tell us?"

"You already know, too. That's the trouble with the living. They only hear the past when they should be listening to the future."

"Oh, great. Mom, you got any dope on you? I can't handle this."

Katy looked at her daughter, whose face was pale green from the interior lights. Her dyed-black bangs were parted, making her look younger than her twelve years. Yet Katy's little Gothling was knocking on the door to womanhood and all the crazy mysteries waiting ahead. Not to mention the crazy mysteries in the backseat. "You promised, remember?"

"Yeah, yeah." Jett sighed and reached to turn up the music again, then changed her mind and settled back against her seat, still leaning away from Rebecca. But she said to the ghost, "So, why did Gordon kill you?"

"Because he loved me. Why else would you kill someone?"

"No," Katy said. "I think the reason is even more selfish than that."

As she compelled the Subaru up the logging road, she thought back to his fascination with myths and old cultures and his ranting about harvest gods and goddesses. No one could be that insane, though. Certainly not a well-educated resident of the twenty-first century. Gordon was plenty strange, but she'd never sensed any type of aggressive behavior in him.

But would the behavior be aggressive, considering Gordon might think offering human sacrifice was the most natural thing in the world? Maybe he viewed it as a pleasant little appeasement ritual that had been too long neglected, thus bringing about the sorry state of the modern environment. Maybe he was trying to follow in the footsteps of his forefather, Harmon Smith, in observing his own peculiar belief system. But hadn't the goats been amazingly fruitful? How many kids had been born on the Smith farm in just the last four months? And the pumpkins, corn, and winter squash had all been abundant.

What if the sacrifice had been noted and *rewarded*?

Katy shivered and looked through the windshield at the rutted road ahead, wondering what sort of god would compel a man to slaughter his wife and maybe others. Surely Katy and Jett would have been next, and would have joined Rebecca in haunting the old wooden-frame farmhouse until the end of time.

"He did it because it was his destiny," Katy said, raising her voice over the roar of the straining engine.

"You're freaking me out, Mom," Jett said.

"Destiny," Rebecca said. "That's as good a name for it as any."

"So, what's your deal?" Jett said to the ghost. "Are you stuck here or something? Why don't you get to go to heaven or wherever?"

"I belong to Solom now."

"Mom, maybe we'd better find a place to turn around. I don't think I want to die here. It would be a real bitch to be stuck in Solom forever."

"We're not going to die," Katy said. "There's a reason for all this. You'll see."

"Does that mean I have to keep my eyes open?"

In response, Katy cranked up the volume on the Westerberg CD and a blues guitar riff tore a hole in the sheet of night.

God had chosen the wrong Tester.

Ray had always known it, and that was the thing that had driven him from the Primitive Baptist Church. God had dropped the bucket in that matter. David had a silver tongue, there was no denying that, but when it came to sheer gumption and balls, Ray had his younger brother beat seven ways to Sunday. True, the congregation made the decision on choosing a new church elder to deliver their sermons, but hadn't God determined all things before he even set the whole blamed shooting match in motion?

So when Ray had driven by the church and seen David crawling around on his hands and knees, mucked up to the eyeballs and looking like he'd been waltzed through a carnival house of horrors, Ray had fought the impulse to go on past without stopping. But blood kin was blood kin. Besides, it wasn't David's fault that God had goofed.

After all, this was the same God who had set the Circuit Rider loose in the world. If all things had a purpose, then God was basically the kind of guy who enjoyed pulling wings off flies, and He made sure there were enough piles of shit around to draw those flies.

David sat in the pickup truck's passenger seat, wiping his face with Ray's orange hunting vest. The interior light was on, and in its weak light David's cheeks were pale and bloodless. Ray's pipe wrench lay in the seat between them.

"You seen him, didn't you?" Ray said. They were brothers. They had fished together, fought together, lost their virginity to Mary Lou Slater together, were baptized together. They hadn't kept any secrets, not until the day the congregation went for style over substance eight years ago.

"Yeah," David said. "I looked in his grave."

"But he wasn't there."

"No, but he came up while I was digging."

"Dumb-ass. I could have told you that. When they looked in Jesus' tomb, it was empty, too."

"I wasn't good enough, Ray-Ray." David had fallen back to using a childhood nickname, proof that he'd been shaken like a rat in a terrier's jaws. "I had the chance to defeat him, or at least give myself and save others, but *I wasn't worthy.*"

Ray bit back his grin of pleasure. Maybe God hadn't blown this thing yet. Maybe the Big Guy had set up the domino chits so the real favorite son could knock them down.

He patted David on the shoulder and gave him the kind of manly squeeze that said, *Yeah, that's some rotten possum you got served, but eat it for your own good.*

"I've got this feeling," Ray said. "A feeling that maybe God has other business for you. That's how you got to look at it. Maybe you're the fish he threw back in so you could grow up big and strong and feed the multitudes."

David nodded, shivering a little. Mist rose off his damp clothes as the night chill settled around them.

"Maybe it's my turn," Ray continued. "God passed me over the first time because he had this job for me. That explains the scarecrow and the headless goats. Those were signs, and I was too red-eyed blind to see them. I'm the one, Davey Boy. I'm the *one.*"

David was drawn up and beaten, the way he'd been after wetting the bed at age five. David had to sleep on the bottom bunk, not because Ray was older and therefore deserved a higher station, but because there was the real risk that urine would dribble off his plastic sheet to the bed below if he'd been on top. David was in an agreeable mood, Ray noted, because he'd seen the light of truth. David wasn't worthy, and that meant Ray was in the driver's seat again. He could hardly wait until next Sunday's service, when David announced his resignation and Ray stepped up to win their vote as the new elder.

Elder. As if that name for the church leader weren't self-evident. It probably wouldn't hurt the congregation to eat a little crow for going with style over substance, as if practically every lesson in the Bible didn't warn against arrogance, pride, and hypocrisy.

Looking through the windshield, Ray saw a faint glow at the top of the ridge, less than a half mile from the church. He'd hunted that ridge for wild turkey, one of the most elusive creatures ever set loose on God's green earth. The glow was more than just a collected pool of moonlight against the granite boulders. It was a spotlight shone down from heaven, marking a center stage where Ray would meet his destiny. With David serving as witness.

"The path has been marked," Ray said. "Narrow is the gate and hard is the road, but the logging road to Lost Ridge is as wide open as Mary Lou Slater's legs." He punched his brother on the shoulder. "And you get to ride shotgun, just like you did that day we busted our cherries. Whaddaya think about that, Davey Boy?"

David may have answered, but Ray couldn't have heard him over the roar of the engine's kicking to life.

Sarah leveled the shotgun at the Circuit Rider, who sat on the flat boulder with his legs crossed like one of those fat Asian buddhas. Four dozen goats knelt before the dead preacher, still and waiting under the glare of the Jeep headlights. That might have been the creepiest part of the whole scene: the Circuit Rider's eyes burned yellow in the light, his waxen face and gaunt cheeks visible under the wide brim of his black hat, and his smile was like a broken snake under his long, thin nose, but goats were never still. They usually twitched and nattered and stomped and kicked, and most of all, they were usually chewing on something. But these animals folded up before Harmon Smith as if they were dosed with tranquilizers and headed for a long drowse. Even the kids among them were motionless and relaxed, scarcely wiggling an ear.

Old Saint was tied to a tree at the edge of the clearing, and it was the first time Sarah had ever seen the fabled creature. He was an admirable hunk of horseflesh, if "flesh" was the right word. He might have been a couple of centuries up from the grave, but he looked as solid as the oak that served as his hitching post. The horse nibbled at a patch of moss on the tree, as if he'd already heard the sermon that Harmon Smith appeared about to deliver.

Sue sat behind the wheel of the Jeep, frozen by the sight that had greeted them upon pushing into the clearing. Odus, who had regained Sister Mary's good graces, sat astride the paint pony to the left of the Jeep. The young man who held some sort of bow-and-arrow stood on the opposite side of the clearing, as if he'd found another route to the top of the ridge. Sarah recognized him from a couple of his shopping trips to the store, where he bought only cheap staples like rice and dried beans. She figured it was no coincidence that the man had shown up here at the same time as her little trio, and had no doubt that the reason for their mutual summoning was buried in the skull space beneath that ragged-rimmed black hat.

If the Circuit Rider even *had* a brain, that was. Sarah suspected if that skull was laid open with a shotgun blast, it would ooze a stinky, sticky tar. The juice of madness and evil, the sort of stuff that might pump through Satan's icy-hot veins. She was tempted to give Harmon Smith a load of bird shot, just to test the waters, so to speak, but she had a sense that the stage wasn't completely set yet. Harmon had a few other pieces to move into the picture, and he seemed in no particular hurry, as if a full-moon Sunday night were just the right time for a nice, peaceful gathering of good company.

"Shoot him, Sarah," Sue said from the Jeep's cab. Young folks were so impatient.

"You don't just up and shoot a man without giving him a chance to explain himself," Sarah said, keeping the fright out of her voice. "Otherwise the gender would have been wiped out years ago. Besides, sometimes it's fun to hear a man open his mouth just to hear what kind of lie comes out."

"I bring only the truth," Harmon shouted, though he was too far away to have heard Sarah, just at the edge of effective shotgun range. But he looked to be in range of the man with the cocked arrow, who raised his own weapon. Sarah saw the man had other weapons slung over his shoulder, and wore a sidearm in a belt holster. He was equipped like a secret agent in a movie that couldn't keep its time period right.

"Do these shit-bag animals belong to you?" the man asked, voice quivering with either fear or anger.

Harmon swept out a casual hand to indicate the ridge and the valley below. "All this belongs to me," the preacher answered. "And other places as well. My road is long and my service is never done."

"Drop the double talk, Weird Dude," the man said. "If these are yours, you've got reparations to pay. Because you trespassed against me."

"Fences are for the living. I go where I want because Solom belongs to me."

Sarah thought the man's release finger on the bow-and-arrow looked a little itchy. "My deed is registered at the courthouse," he said.

"And mine is recorded in the Book of Knowledge."

"Are you with the government?"

"I answer to one law."

"What's with the riddles, man?" He raised his voice, addressing Sarah, Sue, and Odus. "What are you guys doing up here?"

"We're here for the same reason you are," Sarah said.

"To kill some damned goats?"

"They came because of me," the Circuit Rider said. "As do all my creatures."

"Hey, dude, I saw those goats *eating* you."

"I provide nourishment to my flock."

Sarah figured Harmon Smith, back when he was alive, had been touched in the head somewhere along the line, about the time he traded in his Methodist leanings for a belief in fleshly sacrifice. After a couple hundred years roaming the backwoods to visit various Appalachian communities, killing somebody here and there along the way, he'd probably made peace with his madness. The miles were long and the path dusty, but a mission of that kind would require a man to embrace solitude. Even with a horse for company, the Circuit Rider worked alone, abandoned by both God and the devil and shunned by every mortal creature. Then why were those creatures gathering around him like moths drawn to a porch light?

"I have a revelation to deliver," Harmon Smith said, as if he'd looked inside Sarah's head. He drew his ragged wool coat about him with gaunt fingers. "But we'll have to wait for the others."

"Others?" Odus said.

At that moment, Sarah heard a mechanical roar rising from the slopes below and echoing in the cup of the valley. Cars, at least three and maybe more, the rumble of a convoy as the engines whined against the climb. She wondered how many the Circuit Rider would summon tonight.

Harmon Smith sat on the rock in his yoga position, the snake of a smile bending into a deeper smirk. "My children," he said. "All my lovely children."

Jett figured her mom was taking some kind of heavy downer, because she seemed calm as she navigated the narrow, rutted road, looking freaky with her one bruised eye. A couple of times the Subaru had swerved over to the ledge and the valley opened up in a dizzying tableau below. In those moments of vertigo, Jett covered her eyes and imagined what her obituary would look like. She figured her obit would have the same problem as most people's: it would be way too short. Plus it would leave out the cool stuff, like her acid flashbacks and the ghost in the backseat.

Rebecca's ghost had a part in this whole cluster fuck called Solom, and Jett had come to accept that Gordon's goats were evil and the man in the black hat wanted her for some very special and creepy purpose. Solom was the biggest bad-acid trip of all time, and she and Mom couldn't escape until the drug wore off. She was aware that most people used the term *supernatural* to describe such occurrences, but to Jett they seemed completely natural. In a world gone crazy, why shouldn't the dead and the living occupy the same space? Why shouldn't a ghost guide them up a mountaintop in the dark of a Sunday night, even though Mom had been determined to flee this place for the comparative sanity of Florida's crime, congestion, and pollution?

The road leveled out and grew wider. Mom steered the car over a grassy area, though a path appeared to have been tattooed into the dirt. Tire tracks cut twin grooves in the open stretch of land, flattening the wet weeds. The tracks were recent.

Jett turned to Rebecca, still not quite used to the shock of that pale face, the hollow eyes that looked out as if from the bottom of a deep and drowning cave, the thin lips that were as insubstantial as mist. Jett realized that, if the ghost hadn't helped her, Gordon might have caught both Jett and Mom, and then *they* might have been trapped at the Smith house forever. This was some drug-addled scriptwriter's twisted version of a *Scooby Doo* episode, except nobody got doggie treats and the bad guy's mask didn't come off at the end.

"Somebody came here before we did," Jett said to Rebecca. "Do you know why?"

Jett didn't like the way the torn flesh around the woman's neck rippled as she spoke, as if unearthly air passed through her windpipe. "We're all on the same path," the ghost said.

"Yeah, but what does that mean?"

"It means we have to look," Mom said, turning her head for a moment. "We can't just go off and leave a mystery hanging."

"Sure we can, Mom. Remember the scarecrow? Remember the goats? What do I have to do, die or something to get your attention?"

"We can get through this together."

Jett almost choked on the Mom-ism, but decided to go with it this time. After all, she had no choice. Even if she jumped out of the car and survived, she'd still be facing a long hike down the mountain. And then what would she do? Call Dad and beg him to turn around and come back?

No, Dad was out of the picture for the moment. He hadn't believed a word she'd said this morning. A weary sadness had pressed itself over his face, and she knew he blamed himself for her problems, her delusions, her dark imagination. Some family she'd been born into; if either parent had spent half as much energy accepting responsibility as was invested in embracing guilt, they could have made a go of it.

As it was, she took her spiritual guidance where she found it. Even if the spirit in question had to keep adjusting its head atop its shoulders.

"Rebecca, tell Mom this is crazy." Jett recognized the inherent lunacy of her request.

"This is crazy," the ghost said, mouth parting to reveal darkness inside the translucent flesh.

"Yes, but we can't leave until we know what happened," Mom said.

"What *happened*?" Jett gripped the dashboard as the Subaru leaped a vicious rut. "You act like it's already too late to do anything about it."

"It's not too late," Mom said, applying the brakes. "Looks like the party's just started."

Through the windshield, Jett saw a scene that would have made Stephens both King and Spielberg wish they had thought of it first. The man in the black hat sat on a rock, surrounded by goats, while people came walking out of the woods to gather around the ridgetop clearing. Jett recognized some of them: there was Odus, who helped Gordon with farm chores, sitting astride a horse; Jerry Bennington, her math teacher, stood to one side, wearing his bow tie; the man who lived up the road from the Smith house and occasionally rumbled by in his battered pickup hunched at one edge of the clearing, holding some type of hunting bow-and-arrow. Jett saw the old woman who owned the general store, a shotgun across the crook of one knotty elbow. A Jeep bathed the group in light, and as Mom parked the Subaru, its lights joined in, giving the menagerie a strange, stark radiance.

"That's the guy I was telling you about," Jett said.

"It looks like he found us," Mom said.

"Mom, you're tripping."

"No, I'm pretty straight at the moment."

Jett turned to query Rebecca on this weird gathering, but

Rebecca was gone. At least, *most* of her was. Her disembodied head hovered in the rear passenger area, slowly fading to thin air. The last thing to fade was those dark, hollow eyes, and they seemed to hold a challenge and a glimmer of triumph.

Chapter Thirty-four

Odus gripped the reins to steady Sister Mary as more people came out from the trees, vehicles groaned up the old logging roads of Lost Ridge, and a few stray goats staggered into the combined glare of a half dozen headlights. It was like some kind of bizarre revival service, with the Circuit Rider calling his flock. Odus suddenly didn't feel so special. He was ashamed to think that he would be the one to rid the world of the Circuit Rider. He was unworthy. He was just a drunk who couldn't hold down a steady job, a dirty horse thief, part of a bloodline that had squatted on these lands since Colonial times but had not really improved them.

The Eakins boy, the one who owned a piece of property above the Smith place, stood with his compound bow, unsure of which direction to aim. Loretta Whitley and her son Todd each held pitch-forks, looking like frightened members of a mob storming Victor Frankenstein's castle. Amos Clayton sported a shotgun of a larger bore than Sarah's, though he seemed uncertain about using it. Odus wondered if they each had suffered the same delusion, of being called to kill the Circuit Rider and finally lay the preacher to rest, bringing peace to the valley. Or perhaps they had come because they each wanted to offer themselves on the altar of life.

Several more vehicles rolled into the clearing, and the smell of exhaust briefly muted the stench of the goats and the bright, metallic odor of human fear. Odus recognized Ray Tester's Ford pickup, and a sport utility vehicle pulled up beside it. A sheriff's department patrol car, a Crown Victoria, had been beaten up by the rough road, but the rear-wheel drive had dragged the car to the peak. The door on the patrol car opened and a deputy stepped out, half his face blotted by a red birthmark, one hand on his sidearm. Odus figured the deputy would try to take control and restore order, but he seemed as much under the Circuit Rider's sway as the rest of them.

"Welcome, all," the preacher said, standing on legs that seemed to unfold like broken black sticks. In the combined glare of a half dozen sets of headlights, he seemed almost a silhouette in his moth-eaten black suit. He lifted the brim of his hat and turned in a semicircle so that all the assembled could see his face. The skin appeared to be as smooth as hardened wax and just as brittle. The preacher's eyes were the bloodied color of a harvest moon just after sundown.

The crowd fell silent, as if each word might be the one that delivered the Truth. The late-arriving goats joined their kind near the stone that served as the Circuit Rider's pulpit, and they, too, settled into passive and meek positions. The people who had emerged from the woods—Odus saw Marletta Hoyle, the wispy-haired English teacher at the elementary school, carrying an eagle-head cane as if she meant to brain Harmon Smith like a wayward student—drew closer around the stone with an air of expectation. The Tester brothers had climbed out of the truck cab and stood at the outer edge of the goats, David looking a little beaten down but Ray stood with his shoulders thrown back and head held high, like a dog waiting for a treat.

"We're not all here yet," the Circuit Rider said.

A man in the concealed safety of the forest called out, "Go back to where you come from, you black devil."

The Circuit Rider grinned, showing teeth as orange as candy corn. "This *is* where I came from."

The unseen man hollered, "You wasn't born to Solom. The damned Methodists sent you."

"It was a Methodist who rode into this fair valley all those years ago," he said, in a voice that would make any preacher, living or dead, proud. "But that Methodist found other, older ways here. Ways brought over with the first white settlers."

"We're God-fearing folk, Harmon Smith," Loretta Whitley said, slamming the point of her pitchfork handle into the ground for emphasis. "Why don't you go on about your business and leave us alone?"

"This is my business," the Circuit Rider said. "Your church leaders couldn't tolerate my beliefs, so they did away with them the only way they knew how."

"By killing you," Sarah said, surprising Odus with the strength in her voice. "The same way we're fixing to kill you again."

The Circuit Rider laughed, a sound as raw as an owl's screech and as deep as the howling of a red wolf. "We all serve a purpose under God's sky. The tree is known by its fruit."

"What about your goats, Weird Dude?" asked the Eakins boy. The way his hands were trembling, Odus figured the arrow would let fly at any second. Maybe all of them were waiting to see who would attack Harmon Smith first. Then they could all join in with whatever weapons or talismans they had brought. Odus realized he still hadn't decided on a weapon. He had trusted that the way would be shown, but now that the moment was at hand, no voice from the wilderness gave him instruction. Through all his false courage, he was alone. As were they all, despite their number.

"Which one of us do you want, Harmon?" Ray Tester called. "We know you need to take one of us, and we know you've done passed over a few." Ray shot a glance at his brother.

"I want all of you," the Circuit Rider said. "Why do you think I keep returning?"

"You're just a pesky old buzzard," Sarah said. "You pick at the bones of the past. But we don't need you around no more."

"It's not about what you need, Sarah Jeffers. It's about what's meant to be."

"Well, I ain't meant to be standing on the top of a cold mountain in the middle of a September night."

"You're here, though, aren't you?"

Sarah had no answer for that. She thumbed at the hammer of the shotgun as if debating whether to try a shot in such a crowd. No doubt stray pellets would strike innocent bystanders. But maybe, Odus figured, none of them were innocent. After all, they belonged to Solom, and Solom had slaughtered the Circuit Rider. Maybe the years had led to this moment just as surely as the Circuit Rider's route brought him back again and again. While the past drew only further in the distance, the Circuit Rider was caught in an endless loop, playing out his fate with no hope of rest.

Odus was surprised to hear his own voice, not aware his thoughts had slipped to his tongue. "We're here because we have to be."

"That's the same reason I'm here, Mr. Odus Dell Hampton. Because you all need me."

Odus felt the Circuit Rider was looking straight through him, and he was sure that everybody in the crowd had the same feeling. Though the headlights must have been burning his eyes, Harmon Smith didn't squint as he surveyed the creatures gathered on the ridge.

"Let's kill the fucker," the Eakins boy said.

The sheriff's deputy barked in an authoritative manner, "Hold it right there. Nobody gets killed here unless I say so."

Odus wondered if anyone was going to point out the irony of killing a dead man, but the assembly merely waited with half-held breath. Amos Clayton raised his shotgun but it was pointed toward the leering moon above. Will Absher, who had once been Odus's fishing buddy before Odus had caught him stealing change out of his truck ashtray, stepped from the laurel thicket carrying a muzzle-loading rifle that appeared to date to back before the Civil War. Odus wondered if that was the means of sending the Circuit Rider on to heaven or hell or lands in between: a weapon from Harmon Smith's own mortal time. Odus was getting a headache from thinking over the possibilities, and decided his original idea was the best one. The way would be shown when the time was right.

If the time was right, Odus amended. He'd seen no sign that Harmon Smith was bound to die again tonight.

Sister Mary's flank muscles quivered beneath Odus, and for a moment Odus wasn't sure whether it was his own shivering, building until it was transmitted into the horse's mottled flesh.

Another handful of people leaked from the woods, one of them on horseback. As James Greene walked into the clearing leading a mule, the Circuit Rider issued his black grin.

"Well, now that we're all here, let's see who among us is ready to enter the kingdom tonight," the preacher said.

"Holy fucking *frijoles*," Jett said as they came upon the bizarre scene.

Katy forgot to chastise Jett for the expletive, she was so stunned by the cars, people, and goats gathered on the isolated ridge. As she applied the brakes and brought the car to a halt, she saw the man in the black suit, the one Jett had told her about. He stood on the rock, basking in the crisp glare of the various car headlights. Katy recognized a couple of the people who stood outside the circle of goats.

"Those are Gordon's goats," Jett said. "I would recognize them anywhere, especially after they tried to munch me. See that big one, up at the front? With the brown tail? That's Ezekiel."

Katy turned to ask Rebecca about the goats, but Rebecca was gone. Or at least, *most* of her was. Her head floated in the air, ragged strips of ghostly neck flesh tugged by whatever gravity held sway over the dead.

"Hey, don't do that," Katy said. "This was your idea, remember?"

"Sorry, I haven't been myself lately."

"What are we supposed to do now?"

"Get out and listen."

Katy looked at Jett, who nodded. "Guess we might as well get this over with, Mom. Besides, you need to see that I wasn't lying."

"How did the goats get up here before we did?"

"Forget about that. We ought to be worrying about—hey, look!"

A figure moved from the edge of the woods, and the crowd parted to let it through. Katy recognized the battered straw hat and the feed-sack face. "It's your scarecrow," she whispered.

"Told you, Mom. But you wouldn't believe me about the scarecrow, either."

The scarecrow figure held a wicked-looking sickle. Its clothes were torn and rumpled, and straw leaked from the folds with each step of cracked and flapping boots.

Jett unsnapped her seat belt and was out of the car before Katy could grab her arm. "Come back here, Jett."

But Jett was already passing the Jeep and Odus Hampton on a horse, reaching the outer circle of goats.

"Shit," Katy hissed, getting out of the car.

"It's him," Jett screamed, pointing at the scarecrow, which was approaching the Circuit Rider from the opposite side of the clearing.

The Circuit Rider's pale and waxen face turned from Jett to the scarecrow. The grin froze on the preacher's lips. Katy was pushing past Odus Hampton and Sarah Jeffers, noting the shotgun in the old woman's arms. *What in the hell is going on here?* her mind screamed as her feet carried her after Jett.

The goats stirred for the first time since their arrival, snorting and bleating as the scarecrow stomped into their midst.

"You're not supposed to be here," the Circuit Rider said.

The scarecrow's stitched lips gave the illusion of a wicked smile, but surely that was an illusion, because the feed-sack face bore no other expression. The scarecrow hopped over a fat nanny, catching one dusty boot on a curled horn. It regained its balance and leaped onto the stone beside the Circuit Rider.

"Solom doesn't need you anymore," the scarecrow said, in a muffled and rough voice. "We can appease God ourselves."

"Solom needs me," the Circuit Rider said. "Who else can bring the rain and the frost and the wind and the sun?"

"You're not the only one who understands the power of blood sacrifice."

Jett had drawn to a stop among the goats, about ten feet from the stone stage. Katy dodged around the goats, ignoring their sinister eyes and wicked teeth. Her daughter was more important to her than the whole world, and she was nearly oblivious to the strange assembly of people, many of whom held weapons. At least she had proof that she wasn't descending into madness, because if this was a hallucination, it was a communal one.

Katy sensed more than saw the movement around her: the sheriff's deputy reaching in the car and triggering the blue strobes on the car's roof; Ray Tester dashing through the goats like a drunk running an obstacle course, rousing some to their feet as he thumped against them; their reclusive neighbor, Alex Eakins, raising what looked like a bow and aiming an arrow toward the stage; a large old goat that was the spitting image of Abraham, the one that Katy had killed or crippled in the driveway, rising and stomping toward the Circuit Rider like a repentant sinner headed for the touch of a faith healer; Sarah Jeffers moving into shotgun range with the careful steps of the elderly; Odus whacking the paint pony on the flank and urging it toward the granite slab; others circling and drawing closer, wanting to be part of the malevolent miracle, some stretching out their hands like New Testament lepers reaching for the robes of Jesus.

Jett's quoting of the Tommy Keene title "Merry-Go-Round Broke Down" popped into her mind, all the pretty ponies spilling from their poles, the center giving way, the crazy carnival lights bobbing, though the smells were those of fur and forest instead of popcorn and spun sugar. She reached Jett just as the scarecrow joined the Circuit Rider as if wanting to hog half the spotlight.

"These are my people now," the scarecrow said, and Katy recognized the cruel, commanding tone.

Gordon.

"Fucking Christ on a rubber crutch," Jett said. "It's *him.*"

Katy recalled the scarecrow outfit in the box upstairs, the blood in the locked cupboard. She'd accepted that Gordon was capable of murder in the wake of Rebecca's confession, but she hadn't pegged him for a lunatic until now. She figured he was just like any man, vain and cruel and possessive, but she didn't know the possession might have worked both ways.

But why the costume? Why dress up when the most successful killers were those who didn't draw attention to themselves?

Katy had no time to analyze Gordon's motives. She hadn't figured him out in the year she had known him, and she suspected that would be the job for a team of prison psychiatrists over the next thirty years. In fact, all of Solom's residents would probably be scooped up in a giant butterfly net and plopped gently into soft asylum rooms, especially when they started babbling about dead preachers, man-eating goats, and mountaintop revivals where faith was challenged and madness was shared like communion sacraments.

The scarecrow—*Gordon*, she had to remind herself—stood half a foot taller than the Circuit Rider, the brims of their hats nearly touching.

"Have you people had enough of the Circuit Rider?" Gordon shouted, the feed-sack mouth puffing out with the air of his words, the stitched lips moving in a grotesque parody of language.

"Get out of the way and give me a clear shot," Alex Eakins yelled back.

Ray Tester tripped over a billy goat, and the goat snapped at his flesh, teeth sinking into his arm and eliciting a scream. Ray swung the heavy wrench he was carrying as if it were Samson's jawbone of an ass wielded against Philistines. The scent of blood seemed to arouse the other goats, because several of them broke out of their languid stupor and sniffed the night air. Katy looked down at the goats around her legs, noting that their attention was still fixed on the Circuit Rider. The goats around Jett twitched their tails but were otherwise docile. Ray regained his balance and continued toward the stage, holding his arm, blood trickling between his fingers, the bloody wrench clutched in one fist.

Throughout all the chaos, the Circuit Rider stood with his grave-seasoned hands at his sides, his face calm, his eyes burning with the orange and red of coals being fanned to life by an inner wind.

"What has this preacher ever done for you?" the scarecrow/Gordon called to the crowd.

"Is that you, Gordon?" someone said from the edge of the crowd.

"I am the son of Ceres, the daughter of Diana," he answered, in that bombastic, lecturing tone that should have been enough for Katy to call off the engagement. But she had wanted to give Jett a happy, stable home, one far removed from the troubled past, the drugs, the divorce.

All those ordinary failures now seemed so laughable when compared to this supernatural tsunami of danger and death.

Katy reached Jett and tried to pull her back, but Jett stood transfixed. Though it was difficult to tell where the bone-button eyes of the scarecrow mask were focused, she felt burned by his stare, which was brighter and hotter than the beams of the collective headlights. Katy could have sworn the black yarn of the lips arched into a sneer.

"Ah, my sweet little scapegoats," Gordon said. "Come to offer yourself to the old gods? Come to give yourself to the soil so that Solom may be fruitful and multiply?"

The scarecrow put a hand on the Circuit Rider's shoulders and forced him to his knees. "See how hollow this supposed man of God is? A straw man, you might say. *Ha-ha-haa-haaaaa*."

Ray scrabbled the final few feet to the granite slab, pushing past complaining goats. "Take *me*," Ray said. "I'm the chosen one."

"No," Odus said, guiding his horse among the capricious herd. "This is my mission."

"Get off that horse and come back here," Sarah called to him. "I can't get a good shot with so many people standing in the way."

To Katy, the woman sounded almost grateful to have an excuse. Any of them could have attacked the Circuit Rider if that was their intention. He was exposed on the rock, presumably blinded by the glaring lights, unless his vision was guided by unnatural laws. Those at his back wouldn't have to worry about being seen and marked by whatever wrath he might unleash. It was as if the people, like the goats, were under some sort of spell, transfixed despite their hatred of the entity that had brought such pain and suffering to their community.

"See?" Gordon said, towering over the Circuit Rider. "Look how frail is this creature of the night."

Gordon yanked off the preacher's hat, exposing the wiry gray hairs that curled over the pale, crenulated skull. Gordon sailed the hat into the herd of goats, where it caught on the horn of one and hung as if tossed atop a coatrack.

"Look upon his wonder and be disappointed," Gordon said. "Know him by his fruits."

Katy wanted to bring Jett back to the relative safety of the Subaru, but found herself as rapt and awestruck as the rest. This close, she detected not only the electric aura of the Circuit Rider, but Gordon's mad energy that created its own special and strange gravity as well. She wondered if that danger-tinged charisma had been what had attracted her to him, but the thought sickened her.

"What's he doing and why doesn't that policeman stop him?" Jett said.

"Because the policeman's human. Like the rest of us."

Ray tried to climb up onto the stone slab. It was slick with September dew, and his wounded arm prevented him from gaining solid purchase in the crevices. He lodged one boot into a crack and was about to haul himself up onto the impromptu stage when one of the goats in the front row, whose brown facial fur made a raccoon mask, lurched forward and snagged his other leg, tugging on the cuff of his jeans. Another goat rose, this one with crooked beige horns, and began sniffing his calf. "Help me, David," Ray called.

A hissing *thwack* pierced a hole in the night, and the goat with the beige horns let out a bruised bleat of shock. The feathers of an arrow tip jutted from its rib cage, just above its heart. It staggered back two steps, wobbled, and collapsed as if its legs were pipe cleaners.

"No!" Gordon moaned, as though the injury had been inflicted on him instead.

"The fucker munched my stash, man," Alex said. "That was private property. *My* property."

The goats near the one who had fallen began sniffing the warm corpse. One poked out a tentative tongue and licked the wound. The flock began bleating and lowing, giving off restless snorts, several of them rising.

"Come on, Jett," Katy said. "I don't trust these goats."

"I don't trust anything right now."

A grizzled billy goat, one eye made milky by blindness, nipped the air a couple of feet from Katy's leg, brown teeth clacking with menace. She eyed the distance back to the Subaru. The rock slab was closer, but that would put them within Gordon's reach. Gordon pointed his sickle at Alex, the other hand still pressing on the kneeling preacher's shoulder.

Words issued from behind the scarecrow's mask: "You should forgive those who trespass against you."

"Maybe you should take better care of your fences," Alex said, notching another arrow. "*Gordon*."

"I'm not Gordon. I am he who gives tribute."

"With other people's lives," Odus said, guiding his paint pony through the restless goats.

"Gordon's gone squirrel-shit nutty," Jett whispered to Katy.

"I think we all have," Katy whispered, just before the first shot-gun blast ripped through the forest night.

Chapter Thirty-five

Sarah didn't quite mean to squeeze the trigger. At least, that's what she told herself. But an old woman's reflexes, like all her physical responses, tended to decline with every go-round of the sun. A shotgun was a great weapon if you needed to rake down a thief from close range, but the wide pattern of the bird shot all but guaranteed a few stray pellets.

A few bleeding goats might not be a bad bonus, she rationalized, as the echo of the gun's report slapped off the granite boulders and rolled through the trees. Blue-gray smoke swirled in the Jeep's headlights, and the strong bite of cordite drowned out the moist humus smell of the mountain and the stench of the goats. The frail bones of her shoulder ached from the recoil.

She'd meant to take down those goats nearest to Ray Tester, because they looked ready to chomp down on his legs. But what really flipped her was seeing the goat that had raided her store. She didn't usually carry a grudge, and believed all God's creature's had a rightful place in the world. But this was the same world that held monsters like the Circuit Rider. And it seemed Gordon Smith had gone crazy, too.

She'd never quite trusted the man, and it wasn't just because of his bloodline. Whenever he ate a sandwich and took coffee at the store, he always calculated the tip at exactly 15 percent. He'd do the division longhand on the back of his ticket and round it to the nearest penny. Sarah could only guess what that scrawny, red-headed wife of his had gone through. Now he'd slipped into some sort of Halloween getup and had taken to killing folks.

The gunshot temporarily restored the peace that had prevailed when they had first stumbled onto the gathering. But it was a false peace, inflicted through shock and surprise. In that frozen moment, Sarah had time to absorb tiny details just as the night exploded: Sue Norwood opening the driver's-side door of the Jeep; Odus sitting tall on the bareback horse and looking around like a rustler wondering where to direct the stampede; the man with the hunting bow taking aim at either Gordon or the Circuit Rider; Ray scrambling onto the flat slab of stone and crawling toward the Circuit Rider; Gordon in his scarecrow outfit reaching a gloved hand to the Circuit Rider and pulling that sickly forehead back, exposing the dead preacher's pale and knobby throat; the goats rising to their feet as if heeding some silent command; and David Tester running into the midst of the stirring animals, either chasing his brother or making the same obsessed dash toward the Circuit Rider.

Sarah broke down the barrel and thumbed out the warm, spent shell, reaching in her blouse pocket for a fresh round.

Katy sensed the change in the animals after one of their number had fallen. The night was electric, charged with rage and confusion.

Ray leaped for the Circuit Rider and threw his arms around the preacher, shielding him just as Alex launched another arrow. Katy heard the wet *snick* of the arrow as it buried itself between Ray's shoulder blades. Ray's wrench bounced off the stone with a dull *clink*. He gave a soft grunt of surprise, hugging the preacher, looking up into his face as if craving a final benediction. The preacher showed no emotion, just stared back with those beetle-black eyes.

Ray's words were so weak and strained that Katy was sure no one heard them besides herself, Gordon, Jett, and the Circuit Rider.

"I'm the one," Ray said, smiling, dying, slumping against the preacher with the arrow jutting from his back.

"Get him!" Gordon yelled, again pointing his sickle at Alex. At first Katy thought he was addressing the crowd, but the goats turned as one and sniffed the air in Alex's direction. The goats gave out cries and squeaks as they moved. Alex backed away, but the goats nearest him had broken into a trot. There was no way he'd make the relative safety of the woods. Even if he did, the sure-footed goats would have an advantage on the rough terrain.

The horn of a passing goat grazed Katy's wrist, laying open the skin.

"Shit, Mom, you're bleeding," Jett said.

Jett wasn't the only one who noticed. A long-bearded nanny paused, bucking against the river of goats and turning toward Katy. It sniffed, snorted, and kicked up its back legs, clicking its hooves. Then it struggled against the seething tide of animals and headed for Katy as if she had been dipped in honey and oats.

"The rock," Katy said, gripping Jett's hand so hard her own fingers ached.

The nanny negotiated the rumbling herd better than Katy did, because she was busy dodging bobbing horns and stomping hooves. The nanny was gaining, and Katy was still twenty feet from the rock. And even if she reached the rock, what would Gordon do to her? Cut her with his sickle, or toss her to the meat-eating monsters that somehow obeyed his perverted commands?

The decision was taken from her as a passing goat rammed her in the stomach, knocking the wind from her. Above the high-pitched whining in her ears, she heard Jett scream, and a hundred hoofbeats drummed their death march. Then she was lifted into the air, yanked as if by the ray of a flying saucer or the crook of God's swooping shepherd's staff. She blinked the lime-colored sparks of pain from behind her eyes and found herself flopped belly-down over the back of Odus's horse.

"Where's Jett?" she managed to whisper, breath like wet cement in her lungs.

"Can't reach her," Odus said. He slapped the horse on the thigh and said, "Come on, Sister Mary, let's ride out of this stampede."

The horse whinnied and reared, jostling Katy, and for a horrifying split second she thought she would be hurled from the horse and back among the milling goats. But she grabbed the horse's

neck and held on as they waded through the herd, which was thinning now as the stragglers made their way toward Alex.

Another shotgun blast sounded, and two goats bleated squeals
of pain. Katy saw Jett at the edge of the rock, climbing up, finding
handholds on the mossy surface, gaining her footing.

Gordon let go of the Circuit Rider, who was still in the grip of
Ray's corpse. He grabbed Jett by the hair and yanked her against
his ragged clothing. "I'll teach you to leave me," he said.

"We have to save her," Katy said to Odus.

"These goats are crazy," Odus said. "Look. They're *eating* people."

He was right. Alex had reached a beech tree and scrambled up
into the safety of the branches. Two goats butted the tree trunk, but
its girth was several feet in diameter and the tree barely shook. A
man screamed as another shot rang out, and Katy looked around to
see the deputy, a goat latched onto his leg, another biting the hand
that held his pistol. A wounded goat shivered at the officer's feet,
thrown into spasms by a head wound.

The old lady who owned the store had dropped her shotgun and
climbed onto the hood of the Jeep, and several goats tried to clam-
ber up the bumper. An old man in a leather jacket, whom Katy did-
n't recognize, leveled his shotgun and blasted toward the Jeep,
sending pellets scattering across the metal and driving the goats
away. The old woman cursed and gripped her knee.

A woman and a younger man with pitchforks stood back to
back, jabbing at the goats that had them encircled.

"We're all going crazy," Katy said.

"We were already *at* crazy," Odus said. "We've gone way past
that now."

The goats had lost their communal goal and scattered into the
night, chasing the people who had been summoned to the surreal
revival. Their bleats became guttural cries of hunger. Katy saw one
digging its teeth into the neck of one of its brethren that had fallen
victim to a gunshot.

Odus guided Sister Mary toward the logging road, urging the
horse into a trot. But Katy kicked free, falling to the ground, twisting her ankle as she rolled. She struggled to her feet in the rough,

tilled soil where the goats had romped. Goat manure streaked the knees of her pants, and the smell was enough to make her vomit. But she blocked that out, along with the screams of the people and the unnerving cries of the goats. She focused on the rock, where Gordon stood holding Jett, the eerie scarecrow figure seemingly seven feet tall under the moldy straw planter's hat.

Katy limped toward the rock, passing the preacher's trampled hat. A goat trotted past her, a dripping chunk of what looked like potted meat clamped between its buckteeth. "Let her go, Gordon," she said, trying to summon her bitch voice, one she'd packed away in the wake of her divorce.

"Come here and I will," Gordon said. "It's you that I wanted, anyway."

Katy's gaze shifted from the sackcloth head to the Circuit Rider's implacable, waxy face. "Is this why you won't die?" she said to the preacher. "Is this why you kept coming back all those years?"

"It's not what I want that matters," he answered through thin, bloodless lips.

Katy reached the edge of the rock and the Circuit Rider kneeled forward, reaching down a hand that looked the color of rancid soap. She couldn't climb the rock with her injured ankle. She took the preacher's hand, a chill coursing through her as if a dozen icy needles had penetrated her palm. Despite his gaunt, slack flesh, the Circuit Rider pulled with the strength of a draft animal, and Katy found herself lying alongside Ray Tester's cooling body.

"You need to kill somebody," she said to the preacher, "then do it and get it over with. But that means Jett goes free, right?"

Gordon laughed, a sound that somehow echoed the goats' ravenous bleats. "You're praying in the wrong direction, my dear. I'm the one who chooses the sacrifices now. I'm the child of God's favor."

Jett peered out from under her black bangs, eyes wide with fright. Gordon put the tip of the sickle against her neck.

"You killed Rebecca," Katy said, knowing it sounded dumb, as if one murder mattered in a mountain valley where dozens had come to wicked ends.

"She wanted me to kill her," Gordon said from inside his scarecrow mask. "She gave herself up for the greater good. Because she wanted to belong to me forever. To *Solom* forever."

"Then why did she bring us to . . . oh."

The clop of horse hooves sounded on the packed dirt, and Katy thought it was Odus, come to make a rescue attempt. Instead, she saw Rebecca, sitting sidesaddle on Old Saint. The vehicle headlights cut through both her and her mount's bodies as if they were gauze. Rebecca had no head, and Katy thought of Ichabod Crane in *The Legend of Sleepy Hollow*.

"Here's your horse, honey," Rebecca said, but the words didn't come from the body. Instead, they came from the head, which floated just beyond the edge of the granite slab. It wore the preacher's black hat, angled to one side in a parody of fashion. Around her, the goats continued their hunt for human meat.

"I wasn't ready then," Gordon said. "I had to grow my power. More sacrifices, more goats killed, more tribute paid to those who bless this land."

Gordon moved the sickle away from Jett's throat and waved it at the Circuit Rider. "Just like you did," he said to the preacher. "Only you killed reluctantly."

"I just want to rest," the Circuit Rider said. "Put my three graves together and you can have Solom. And all my other stops."

Gordon kicked Ray's limp body. "They're still willing to die for you. Use it."

The Circuit Rider shook his head. "My rounds are over."

"You weren't fit to carry the Smith name."

"None of us are worthy."

Katy eyed the distance between her and Gordon. Even with two good legs, she wouldn't have been able to reach him before he cut either her or Jett. And a man who could order goats to kill and ghosts to do his dark deeds probably had few limits, anyway. But she had to try. Damned if she would give herself up as Rebecca had.

Not to mention her daughter.

She thought of the promise she'd repeated to Jett so many times that it had become a mindless mantra: *we'll get through it together*.

She just hoped it wouldn't be death's door that they would go through, side by side, hands held in fear of the waiting unknown.

* * *

The buck-toothed bastards had him treed like a lost coon.

Alex had dropped his Pearson bow when the flock started chasing him. He'd had one decent shot at Weird Dude, but that other guy had gotten in the way. Alex figured if Weird Dude was some sort of secret government agent, there would be a cover-up and nobody would ever find out about this little gathering on the mountain or the existence of intelligent, mind-controlled killer goats. If only the government wouldn't have bred or genetically implanted in them a craving for marijuana, Alex would have figured "Live and let live." But that was just like *them*, to use their power to intrude on people's peace and property.

He looked down at the bleating, sneering creature closest to him, who was reared up on the tree trunk. The strange eyes with their boxy, oblate pupils glittered in the gloomy sweep of headlights.

"Yeah, you'd eat the original U.S. Constitution if it was right there in front of you, wouldn't you?" he taunted. "The powderheads wrote it on hemp paper, and I know how much you fuckers love hemp."

The goat twitched its ears in fury, and another goat butted the tree, horns clacking against the bark.

Alex wasn't in position to work the submachine gun, but he undid the snap on his hip holster and drew out the Colt Python. The Circuit Rider and Gordon Smith, who was dressed in a freaky scarecrow costume like an acidhead on Halloween, were still on the rock and were out of pistol range. Not that Alex had any personal grudge against his neighbor, besides the fact that Gordon's fence had failed. But the goats seemed to obey Gordon, not Weird Dude. And now Gordon was holding the little Goth girl, the one who had moved in along with the redhead last summer. A man's private business was a man's private business, but it didn't look like your typical Hallmark Special moment.

Alex aimed the pistol in a two-handed grip. The goat stared back along the length of the barrel.

"You are one ugly piece of work." Alex squeezed the trigger and a brown dot appeared on the animal's forehead. He knew goats had thick skulls because of their bizarre mating rituals that sometimes caused them to butt heads until one of the males dropped from exhaustion. They weren't symbols of depraved lust for nothing. But a Python bullet was more than a match for the thick plate of bone, though the entry wound was a little messier than usual. The back of the goat's head exploded, raining bits of meat and bone on the half dozen goats surrounding the base of the tree.

The goat's lips peeled back in a grin.

Leave it to the government to build a goat that wouldn't die.

David had it all wrong.

He figured the Circuit Rider would claim a victim and then drift on into the night, continuing his eternal rounds. It was one of life's constants, and the people of Solom had adjusted to it over the years. People measured the course of their lives with his visits, along with the September frost and the May buttercups and the first cut of hay in June, the annual flock of tourists in their tinted-window sedans, the final snow in early April that was often the largest of the year. The Circuit Rider was evil, unholy, and murderous, but he was *theirs*.

So Ray's death should have ended it. Because Ray had died for the Circuit Rider, accidentally or not. David had made the offering of his own life, which would have spared the others who were now being attacked by crazed goats. But his own soul had been found wanting, his faith weak, his meat unworthy of the great banquet prepared by Harmon Smith.

Except . . .

David had climbed back into Ray's truck when the goats went wild, and three of them battered at the driver's-side door, taking turns launching their horns against the sheet metal. Ray's truck bed had no tailgate, and a shaggy-faced billy had climbed into the bed among the rusty chains, boards, and hand tools. One blow of those curving horns would shatter the rear windshield.

But that was okay.

David understood now.

It wasn't the Circuit Rider who was calling the shots. Gordon Smith had somehow usurped his ancestor. Gordon, a student of myth and ritual, had claimed whatever tilted pulpit granted the power of life and death in Solom.

But all actions had been set in motion long ago by that larger, unseen Hand that slept behind the stars.

The One who wielded that same Divine Hand, the One who hadn't found David a worthy sacrifice, triggered a blinding rage. He'd lost his brother, Gordon Smith had been granted some bizarre supernatural power, and goats were ravaging his neighbors and the members of his congregation. Sure, there was a satisfactory number of Free Willers and Southern Baptists among the victims, but God was filling up the good spaces in heaven with those who had spent life on their knees, not those who had accepted his grace without doubt or the craving for mortal intervention.

Hooves rattled in the metal bed of the truck, and the rear windshield exploded behind him. Glass showered down the back of David's neck. The goat's horns caught in the gun rack, and David leaned toward the passenger side out of reach of the animal's frantic jaws. The goat's breath stank of bad blood and sulfur.

The sheriff's deputy had fallen and two goats were tugging him in different directions, like dogs fighting over a string of chitlins. The deputy's pistol lay just outside the glare of headlights, but each blue sweep of the patrol car's bubble lights reflected the sheen of the barrel. David wasn't sure God required His creatures to make such decisions, but the pistol was within his reach for a reason.

He flung open the truck door and dove for the gun. One of the goats dropped the deputy's arm, which flopped against the leaf-covered ground and lay still. The goat tossed his head and charged, pointing its whorl of bony horns at David. David reached the gun, not knowing whether the safety was on or off, then remembered that the deputy had squeezed off at least one shot. He brought it to chest level and fired wildly, punching three holes in the goat's back and neck. It didn't slow at all, closing the ten feet between them before David could draw a breath, and then the stony head knocked him in the chest and he lay stunned in the damp leaves of the forest clearing. Above the strobing blue lights were the scatter of stars and the bloated eye of the moon.

And, above it all, the eye of God, looking down.

He was dimly aware of hooves drumming, of large shapes hovering around him. He was just regaining his breath when teeth latched onto his throat.

We are loaves and fishes feeding the multitude, he thought, the pain blending with the bruised ache in his chest. As other mouths set to work in the serious business of feeding, a final thought brought a crippled smile to his face:

I have been found worthy after all.

Gordo is nutso, plain and simple.

But worse than the nutso is, like, the power to make goats kill people.

Besides the fact that he wants to kill me and Mom.

Jett could smell Gordon's pompous aftershave beneath the musty, dusty scarecrow outfit, and that sickened her almost as much as her anger and fear. Her throat hurt where he'd stuck the point of his sickle against it, and a warm trickle descended the slope of her neck. The persistent *wah* of the police lights made her dizzy as screams and frantic bleats blended into a muddy music. If she closed her eyes, she could almost imagine she was at one of the industrial raves from her druggie days in Charlotte, with her heart providing the driving bass beat.

But this rave was the kind that killed.

She met her mom's eyes and could read the look. That sappy old "We'll get through this together," but for the first time, Jett welcomed it and *needed* it.

She didn't think it would work on a ghost, but it might on a guy who had more balls than sense. She stepped to the side while Gordon was focused on the Circuit Rider, then launched one of her feet, clad in a heavy black lace-up boot that Gordon had so often ridiculed, and planted it firmly in his crotch. The air left him like a pinpricked balloon and he folded up.

She couldn't be sure, but the Circuit Rider's grim lips might have lifted in a smile.

"Run!" Katy yelled, and Jett jumped from the stone. The goats had scattered enough so that she had a clear path to the Subaru, or to the woods if she thought the trees offered more protection. But she didn't want to leave Mom. That "together" thing bit both ways.

"Come on, Mom," she said.

Gordon recovered and reached for Katy, catching her by her long red hair. He yanked, and she was jerked backward. "Come here, bitch. My things never leave me, even when they're dead."

He raised the sickle, and its blade caught the blue light and reflected a curve of icy fire.

That's when the Circuit Rider erupted.

He rose in a vengeful flurry of black-clad limbs, his pale head nearly luminescent in the headlights, eyes two cold pools of diseased ichor.

"You want to ride in my saddle," Harmon Smith said. "But are you worthy?"

Startled, Gordon turned to face his deceased ancestor, still gripping Katy's hair with one gloved hand. But "face" wasn't the right word, Jett thought, because Gordon's was hidden by the coarse cloth and the Circuit Rider's waxy lumpen features could hardly be described by that word.

"I've proven myself worthy," Gordon said. "Know me by my fruits."

"You don't know Solom," the Circuit Rider said. "And your tree is diseased."

Jett heard thundering hooves and thought some big billy goat— Methuselah, Seth, Jacob, or whatever Old Testament fucker Gordon had picked for a name—was charging. She looked away from the stone stage to see Rebecca and Old Saint galloping toward her. Rebecca wore her head again, but her skin had gone grave-gray and mottled, the ragged flesh of her neck flapping in the breeze, her long dark hair billowing behind her like the threads of a ragged burial shroud.

Before the ghostly horse and rider could reach her, Odus rumbled in on his paint pony, hunched over the pony's neck, whispering in her ear, then raising his voice to a shout. "I knew you'd send the right tool," he shouted at the sky, and Jett figured he was just one more squirrel-shit-nutty Solom inmate, except he rode like a holy warrior on a suicide mission.

As she watched, Old Saint grew more solid, his hooves hammering thirty feet away, clumps of dirt flying in his wake. Rebecca, too, grew more solid, though still bloodless, her lips black, skin withered, face shrunken by decay.

"These are *my* people," the Circuit Rider said, and Odus narrowed the gap, the two horses charging as if their riders were competing in a lanceless joust.

"I'll never need drugs again," Jett whispered to herself just before the horses collided.

Chapter Thirty-six

Sue waved her climber's pickax in front of her as if it were a charm, but the three goats circling her seemed wholly unimpressed. She'd had the idea—absurd in hindsight, though she'd wasted little time in retrospection—that she could scare the goats away long enough to get Sarah down from the hood of the Jeep. But Sarah was sharp enough to save herself. A woman didn't live to get that old without a strong sense of self-preservation.

Sue didn't pay much attention to the doings in the center of the clearing. She was too intent on getting Sarah to safety and then making a beeline down the mountain. But as Odus Hampton and the creepy woman sped hell-bent toward one another, Sue couldn't help but look. So did the goats, and Sue noted that the woman was *dead*, sickly pale, rotted, the skin drawn tight around her skull. Sue clambered onto the hood, the pickax in her fist. Hearing the *thrump* of metal, the goats turned again and leaped up onto the Jeep, trying to get a foothold on the dew-slick front bumper.

"About time you came to the rescue," Sarah said. "I thought I'd hooked up with the wrong spunky sidekick for a second there."

"I haven't rescued either of us yet," she said, digging the point of the pickax into the Jeep's soft-top. The vinyl-coated fabric ripped and she pulled back on the climbing tool, working the gap wider. A new top would cost her five hundred dollars, but she was sure she'd find a way to write the expense off on her taxes. Surely there was a category for supernatural casualty.

A goat gained enough traction to leap forward and nip her shoe. Sarah stomped on the animal's head, bouncing it like a coconut and with about as much effect. Sue peeled the top back. "Get in," she said, and as she helped Sarah work her knobby limbs over the windshield and into the Jeep, a siren scream of twin whinnies slit the night.

Odus figured the tool would be given, the sword put in his hand at the moment of truth. High philosophy had never been his strong point. He was more comfortable with the kind of mental ramblings brought on by the bottom of a whiskey pint, and his truths were those of nature: trout bit better just before a storm, wild turkeys were smart enough to walk around in a hunter's tracks, marigolds and onions kept bugs out of the garden.

Now he faced a truth that *was* nature, grown wild with the night, legs flailing, tail twitching, neck hunched low as she charged. Odus wasn't sure if he'd guided Sister Mary or if the horse had propelled itself through some inner command. Either way, the paint pony had enough giddyup to break both their necks. As the distance narrowed, he got a good look at the thing riding Old Saint. He'd worked for the Smiths before Rebecca had been killed, and had always thought her the sweetest of ladies. Plus she cooked up a mean parsnip pie.

But now she looked to be serving up a different kind of meanness, one brought by the anger of the grave.

Odus wasn't sure what was going to happen, but the showdown felt right. Maybe he wasn't supposed to take down Harmon Smith after all. Maybe Odus was just supposed to knock the preacher's legs out from under him in the form of his horse.

But Old Saint looked massive and solid, not two hundred years dead. Twice the weight of Sister Mary, the horse was liable to knock them into next week, skipping Sunday on the way.

Odus was close enough to see the steamy breath pluming from Old Saint's nostrils and to look into the cruel caves in Rebecca's skull where her eyes had once perched.

Fourteen hundred pounds of horseflesh met and the forest shuddered.

Alex had used up the rounds in the Colt Python, but the goats still circled below him. A couple had fallen, those whose limbs had been clipped by bullets, but none of them had died, despite shots that landed between the eyes or dead-on in the heart. Sure, the wounds slowed them down a little, but they also made them angrier, like a hive of bees that had been smoked. The marijuana they'd munched must have made them ornery instead of mellowing them out.

Alex adjusted his position in the branches and fumbled the AKR submachine gun into his lap. He kicked back the lever and surveyed the clearing. Weird Dude Walking and the scarecrow creep were going at it like a Republican and a Democrat fighting over a defense contract. The little neighbor girl, the Goth with the dyed-black bangs, stood alone in the clearing as the two horses smacked into each other.

The thunder of slapping meat was like an artillery blast in the September night.

The horses collided, and for one long second, they merged. The spotted horse and the giant black horse were a tangle of knotted knees, forelegs, hooves, and stringy hair. They appeared to be one quivering mass of flesh, and the fellow who worked on the Smith farm was thrown clear, rolling toward the Goth girl. Rebecca, or the rickety rack of skin and dry bone that wore her features, became part of the orgiastic wad of insane magic.

To Alex, it wasn't supernatural magic or illusion, just another test run for the government. No doubt he'd have to be deprogrammed (if they took him alive, that was, and he hadn't made that decision yet) after it was all over. But for now, he had a pouch full of ammunition and enough goats on hand to just about repay the property loss he'd suffered.

He locked down on the trigger and the Russian-made submachine gun kicked out its sweet staccato song.

*   *   *

Katy tugged away from Gordon, but his fingers were hooked into her hair. She screamed at Jett when the horses slammed into each other, but Jett had already jumped back.

"I take back what is mine," the Circuit Rider said.

"It's not yours anymore," Gordon said, sweeping the sickle down toward Katy. She felt the tension of his muscles more than she saw the descending blow, and she twisted away, the back of her skull on fire where the roots of her hair gave way. She cringed, anticipating the cold slice of steel, but the Circuit Rider reached out and caught Gordon's wrist like a frog's tongue snatching a mosquito out of the air.

"I take back what is mine," the Circuit Rider said.

Gordon released Katy as he and his unnatural ancestor struggled. A metallic hail rained down on the night, and Katy recognized it as automatic gunfire. Slugs whined through the night air, *thwacking* into trees, pinging off rocks, and ripping into vehicles.

"Get down, Jett," Katy yelled.

The Circuit Rider forced the sickle to Gordon's face, dragging the tip down so that it cut into the scarecrow mask, dissecting the black stitched lips. Blood appeared around the tear, darkening the coarse sackcloth.

"Show your face," the Circuit Rider said.

Gordon used his superior height and weight to bend the Circuit Rider back, grunting with effort. Katy realized she was pulling for the dead preacher. Despite his reputation, he seemed the lesser of two evils at the moment.

She knelt over Ray Tester and yanked the arrow out of his back, and the tip emerged with a wet *sloosh*. She gripped the blood-slick arrow in both hands and spun, ramming it up into Gordon's gut. He jerked in a spasm of pain, and in that motion, the sickle swept into the Circuit Rider's neck. The pale, waxy flesh tore like paper, and a black powdery substance spilled out. Except it wasn't powder: the tiny specks were alive and crawling.

Katy jumped down as Gordon lurched across the stone, conducting a crazy scarecrow waltz that might have mimicked those sacrificial harvest celebrations of long ago. He tottered and fell, planting the arrow more deeply inside him.

The Circuit Rider stood, his hands spread wide, the black scrabbling creatures leaking from his wound.

He smiled at Katy, as grim and dark an expression, but also as peaceful, as she'd ever seen. "You are the light of the world," he said.

Then he was gone.

"Get this jalopy in gear," Sarah said, as Sue started the Jeep.

Sue punched the accelerator and popped the clutch, parting the goats that were climbing up the bumper. The Jeep's knobby tires gave a satisfying bump as they rolled over one of the creatures. Most of the people, at least those who weren't being eaten by goats, had fled into the woods.

"I've always hated them damned critters," Sarah said. "Never could trust something with eyes that looked twenty ways at once."

Sue wasn't sure where the gunfire was coming from, but she figured moving fast and crazy was the best course of action. A man fell to his knees, clutching his belly, and goats converged on him. Sue figured it was too late to save the man, but not the others. She guided the Jeep toward the redheaded woman on the rock just as the Circuit Rider and Gordon tangled, and Gordon performed his St. Vitus dance of death.

"Did you see that?" Sarah asked.

"No, and neither did you. I don't want to spend the rest of my days in therapy."

"You ain't crazy. I guess you've just been officially welcomed to Solom."

Sue brought the Jeep to a halt beside the girl and Odus, who was woozy but appeared to be in no danger of sudden death. Unless one of those stray bullets caught him. Sarah opened the door and crawled into the back, leaving room for the girl to help Odus into the Jeep.

"Where's my horse?" Odus said, as groggy as if he were on a two-pint drunk.

"Went up in smoke along with Harmon Smith," Sarah said.

The driver's-side mirror took a bullet and shattered. The gun fell silent, and Sue figured the shooter was reloading.

"Hurry, Mom!" the girl yelled, and the redhead jumped off the stone and pushed the girl into the Jeep. Clinging to the roll bar, half of her body hanging out with the door flapping against her, Katy said, "Roll!"

Sue did.

Alex had a terrible dream. In the dream, he'd been brought to a secret bunker in Roswell, New Mexico. He was escorted by two men in blue uniforms, each wearing enough brass and doodads to win an "Unsung Heroes" contest. They led him down a long concrete tunnel, whose recessed lights threw off a smoky blue color. The air was stale, as if it had been recycled for weeks. A set of double metal doors slid open and Alex was escorted into an office.

An oval office.

The president sat behind a large cherry desk, the wood surface so polished that the president's shit-eating, frat-boy grin and pointy chin were reflected.

"Welcome, Agent Eakins," the president said in a Texas drawl as he stood. "The United States owes you a great debt of gratitude, or a date regret of attitude, dude, or something like that."

The president reached over the desk to shake Alex's hand. There was only one thing to say. So Alex said it.

"Vote Libertarian, you weasel-eyed fuck-face."

He jerked awake from the nightmare to find himself in the tree, his arms wrapped around a branch, the AKR cold at his side. The sun was just now dragging its lazy orange ass over the horizon. Blue jays squawked and wrens twittered in the trees. The forest was otherwise quiet, besides the soft rustle of wind in the last of the dying leaves.

Weird Dude was gone, and the scarecrow creep was lying in a puddle of blood in the center of the granite stone. A couple of vehicles were still parked at the edge of the clearing, their headlights faded to a weak pumpkin glow.

Below him were the white-and-brown lumps of dead goats. Somewhere during the spree, the goats' protective powers must have worn off, proving that even the almighty government was fallible.

Also scattered on the churned-up ground were a dozen or so

people, lying still in the dawn, their clothes moist with dew. A few of them had visible wounds in their bodies, but Alex couldn't tell if they'd taken friendly fire or had been chomped by mutant goats. For all he knew, the feds had pulled a Ruby Ridge and taken down some innocents, then slipped back to Washington without apology, leaving someone else to clean up the mess.

Strangely, the sight was a calming one. This was reality. He could handle it. Just don't ever put him in a government bunker and he could deal.

He reached into his pocket and worked up a joint, then fired it with his Bic. As he bathed in the luxuriant blue smoke, he considered the old saying that revenge was a dish best served cold.

Alex decided he liked the taste either way.

"Told you we'd get through it together," Katy said.

"Yeah, but now what?" Jett applied a crumbly smear of purple lipstick. She decided she didn't need eye shadow today; the weary pouches were offensive and startling enough. Mom had let her skip school. They decided to regroup at the Smith house, where Sue had dropped them off.

"Well, first off, I guess we better tell your dad."

"Cool. Are you guys getting back together?"

"Honey, if I ever taught you anything, it was not to repeat your mistakes."

"Well, look at the ass-wipe you married the second time around."

"Watch your language. I'll be sure not to ever marry another psychotic, wife-killing maniac who likes to dress up like a scarecrow. How's that?"

"It will do, for starters."

They sat on the porch, though the morning was cool. Katy didn't feel like going in the house, though she was sure Rebecca would never be back. Rebecca had followed the rest of them into the netherland where the Circuit Rider's flock grazed for all eternity. Gordon might be there, too, for all she knew. The future wasn't fixed. It was, if anything, a great crippled wheel, dipping here and there, throwing off those who didn't cling tightly enough.

A merry-go-round broke down.

"Sure is peaceful without all those goats around," Katy said.

"Yeah. Almost makes me want to check out the barn, just to be sure none of them are lurking around. You know how in the cheesy horror movies, the end is never really the end."

"We're staying out of the barn, little lady." Katy swept Jett's bangs from her forehead and planted a kiss. "Tell you what. You put on some music, and I'll make us a bite to eat."

"No Smith family recipes?"

"Promise."

As Katy prowled the fridge between the butter and the olives, the biting riff of a Replacements tune blasted from the shell of Jett's room: "Merry-Go-Round."

Maybe the crazy carnival ride still had a few turns on it after all.

Arvel Ward opened his cellar door. He'd spent a sleepless night downstairs, the bare bulb burning, the air ripe from the earthen floor's odor, jars of jelly and pickled okra lining the shelves. As morning's first light leaked through the narrow, high-set windows, the warmth of joy replaced the autumnal chill in his heart.

He'd survived.

The Circuit Rider may have walked up the stairs and taken Betsy, just as the preacher had taken his brother Zeke all those years ago, but Arvel had made it. Arvel was safe until the next round of the circuit, and with any luck and by the grace of God he'd find a natural grave before then. There was comfort in the sleep of dirt and worms, but until then he would get along as best he could, living right and keeping his tools clean.

Arvel went into the living room. When he'd gone into hiding the night before, he'd forgotten his chewing tobacco, and the ache was on him strong. He opened the foil pouch with trembling fingers and stuffed a wad of shredded leaves inside his cheek. The nicotine bit sweet and hard.

He almost swallowed the wad when he turned and saw the Circuit Rider sitting on the couch. Betsy had draped an oversize knitted doily over the back of it, and somehow the preacher seemed even more of an intrusion, sitting there among the tidy pillows.

"Not expecting company?" the Circuit Rider said, thumbing the wide brim of his black hat. The preacher smelled of spoiled meat and rotted cloth, and his fingernails were dark with dirt, as if he'd clawed his way up from the grave. Up close, Arvel could see the holes in the Circuit Rider's wool suit. There was no flesh behind them, only an emptiness that stretched as long as every nightmare road ever traveled.

Arvel spat out the tobacco, but his involuntary swallow sent a slug's length of bitter juice down his throat.

"It ain't my turn," Arvel said. "Take Betsy. She's upstairs, helpless as a cut kitten, and she ain't going to put up much of a struggle."

"Neither will you."

Arvel backed away, wondering if he could reach the fireplace poker and if the steel bar would do any good against a creature that seemed to be built of *nothing*. "You can't take me," Arvel said, nearly giggling in relief. "The sun done come up."

The Circuit Rider stood, seven feet tall and gangly. "I don't make the rules, Arvel," he said.

"But you've already claimed a soul for this trip around."

"I've claimed nothing. Solom has."

"It ain't my *turn*." The tears were hot and wet on his cheeks, the living room blurred, and Arvel took in the familiar surroundings of his house, a place that he knew he'd never see again. At least, not from *this* side of the border between dead and alive.

"Hush, now, or you'll wake Betsy. She needs her rest." The Circuit Rider gave a tired, benevolent smile and reached his long, waxy fingers toward Arvel.

Harmon Smith unhitched Old Saint from the lilac bush. Harmon considered letting the horse munch on the fading, frost-browned flower bed a little longer, but Betsy had suffered enough already. She'd need the busywork to distract her from the loss of her husband, whose body lay cooling on the kitchen floor, near where the goat had attacked Betsy. If the authorities were summoned, they might rule it a heart attack, or they might say it was an accidental fall. Most likely, they'd say, "That's Solom."

Calling them "authorities" was a silly, mortal concept anyway. Only one authority existed, and Its hand had set the wheel in motion. But such things didn't trouble the Circuit Rider. His duty was given, and he was a good servant. He hauled himself up into the familiar cup of Old Saint's saddle.

"Come on, Saint, we've got places to be," he said, giving a gentle lift to the reins. He didn't have to point toward a destination. The horse, fat on souls and shrubs, knew the route as intimately as Harmon did.

Narrow is the gate and hard the road that leads to life and light, truth and heaven, but all other roads are open and endless. And on these trails, the Circuit Rider travels alone.

Feel the Seduction Of
Pinnacle Horror

When Darkness Falls
Grab One of These
Pinnacle Horrors

Scare Up One of These
Pinnacle Horrors